CARDINAL CAGED

Book 2 of The Cardinal Series

Mia Smantz

© 2020 Mia Smantz

All rights reserved. No portion of this book may be reproduced in any form without permission from the publisher, except as permitted by U.S. copyright law.

Independently published.

ISBN:

For more information visit:

https://www.miasmantz.com/

Dedicated To

My brother who was arguably the coolest person in our crazy family. Loved, but not forgotten.

Prologue

It was dangerously hot in the school, a ticking time-bomb waiting to go off. Tempers were abnormally short and quick to boil. My bully, Bryan Weltz, had already been in three fights—all undetected by teachers. I was doing my best to stay off his radar. Of course, that was the least of my troubles that day.

The day before, they canceled school for something other than snow. That was unusual here in Pennsylvania. It couldn't have been avoided though. The place was built like a greenhouse—not something you'd notice until the air conditioning putters out on one of the hottest days of the year.

Say what you will, but the teachers were resilient. Hopeful students had kept a weathered eye on the news for another cancellation. When it wasn't announced, everyone showed up surprised and disappointed. They were even more disappointed when they saw the eclectic and numerous fans that had popped up like a fungus all over the sweltering building. Nothing had been fixed, they just didn't want to cancel again.

Tempers were short in direct correlation to the soaring temperatures. Kids without deodorant were repelling the river of students during passing periods as if they had their own personal force field.

There had been several fights before the tardy bell even rang at the start of school.

I had decided to hole up in the computer lab during lunch. No way would I try to face a hot, middle school cafeteria where Bryan Weltz, my number one bully, would be.

I wiped at my forehead as I logged onto the school computer. My hands were sweaty and not because of the heat. I was doing something illegal, but it was with the best of intentions.

If I got caught, maybe they would go easy on me. I was a good person. I hadn't even been to the principal's office before. They'd at least give pause before throwing me into prison...right?

It didn't matter. I had to do this.

Yesterday, Dad sat me down to ask a favor. He told me that he wasn't really my dad. He said that Mom tried to tell him that I was his, but he'd had a vasectomy before their marriage.

At the time, I'd felt a little bit relieved. All my life, he hadn't been very warm to me, and maybe this was why. I tried to understand what it would be like to live with the woman you loved. Yet, there I was, the physical manifestation of lies and deceit.

I felt guilty and responsible in a way because my mom was my biological mother. I was ashamed at what she had done to the man that had always been there for both of us.

My dad told me that he'd sacrificed a lot to raise me. He reminded me of all the things he'd done. Mom had always been a stay-at-home mom. We'd been sponging for years off the man she'd betrayed. I admired him for the care and devotion he had shown by not leaving. It wasn't a surprise he'd been so aloof with me.

I was eager to help him out and make him like me. I could right the wrongs. I'd scoured the internet most of the night, looking for the password breaker that I'd need to do this thing for him.

At first, mom hadn't wanted me to have access to a computer. She'd been adamant, but Dad insisted. It was the only time I remember him putting his foot down. As a compromise, he'd installed hefty parental locks and filters to appease her. She hadn't argued with him. With my new-found knowledge, I wondered if it wasn't because she felt guilty for what she'd done to him. As far as I knew, she didn't know he couldn't have children, so she still thought it was all a big secret.

With that compromise, Dad had won. I'd had access to a computer.

I'd put to use my knowledge from the Coding for Dummies book Dad had gotten me for Christmas. I took to it like bread in water. Even when I wasn't looking at a computer screen, I was seeing code.

After some small attempts to hack into people's social media accounts, I felt that I was ready to delve in deep.

The parental filters had been the first thing I'd hacked, out of curiosity. That had been a colossal mistake that I was still scarred from. With the filters down, the internet was a dark and scary world. My anger and indignation towards my mother had softened a little bit after that. But, Dad needed me to do this thing for him, so I braced myself, got back at it, and put the parental filters back up.

But, I altered them to fit my needs. It was hard to search for anything with such an overzealous filter. I smartened the coding up, made it better able to sort out the bad stuff by expanding its contextual knowledge.

I'd been able to do that with minimal trouble as I stumbled across a dad that was a hacker during my research. The hacker-dad, Wicked_1, had been less than impressed with parental filters as well. He complained that his kids couldn't even search the word "analogous" because it had the word "anal" in it. He compiled his own list of phrases and terms. Most of the words and phrases on the list had boggled me when I glanced over it in curiosity. I decided that I didn't want to understand and left it at that. But I did use his work to try to keep from seeing things I'd stumbled across that one time.

It worked like a charm with my coding sequence. Wicked_1's list was static—only able to block the things he'd added. That issue was fixed when paired with my program. The hybrid program could learn from the list he'd made, see other terms on sites with those phrases, and add to itself. It was a software inspired by Google's search-suggestions function.

Since then, I hadn't run across anything bad, and I'd had access to endless amounts of information.

All thanks to my dad.

He was the only one in this world that truly, selflessly cared about me.

I had to do this for him.

He wanted to be able to divorce my mom. He couldn't deal with the lies anymore, but he didn't want to abandon me either. He wanted to take me with him. He worried that if he did, Mom would demand a paternity test, and he'd lose all rights to me. Dad told me that it would kill him if that happened as he'd grown to love me as his own flesh and blood. We needed to avoid that. Dad said that it would be best if we could disappear and start over somewhere where she couldn't find us. All I had to do was make that possible.

The internet loaded on the computer, and I made sure to bypass the need to use my own credentials to log in. It would've defeated the purpose of waiting to use a more anonymous computer, only to sign in under my own name.

I found my elementary school's website. They'd been in the process of digitizing all the records, shredding hard copies of files and uploading everything to the school's database. It was perfect for me because that meant the only copy of my record was online already.

But first I needed to break in.

The school's filters blocked the password breaker app, so I had to spend a good ten minutes trying to bypass it. I was in though, and the program was doing its thing. I just had to wait.

I sat back and glanced around. There was a redheaded boy in the corner, mousy and smart. I thought his name was Grayson. I was still learning everyone's names at the middle school, same as everyone else. In fact, the only reason I recognized this boy's face was that he was usually here with me during lunch.

The program dinged, drawing my eyes back to the monitor. I typed a few things and gained secretarial access to the records. It would be all that I needed to accomplish my goals.

I went in, searching for my file.

Curiously enough, there was an annotation in my file by a few of my teachers about how advanced I was in math while I was behind socially. It was embarrassing to know that my teachers had noticed enough to write that down. I thought I'd gone by invisible.

There was also a note about keeping me separated from Bryan Weltz, the guy who'd always pull my bows out and bully me. The same one that'd been in three fights today. The same one that I'd been eating in the computer lab to avoid. It'd started in kindergarten and hadn't gotten better over time. In fact, it'd only gotten worse now that we were in middle school. He had more friends, meaner friends that were quickly becoming just as bad as him.

I shook my head and deleted my file. I felt bereft and ambivalent, unsure of how to feel about the situation. In a way, it was cathartic. It was like erasing my files was deleting my past completely. It also felt like I was eliminating myself from all the good memories I'd had as well. It was like eradicating the good memories when I'd thought my family was perfect even if my dad was aloof and my mom caved in too easily. In some ways, ignorance was *bliss.*

Either way—good or not, it was done. There was no way to retrieve the file now, not the way I'd deleted it. It wouldn't do for anyone to find a way to restore the file after Dad and I disappeared.

I cleared my history and switched computers just in case, creating a short history of sites in my name to give me a bit of an alibi. I even altered the time stamps on them so that I would've had to be in two places at once to be responsible for the hack.

Once I had done that, I pulled out my well-worn book on the Russian language. I had been learning Cyrillic lettering. I was interested to see how a different language might affect some coding sequences I'd been working on. So I worked on that a bit. It had become a hobby of mine when math started getting too easy and a teacher gave me detention for "not looking studious."

I pulled out my homework for The Giver *and translated my answers, practicing the phonetics of the Russian lettering in my notebook.*

Five minutes before the bell rang, Bryan Weltz showed up with his friends.

I'd hoped that he wouldn't be able to find me in the computer lab during lunch, and it'd worked for a while. Now, I'd have to find a different spot, it seemed.

There was a teacher's aide in the corner. She was charged to watch over the room in case students needed to print or finish online homework. As a poorer school district, many students didn't have access to technology at home. The aide looked like she was engrossed in the computer, only giving Bryan and his group a cursory glance as they strolled in. In fact, Bryan complimented the teacher, and she actually gave a smile as she waved him on.

My palms sweated. I stared straight ahead, pretending to be engrossed in the website I'd randomly pulled up. I could feel my cheeks heat up. I licked my lips.

Dread loomed when the chair next to me was pulled out and a large body dropped in it. He'd grown a lot over the summer. I knew it was him though. I could feel his stare and smell the cinnamon gum he always seemed to be chewing.

"Hey," he said, his voice much deeper than most of the boys in our grade. It was nerve-wracking. He already had facial hair, and half of the boys still sounded...well, like boys.

I didn't say anything. My throat constricted in fear as adrenaline flooded my veins. I wouldn't be able to do more than squeak and squawk with how terrified I was.

In fact, I did squeak when Bryan grabbed the back of my chair and turned me to face him.

He frowned. "What's wrong? You sick or somethin'?"

I nodded, my hand going up to my throat. I never knew what to say to people, and especially not to guys like Bryan Weltz. At least, he wouldn't expect me to say anything if I faked a sore throat.

One of the guys behind us snickered. "More like she had a busy night. Your knees sore too?"

I frowned, understanding that he was likely being crude by the tone of voice. But I wasn't sure what he was implying.

Bryan frowned for a second, his thick brows drawing down. Finally, he snapped, "Don't talk to her like that."

I blanked.

My mind was trying to decipher his words as if it was some sort of code and I was missing the key. Bryan—Bryan Weltz—the guy that had picked on me and shoved me and pulled the bows from my hair since kindergarten, was defending *me?*

I played with the bottoms of my hair, unsure.

Bryan's body language was defensive. His friend's was not. It said that what they were referring to was definitely related to that brief flash of a webpage I'd had after disabling the parental filters.

I chanced a glance back at the guy that Bryan was glaring at before looking around. Grayson was in the corner, but his head was turned to the side as if he was listening in to our conversation.

"Fine, whatever," the other boy grouched under the weight of Bryan's look.

Bryan turned back to me, and, just as he went to talk, the door to the lab crashed open.

Everyone turned to the commotion, trying to understand what we were seeing.

Shoulders spanning the entirety of the doorway, was a large man. He was tanned, bald, and muscular. He wore a black t-shirt stretched tight and tan cargo pants. There was a gun and large combat knife the size of my forearm strapped to his waist. He didn't even bother to hide the weapons, his t-shirt tucked into his utility belt to allow quick and easy access to any of the things strapped there.

Everyone froze, including the teacher's aide.

Guns weren't allowed at school. There also was no visitor badge on him—something that you had to get before you were allowed to leave the office.

Apparently, he'd found his own way in the building because he clearly wasn't a teacher. And though he didn't have either the knife or gun in his hands, he was a lethal weapon himself. He moved with precision, a tightly-wound mass of muscle and training.

The teacher started to protest, but the stranger cut her off with a look. "You, beat it. Go run to the principal's office so you can call the police or whatever it is you want to do. It won't make a difference. I'm armed to the teeth and pretty unstoppable." His eyes zeroed in on me. "You, you're coming with me," he said, a slight accent to his voice.

I stiffened in shock, unable to comprehend what he was saying. I was a nobody, invisible. How could he possibly know of me, let alone go to the trouble to—what, kidnap me? From school? This couldn't be real.

"Hey now," Bryan said, standing up. He was large, but he looked like a child standing up to this man. "You can't just take her," he turned to me. Eyes that I had only known to hold anger and hatred, now looked at me with protectiveness and curiosity. "Do you know this guy, Callie?"

I shook my head, staring at the strange man, trying to solve some complex equation. He couldn't be some long-lost relative—like say, my long-lost biological father. There would've been more of a resemblance. This man's black eyes and darker skin tone, along with the accent let me know that he was from lands far away. With my pale skin, brown hair, petite frame, and hazel eyes, we couldn't look less alike.

At the shake of my head, Bryan stood up straighter, and his friends, to their credit, fell in beside him. It wasn't much, but it was enough to let everyone know they would back their friend up. Their unity was a futile action, but it shocked me nonetheless. Especially when quiet, mousy Grayson stood up to join them.

The guy flashed a blindingly white smile and said. "You prepubescent chil-dren think you can take me? Cute." His face completely changed, the smile fading way to a deadly calm. "Now step aside. I'm only here for the girl."

Grayson looked terrified as did the rest of Bryan's friends. But, Bryan kept strong—even when the man pulled the gun on him. The aide cried out, picking up the phone and dialing the office. The strange man didn't even seem to care that help would be on the way. He didn't even bat an eye at the staff's actions.

I had to swallow twice to squeak out a comprehensible, "No!"

The man moved just his eyes to analyze me.

I swallowed again. "Don't. I'll go. Don't hurt anyone."

"Callie," Bryan warned, unhappy.

I jumped up to slip past the ring of protectors. It was incomprehensible how people that'd made me feel so uncomfortable were now my pseudo-heroes. Even if they hadn't stood up for me, I would've gone with the guy anyway. I didn't want anyone to get hurt. That was guilt I didn't want on my conscience.

Bryan reached out to grab me, but it was too late. I was within the man's grasp, and he wrapped a large hand around my arm, pulling me to him before Bryan could stop me. He addressed my classmates. "You guys have balls, and I respect that—but if you try anything, and I do mean anything," he tugged me to his side and pointed the gun, "She dies."

He yanked me out of the room and into the hall. He made sure I wasn't going anywhere—how could I, my legs felt like jelly—and then wedged a lock into the door. "Don't trust them anyhow. Nothing but hormones in the drivers' seats at that age. Let's go, girl."

He yanked me along, not seeming to care that he was pretty much carrying me. He went down empty hallways and up to a door that was still intact. Either this hadn't been his way in, or someone had let him in.

Outside, the late-August sun of Pennsylvania blasted us in the face. The air was so hot and humid that it felt like I was trying to breathe through a straw. It took a minute for my eyes to adjust to the glaring brightness.

When my vision cleared, I looked around, praying a police officer would be nearby.

There wasn't. The only thing was a nondescript white van, parked by the sidewalk, that the man shoved me into.

My eyes then needed to readjust to the dark before I could see anything. The temperature was cooler in here, raising goosebumps along my arms.

I knew that the air conditioner had to be running full blast and that the van had to be running, but I couldn't hear it. My blood was pumping with a loud beat. I was blind and deaf in a situation where seconds could make the difference between escape or...not. I was desperately avoiding thinking about the "not."

I was terrified. The gravity of the situation was settling in, and I was realizing that I truly was being kidnapped. I turned back to the door behind me, ready to try the handle, but a voice stopped me.

"I wouldn't," the deep voice said. "Well, actually, that's a lie. If I were in your position, I would, but I'm telling you now that there's no way out, so don't bother."

I froze. It was a different man in the back with me, confirmed twice-over when the van shook as the front door opened and shut. A quick glance verified my thoughts as I saw my original kidnapper in the driver's seat.

I finished turning around, spotting the man I hadn't noticed until he'd spoken up.

"Hello," the man grinned a wide, dimpled smile. "It's nice to finally meet you."

He was older, had a dark beard, and was of the same complexion as the bigger guy that'd dragged me from the school.

"Run into any problems?" he questioned, and I was guessing he wasn't asking me even though his eyes hadn't left me.

"Nope," my kidnapper said. He started the van up. He looked in the rearview mirror. "Where to, boss?"

The man leaned back in his seat, slow, relaxed, and smug, his eyes studying me as he answered. "Well, Andrea, Pennsylvania's getting a little too hot for us. I think we need to take our show internationally, and, with our secret weapon here... we just might be ready."

He paused and leaned forward, staring. "But how to get you out of the country?" he asked himself. "No social security, no birth certificate, no ID, no passport"

The more he talked, the more nervous I became. Dad said he knew someone that would take care of the physical copies with the government. However, my first task of disappearing had been to make the digital footprints of those documents go away for good. I'd only deleted them last night.

How did this man know? Had I tipped someone off? It couldn't be a coincidence that they were ready to get me almost immediately after I finished deleting my school history, the last digital record of my existence.

Would Dad go to prison? Would they think that he'd coerced me to do it since I was a minor?

My breath caught in my throat at the thought. I forced myself to speak around the tightness that had settled in my chest. "W-who are you?"

The man's smile widened. "My name is Tarik Veseli, and I've gone through a lot of hoops to get you, Callie Jensen." He turned away from me for the first time since the other guy had shoved me in. "Head to the shipping dock in Boston, Andrea. We've got a package to prepare."

I fell back against the door, terrified that he knew my name. It only confirmed I'd been sought out instead of randomly snatched. No matter how unlikely, I'd still been holding out hope.

Tarik Veseli just smiled a slow, devilish grin, his eyes full of hidden laughter.

Chapter 1

C allie," the person said, snapping me from my thoughts.

I looked up, meeting Dr. Harper's kind gaze. Dr. Harper was one of two "doctors" assigned to me after my rescue not long ago.

Dr. Harper worked for a clandestine organization called Delta, a sister company to the United States' very own Central Intelligence Agency.

Dr. Harper was a mind doctor. The other was an animal doctor, hence the quotation marks. It was somewhat amusing to me that I suddenly had two doctors after a lifetime without hospital visits. And neither of them was an actual M.D. Dr. Scott was a veterinarian, and I'd found out during my mandated therapy sessions that Dr. Harper was a psychologist—sort of.

"I'm sorry what?"

"I said," he repeated. "Are you going to tell us about the person that kidnapped you? You've only mentioned his name, uh," he looked down at his notes.

"Tarik Veseli," I said, somewhat sad all my injuries had healed. The bandages gave me something to play with when I was nervous. I fiddled with the bracelet on my wrist instead.

"Right," Dr. Harper said, looking up again. He studied me for a moment as I stayed quiet. "Listen, Callie." He closed his notebook. "Psychiatry is not my strong suit. I only minored in it. My doctorate was in art if you can believe it, but I can help you if you let me." I didn't say anything. "You sang like a bird when it came to Nikolai Ivanov, and Karl is using that information to the best of his ability. We'll find Ivanov before he can get to you… but you need to tell us about this Veseli character."

"I told you," I said. "He's dead. He had a two-man empire. It was all smoke and mirrors that he had me create digitally so that people wouldn't challenge him. Two men," I repeated, "And the other guy is dead as well."

"So, if someone is dead, we shouldn't talk about them?" Dr. Harper asked. He leaned forward. "What about Kaz?"

My heart wrenched itself into a tight fist in my chest. I looked down, playing with the twine bracelet, Kaz's bracelet. As far as I knew, the seven-year-old boy had been buried with the matching one that belonged to me. I wasn't sure though. I hadn't been brave enough to ask.

I swallowed, dropping eye contact. "I don't want to talk about Kaz."

"It's healthy to talk about the dead, Callie. It's good to remember the happy memories."

"It's the unhappy one that I'm worried about. It took me weeks to stop seeing his death every time I close my eyes. I… I need more time."

"Fair enough. It takes time to heal. Sometimes it takes years. And a lot of times, we never get over the loss of a loved one. But, I will say that bad memories become fuzzier, and the good memories less painful. When you are ready, I have the information on where he is buried."

I let out a breath of relief knowing that the Delta organization had kept their word on giving Kaz a proper burial. Even if I wasn't ready to visit the grave, if I ever would be—I still was on house arrest for my own safety.

Dr. Harper let me process before going back to his previous topic. It was his topic of choice for the past week and a half since I first made the mistake of mentioning Veseli's name. I blamed my sleep-deprivation. I could almost think about Kaz without bursting into tears now, but the nightmares were vivid and detailed—as they should be since he was killed in front of me.

Dr. Harper cleared his throat. "But what's your excuse for not wanting to talk about your first kidnapper?"

I didn't say anything.

Dr. Harper frowned. "It's not about putting a criminal behind bars. Though I'd very much like to see justice done to the kind of man that would--" he cut himself off, gathering his thoughts. "Callie, this isn't vital information. Lives are not hanging in the balance. You need to talk about Tarik Veseli simply to talk about it. It's not healthy to hold in everything that happened to you. Even when you tell us about Ivanov, it's only the information that's related to his crimes. I want fewer facts and more feelings, as cliché as that may be."

I looked out the window. The two-way mirrored glass was a good way to view the city of Norfolk without outsiders looking in. They wouldn't see anything but an abandoned building.

"I don't see what the point is in rehashing things that are in the past."

"The point is to help you work through the things done to you...the things that you had to live through."

"What about all the stuff that *I've* done?"

He leaned forward, eager and supportive. "We can talk about that. You have this guilt that no one has been able to guess at. We could talk about why you feel that way."

I shook my head.

Dr. Harper sighed again before leaning back in his chair. "Okay, let's talk about your life now, here at Delta. How are you adjusting?"

"Well enough," I said.

"You've healed up nicely, or so I've been informed since Dr. Scott insists on handling all your check-ups." I cracked a smile at Dr. Harper' jesting exasperation with his protege. "You start training soon, right?"

"I start tomorrow."

"And how are you feeling about that?"

"Well, I'm not allowed to take any computer classes yet. I think they're afraid I'll try to track down Ivanov by myself or something. I'll take physical training and some elective classes that I could choose—

so basically any class that doesn't involve a device with Wi-Fi. The classes might be fun. I like to learn. Physical training is...well, I'll like seeing Brock and Jace. I've missed them. I've missed all of them."

"It's been, what, a month?"

I nodded, not wanting to correct him that—aside from the home check-ups with Doc Scott—it had been well over a month. But hey, who was counting?

Dr. Harper smiled. "Well, good. I'm glad to see that you've made connections. That's healthy. Speaking of, how are you connecting with the Cardinals?"

"I learned their names," I hedged.

"You're not calling them by their Disney princess names any longer?" Dr. Harper asked, a bit of a twinkle in his eyes.

"No, at least, not out loud," I said. "They started calling me Wendy Darling and said I was moping around for all of my Lost Boys. I learned their names quickly after that."

Dr. Harper choked on the sip of water he had taken. He cleared his throat a couple of times. "Lost Boys?" he asked. His voice was neutral, but there was this glint to his eyes. "You mean the men on the Tate and Emerson teams? Including your very own Dr. Scott?"

"He's not *my* doctor. He's a veterinarian. He's not even a doctor. Well, I mean, he is technically *my* doctor, but—" I bit my lip. "You can't tell anyone! The doctor-patient privilege or something, right?" I prodded again when he didn't give me an answer. "Right, Dr. Harper?"

He grinned at me but didn't answer my question. "You haven't started doing any of the team-building training yet, have you?"

"No, Karl said that it would be better for me to build up my strength first as an individual. Something about needing to learn myself before I could be a good team player," I mumbled.

"That's good advice. You're lucky to have him as a mentor."

I shrugged, but it was true. Karl and the guys had blown into my life at my lowest point, saving me in ways I could even begin to imagine. "He's a good guy. I don't know how I could repay everything that he has done for me."

"Well, Karl is in a pretty self-sufficient place right now. But you don't have to help him. Perhaps...have you heard the saying: pay it forward?"

I shook my head, so Dr. Harper explained. "It means that if someone is kind to you, you can always pass that kindness along. Karl helped you, but you can always support others. That would benefit your self-image. I also think it would help you deal with the misplaced guilt you are still carrying around. Of course, talking about it would help as well. I don't suppose you're ready for that...? No, I can see you're not. Okay, well, if there isn't anything else, our time here is up. You can be on your way. What's your schedule for today?"

I toyed with Kaz's bracelet. "Well, I'm still on a sort of house arrest, though that should be lifting with my healing all finished up. They're letting me take these classes here at Delta, but they wanted it to be a gradual change. I don't have anything planned until my training with Brock and Jace tomorrow."

"Good, that will be good for you," he said.

"I'm just glad you don't have to meet me at the Cardinals' house anymore."

"Why do you say that?"

Dr. Harper...always analyzing everything I said.

He might claim that psychiatry wasn't his strong suit, but that only meant it either came to him like breathing air or he was lying.

"Well, I was going stir crazy. I hadn't left until today with you. It was good for a while, to heal and...and come to terms with...Kaz," I swallowed past the ball of grief that had wedged itself in my throat.

Kaz was the seven-year-old son of Nikolai Ivanov. Even as a hostage under Ivanov's thumb, I'd grown close to the boy over the three years I was there. And Ivanov had killed him, his own son, to punish me and show his guys that he wasn't to be messed with.

I cleared my throat. "But I think I'm ready to get back on my feet. Karl keeps going on about how I need to get to know 'Free-Callie,' but it's hard to do that from a gilded cage."

"Quite right, Wendy Darling."

That cheeky, sly...

Dr. Harper chuckled. "A fair warning, Miss Callie. Your face is such an open book. You might be careful about how you mentally prepare my demise, lest you give away your plans to the intended victim."

I groaned, giving up my dark fantasies that hadn't been well-thought-out anyway. I'd stew over it later.

I got to my feet. Already I could that my team's moniker for me would be spread around the Delta hub before lunch to those that knew of me. So, just the guys, since they were still trying to protect my anonymity. Dr. Harper was an unashamed gossip. He felt things within Delta worked like one big family, so patient-confidentiality...about something like an embarrassing nickname? It didn't exist.

It seemed I would be officially joining the ranks of the Disney Princesses. But...so would the guys as well. I wondered how they'd feel about being referred to as my "Lost Boys."

I stopped and turned, fiddling with the twine bracelet. "Dr. Harper?"

He looked up from his paperwork, his reddish hair shining in the lights.

"Is it pretty?"

"Beg pardon?"

I looked down at my wrist. "Kaz's grave. Is it pretty?"

The confusion cleared from the doctor's face like curtains pulled back on stage. "They found a very scenic resting place for him. It's nearby, in fact."

Tears welled up in my eyes, but I'd had over a month's practice at not letting them fall without my consent. "When I'm ready..." I swallowed again. I swiped at my cheeks. My hard-earned control was wavering today. "Will I be able to...?"

Dr. Harper took pity on me and guessed at my thoughts. "Will you be safe to go visit him? Of course. Ivanov doesn't know where they buried his son. It's a very secure location, inside of Delta's own memorial site. They placed little Kaz in with the other fallen heroes."

I lost all control at that.

I cried.

Chapter 2

I wiped away the last of my tears and opened the door, taking the time to glance around. I'd been rushed into Dr. Harper' office as we'd been running late, courtesy of Yolonda Bernard, a.k.a. Princess Belle, primadonna that she was.

With it being my first time out of the Cardinals' house in a while, I hadn't been able to really take in anything of the smoke-and-mirrors Delta building to my satisfaction. I was curious. I had been ushered from point A to point B both today and the first time I'd been here over a month ago.

So, I drank my fill of it now.

Via the Cardinals, I had found out that Delta was actually called Delta because of its rank of letters in the Greek alphabet. It was Delta to the CIA's alpha or some sort. Technically, there was a "beta" and "gamma" in between alpha and delta…so maybe there were other secret organizations out there the CIA had created. Or maybe… the CIA wasn't the alpha after all. Maybe it was having its strings pulled by someone higher up.

Either way, Delta was part of an acronym that stood for Delta Intelligence Training Organization, or DITO. Most everyone called it Delta though.

Delta was in a building that appeared abandoned on the outside to maintain its secrecy. Because of that, all the windows were one-way mirrors. People wouldn't be able to see in during the day, but Delta people could still see out. At night, they pulled blackout shades over the windows. It robbed workers of a beautiful night view, but it was necessary since light inside at night would be visible through the mirrored glass.

I was in the hallway and headed to the common area. I thought I'd spotted a juice bar in there and was hoping to buy something when I met up with the Cardinals.

There were several rooms down the hallway I'd been in. Many of them were open to allow glimpses inside: a flash of a person's office, someone calling a flower company, one guy buried within a bunch of technology.

I gave the computers a longing look. I missed access to the internet but was in a place now to understand why my communication had been cut off. To tell the truth, I'd been so traumatized and devastated when I first got here that I probably *would* have sought Ivanov out on my own.

A wistful sigh escaped my throat before I shook my head and carried on. The next room had a smartly dressed woman on the phone. She met my gaze and gave me a commiserating look, rolling her eyes at the person on the other end of the line.

It felt weird to be included in such an interaction. I'd been given a lot of orders, told to always blend into the background, and surrounded by strangers for a lot of my life. I had not really felt on the inside of anything before, not even to commiserate with someone.

There was a soft thump from behind me as someone caught a door jamb to stop themselves.

"Callie?"

I froze, turning around.

Standing in the doorway of the technology room I'd passed was CJ Tate.

I didn't move. I couldn't believe that it was really him. CJ was still tan somehow and every bit as filled out as his twin brother despite the love for technology that took up a good chunk of his time. He was the very essence of a golden-boy. His sun-kissed curls were mussed up a bit like he'd been running his hands through them. His golden-brown eyes were smiling at *me*, Callie Jensen. His skin even had a golden glow about it.

I had to wonder how CJ pulled that last one off. I probably spent the same amount of time on computers as CJ, and I always looked pasty and translucent in the bluish glow of a computer screen.

My breath caught for a moment as I realized how handsome CJ was.

For a split-second, I was unsure how to react around such an attractive guy. Then, I remembered all of our encrypted communications and our in-person interactions.

It was CJ. I knew CJ.

I grinned, and he was rushing me. He nearly tackled me with his overexuberant hug. Instead, he caught both of us and stood. My feet dangled in the air a good bit above the ground since he was six-foot-even, and I was barely five-foot-nothing wearing shoes.

"Callie, I'm so happy! I've been...there's so much...Callie! You're here! You're really here!" He put me down on my feet and grabbed up my hand, pulling me along with him to the tech room. "I want to show you something."

Barely able to catch my breath, I went along, trying to suppress the urge to cry. I was so stinking happy that it was like my emotions were too much, seeking any type of outlet just to relieve the expressive pressure.

I basked in the scent of lemons and bergamot, trying to commit every single detail of this moment to memory. I'd spent a lot of time with the guys that had rescued me, but I hadn't been in the clearest of headspaces. It was a point of regret I'd carried with me over the past— ahem, 43 days—*not* that I was counting.

We entered the office he'd ran out of. It was surprisingly well-lit with floor-to-ceiling windows on the back wall. It wasn't some dark, isolated room where he performed his mad hacks. Other than the sheer amount of technology spread across his dinner table-sized desk, the room was open, light, and airy.

"Is this your office?"

"Yeah," CJ said distractedly, taking me right behind that gargantuan desk of his. There wasn't an available surface in sight. It was beautiful chaos.

"Look, look," he said, gesturing me over. He realized that there wasn't another chair and pulled me into his lap without much thought.

I paused, holding my breath.

I was *sitting* in his lap.

We both froze as his casual, instinctive gesture turned awkward as the situation sank in.

Would it make it more awkward now if I stood back up? Probably. And honestly, I wasn't in a huge hurry to stand up anyway. It felt nice sitting sideways across his lap, my shoulder brushing against his strong, broad chest.

CJ, bless his cyborg-heart, cleared his throat and tried to diffuse the situation. He pulled up something on his computer that had me freezing for an entirely different reason.

On the screen were the faces of my old family. Of course, my eyes had no choice but to be drawn to the person I'd had the most interaction with. My mom was older and thin with gaunt cheekbones and haunted eyes. It looked like a deeper pain than she'd carried around before, and I had half a thought to wonder if it was because of me. My dad was much older looking as well, his hair greying at the edges and starting to pepper all over. It was hard to even look at him—knowing what I did now.

I swallowed three times before croaking out, "What...?"

CJ's tone was very pleased. "Well, I wasn't able to find anything about you, but I was able to narrow down what I thought could be your family. You told me you were from Pennsylvania, right?"

I was silent. I remembered him asking me as much information as he could since I didn't have a social security number or birth certificate. Honestly, I hadn't wanted my parents found. There was nothing there for me except an entire childhood of betrayal and deceit. If I had thought that CJ would've had a snowball's chance in hell of finding them, I wouldn't have told him anything.

CJ broke me from my shock when he asked. "Well, is it them? Are these your parents?"

I stared at the screen, not taking my eyes off it to answer. "No, it's not."

He watched me for a second before he sat up straighter, closing the pages rapidly.

I sagged in relief. If he didn't keep digging, maybe he wouldn't find out the truth. I would be mortified. If he'd been able to find them, then he'd be able to discover a lot of things better buried in the past.

"Um, Callie," he said. "I hope you don't mind my looking for your family. I wanted to do something nice for you, surprise you. I've been worried about you, and I needed to do something to keep me occupied."

"It's okay," I said, a knee-jerk reaction. Then, I thought about it a little more. Living with the Cardinals, I'd been learning more about myself. I didn't need to please and acquiesce to everything and everyone. I wasn't that good at standing up for myself yet, but I could do it on important matters. "Actually, do you mind not looking into it?"

CJ stared at me, almost eye-level even though I was sitting on his lap still. "Can I ask why?"

"I don't have a family."

"But--"

"I'll tell you about it one day when I'm ready. I promise, but you should know that the family that raised me...they're not my family. Not anymore," I said with conviction, trying to get my point across through sheer eye-power alone.

CJ pursed his lips like he didn't want to let it go, but then he finally nodded.

"Well," he said, changing the topic. "Good thing that's not the only thing I've been doing." He pulled out a very familiar thumb drive. It was the thumb drive that I had saved every bit of information that I could about Nikolai Ivanov. Before I'd been caught, it was with the hope of taking him down.

CJ had kept it safe in all the chaos overseas. Later, I'd given it back to him for safe-keeping before retreating on my healing-hiatus at the Cardinals' house.

"Of course, there was some water damage, but it didn't take much to get it up and running again."

My eyes watered, and I threw my arms around his neck, burying my face in his shoulder. Hesitantly, his arms came up to encircle me before squeezing me back just as tightly—if not more so.

It felt good to be held. I'd gone so many years without any positive physical contact. Over the last month one of the Cardinals, Beatriz Josefina Catalina Moreno—Triz for short, a.k.a. Moana—had been building me back up with hugs and touches and hand-holding. She was an exuberant, lovable force to be reckoned with. It reminded me of the guys I'd grown so close to in such a short amount of time. She had filled a space they'd left in their 43—sorry, 44-day absence. With her perseverance she'd not only replaced an empty space, she carved her own space entirely into my heart. Triz had done a lot to make up for my lack of affections for the last seven years of my life.

Since then, I'd come to crave it.

I let myself relax into CJ's hold a tiny bit before pulling away.

I sniffed and sat up. "Was there anything useful on it?"

CJ's eyes grew serious. He looked so much like his twin brother at that moment. I always thought of CJ's eyes as golden-caramel brown, whereas his twin, Jace, had dark-chocolate eyes that were serious when he wasn't being sarcastic. It wasn't true; they were identical twins, down to each and every freckle, as far as I knew. Yet, my mind refused to believe it, except for right now, apparently. I had to remind myself we were surrounded by computers and that this twin smelled like lemons and not oranges. It was CJ, not Jace.

"No," he said. "I'm almost through all the information. It's been a long process. When I go into the different businesses and contacts—Callie, you stockpiled a wealth of information on here," he said impressed.

"Well, there would've been more, but it was a spur of the moment decision to do it. I tried to take the most important information," I said.

"I can see why Ivanov threw you in the tank then."

I shuddered at the thought of the tank. It was a steel box, filled to a few inches from the lid with rancid water, Ivanov's favorite form of punishment.. He'd throw people in there to kill him, drowning after days of treading water and exhaustion. He liked to leave the bodies in there for a while to flavor the water for the next visitor.

CJ continued on, "No doubt when he threw the thumb drive in, he wasn't expecting you to be found. He may have scrubbed the loose ends and be untouchable, but you definitely crippled him. There's no way these connections and resources were a blip on his radar. As you know, it's nearly impossible to eradicate things completely. There's not enough there to implicate Ivanov, but with the lines already drawn, I can get a pretty good idea about their use and value to his empire. Of the little I checked, some of the political figures alone were extremely high in power."

He started pulling up different web pages of obscure references—a birthday celebration in a newspaper article, a review from a college student about the new head of power, an official that visited an elementary school for a reading day.

"Callie, I think some of these people were even a part of the Russian Federation...that's just...it's mind-boggling...and Ivanov's had to cut ties with all that because of you," CJ looked at me, waiting until I met his golden eyes before he continued. "Because of *you,* Callie."

I felt an overwhelming urge to cry once more, but he wasn't finished.

"And it's not just his contacts either." He pulled up countless pages and articles. "Aleks has been helping me translate a lot of these. Warehouses, bank accounts, weapons caches, cover-ups...all useless with the information on this thumb drive—a thumb drive that you created on the drop of a dime."

I flushed a bit, embarrassed and just all around relieved that we'd been able to make it out of Russia. I was thankful that Nikolai had been so arrogant to leave the flash drive with me in the tank. He'd been sure die. Like CJ, he must have underestimated the extent of the data I'd collected, or he might not have taken the chance.

I wondered if the hacker he'd needed to replace me would have survived the temper that must have followed that little bit of news. "Don't kill the messenger" had never really applied in Ivanov's book, and when his new hacker would've finished figuring out just what all I'd stockpiled...

He was dead. In my mind, I knew that person would've been killed in Ivanov's anger. He didn't like having his authority tested.

"What about the cover-ups?" I asked. "The people framed for his crimes?"

"That's a little trickier. Even if we could get those people exonerated based on your evidence, most of the prison staff are in Ivanov's pocket to some degree. You weren't just being paranoid when you wanted to leave Europe as soon as possible."

"I wish," I said.

CJ tapped his keyboard in thought. "What if we got them extradited to the US? The ones that are alive, we could possibly put them in witness protection..." he trailed off because I was already shaking my head.

"I have no idea how Karl managed it the first time. Even if he *could* get that paperwork pushed through again, it would be very difficult to get them out of prison. Word would reach Ivanov, and he'd order them dead. It would be mass 'suicides' and lethal inmate brawls. He wouldn't even have to lift a finger. Spread the word through the right channels that Ivanov is looking for a favor, and people would be climbing the walls to obey." I froze as I had a bad thought.

"What?" CJ asked, picking up on my tension.

"I had planned to let any surviving families know about the cover-ups. They might have loved-ones that were killed or wrongly convicted. I guess I hoped to give them some peace of mind. I won't be able to do that. What if in their grief they tried to challenge Ivanov or caused a ruckus? I'd condemn entire families to death."

I was so upset because that had been my plan. Not knowing if I'd be able to freeze any of Nikolai's assets, I had at least hoped to put some minds at rest.

"You should still tell them," CJ said at a low, calm volume. "I'd want to know if...if my brother…"

I shook my head. He was talking like a hero, but I was playing in the real-world's sandbox, a sandbox dominated by Ivanov.

"Don't contact any of the families," I said. "Promise me? You saw yourself how far Ivanov's reach is. He's got people in the *Russian Federation.* You can't do that to those families. A lot of them are innocent and didn't even know what kind of business their loved ones got up to. The ones that were savvy of Ivanov's corrupt power would have to decide to seek justice or say nothing and survive. Women, grandparents, children...promise me, CJ," I demanded. "They're better oblivious and alive than dead. Don't make them have to carry the responsibility of a choice like that."

CJ frowned, not saying anything for a long time, until he gave a short nod, looking mad.

I felt bad for angering someone so happy and hopeful, but I'd do what I could to protect those still alive. "Thank you."

"Do *not* thank me for this. Not for this," he said shortly.

I hesitated, caught by surprise from the vehemence of his reaction. Guilt settled over my shoulders like a weighted blanket.

I swallowed the best I could through a suddenly tight throat and started walking towards the door. At the last minute, I turned back. "Can I have the thumb drive? One day, I'll get access to the internet again, and I would still like to research how to take Ivanov down."

At first, CJ looked like he was going to refuse me, but he pulled the thumb drive out and handed it over to me without a word.

I left, feeling the familiar guilt I'd racked up as Byte-Syzed, the unknown hacker. I thought I'd be able to absolve it if I worked hard enough, helped enough, and sacrificed enough. Maybe that had been hopeful thinking. It'd been over a month since I'd learned anything about Free-Callie. The pain helped hone the message that Free-Callie was a hopeful mess, and the backlash from that hurt.

Like a bullet to the stomach.

I should know.

Chapter 3

I was back at the Cardinals' house, laying on the bed I'd been using for the past month. No longer interested in the juice bar after my run-in with CJ, the Cardinals had been perceptive and brought me back to the house without any questions.

I was on my back, staring at the ceiling. My mind was unable to comprehend how CJ and I could've had such different opinions on the whole matter. I was trying to protect people's lives. Why couldn't he *see* that? I hated that he was mad and disappointed with me. It made all the guilt of the bad decisions I'd made as a hacker feel lemon-fresh in my mind.

There was a knock at the door, interrupting me from my thoughts.

"Callie? We made your favorite. Blueberry muffins. Why don't you come down to eat with us so we can talk?"

I turned my gaze to see who'd been sent to fetch me. It was Beatriz, or Triz, emphasis on the Portuguese pronunciation. Triz was very close in my mind to Natasia or Tasia, the Russian girl on the team. It was difficult for me to not call them the others' name by accident even though they were like night and day.

Triz was from Brazil and looked like Disney princess, Moana. There was no other way to put it. She had large brown eyes, mocha skin, full lips, long wavy hair, and an endearing smile. Her figure was short and voluptuous figure with curves in all the right places. She was the friendliest, most open person I'd ever met.

On the other hand, Natasia was tall and slender with sharp cheekbones, platinum blond hair, sculpted eyebrows, and ice blue eyes. With a pang of longing, I'd noticed that her eyes were only a shade darker than another Russian Delta member I knew. Natasia's thin lips were always in a serious line, rarely cracking a smile, and her personality matched that. Her frosty demeanor at first impression along with her pale complexion had earned her the Elsa nickname from fellow Delta members.

It was sad how long it'd taken me to stop mixing their names up with all those differences.

I got up from the bed and made my way towards the door. I avoided looking at the large mirror above the vanity. It was the only furniture in here other than the bed. I'd inherited it from Triz when she'd moved out to give me my own room. I didn't want to glance at my reflection at that moment and have to deal with the person that I'd become, keeping secrets to protect people. I hadn't liked it when it'd been done to me, so who was I to choose what these grieving families could and could not know? Maybe CJ was right?

When I got to the doorway, Triz threw her arms around me in a hug. We were about the same height, so I was able to briefly wrap my arms back around her with ease and smell the acai fruit and coconut in her long, wavy hair.

Thankfully, I'd gotten used to Triz's hugs. She came from a "huggy" family. I wondered what it would've been like to be a part of such an open and affectionate group of people.

Without a word, Triz took my hand and led us both down to the kitchen.

The Cardinals' house was a homey place that made up for in acreage what it lacked in square footage. It had been purchased specifically for the seclusion and ease of defense or escape if Natasia's Russian-mob father ever came knocking. Likewise, it was great for me, also on the run from Russian crime-lord, Nikolai Ivanov. So, even though there was a lot of land, the house was small. It had four bedrooms, one and a half baths, a living room, and a kitchen.

Triz led me to the kitchen.

The rest of the Cardinals were already down there.

When I'd been brought into Delta protection, I'd had to pick a team to stay with for my own safety. There were two teams that I'd been tempted to choose, the Tate team and the Emerson team. I'd grown to care for all the eight guys and had been unable to choose between the two groups. That's how I ended up with the Cardinals which was actually a great fit.

There were five girls that made up the Cardinals before I came along. They were called "Cardinals" because of a famous polyglot, Giuseppe Mezzofanti, an Italian cardinal that was renowned for knowing so many languages.

Each of the Cardinals on the team knew at least three or more languages, including me, so it was like fate in some ways.

My eyes immediately found the sculpted, svelte form of ice-princess Natasia Mirov. Next to Natasia, was the leader of the Cardinals, Sabra Jaheem. She said it was okay to call her Sarah, but I liked the uniqueness of her name and had made the decision to call her that. She was nicknamed Princess Tiana at Delta. She was imposing and built like an Amazonian warrior. She was dark-skinned, muscular, and had full features—large, open eyes, broad cheeks, and incredibly gorgeous filled-out lips. She gave me a look that was somehow both encouraging and stern, leaving me uncertain about if I should feel scolded or praised. I probably felt both. She was a woman of few words, but she had single looks that spoke entire stories.

Pulling a tray out of the oven was Darcy Gallagher, a.k.a. Princess Merida. She was from Ireland, had snow-white skin, freckles, bright blue eyes, and wild, untamed red curls that went down to her waist. She was of medium build and stature except for the very generous portions of her, uh, bust...area. She gave me a wink as she saw me. "Callie," she chimed with her Gaelic accent.

This caused the last Cardinal to turn around. Her name was Yolonda Bernard, and she went by Yolo, making it her life's mission to...well, live up to her philosophy: you only live once, YOLO. She was petite with a short hairstyle that was constantly changing shape. Today her medium brown hair was done in a stylishly messy...bob-do-thing swept to the side. Her brown eyes were lined with dramatic makeup that I'd been told was a smoky look. She was French and brunette, so her nickname was Belle, though she wasn't bookish in the slightest. She was an independent femme-fatale as lethal as she was attractive...mysterious and inviting...to everyone but me. I think she found me too cautious for her tastes, but she was polite to me either way.

"Come have a seat, *a chara,*" Darcy said, her Gaelic endearment coming out with a thick brogue. "We made your favorite."

Triz ushered me to her seat and went to get another one for herself from the pantry. Darcy plated me a blueberry muffin the size of my face. I couldn't hope to eat it in a week, let alone a day, despite my increased appetite over the past 44 days.

I knew better than to protest though. Darcy was still holding an oven mitt, and I didn't want to test her passionate temper which was Irish-strong and redhead-short.

"Thank you, Darcy," I said softly.

Natasia leafed through the paper in front of her, forgoing all meals except dinner when she loaded up on sausage, animal fat, lard bread, and soup. Despite not eating, she was sitting with us anyway sipping water.

Yolo was eating a grapefruit, croissant, and espresso as her late breakfast. I was fairly positive that she was a vegetarian but hadn't really had the courage to ask.

Sabra left her muffin on the plate, looking around to address the team. She was a business first, fun never kind of person. "Okay, today was Callie's first time outside of the house. Miraculously, the world didn't collapse, so we can celebrate that."

"Did you have a good visit with Dr. Phil," Natasia asked, sipping at her water, her icy eyes studying me.

"Dr. Harper," I corrected. I'd gotten along rather well with Natasia, despite her frosty personality towards most people. It was why I felt comfortable enough to correct her.

Natasia didn't crack a smile, but the corner of her thin mouth twitched the slightest bit. "Fine, did you have a good visit with Dr. *Phil*-lip Harper?"

I shrugged. "I guess he's upset that there's still stuff I don't want to talk about. I just don't see the point in talking about them."

"Right, and you got your medical degree...where exactly?" Yolo asked idly, not looking up from her plate.

"Yolonda," Sabra scolded, her voice sharp.

Yolo didn't acknowledge the reprimand as she dug into a grapefruit the size of her plate.

I didn't let Yolo's comments get to me. I'd grown a pretty tough skin in my life. "It's okay, Sabra. She's right. I should talk about my past. I just don't want to, I guess. It won't change anything."

"But it'll make you feel better, *maninha*," Triz said, calling me 'little sister' in Portuguese while stealing a strawberry off my plate.

I frowned at her. "I'm pretty sure I'm older than you. *And* taller than you," I added, proud that there was someone around my age that I was taller than.

She flashed her big, unrestrained smile. Her perfect and bright white teeth were blinding against her flawless, freckled mocha skin. It reminded me of a certain, shameless veterinarian. "And?" she asked.

"I know what *maninha* means. It means little sister."

She stole another strawberry from my plate. "It suits you, *maninha*."

"I agree with her, *mladshaya sestra*," Natasia added, not looking up from the newspaper.

I groaned internally and blocked Triz's next swipe with my fork. "Speaking the same thing in Russian doesn't change the fact it's not true."

"But, by your own argument, I am taller than you, so that should make you the little sister, *da*?" Natasia asked, a sharp brow raised.

I stabbed at the muffin on my plate.

"This topic you won't talk about," Sabra said, focused on cleaning her plate. "Is it about Tarik Veseli?"

I sat up a bit. "Yes," I said in a soft voice. "Dr. Harper wants me to tell him about when I was first taken."

"That's a big part of your life, *mladshaya sestra*," Natasia said. "And Dr. Phil knows what he's doing. He wouldn't lead you wrong."

"You know he doesn't like it when you call him that, right, *bol'shaya sistra*," I said back.

"Ha, that is not a truth, Callie. That is a layer, like Russian matryoshka doll. Dr. Phil says he doesn't like it, but on inside is another layer that is very pleased with the compliment. Like when you call me big sister. You say it sarcastic, but I think you are happy on inside layer to use it."

I didn't say anything to that. I was afraid to admit it to myself, but I was starting to feel like I could make a home here with the Cardinals.

And it absolutely terrified me.

Chapter 4

The following day, the car ride to Delta was dead silent. Sabra and Natasia had left early on a case translating via phone conference for a job. Darcy was called in ahead of schedule to the restaurant she bartended for, and Triz had to go to the car shop for an emergency repair on a loyal client's motorcycle.

That left Yolo as the person to give me a ride to Delta for my first training...hence the silence.

Today, Yolo's hair was straight, parted on the side, and draped over to hide one of her sultry, dangerous eyes. She had on a large, billowy shirt, cut on the top and pulled off of one shoulder to continue with the asymmetrical look. Finishing the outfit, she had on ballet flats and plum colored skinny jeans.

Even though that was a casual look for her, I still felt underdressed in my shorts and t-shirt. I wasn't dressed down from a lack of funds. Buying new belongings for me had been one of the first things the Cardinals had done. In fact, Yolo herself had been the one to take me to the shopping mall for clothes and things for my room. However, I had only felt comfortable buying the necessities. It was what I was used to. Not only that, I felt guilty about spending their money even with their numerous assurances that it was mine to use.

I looked out the window. Memorizing the way to Delta on my trip yesterday had been a priority. I had firsthand knowledge about the necessity of it. Today, I spent my time studying the streets and landmarks in case I ever found myself stranded as I'd been after that CIA agent, Branson Grinley, had taken me.

Yolo pulled into the parking garage for the hospital, whipping her little, vintage beetle into a space before another driver could take it. She ignored the angry honk and proceeded to get out, her head held high considering she was only half a head taller than me.

I scrambled to undo my seatbelt and follow after her. I wasn't 100% sure she wouldn't leave me stranded if I didn't keep up, unable to access Delta without her key card.

I didn't want to be late on my first day.

It had nothing to do with the fact that I was going to be seeing Brock Johnson and Jace Tate, CJ's twin brother—both of which I hadn't seen in 44 days.

Not excited at all.

The angry owner of the silver car gave another honk for good measure. I'd been crossing in front of the car, near the hood, so it made me jump and startle. I bit my lip so hard that I drew blood. I glanced at the windshield but only saw my own wide-eyed expression mirrored back at me in the darkly tinted windows.

I gave an apologetic wave and rushed to catch up with my impatient escort.

I reached Yolo right before she entered the stairwell. We went to the 4th floor at the hospital, entered the designated elevator, scanned her card, and walked out into Delta through the elevator's back wall. The mirrored doors shut behind us, obscuring the covert entrance once more.

It was bustling and busy inside Delta—busier than I had seen it my two times here.

I wondered if CJ would be in today. I had a hard time sleeping last night after our disagreement—unwilling to budge but wanting to smooth things over. He was one of my few friends.

With confidence, Yolo headed towards another set of elevators.

I frowned in confusion but didn't say anything.

"Just ask the question if you have it, Callie," she said shortly in her sultry French accent, pushing the button for the fifth floor. "You're too cautious."

I did a double-take at the buttons. The elevator between the hospital and Delta only had four floors, mostly because the hospital only had four floors. However, I kept forgetting that Delta had eight floors plus a basement and possibly a subbasement.

I cleared my throat, not sure how Yolo had known that I'd had a question in the first place as she hadn't looked at me once this morning.

I tugged at Kaz's bracelet. "Well...I sort of already figured out why we needed this elevator to go up. The hospital only has four floors, and we're going to the fifth…but I guess I was also wondering what was on the other floors."

"Well," she said. "That's classified."

"Oh," I said.

She gave me a weird look. "I am kidding, of course. Callie, lighten up. There are different classes on the floors, the fourth floor is admin and conference rooms. The fifth floor is the gym—or dojo as your Lost Boy, Brock Johnson, would call it." I blushed at that, but she didn't notice as she was carrying on. "There are a short shooting range and bomb tech departments in the basement, completely soundproofed. You'll learn the different levels soon enough."

I processed that information, realizing that CJ's office was on the 4th floor, the admin floor. He was very young to be the head of a department, but maybe Delta worried about who was best for the job, despite age?

The doors opened up to a hallway running perpendicular to the doors. Hanging up on the wall right in front of us was a sign saying that the gym was closed for the next two hours. It directed people to use the secondary workout room on the seventh floor.

Had the entire gym been closed...for me?

"Girls' locker rooms are to the right," she said with a nod, turning to leave.

I felt nervous like it was the first day of school, and I was going to gym class. I was never any good at sports, even after defense training with Veseli and Ivanov's people, I had two left feet. "How will I find you when it's over?"

Yolo's accent became stronger as she grew impatient. "Just go to ze fours floor when you are done. Natasia and Sabra weel be zare. You can wait in ze common area. Get a juice or somezing," she said, fishing out a twenty and handing it to me. "And *non*, just take it. You are always so damned modest. Is zare even a mean bone in your 4'11" body?"

Yolo shut the doors, leaving me in the hallway alone.

"4'11 and 3/4"," I said a second too late to a closed door. I sighed, tucked the money into my bra, and headed towards the girls' locker rooms.

The room had painted concrete, dim lighting, and wall-to-wall navy-blue lockers. Some lockers were open and empty, others had stuff stored in them. A mixture of different perfumes and body sprays assaulted my nose, so I didn't stay long. I didn't have anything to change into anyway.

I headed past the bathrooms and showers and entered the gym. Inside was a long room with padded floors, workout machines, and two walls of mirrors. The area was open and well-lit with the floor-to-ceiling windows on the exterior of the building.

My eyes stopped on the two figures in the middle of the room.

Brock and Jace.

They hadn't changed at all, except their hair was the slightest bit longer since I'd seen them last.

My first instinct was to run to them, but then I remembered my fight with CJ. Jace was his twin brother and teammate. Would he be mad at me as well? Would they have told the Emerson team also? Would Brock be angry?

I stopped in place, filling the doorway and not entering the room.

Jace was the first to spot me, and when he did, his reaction erased all doubts from my mind.

"Hey, Damsel," he said with a smirk. Identical to his brother, he was six-foot-tall, tanned, and had sun-kissed blond curls. He liked to call me a damsel in distress for the one time—*one time*—that he saved me, according to him.

He walked over and pulled me into a bone-crushing hug that felt like coming home. I took in the familiar scent of synthetic oranges as I returned the hug, only able to get my arms around his neck. I could've been blasted to smithereens by a bomb at that moment and been happy to go.

"Is she...purring?" Brock's voice came from close by.

Brock's proximity, along with his question, snapped me out of the trance I'd been in. I let go of the bone-crushing grip I'd taken without realizing it.

"Don't worry, Damsel. You can hug me any time you like. I don't mind," he said, setting me on my feet with a wink. I blushed, avoiding his dark chocolate eyes.

I didn't get much of a chance to settle before Brock swept me up from behind, holding me to him in his own hug. His strong forearms wrapped around my waist, just under my chest. Brock, like me, wasn't a touchy-feely person, but he and I seemed to have made an exception for each other in the short, intense time we'd known each other.

He leaned in to talk in my ear. His tone was casual and his words were friendly, but the sensation of his permanent 5 o'clock shadow scratching my neck left me shivering. "Callie, we've missed you. You ready yet to leave your *temporary* team."

I shuddered as goosebumps broke over my skin. I patted his arms, taking in the scent of aftershave and rain. "The Cardinals are very nice actually. They've really taken me in under their wing."

Brock grunted at that, holding me for a bit longer, before letting me go when Jace cleared his throat with exaggerated force.

I glanced Brock over. He was tall, pushing six and a half feet, and had thickly stacked muscles everywhere. He had a black belt in some form of fighting, and it showed in the clearly defined muscles underneath his gray shirt. Brock was a very masculine guy. He had short black hair that he ran his hands through a lot, so it usually stuck up a bit in the front. He had a strong jaw, dimpled chin, thick brows and neck, and winter-gray eyes.

"Okay," Brock said. "We've got the gym to ourselves for the next two hours. We're going to make the most of it. I need to assess your levels first before I can plan out how to train you."

"Blah, blah, blah," Jace said and nudged me. "It boils down to this: you get one-on-one...well, two-on-one *private* training. You should feel very special."

"Yes," Brock said. "Usually you would be in a class with about thirty other people at your level, but you're what the CIA calls a spook so you get preferential treatment. Though *two-on fucking-one* is a bit excessive." Brock shot a pointed look at Jace.

Jace held his hands up. "Hey, the top brass said I could be here to help."

"I've never needed help, and you've never offered help when I taught other classes," Brock said. "*And* they only said you could be here because CJ cashed in a favor--"

Jace wrapped an arm around my shoulders, leading me to one of the treadmills. "While Brock pouts, let's get started."

"I'm not fucking pouting!"

"Okay," Jace said. "The first test measures endurance. Basically, you run until you fall off or puke. Stopping before that point is unacceptable."

Brock interrupted at my wide-eyed expression. "Don't fucking listen to him. That's not how we run our endurance tests."

"It's how I run mine," Jace said with a smirk, hands in his pockets.

"Yes, well, you teach the advanced classes," Brock said. "For a baseline, all you have to do is run as much as you can in thirty minutes, *dušo*."

I still had no idea what Brock was calling me when he said that. I could speak several languages, but I couldn't get a read on what language he was speaking. He spoke Russian and German, but it wasn't either of those. I spoke Russian and had checked in a word-to-word German dictionary for the other.

Brock continued, stressing his point. "That's more than enough for most cases where you'll need to run anyway. If you're ready, climb on."

He helped me mess with the settings, showing me how to use the different buttons with Jace adding in short, sarcastic remarks the entire time that had me struggling not to smile.

Finally, I pointed to him and said, "Hush."

Jace's jaw dropped open, shocked at my reprimand since I was usually so quiet around him.

Brock smirked.

Jace had recovered and sent a frown Brock's way as he crossed his arms. "Ha, ha," he deadpanned. "Don't come crying to me when you need a hero to save you, Damsel." And with that, he turned the treadmill on to a very, *very* brisk pace.

Well, someone was a bit disgruntled.

I scrambled to take off running and avoid being catapulted off the machine.

Brock had finished beforehand explaining all of the functions, so if I'd needed to, I would've been able to slow down the speed. As it was, I wanted to challenge myself, so I left it alone. I knew I wouldn't be able to make it the full thirty minutes at that pace, but I was going to try. I didn't want to disappoint anyone else like I had CJ.

I surprised myself by nearly making it. I was nearing that point Jace mentioned where I would either throw up or get vaulted from the machine after collapsing in exhaustion. Thankfully, neither of those happened as it was Jace himself who reached over and turned down the speed to a brisk walk without any prompting on my part.

I glanced at him the best I could. There was only time to glimpse a small frown on Jace's face before I had to concentrate on putting one shaky foot in front of the other.

"Time," Brock said, staring at the stopwatch and recording something down on a clipboard. I hunched over, gasping for air with my hands on my knees. Brock also seemed upset about something, but he must have chosen to keep it to himself because he said, "Good job, Callie. You're right about where you should be on endurance—which is surprising considering how you've only just finished healing."

I nodded, trying to regulate my breathing to not sound so out of breath, but I was doing so at the risk of passing out from lack of oxygen.

"Okay," Brock said. "I think we'll spend some time on the weight machines. The last hour we'll do some practice sparring and basic defense." He walked off, completely missing my incredulous look.

Last *hour*? There was *more*?

Jace didn't miss my look though, and he smirked at my expense before handing me a towel and water. "Don't drink too much too fast, unless you want to become close friends with the toilets in the girls' locker room," he said sagely.

I hung the towel around my shoulders and used a gargantuan amount of self-restraint to avoid guzzling the whole bottle down. I *really* didn't want to get sick as Jace had implied.

Brock was setting up one of the weight machines for me, and I swore that my legs trembled in protest.

Dutiful and resigned, I headed over.

"Hey, Chuck Norris," Jace called. "Before you go all dastardly drill sergeant, why don't we do some stretches instead."

"What? Stretches aren't until the cooldown," he said. "And I don't even assess them."

"Well, that's your flaw, not mine," Jace said. "Flexibility is a very important skill. What good is it to put some distance between you and a bad guy if you can't squeeze yourself into a halfway decent hiding spot?"

Brock turned and opened his mouth to refute Jace's claim but stopped when he got a good look at me. I must have made a pretty pathetic sight because he conceded without argument. "Fine. We'll do ten minutes of stretches."

"Twenty minutes," Jace said. "And it'll be yoga."

"The fuck? Yoga?" he asked, incredulous.

"Why not? That's what I use to assess most of my students. It's not always about how much weight you can lift, but what you can do with your own body."

"Watch it," Brock growled.

"Oh, come on, I didn't mean it like that," Jace said. He tilted his head a little bit, staring off into space. "Although…"

"Stop!" Brock said. "Fine."

Jace shook his head, focusing back on the conversation. "Fine, what?"

Brock gritted his teeth. "*Fine*, you can do the yoga thing."

"What do you mean 'you'? I didn't realize that I said it was optional."

"I'm not doing it."

"You're doing it with Callie and me."

"What the fuck!" At Jace's innocent look, Brock continued, "Really? You going to pretend you didn't just say what you said? Again?"

"Don't know what you're talking about," Jace sing-songed.

"Nope," Brock said, brandishing his clipboard like it was armor. "I'm assessing, so fuck off."

Glad that I was getting a short reprieve to replenish the oxygen to my brain, and not wanting to upset Brock, I said, "It's okay if he doesn't want to do it. It's probably too easy for him."

Jace scoffed. "Too easy? More like too challenging, but whatever." He shrugged his shoulders and started to get into a stretching position.

I went to mimic his actions and was surprised to hear a dull thud as Brock's clipboard hit the ground. Not long after, Brock settled in beside me, copying our pose.

Jace named out different poses that we were doing and what muscle groups they stretched as he coached us to breathe through the poses: downward facing dog, seated forward bend, lunge—well, actually Jace called it the "tight-end rear-end move." We transitioned into cobra and then king cobra.

After some mental consideration and approval, Jace informed us that we were switching to more advanced moves. He called them out and talked us through the thirty-second holds: king pigeon, lord of the dance, shoulder-press, and—after some debate—the firefly.

Then he ended it with the peacock pose.

That was when we lost Brock. He collapsed with a loud thump on that pose before the thirty seconds were over, drawing my attention to him. I hadn't even realized he'd been struggling, but his face was sweaty and red. I moved from the position to check on him. "Are you okay?"

He nodded, laid on his back, and ran his hands through his hair, causing it to stick up in places.

Jace's smug voice floated over our way. "Too easy, huh?"

Brock sat up, his impressive abdominal muscles flexing under his loose gray tank. "Okay," he admitted begrudgingly. "Yoga is tough shit."

Jace smirked. "Don't feel so bad, Johnson. Those were some of the hardest poses there are. Damsel surprised me so we kept going," he said, pulling me into his side to ruffle my ponytail.

"Well, Callie," Brock said. "If you can do all those poses, you're pretty strong...and...flexible," he cleared his throat, seeming uncomfortable. "But, there's always room for improvement, so let's see where you are on the weights."

He led us over to the machines. "This is the bench press. The bar alone weighs forty pounds, so I don't have many weights on the ends." He got down on the bench, describing the proper pose and form for doing a set. Not counting the bar, there were sixty pounds on there, according to him, and he went through about ten presses without even looking put out.

It was...impressive.

When it was my turn, I got on, and Jace got in position to help me in case I couldn't lift the weight off my chest. In reality, he needn't have worried about me getting the bar stuck on my chest because I couldn't get it off the stand.

Brock spotted my struggle before I did and stopped me. He took off the tens and put on fives. It was much more manageable, though he still stopped me at that and took those off as well, leaving exactly zero weights on the ends.

Forty pounds.

I could only press the forty-pound bar.

The rest of the machines were similar with Brock making them look ridiculously easy and me struggling through the repetitions.

In the end, Brock declared me under average but much better than expected considering the circumstances.

"Are you done asserting your masculinity after your embarrassing yoga attempt?" Jace asked dryly.

Brock's ears tinted red.

"Right, now onto sparring," Brock said without responding to Jace's quip.

"I'll take that as a 'no'," Jace said, being ignored by Brock once more.

Chapter 5

Brock stood across from me on the padded mats. Jace was just a bit off to the side, arms crossed and mostly observing.

I was nervous about sparring, but probably not for the reasons they thought. When I'd been taken, it had been for the fact that I had essentially made myself non-existent. Basically, I'd facilitated my own kidnapping by my history. Later, my language skills were just icing on an already all-too-tempting cake.

Because of my absolute anonymity, I'd been trained in different escape and evade techniques. My jobs were to infiltrate and escape. Then later, with Nikolai, simple defense techniques had converted to maim and kill, do serious damage, and get the job done at *any* cost.

I didn't just have fight-or-flight. I had kill, maim, or die trying. Ivanov's men did *not* get caught. Period. If they were caught and did not kill themselves, they were taken care of in a much less pleasant manner with the same end game: dead. That was part of the reason why I was so well-acquainted with the tank. Killing people disagreed with me, and Nikolai Ivanov disagreed with that. That's why I'd been in the tank the last time. Ivanov had reached his limit when he found out I'd hesitated to kill that security guard at the hotel in Paris and Dell had to cover for me. Again.

The point was, I could somewhat passably fight, even if I abhorred it and refused to do it whenever possible. Due to my small stature, I had been hardwired on targeting areas with the most impact. Honestly,

I wasn't a very good fighter at all. Against Ivanov's men, I'd never once won a fight. Out on a heist, I'd done okay because most people hesitate to harm a small, young girl. My skills relied on people being fooled by my appearance so that I could inflict the most amount of damage as quickly as possible. I most certainly wasn't going to use any of those techniques here.

So, when Brock got to the center of the mat and motioned me forward, telling me to attack him, I drew a blank.

His mass was so much more than mine. I kept going to the classic, three-hit move: shin, throat, and groin in that order. It was effective because it used a person's own reflexes against them. They would hunch forward because of the kick to the shin, making the punch to the throat that much more effective. Inevitably, when their hands went up to protect their throat, it left their groin vulnerable to attack.

Needless to say, I was determined to not use that on Brock. Instead, I stood there, lamely, shifting back and forth on my feet.

Jace didn't seem to share my reservations. He cheered me on from the side, trying to get me riled up. "Come on, Callie! Give it your best shot. Pretend he killed your puppy to it wear as a hat."

Brock shot Jace a dirty look but turned back to face me, bouncing on the balls of his feet. He shrugged his massive shoulders to loosen himself up a little bit. He did a couple of dodges, light on his feet despite his size. He could be twinkle toes in a sparkly tutu.

The random thought of imagining Brock dressed up as a ballerina absolutely killed any aggression Jace was trying to draw forth with his taunts.

Logically, my mind recognized that he was a big man. He had muscles on his muscles' muscles. And he was only an inch or so shorter than the tallest person I knew—Aleks. Not only that, there was the major detail that he had at least one black belt that I knew of. After it'd been pointed out to me, more or less, it was hard not to see it in every movement he made. Every tick of the muscle, every step, every action was so fluid and coordinated that they all seemed to be calculated for the best impact. It was disconcerting, to say the least.

I knew all this and accepted it, but I couldn't really *feel* threatened. I didn't feel threatened by *anyone* on the Emerson or Tate teams.

I'd had nothing to do the past month but over-analyze every interaction with an increasingly clear mind, and I had sorted them into a schema in my head. They wouldn't hurt me. They were protectors.

"You've got this, *dušo*. Don't hold back," he said. "Pretend I'm Ivanov or that fucker Grinley."

I couldn't muster up any anger, but I didn't want to outright disobey him either, despite my conviction to not fight.

I walked forward. Brock kept his stance loose and non-threatening. I pulled my fists up close to my face and jabbed one at him.

He didn't even give me the pretense of having a chance. He moved so fast that I would've missed it completely if it weren't for the sudden, iron-grip he had on my loose fist. And yet, I still didn't feel like I was in danger.

I tried to pull my hand back, but he kept a hold of it until I looked up at him. "I'm serious, Callie. Don't restrain yourself. You won't be able to hurt me. I need to test your skills."

At my nod, he let me go. I put about five or six feet of distance between us.

I wouldn't be able to hurt him.

Our eyes met before I started to run. He lowered his center of gravity and shifted forward, bracing himself. I took a running leap, sailing straight for him and... was flipped mid-air, slammed down onto the ground, and was left staring up at the ceiling while gasping for breath.

I got lost in my memories.

"Step forward please," Nikolai Ivanov said with polite calm.

I hadn't been here very long, but from what I could tell, everyone at this compound had been gathered except for the bare-bones amount of men still needed to guard the place. Ivanov didn't seem like the type of person to leave himself vulnerable, so I very much doubted that he'd call everyone in for this impromptu meeting.

Memories of Veseli and Andrea threatened to make tears spill over. I swallowed the emotion back down, determined to keep a brave face. It wouldn't change anything to cry over them now.

Ivanov hadn't had much contact with me since kidnapping me. He didn't have much contact with anyone except for the British guy, Dell, that had been at the warehouse I was kidnapped from.

Ivanov was on the mats, waiting.

Dell stepped up to the middle of the floor, his booted feet sure and precise as he distributed his weight.

Ivanov stood there, still and intense with his eyes focused on his opponent.

Ivanov was dressed in something other than a three-piece pinstriped suit which was what I'd always glimpsed him wearing over the two weeks I'd been here. While Dell was wearing tactical clothes and boots, Ivanov wore sweatpants and was barefoot.

And yet Ivanov looked more deadly between the two of them.

I was confused until I realized that they planned to spar.

The murmurings all around let me know that this was a rare occasion.

Dell nodded his head at Ivanov, and that was their cue. The match started.

Their moves were lightning-fast and vicious. It was almost as if their bodies blurred. They were so quick that by the time I noticed Dell's broken nose, blood had already run down to the neck of his shirt. Ivanov didn't have a scratch on him.

They weren't holding back at all.

The punches were a grotesque soundtrack that I couldn't tune out. I didn't want to be here. I wanted to be anywhere else but *here. I would gladly go back to Veseli and Andrea.*

Since coming here, I'd been starved, sleep-deprived, and isolated in a cell well away from all activity at the compound. I was dirty, shocky, and weak. My senses were overwhelmed. Every sound louder, every light brighter, every touch jarring.

The first day they took me out of isolation, they showed me the tank. It was a torture device. Plain and simple. A man was being punished for letting Ivanov down somehow. At least, that was my guess as far as I'd been able to gather from the fully-grown man hysterically yelling as he begged for his life. My Russian skills were still choppy, but it's hard to miss the meaning behind the sound someone makes with that sort of plea for mercy.

The cries hadn't moved any of Ivanov's men to compassion.

They'd reeled the tank open, click by click. The smells that plumed out were putrid, horrid. Dell had dragged me up the stairs with the terrified offender. At the top, I saw that the tank was nothing more than a metal box filled with rotting water to the top. With the lid shut, there would be maybe six inches of breathing room if the person stayed still. I thought at first that I was going to be thrown in with him.

I wasn't. They just wanted me to see what the punishment would be if I failed Ivanov.

They'd thrown the man in and lowered the lid.

With a sick stomach, I asked the British man how long they would leave him in.

He hadn't answered me then, but I found out later when they pulled the unrecognizable body from the water several days later.

A series of sickening cracks made me look up.

Dell's arm was dangling uselessly by his side from an armlock. He'd popped his own shoulder out of place to escape. He didn't stop fighting though. He wiped his face with his good forearm and went back at it.

Ivanov was still cool and collected, calculating. I imagined if I saw a leopard in the jungle, it might have the same look on its face as it tried to suss out weakness in its prey. He put one arm behind his back and kept it there as if he was fencing instead of giving a brutal mauling to his right-hand man.

Even with the self-imposed handicap, Ivanov looked bored with the situation and decided to end it. He feinted, dodged, and went in for the kill, audibly snapping Dell's collar bone.

Dell stumbled. Ivanov went berserk. It was like he blurred and Dell's body would react to the punch after a short delay.

Punch. Dell's head snapped back. Punch. Dell's already broken nose knocked completely sideways. Punch, his jaw trembled to the side. Punch, he hunched forward to protect his gut. Punch, his knee dislocated. Punch, he was huddled on the ground being wailed on.

Ivanov slowed down now that his prey was on the ground. He leaned over him and picked him up by the collar of his shirt. He punched him straight in the face. Dell fell back on the ground. Ivanov picked him up again—another punch to the face.

He repeated this cold, brutal beating. Even closing my eyes, I couldn't drown out the clear, sickening sounds of the punches hitting flesh and bone.

Dell's face was almost unrecognizable hamburger by the time Ivanov decided to stop playing around. He delivered one more precise blow.

Dell's body went lax.

The cheering and jaunts silenced as Ivanov stepped to the side. He kept the unconscious Dell in his peripherals while also surveying the audience.

His piercing eyes landed on me. He spoke in English for my benefit. "Dell will be in charge of Callie's training." He nudged Dell until he stirred, groggily looking out through one half-swelled eye. Ivanov continued. "Each time, it will be as if you are fighting to the death. If I find out that you held back, my friend, I will end you and find someone else to take your place."

Dell didn't say anything. He just snapped his broken nose back into place in response.

Ivanov continued, speaking directly to me now. "You will fight every day. If you haven't managed to beat Dell by the end of the week, you will spend your weekend in the tank."

The tank?

I shuddered.

Dell just had his body mutilated, dragged across the coals, and sent through a shredder. I'd been trained by Veseli and Andrea, and yet Dell could've taken on both *of them with his dislocated shoulder and broken nose. Easily.*

I had a feeling I'd become really familiar with the tank.

"Come Monday, you will be out, ready to go again. This will repeat until you can defeat him." He smiled an ice-cold smile. "Welcome to my world, Callie Jensen."

My ears were ringing, and I was having a difficult time trying to get my body to obey my commands, so I laid there for a second. When I was able to focus, Jace and Brock were kneeling down on the ground near my head, asking if I was okay.

"I'm fine," I wheezed. They watched me as I took deep breaths and tested the mobility of my limbs. I shook my head to clear the memories from my mind.

No longer worried that there was a dangerous injury, Jace's attention shifted. "What the hell was that?" he shouted across me at Brock.

Brock looked angry. "Fuck off!" he shouted back. He turned his winter-gray eyes on me. "What the hell, Callie? You shouldn't have run at me like that if you didn't know how to stop a flip. Fuck! I could've seriously hurt you. Maybe I *did* seriously hurt you. Fuck, we need to take you to see Doc Scott."

I shook my head. "No. No, I'm fine. Really."

Jace apparently wasn't appeased with Brock's answer. "Why would you expect her to have any training? That's the whole point of what we're doing!"

"I made a mistake. Fine. But back the hell off! I wouldn't fucking hurt Callie on purpose."

"Guys," I tried to yell, but I didn't have enough breath in my lungs yet to reach a louder volume. "Don't fight!"

"See? You broke her voice, you idiot!"

"No, I didn't!"

"He didn't!" my voice was cut off again, easily drowned out by the maelstrom of testosterone rushing around the room. Finally, I stood up and shoved Jace with all the strength I had. He only fell back a half-step, but it got his attention. His dark chocolate eyes locked on me.

"Stop," I said, easily heard in the dead silence that had stolen over the room. "I'm fine. He didn't hurt me. I just got the breath knocked out of me. Besides, if he had hurt me, it would've been an accident. Brock wouldn't do anything like that on purpose. None of you would. Think about that before you go slinging hurtful accusations that can't be taken back."

Jace seemed to take my words seriously, tilting his head as he thought them over.

"Furthermore," I stressed. "If this is going to be the standard reaction every time going forward, it might be best to not have both of you training me at the same time."

Jace stiffened. "You don't want me to train you?"

"No! I'm sorry. That came out wrong. I'm not very good with social—um, that's not what I meant *at all*. Look, Jace, you're very skilled and talented and a great teacher--"

"Keep going."

I gave him an unamused look before continuing. "I think you *both* are. And I'd love to learn as much as I can from you two. You each bring something useful to the plate. I value the different styles and perspectives. Two heads are better than one, they say."

Jace coughed into his fist, trying to hide a smile, and Brock slapped him on the back of the head.

I frowned at the action, but it didn't seem as if they were being aggressive like before, more like playing around.

"Well," Brock started. "I would like one-on-one time with Callie, but I—I can't believe I'm saying this—I wouldn't mind working with you to train her." At this, he looked at Jace. "I mean, that yoga shit...that was hard. And I can see the benefits of it."

I smiled a small smile at that, somehow drawing both of the guys' eyes at the movement. My smile shrank carefully as if it was trying not to spook a wild animal.

Brock cleared his throat and looked away.

Jace continued to stare at my lips. Nervous, I licked them, and Jace's own lips parted the slightest bit. I was entranced by the action. I could see his pink tongue just inside his mouth, behind his white teeth. It looked so soft, and his lips were so...

Brock dropped a barbell, making me jump and drawing Jace's glare. "Oops," he deadpanned, bending to pick up the ten-pound weight. "We're at a good stopping point for today. *Dušo*, you can go shower and change. And before I forget, any locker that's open, you can use. Bring a lock next time so you can lock your stuff up. And, we'll see you again. Same time, day after tomorrow."

I nodded and made the executive decision to *not* tell him that I hadn't brought anything with me. It was embarrassing enough that I hadn't thought to bring clothes, so I just said my goodbyes and headed towards the girls' locker room.

Jace and Brock's voices faded out as they began to discuss their observations. They were still talking when the door closed behind me and cut off their deep, almost harmonic murmurs.

In the privacy of the girls' locker room, I gave myself a short, cautious sniff followed by a more substantial one to assess my state. I didn't smell bad, but I decided to do a quick rinse anyway. Being submerged for days on end in a tank of water had wreaked havoc on my mental state. Showers were manageable, but I had a fear of large bodies of water, enclosed spaces, and the dark. It was especially bad when they were all combined at once—a.k.a. the tank.

I showered off and reluctantly put the damp, cooled clothes back on. They clung in awkward places. Note to self: always bring spare clothes.

As good as it was going to get, I left the locker room and headed back to the elevator. Thankfully, it was not the elevator between the hospital and Delta, so it didn't need a key card to operate.

I pulled the twenty out of my bra while I was in the relative privacy of the elevator, deciding not to feel guilty about using it. I was parched and was going to be stuck here for a while until Sabra and Natasia finished up their interpreting job.

The elevator dinged and let me out on the admin floor. I was both hopeful and terrified that I would run into CJ, but even if he was around I might have missed him anyway. It was about noon, and the place was crowded. The little bistro and juice bar to the right of me was packed. Straight across, I could see that most of the couches and tables were full as well. People young and old were socializing, reading, eating, or observing like me.

The sweet aroma of fresh-baked bread, coffee, salty meat sizzling on the grill, and a variety of different citrus fruits being blended into shakes… it was heaven. My mouth watered, battling out my anxiety of so many people. I made my way to stand in line, gripping the twenty in my clammy fist until it was crumpled. All around conversations were taking place and the voices blended together into a dull roar.

That was why it took me so long to realize that someone was saying my name.

Chapter 6

Dr. Duane Scott, the veterinarian, was standing there, smiling at me. How could such a devilish, flirtatious grin fit on such an angelically perfect face? I could live a thousand years and not have an answer for that. One thing I did know was that any time I saw his smile, it sent my heart into ominously strong palpitations.

How self-serving: a doctor that propagated the need for medical help. I could be perfectly fine, and then—cue roguish smile with intense obsidian eyes and those straight, perfect teeth that stood out against his mocha skin… he could've been making millions in dental commercials—instant heart attack.

"Dr. Scott," I said with overstated politeness, moving forward with the line. If I focused on the food, I could probably calm my self-destructive heart. At least, I was hoping so. The appetite after Brock and Jace's hellacious workout was no laughing matter. It should be distracting enough...

"Don't you 'Dr. Scott' me, Babygirl. How many times have I asked you to call me Duane?" he asked, stepping forward to keep abreast of me.

"I've lost count, Dr. Scott."

"Duane, leave the poor girl alone," a female said from behind me in line.

He glanced back at the person behind us. "I will not. She's my patient. I'm checking in with her."

"Is *that* what you call it nowadays?" the voice was wry. "Besides, I thought you had animal patients, not patients of the female variety."

"It's a recent development. I'm sorry, Julie, but do you mind if I cut in? I'd like to check in with Miss Callie," he said, flashing her a smile that was so bright it gave me a secondhand daze. Under the full brunt of it, poor, twitterpated Julie didn't stand a chance, giving a stilted nod as her consent and looking away.

Doc Scott smiled a crooked smile and stepped into the long line behind me. "Well, Babygirl, how are you feeling? Brock said he slammed you pretty hard."

They'd already talked?

"It was an accident. I'm fine," I said, now desperate for a distraction and squinting at the menu. The problem was that Doc Scott himself was entirely too distracting for me to be distracted.

Uh...wow.

In addition to the traitorous, failing heart, could he check me over for mental issues? My brain seemed to be short-circuiting—again— probably due to his close proximity.

He spoke from over my shoulder, causing me to jump. "The mozzarella panini is my favorite. It's got fire-roasted tomatoes, Italian seasonings, and a balsamic glaze that just makes the mouth happy. Though, Bryce claims the chicken feta is the best, and if you know anything about Brock, you'll know he likes the cinnamon roll panini."

Unable to help myself, I turned back to him. "Cinnamon roll panini?"

Doc Scott grinned a crooked smile and folded his large arms across his chest. It pulled the navy-blue shirt taut, the short sleeves straining around his biceps. "If there's cinnamon anywhere, Brock will suss it out like a bloodhound on the trail. I'm pretty sure Miss Maggie added cinnamon roll paninis to her menu solely for our little Brock."

His use at the word "our" threw me through a pointless loop of excitement and surprise until I figured that the "our" was referring to his team. After all, what sort of ownership would I have over the tall, dark, and handsome black-belt man?

I turned back around to avoid staring at his smooth skin...the strong, pronounced jawline, the thick s-shaped brows, the shaved head... I coughed and practiced mentally saying my next statement a few times before I felt like I could get it out without embarrassing myself. "You guys must be pretty close if you know what they'd order."

"That's how Delta works. You spend enough time with your team, training and doing jobs...they become family. You know everything about them, and they know everything about you." He paused here, and I didn't dare turn around. It was hard enough to think *without* looking at him. He cleared his throat before he spoke again, a forced casualness to his tone that immediately piqued my attention. "You could learn what their favorites are too, you know? All you have to do is say the word. I'll make it happen, Babygirl."

My shoulders froze as my mind tried to decode the meaning behind his words. My heart raced into overtime, and a surge of energy suffused my body. I felt jittery like I could go another three rounds with Brock's horrible treadmill of death that'd almost claimed my sad little life.

"Excuse me, hun, can I help you?"

I looked up. I'd made it to the front of the line without even noticing. I also realized that I hadn't had a chance to read the menu. At all. I panicked.

"Mozzarella panini," I shouted, feeling like the student that had been caught sleeping in class. Then, I didn't want to give the cheeky and smooth-talking vet any ideas. I could *feel* the crooked smile forming on the roguish face behind me after I ordered his self-proclaimed sandwich, so I added. "And a cinnamon roll one!" Okay, I needed to calm down. I took a breath. Then I worried that word would somehow get back to Bryce, and I didn't want him to be offended at being left out, so I added, "And a chicken feta panini!" *Seriously, calm down, Callie.* "Please," I tacked on at a more reasonable level.

"Thas quite a bit o' food, guhrlie, ahre ya sure you can put it away?" she said with an Irish accent.

Fervently ignoring the cough-chuckle from behind me, I nodded, and she didn't even bat an eye. She totaled me up, I handed over the crumpled bill, and I was good to go. I shuffled down the counter to wait for my order. I was determined to avoid all eye contact with...well, everyone, but I couldn't stop the morbid curiosity—like looking at an accident on the side of the road. His presence was practically magnetic in its draw. I had to look. There was no choice, really.

My quick glance was more than enough to light my cheeks aflame.

Dr. Scott's crooked smile was loud and proud on his roguish face. His black eyes were full of suppressed mirth as he watched me, and it seemed that even his thick eyelashes were amused and laughing at my expense. He had to cough a couple of times to hold back what sounded suspiciously like chuckles.

The ground could have swallowed me up, and I wouldn't have minded at that moment.

Ordering the two other paninis hadn't done a thing to persuade him that I hadn't ordered the mozzarella panini because of him. It was like I could hear the mental thoughts that had to be going through his one-track mind.

I opted to take my three sandwiches to go.

If I stumbled a little as I scampered away with my order as fast as possible, I was sure that no female would judge me. I found a secluded corner in the lounge area and dug in with gusto.

I did end up eating all the food that I'd bought—relishing the cinnamon roll one. Brock was onto something there. It had a sugary cinnamon goo filling, the bread tasted sweet like yeast bread, and the outside was drizzled with warm, vanilla icing. Delicious. If I hadn't ordered two other paninis, I would've gone back for a second or third cinnamon panini.

After I finished, I spent a good amount of time just people watching and wondering how I was going to find my teammates. I knew I wasn't going to be spotted in my little hideaway cove, though it was a close call. Dr. Scott had meandered by, leisurely looking around before heading towards the hospital. He could be volunteering there today.

I waited ten more minutes to be sure I wouldn't run into him though. I wouldn't be able to survive two close encounters of the mortifying kind in one day. Eventually, I decided to wander around and hope I'd run into the Cardinals since I wasn't sure what room they'd be in.

It turned out that I didn't have to wander far. I'd taken the maze of hallways on the right. I figured if I was already avoiding Dr. Scott, what difference would it make to also avoid a certain six-foot computer genius that could still be mad after our argument?

Choosing the hallway that didn't have CJ's office ended up being a great decision. As I was wandering past, there was a small office room with a conference call going on. There were three phones set up in the middle of the table with all the lines open. Scattered among the five people in the room were Natasia and Sabra.

Since the door was open, I assumed it wasn't top secret and listened to the conversations.

Sabra was translating for a guy on the first phone, speaking Arabic. Natasia would listen in and translate to Chinese for the person on the other phone. The third phone remained silent but open, so I assumed someone was listening in on the whole conversation.

It was interesting to see the Cardinals at work.

They were helping to facilitate some sort of foreign exchange program for local schools, but Sabra was struggling with the Arabic translations. I played with Kaz's bracelet as I debated. I listened carefully to the Arabic speaker and his dialect. I didn't want to volunteer to help, and then find out that I had been overconfident and couldn't speak his dialect anyway. After a few more minutes of conversation to confirm the dialect that he was speaking, I got the courage to announce my presence.

"I can help," I said.

The room grew silent as eyes turned to me, though the guy speaking Arabic carried on, unaware of the suddenly tense silence on our side of the line.

No one said anything, but I stood my ground. I knew I could help. My gumption could probably be credited to the leftover jitters from my run-in with Doc Scott. I cleared my throat. "He's asking about the student's accommodations and the possible transfer of credits for classes that the student might take while he's at their school," I said. The silence in the room grew. I shifted in place worried I had made a big mistake. "I uh...I think he's Palestinian, but I speak Levantine Arabic, so I can understand him pretty well..."

Sabra's face didn't change but she pulled out a chair for me between Natasia and herself. I was grateful and moved to the seat, only taking a quick glance around at the others to gauge their reactions. It seemed like they were trusting my team to make the decision, so they went with it.

I started translating in earnest. I'd relay the information in English to Natasia and listen to her translate it into Chinese for the female on her line.

The lady asked a return question, and I went ahead and translated it into Arabic for the other guy. I had done loads of interpreting jobs before of a much *less* innocuous nature. It was rote memory for me, and I got into a good, steady rhythm. In a way that I hadn't expected would be so impactful, it felt good to somehow be using my skills to help people, *good* people. Maybe I could start working to pay back all of the hospitality the Cardinals had shown me over the last weeks.

I translated the response back to English, waiting for Natasia to translate it to the Chinese female. She didn't. I looked up. Both Natasia and Sabra were staring at me, as well as the rest of the room. "What?"

"You know Mandarin?" Natasia asked, but it didn't actually sound like a question.

I realized then that I hadn't waited on Natasia to translate the female's question before I'd interpreted it into Arabic. "Oh, um...yes?"

No one said anything, and I could hear both of the people on the phone asking if we were still there. Trying to break up the silence, I nodded towards her phone. "Are you going to...?"

Natasia raised a sharp, professionally plucked brow, her lips twitching up a fraction at the corner. "No, *mladshaya sestra*. If you know both, that makes my job easier." And with that, she sat back in her seat with her hands clasped together in her lap. If we'd been at home, I suspected she might have been tempted to kick her chair back and put her feet on the table.

Uncertain, I looked over to Sabra. She gave me a regal nod with a slow blink.

"Uh..." I was distracted from trying to figure out if they felt like I'd stepped on their toes by the voices on the phones. I leaned towards the Arabic line. "*I'm sorry. We're still here. One second, please.*" Then I leaned over to respond to the other line, seamlessly switching to Chinese. "*Hello, yes. Sorry about the wait. He said...*"

Chapter 7

I had a headache and was dead-tired by the time the phone conferences wrapped up an hour later. It was a mental strain to go back and forth between two languages like that. I was pretty good at Chinese since I'd had to use it so much, but I hadn't had a lot of experience with Arabic. Not only that, but it'd been a while since I'd had to use it. It definitely wasn't one of my stronger languages. It wasn't even in my top five.

My skills were enough to get the job done though. All the details had been arranged between the two institutions. After they cut the lines, the previously silent phone had thanked us and said that they would wire us the money into our team account. That had felt good. Not that I needed the money when the Cardinals had been providing everything under the sun that I could ever need. It just felt good to contribute.

Sabra said that they'd meet me by the elevators, effectively dismissing me.

I was more than okay to high-tail it out of there while they wrapped up with the procedural stuff and talked to the well-dressed big-wigs that'd been present. Maybe they had to validate their reasons for letting me take over the job. I'd rather not be there for that conversation.

The commons area was much less crowded now with the cafe nearly empty. I ordered water while I waited and was sipping it when a hand on my shoulder startled me. I gasped, inhaling my drink. I coughed a couple of times, sadly accustomed to the sensation of breathing water without meaning to.

"Callie," said a smooth, melodic voice. I smelled tea leaves.

"Bryce?" I asked when I'd gotten my breathing back under control, turning and craning my neck up a ridiculous distance before I saw a face.

Bryce Rost of the Emerson team was standing there with a regal poise that stemmed from his proper and polished upbringing. It warred with the image that his ripped skinny jeans, long black band shirt, and numerous piercings represented. He'd told me that he liked to dress like this to pester his father. His mother found his "little rebellion" endearing and amusing.

Bryce had shiny, dark brown hair that was so smooth it probably never tangled even though it was long enough in the front that he had to whip his head to the side every now and then to get it out of his eyes. But what a treat it was when he did. That aristocratic nose, arched eyebrows, and dark cobalt blue eyes came into view.

"Hello," I said, "How are you? I haven't seen you in a while."

I was casual on the outside and definitely didn't mention the exact number of days it'd been.

"We had a pretty tough mission that the Tate team collaborated with us on. It took a while to organize and execute, so we haven't been able to do much else besides that," he said, avoiding eye contact for a second. He was usually so straightforward and confident with himself. "But enough about boring work stuff. What about you?"

"Oh, I just finished my class with Brock. And I ran into Doc Scott."

It was okay for me to call him Doc Scott when he wasn't around. It bothered him more when I called him Dr. Scott, and I found that to be a nice type of revenge for the man's ability to render me completely stupid in his presence.

Bryce's proper smile became sly. He took a step closer to me, making me feel short. He was the shortest of the Delta guys that I knew, but he still towered over me by about ten inches. "So, I hear you tried the chicken feta panini?"

I blushed, hot and fast, as my mind ran through what Doc Scott would've shared with his team. There was a devastatingly embarrassing amount he could have told. He'd at the very least already let Bryce know about what had happened earlier. I wondered if Brock was told the story as well, or possibly the rest if his team as well, Emerson and Corbin.

Either way, I was mapping out my plans for damage control. "I had other sandwiches too!"

Bryce leaned in, his dark blue eyes flashing in amusement as he pinned me in place with just a look. I couldn't breathe. He got close enough that I could smell the mint on his breath over the scent of tea leaves. "And," he drawled. "Do you find that you preferred *my*...sandwich*?"*

His tone implied innocence, but his face belied anything *but.* My own mind couldn't help but draw similarities to preferring his sandwich to preferring the guy in front of me with a presence hot enough to melt chocolate on a Siberian winter day.

I blushed, hoping against all odds that my face wasn't an open book to my less-than-innocent inner monologue.

My face must've betrayed me, though, because Bryce's smirk grew into an almost smile. "Just *food* for thought, Callie."

His innuendo was so cheesy, that it actually startled a laugh out of me.

His smirk changed from sinful intent to a light-hearted joy. His eyes were definitely dancing with amusement now, sparkling like blue sapphires. "You have a nice laugh."

"Stop fucking flirting with her."

I turned, seeing Brock approaching. My cheeks lit up as I went back to my previous train of thought, wondering if he'd run into a certain chatty veterinarian. Had he been told about me ordering his favorite panini as well?

Brock paused when he caught sight of my face. "You're blushing," he said, drawing up in front of me at his impressive height. His winter-gray eyes were zeroed in on my face, causing my blush to deepen. His hair was wet from a shower and mussed up so that it was standing on end. He smelled fresh and clean.

"Uh," I said, unable to think past that.

"Don't let him flirt with you. He'll never stop," Brock growled. "He doesn't need any encouragement, *dušo*."

I processed his words. My thoughts cleared up, leaving my brain functioning once more.

"Don't be mean. He was just being nice," I defended.

"That shit wasn't nice. It was flirting."

"Maybe she was saying that the flirting was nice," Bryce drawled, giving me an amused look.

My cheeks heated right back up. Did that mean he *was* flirting with me?

"Then again," Bryce said, drawing the words out, "She could just really likes my feta cheese sandwich."

Brock crossed his massive arms over his chest. "Feta, Bryce? I heard that she prefers the *cinnamon roll* panini."

Well, that answered that question. Brock had been told. My, my, my, but a certain veterinarian had been rather busy today.

My cheeks reddened even further as the two debated over the merits of their sandwiches. I wasn't even sure that they were talking about their sandwiches anymore either.

I didn't want to jump in to break up the heated discussion, and I didn't have to because a voice spoke up from above my left shoulder.

"You know, Callie, the turkey panini is pretty good too. Wouldn't you like to try the turkey panini?"

I spun around, not sure how I'd missed Corbin's approach, especially now that I recognized the sweet smell of sandalwood and pine. It scared and thrilled me that he'd managed to get so close without me noticing. Corbin had a goofy smile on, his head tilted to the side as if he was waiting for a response.

Corbin Myers was the fourth person on the five-man Emerson team. Corbin had sky blue eyes, thick eyelashes that would be the envy of any girl, a round, tanned face with barely-there freckles, and a messy mop of amber hair. He wasn't the shortest person on the Emerson team, but he was the skinniest.

"*Dušo*," Brock started to say, drawing me from my inspection of Corbin.

"*Broccoli*," I said impulsively in Bengali and immediately wanted to face-palm. It was the first thing that popped into my head as a nickname for him. At least it wasn't boulder or rock as Aleks liked to call him. I was still in trouble if Brock ever translated the word.

I couldn't get too mad at myself though. I'd wanted to see how he liked being called a nickname when he didn't know what it meant. And considering I'd just called him broccoli, I wasn't about to tell him what language it was so that he could go translate it. As far as I knew, no one around here at Delta spoke Bengali.

Brock frowned for a little bit. He looked suspicious, and for a heart-stopping moment, I was afraid that he actually did speak Bengali. I wouldn't put it past him. He spoke German, Russian, English, and whatever language *dušo* came from.

Heck, even if he *didn't* speak Bengali, he might still be able to guess the meaning. The word for broccoli was literally *brōkali*. Broccoli was one of those rare words that was recognizable in nearly every language.

I sweated it out for a long ten seconds, but thankfully the lack of context threw him off. He shook his head and raised a brow. "I'll figure it out."

I really, *really* hoped not.

I cleared my throat. "Well, I'll beat you to it. I'm already a step ahead of you. I at least know what language yours is from."

That was a lie, but he didn't need to know that.

"I could ask your team what language that is."

I frowned a bit. "They just discovered today that I spoke Arabic and Mandarin. They don't know everything about me yet."

"So, it's Arabic or Mandarin? I know it's not Russian or German, and you obviously don't speak Serbian," he deduced, enjoying our conversation if his relaxed, reclined posture against the wall was anything to go by.

Serbian! He spoke Serbian!

I tilted my head, trying to keep my face calm. "It might be. I know a lot of languages. It's sometimes hard to keep them from mixing."

Brock shifted. "Just how many languages do you know, *dušo*?"

He was smart, trying to narrow down his options.

"What's your definition for knowing a language? Fluently? Conversationally? Academically? Do I have to know how to read and write it as well?"

His eyebrows went up, and he let out a low whistle. "You must know a lot of fucking languages to be deflecting like this."

I smiled at him. "That, or maybe I only know four. And since you already said it's not English or Russian, I'd hate to narrow your list down to Arabic and Mandarin."

He shook his head at me, and then *bopped* me on the nose. It was such a cutesy move from such a large, masculine person that it stunned me into silence.

Corbin cleared his throat. "Uh, can we go back to talking about *my* sandwich now?"

"Whatever it is you're implying, Corbin Myers, unless you'd like to explain it to Sabra, who has become very protective of Callie here, I suggest you back off," Natasia said. She stepped up and wrapped a long, slender arm around me. Her peppermint smell suffused the air, as icy as her outward demeanor. "We've got to go, Callie. Say goodbye to the Lost Boys."

"Lost Boys?" Bryce murmured.

"Wait, wait, wait! Before you go, Callie, give me your phone. I'll put our numbers in," Corbin said.

My hand reached up to fiddle with Kaz's bracelet. "Uh..."

"Nice try boys. But she doesn't have one right now. Part of the plan to keep her safe. You'll be the first to know if that changes, *da?*" Natasia said.

She steered me towards the other elevator. I turned my head, giving what I hoped was an apologetic look towards the guys. Natasia felt the movement, followed my look, turned back around, and tucked me closer to her side, a small smirk on one corner of her lips.

It seemed like she'd pulled me closer for the boys' benefit and not mine. I frowned a bit. "Why are we going towards this elevator instead of the hospital elevator? Aren't we leaving?"

Natasia smiled. "Nope. We've had a change of plans. Karl came in today. He has news to share, and he also wants us to start team-training. We might have a big mission coming up for the team, and since you're a part of the team, you would need to participate as well."

"How could I help? I'm a wanted terrorist. And I don't have access to a computer. I'm an artist without a brush. A pianist without a piano. A--"

She just smiled and guided me in the elevator. Once inside, she pressed the button for the 8th floor—the top Delta floor. So far, I'd only been as high as the 5th for my training with Brock and Jace.

I wanted to ask Natasia what was on Floor 8, but I figured I would be finding out for myself in a second anyway. I kept quiet, thinking over my conversations with the guys.

With a cheerful ding, the doors drew back to show a wide-open, spanning space interspersed with support pillars. Immediately, I could spot the rest of the Cardinals as they were around the only furniture currently in the room: a portable table and some chairs.

Along with my team, there was Karl. Karl looked much more put together than he had been the short amount of time I'd spent with him. His brown hair was not as disheveled, and his suit and tie were actually straight and pressed. Even his shirt was tucked in. His bright blue eyes spotted me as a grin stretched his face.

An answering grin spread across mine until I realized there was one more person in the room that I hadn't noticed. CJ stood up, seeming to take forever to reach his full six-foot height from where he'd been crouched, hooking wires together for the computers on the table.

I shifted on my feet, looking to the floor at the same minute his eyes started to travel up to my face. He'd spotted me.

There was a moment of silence.

"What," Karl said. "No hello?"

"Hello," I said, my voice no louder than it had to be.

"*A chara,*" Darcy said, her Irish accent pronounced. "Are you okay?"

I nodded.

"Alright," Yolo said, impatient. "What is the deal with having the team training up here? We could've easily had it in any of the other conference rooms. It is one of the VR sims, *non?*" Only, with her laying on the emphasis with her normally slight French accent, it came out sounding like: What eez ze deal wiss having ze team training up here? We could easily haf had zis in any of ze ohzer conference rooms. It eez one of ze VR sims, *non*?

I wondered why at home her French accent was nearly non-existent unless she was impatient, but in public it became more pronounced.

"Right," CJ said, clearing his throat. "It is, in fact, one of the VR sims, but it's undergone some...upgrades. We're doing one of the training segments I've put together for working in a foreign territory. We'll give you a set of directives, and you'll need to carry them out."

He went over and picked up a large, sophisticated headset. "You'll all be linked to my computer through the headsets. You'll be able to hear and interact with each other, so treat the whole thing as if it was a real situation. Karl and I will be able to record, watch, and listen in on your interactions as a team. Then we'll give you a breakdown of how you handled the situation. Likewise, we'll send these segments to other team leads for them to analyze as well. The training today was rather short notice, otherwise, we'd have some of those team leaders here with us to give you instantaneous feedback."

Someone pulled me from Natasia's side to give me a hug during the demonstration. Their same-height-as-me stature let me know who it was immediately. Triz. Her acai berry and coconut scents were undetectable under the smell of engine grease and gasoline from her day job.

I got a good look at her when she pulled back. She'd come directly from the shop, still covered in black smudges and wearing her navy-blue overalls tied around her waist. Her dark, wavy hair was pulled up in a ponytail to keep it out of her eyes.

"You're probably nervous, *maninha*, but there is no need. We've taken tests like these lots of times. It'll be easy, ya!" she said with a bright smile.

Darcy rolled her eyes at Triz and pulled her away from me. "Enthusiastic lil' thing, aren't cha? But, she's right, Callie. It'll be a piece of cake. We'll go in, kick ass, and take names...it'll be grand."

"So," CJ continued, managing to avoid my glancing gaze. "I've input your guys' stats into your abilities—at least, what stats I had. Brock and Jace were only able to learn so much in a couple of hours from Callie's session earlier, but it should be realistic enough. The program today is based off of live audio recordings of a dangerous mission one of our international teams was sent out on, so it's all-new. There may be some glitches I haven't worked out yet--"

"*Nyet*, Tate. We all know you are a perfectionist," Natasia said, a warm tone to her normally cold voice. Apparently, CJ's personality could thaw any icy exterior. He was the first person outside of the Cardinals—apart from me—that I'd seen her speak to with fondness.

CJ blushed, and it made my heart ache to think that I had upset someone so generally kind and agreeable.

"Thank you, Natasia, but I wanted to let you guys know in case. Anyway, the mission is that you are going to a city. The audio is in a foreign language, so you'll have to rely on reading the situation and body cues. You won't have any contact with your 'base' to give us the best idea about how you guys would work together and adapt to a stressful situation. Any questions?"

"Yes," Yolo raised her hand, though she didn't wait to be called on. It wasn't like it was a classroom anyway. She looked at Karl. "Why is Callie involved in this?"

My stomach clenched, and I felt my cheeks flush in embarrassment. I had grown used to her aloofness towards me, but it felt worse now that she was doing it in front of both CJ and Karl.

The worst part was that it was a valid question. Hadn't I asked the exact same thing on the way here?

"She's on your team," Karl said sternly.

"*Oui*, but this is because there is a mission coming up that we will need to go on, *non?*" she asked with a sultry voice, her accent so thick it was nearly incomprehensible as English.

"Right," he said, indifferent or oblivious to Yolo's husky tone and sensual smile.

"So, why involve Callie at all? She is the wanted woman. And not in the...*good* way, if you know what I mean," she purred.

"Yolonda!" Sabra said harshly. "You know that we are more than a team, and if we are involved in something, Callie needs to be as well."

Yolo outright glared back, raising her voice. "It is a lee-jit-a-mit question, Sabra. You cannot expect me to go along with zis."

"I can, and I will," Sabra said, stepping closer and towering over Yolo as they both stared each other down.

I wanted to say something to diffuse the situation, but I feared anything I said would only make it worse. I could almost *feel* CJ's gaze on me as I studied the floor. Natasia put her arm back around my shoulders, and Triz moved up to my other side to hold my hand.

"It *is* a fair question," Karl said, breaking the standoff. "Though rude as hell and extremely insubordinate. Look, I know that you're this entitled heiress of some French duke or some other asinine B.S., but this is Delta where we're all equals within your teams. We all bring something to the table. You need to focus more on what Callie can do for your team instead of trying your damnedest to ostracize her."

My eyes were round. I hadn't heard or seen Karl get mad except when I had to tell him that Agent Grinley had killed his good friend and colleague.

The others hadn't witnessed his anger much—if at all—either. You could hear a pin drop. Yolo's sultry smile had turned into an angry pout. She crossed her arms and looked away.

"Besides," Karl stressed, not satisfied with the dressing-down quite yet. "Callie is no longer a wanted woman." He paused, his head tilting. "At least, not here. We couldn't do anything about the other countries. I don't even want to know *how* you managed to make the Algerians mad." The last bit was directed at me.

I didn't try to defend myself at the subtly probing non-question. It was a logical conclusion to think it would be hard to get on a banned list for that country. You had to do some horribly bad, public things to get on their bad side.

The thing about Karl was that he wasn't judgmental and didn't dwell on things. He was also fast on the uptake and highly intelligent when it came to social cues and emotions. In other words, he was my exact opposite. He immediately sensed my intention to keep quiet on the subject and moved on from the lingering statement before it could turn awkward, taking me out of the spotlight.

I glanced at Yolo. She wasn't looking my way. She usually didn't. I squeezed Triz's hand before letting it go and stepping away from Natasia to stand on my own. I was strong. I had thick skin.

I was used to people not liking me.

...I wasn't used to being embarrassed by it. ...and wondering what the people I *did* care about would think.

I felt the air displace around me and smelled lemon and bergamot. CJ had moved by my side.

He wouldn't do that if he was still angry at me, right?

My shoulders sagged a bit in relief. My eyes wanted to water, but I blinked rapidly to stop that. Fingers pushed up on my chin, trying to raise my gaze to his.

I deflected, trying to focus in on the important conversation as Karl explained how the Tate and Emerson teams had worked together to eliminate the paper copies of me from the CIA. In addition, Bryce's influential parents had pulled some strings, and Agent Grinley had been fired, and, and...

I couldn't concentrate.

"Callie," CJ breathed, his cool breath breezing across my face.

I closed my eyes, resigned to having to confirm or confront the fact that he might hate me. I opened them. "Yes?"

He glanced up at the others in the room, talking among themselves as Karl explained more about the situation with my paperwork. CJ gently grasped my arm and led me further away out of hearing range.

"I'm...I'm sorry I got mad. I've been with Delta too long. It's easy to think in terms of right and wrong and lose sight of the struggle people might be facing when they're not in the same secure place. I don't blame you for the way you were thinking. I felt awful after you left. You're...you're my friend, Callie. Long before I met you, I *knew* you. Or at least, I thought I had. That's why it hurt me so much when you said that stuff yesterday. I'd built a pedestal, and when you didn't fall into my idea of you, I was angry. I hate myself for it, especially since it happened so many times to me as a kid."

He rubbed at the back of his neck and looked down. "Before I was old enough to remember her, my mom took Jace and left for Europe. Dad raised me on his own. He did a great job, too. We were always doing something, going on vacations, visiting museums, doing summer camps. But that didn't make a difference to most of the people in my hometown. It was small, and people judged everything. They thought because I was raised by a single father, that I would be an uneducated, unruly heathen. It didn't matter how well I did in school or how much I tried to be a good person. They had put me in this box and labeled me as a trouble-child."

It hurt my heart to hear this story of his childhood. Anyone who knew CJ for even a second could tell how genuine and kind he was. Case in point, he'd thawed Natasia's perpetually cold exterior with his warmth.

"The ironic thing is that they never once assumed that Jace was the one who had it bad. Four-year-old Jace was with our mom and supposedly better off, but she was flighty, irresponsible, and always gone late at night trying to make money. Jace had to pay the bills to make sure they didn't end up on the streets. Even then, it still sometimes happened when she'd binge or party too much to save the child-support money for rent."

My throat constricted, and it became hard to swallow without tearing up.

"It took seven years for our dad to win custody of him—all because of people's judgment that a single-dad had no business raising kids on his own. I swore to myself I wouldn't do that to anyone but look what happened. I expected you to be this perfect soldier that would always do what was right, even if it meant people got hurt. And…you're right. People will get hurt. I couldn't be more removed from what happened, and I still had a strong, emotional reaction. A grieving family…they wouldn't stand a chance. So…I was wrong on so many levels. Callie," he took my hand, his golden-brown eyes beseeching, "Can you forgive me?"

"Yes." My throat was so tight that the words came out a little garbled, but he seemed to understand. "You know, you're pretty in-tune with your emotions for someone who was raised by a single father."

He gave me a look and a slight shove. "Funny."

"Thank you, for sharing all of that."

CJ shrugged, stuffing his hands in his pockets. He couldn't understand how much I valued the fact that he'd given me so much of himself. I could picture young CJ in class, participating and raising his hand to volunteer an answer, only to be overlooked because of a label. I could imagine Jace, having to grow up at such a young age to live in a tough world that was unsure and unstable with a street-mom.

It explained so much about how the twins had such different personalities—why Jace was so reserved and CJ was so unassuming and open.

I thought back to what CJ had said at the beginning of his heartfelt speech. "I-I think of you as my friend. One of my best friends."

His grin stretched across his face a mile-wide, his eyes sparkling as he looked down at me. He held up his hand, pinkie out. "Promise?"

I remembered people doing stuff like this in grade school, giggling on the swings at recess. I clasped his finger with mine the best I could. His was really large, and mine was really not.

He laughed at my struggle bringing—what else—a blush to my cheeks.

I looked away, noticing Yolo watching us, her head tilted to the side and deep in thought.

"Well, let's get ready to do this then," Karl said, excited.

Chapter 8

"CJ, why don't you explain the updates the VR system has undergone."

"Right," CJ said, walking over to what looked like a Jarvis Junior-offspring in laptop form. Jarvis Junior was why I called CJ's computer because the thing was a beefed-up, modified brain. This particular computer was a laptop with a system of wires and boxes sprouting off of it, hooked to different terminals. Lights flashed on the various boxes and the screen was mirrored to six separate monitors.

CJ hit a button and the monitors lit up, showing a densely populated city street that looked somewhat familiar. I studied it a moment, but when you've traveled to so many places, the cities' features sometimes blur together. If I had to guess it looked Asian, somewhere on the outskirts of the Middle East. It could even be a place in Africa.

"So, as I said, this is based on a team's mission a few weeks ago. I have to warn you though I'm not supposed to. Their assignment was planned out to be a simple mission, but things ended up going horribly wrong," CJ said with a solemn face.

"We're giving you this training," Karl jumped in. "Because we want to see how well you mesh together as a team under stress but don't have time to do it the traditional way. We could be sending you to South America soon—don't worry, Callie, not one of the countries you're wanted in—and we need to know if you're the right team for the job. We hope you are since Triz will know the area really well, but we want to be objective. Consider this your official tryout."

Triz knew the area? I wondered if we would be going to Brazil where she was from.

Karl paused to make brief eye contact with everyone before continuing. "That being said, the actual mission this simulation is based on is still ongoing. We have several teams working on it right now to loc—well, I don't want to give too much away until after when we debrief. During the sim, we want your reactions to be as authentic as possible, so we can't explain any more than that."

"On a normal day," CJ said, "We wouldn't even have access to this footage from the assignment until it was all wrapped up. Due the nature of the mission and Delta's specialty in helping others out, they agreed to let us turn it into a simulation to expose it to more people. You know, two heads are better than one. By releasing this while it's still ongoing, they hope someone with fresh eyes will be able to pick up something they missed."

I was very nervous even though this was a fairly low-stakes training. No one could actually be physically hurt with VR, and likewise, being hurt mentally would be a stretch as well since it was a simulation. The only thing I was afraid of was letting the Cardinals down.

"So, the sim is much more upgraded now. We've made pods— they're small, portable rooms that we've moved here to the multi-purpose floor."

Looking around, I could see what CJ was talking about. There was a row along one of the walls with 10x10 rooms.

"You each get a headset, a suit, and headphones. The coding within the program has been updated to give a virtual landscape with mirroring sound."

"I speak many languages, Tate," Natasia said. "Nerdling is not one of them."

"What that means is," CJ clarified, giving her a mock glare that was ruined by the twinkle in his eyes. "You'll have a fake GPS location within the scape. So, sounds will come through the headphones corresponding to your location. For instance, Natasia, if you're standing to the right of Darcy in the virtual landscape talking to her, she'll hear you from her right earbud. Likewise for any other sounds in the program."

"All this is run off of mini Jarvis Junior there?" I blurted out, staring at the laptop and highly impressed by the sheer complexity of coding those functions would take. The processing unit had to be external—maybe one of those boxes wired up to it. There was no way any processing unit compact enough to fit inside that laptop would have the capacity to handle that much data and information at once— even if CJ had built it from the circuit board up with his Midas touch.

CJ tilted his head to the side. "Mini junior?"

"Well, I sorted of dubbed your normal computer Jarvis Junior."

CJ's lips parted the smallest bit as he looked at me. He was uncomfortably silent as he held the stare.

I fidgeted, wondering what I'd said that had him like that. Karl cleared his throat, breaking CJ from some sort of trance as his ears and cheeks tinted pink.

"Uh, um, ah, right. Er...right. Uh..."

"You were talking about how badass your *program* was," Darcy prompted, mirth dancing in her blue eyes as she fluffed her curly red hair.

"Oh...well, I'm not trying to brag. I'm trying to warn you," CJ defended.

"How real can it be, *ma chérie*? It is a simulation, *non*?"

"*Non*," CJ said, mimicking Yolo's French accent. He looked back towards the rest of us, relenting a bit. "At least, not like you've experienced. Look, the sound bit was impressive to you, but that's not even the half of it. It--"

"Kid, let's just let the program do the talking," Karl said. "They'll figure it out for themselves. Besides, it's hard to explain since they're the first ones to use it."

CJ hesitated before he nodded. "Okay, follow me."

He led us over to the rooms. I was put in the fourth one and told I had five minutes to suit up before the simulation would start. Also, he warned us to put any metal or jewelry outside the door in the specified boxes until after the program was over.

Right. Because *that* wasn't ominous at all.

I closed the door gently, noticing that the noise instantly cut off from outside. There was a soft blue glow to the room from LED strips that ran along the perimeter of the ceiling. It was just enough light to let me get a good look around the room.

The gear was hanging on the wall. I put it on, starting with the suit that was somewhat tight and had about 30 buckles. The buckles snugged the material even more, pulling the leather straps with metallic dots close to my skin. By the time I'd finished latching all of them, the timer on the wall let me know I only had thirty seconds to finish. I put on the headgear, only briefly glancing at the room before it was blocked from view. It looked like it'd had lots of silver dots on every available surface, similar to the ones that covered the suit. I remembered the time constraints and hurried to plug in the headphones just in time to hear Karl's voice.

His voice came through both earbuds: *Your mission is to go to this place. CJ has sent the coordinates to you. You should see them somewhere to the side of your view.*

I did see them. In a small circle, it had each of our locations superimposed over a map of a city. Mine was a white dot. I looked down at my body, seeing a white, gridded avatar-body that moved when I did.

CJ's voice popped in as well: *Sorry, Callie. I didn't know what your favorite color was, so you're white.*

"It's purple," I said, not really worried about it.

I looked to the others. Their avatars were different colors with a profile picture of them where their faces were. Sabra was gold, Natasia was light blue, Darcy was grass-green, Yolo was rose pink, and Triz was a lime green so bright it was all but glowing.

There was a short "ta-da" sounding ding, and my gridded body became lavender-colored. I grinned.

Karl's voice continued: *When CJ starts the sim, you'll be placed in a cafe and have to make your way down to the specified location. You are not in hostile territory. It is a safe country. In fact, you'll find the people to be very helpful. Your objective is only to talk to the contact and get the information they have. It's low-risk. They are only giving you information for a company that is hoping to expand. Any questions?*

No one said anything.

Good, then. Roll call, just to make sure your mics are working.

Sabra spoke up. "Yolo?"

"Here," she replied, her voice actually sounding like it'd come from her avatar to the left of me instead of three rooms down where she actually was. The technology was astounding.

"Triz?"

"Here," Triz said with a small, energetic jump.

"Callie?"

"Here," I said softly, hoping the microphone had picked it up.

"Darcy? Natasia?"

"Here," they said simultaneously.

A robotic, feminine voice came through our headphones: *The simulation will begin in five, four, three, two, one. Have fun.*

We appeared in a cafe. It was certainly not high definition, more like 32-bit. Something about the rendering process to change the static data of a video feed into an interactive training simulation left the resolution quality poor. It was graphic, blocky, and pixelated, but there was a good amount of detail, right down to the cup of tea sitting on the table in front of me. It was an odd moment for me to not be able to smell it. Likewise, the Cardinals were right next to me, but I couldn't smell their familiar scents either. It was disorienting as well as eye-opening to learn how much I depended on my sense of smell.

I went to reach out my hand to touch the table, curious to watch it pass through, but my hand was stopped. I was seeing my hand sitting on the table, but I could feel the leather strap on my gloved hand holding my hand in place.

My teammates must have been noticing the same things because their avatars were letting off sounds of surprise and exclamations.

Karl's voice filtered through our headphones: *CJ did try to tell you.*

"How?" Sabra asked, sitting down in a chair and seeming awed by whatever she was experiencing.

The rooms you're in have hundreds of switch magnetics that work in tandem with the highly accurate location and spatial software to give you the feel of gravity and add layers of realism to the VR sim.

"What happened, CJ? Get bored one afternoon?" Darcy asked.

Ha. Ha, CJ said. *I'll have you know it took teams and teams months of--*

Right, I'm going to interrupt him before he goes off on a tangent that no one is really that interested to hear, Karl said.

"I'm interested," I said.

"Of course, you are," Yolo said, offhandedly. She was waving her hand in front of one of the café's customers, poking and prodding at them.

You can flirt with them all you want, CJ said to her with a bit of a bite to his tone. *They're not going to respond to you in here.*

Karl cut in. *Before this conversation can devolve anymore, you guys are good to go.*

Sabra turned to us. "Callie, you are the newest, so for this, I want you to watch and observe how we work. Also, if you have any insights or ideas to share, make sure to speak up."

I could only see the smiling photo of her in the vicinity of her actual face. When CJ said he put our specs in, I didn't know he meant everything, including our heights. However, though I could only see Sabra's frozen smile in the picture, I could most definitely imagine the stern face she was wearing to match the tone.

"Okay," I said, my hand moving up to mess with Kaz's bracelet but stopped when I couldn't get to it because it was under the magnetic suit.

Yolo snorted to the side of me. "Ugh, even in VR I have to see her 'timid' mannerisms."

"Yolo," Sabra said sharply. "You'll bring up the rear. Keep an eye on our backs. Since we're in a safe area—at least, assumed to be safe—we'll have no choice but to have a normal formation. That means the rest of us will be in a group. CJ did give us a head's up that not all is as it seems, so we can be more alert, but we can't take any other precautions that we wouldn't have normally taken in this situation."

"Agreed," Natasia said. "Darcy and I'll flank, Triz and Callie will be in the center. With Yolo floating, Sabra, does that mean you'll take point?"

"Yes," she said solemnly. "We have our coordinates, let's head out."

I went to move, but then remembered we were in a VR. I frowned in confusion, wondering if I was supposed to walk in place.

Triz's lime green avatar held her hands out as she took some steps. She ran into a table, stopped, and cursed in Portuguese. "That is going to take time to get used to. Don't run into any of the things. CJ's magic-magnets will stop you when you get to them."

"Noted," Darcy said, her grass-colored avatar holding her arms up and in front of her as she navigated the room. "I think the floor is some sort of treadmill? I should've run into the wall by now."

"Okay," Sabra said, carefully walking around the tables. "So just move normally."

Yolo seemed to pick up on it with ease, confidently making her way towards the exit. Even though she was just a pink grid with a vague body-shape, she still managed to somehow sway her hips in a sensual stroll.

I wasn't the only one to notice that either.

"What the hell?" Darcy asked, indignant, her grass-green arms held out at her sides for balance. "You're a hideous salmon, amorphous blob-shape, and yet you still project sex-kitten on the prowl? How is that fair? I feel like a newborn colt that drank one too many Guinness."

Yolo's response was smug as she posed herself leaning against the door jam. "I was born this way, hey. And it's not hideous salmon, it's rose. Get it right."

CJ must've done something because the wall Yolo had been leaning against seemed to stop supporting her. It looked like she phased through the wall, falling backward out of sight with a short cry of alarm.

I tried not to smile. Really. I did.

I took a couple of steps, feeling the floor move a little bit beneath me and was glad for once about being short because my center of gravity was so low. I would've toppled over otherwise. Before taking more steps, I carefully scanned my path for obstacles. I didn't want to see for myself how real this reality felt. Gauging off of Darcy's heavily-accented Irish cursing, it probably felt pretty real. She'd run into at least half a dozen things so far.

We made it to the exit and out to the crowded street. Yolo was standing there, her gridded arms folded as she waited on us.

I glanced around.

I was once again hit with the thought that the architecture, though highly simplified in its rendering, still looked a bit familiar. The people walking the streets had more advanced designs than our simple color-schemed avatars. They had dark hair, medium-toned skin, and quick white smiles. We were definitely somewhere middle east if the graphics were to be believed. Their eyes weren't quite the almond shape of far eastern Asia.

Noises filtered in through the headphones. Different conversations started up as background noise at first and grew louder as we walked by people on the street. I passed two men bartering about the price of a necklace before I realized that I understood the language.

They were speaking Bengali. We were in Bangladesh. I looked around again, realizing that I even knew where we were. I'd been here before. We were in Bangladesh's densely populated capital, Dhaka. The symmetric and decorative styles of the Mughal architecture became distinct the more I studied the scenery. There was even the unique look of the national flag, green with a large, red circle.

I faltered in my steps, looking around at the Cardinals. Like planned, I was flanked by Darcy and Natasia with Triz to my right, Sabra in front, and Yolo...well, she had disappeared into the crowds the moment we left the cafe.

Going by their mannerisms, the Cardinals didn't seem to understand any of the conversations going on. I debated whether I should tell them.

Was it cheating if I knew the language? CJ had said it would be in a foreign language. Was I not supposed to know? Should I not act on the information?

I bit my lip. I didn't have much time to think about it though because we were at the meeting place.

"There's our contact," Sabra said, pointing out a young man by some street vendors. The young man was wearing a button-up, plaid t-shirt, and loose pants. He gave a big smile and waved us over into the sandy street. He was much more detailed than the other 'people' wandering around.

As we got closer, I could hear the food sizzling from the food cart he was standing next to. I could see the fried fish, tomatoes, and naan bread, and my mind seemed to fill in the smells of mustard paste, curry, and spices that I remembered from the cuisine there.

The soundscape was amazing, giving so much detail. If the graphics were any more detailed, I would swear that I was back there in that hot sun, about to order a chai latte.

The contact greeted us warmly. It was strange to feel the press and pull of his hand as he shook ours, making me all the more impressed with the magnetic rooms.

"Hello," he said, "I am here to pass along this information. My father, he want to build big business. Uhhm...he? He like to...how do you say...make bigger?"

"Expand?" Sabra asked.

"Yes, he want to ex-pand. You can...no, no, not 'you can'...uhhm...can you help?"

"Yes," Sabra said. "We'll help. What do you need help with?"

"Two buildings. Empty? No one in buildings. Want know...buildings are good, uhm, location? Yes? No?"

A document with photographs of the buildings popped up to the side of my view. There were timestamps and comments written in, detailed ones with the names redacted, and I wondered if these were the real reports filled out by the original Delta team. I scanned through the documents, reading the information. It seemed like the buildings were abandoned, in sound condition, and at a busy location. They would be ideal for a new business.

Sabra spoke. "My team scanned the buildings. They would be perfect for your father's busin--"

A shot rang out, deafening in our ears. I jumped, backing away though I wasn't sure where the sound had come from. It'd ricocheted equally through both of my earbuds. The tall buildings and narrow streets had confused the directional waves of the sound.

The guy that had been talking to us dropped to his knees before falling to the ground. His face pixelated and became blurry. There was shouting all around the street. Civilians scattered as hostiles filled in through the voids. There were at least a dozen masked, armed men. Sabra was to my left, shouting information into her earpiece, but there wasn't any response.

Had comms been taken down for the original team as well, or was this part of the training?

Men were shouting, and all my team could do was react to their body language. They didn't know that I could understand them. They didn't know that they were shouting back and forth about grabbing one of us to take hostage. They weren't aware that Darcy, the one closest to the shouting figures was about to be taken for questioning. Questioning that was probably going to be very similar to how Agent Grinley had 'questioned' me.

They didn't know any of this because I hadn't told them. I didn't even know if I was supposed to act on it or if it was cheating.

Instead, I could only watch as Sabra shouted out for the team to protect me, distracting Darcy even further from the encroaching threat behind her.

A scuffle broke out from behind the hostiles, two of them taken down in rapid, precision with one move. Several of the men turned in confusion, trying to find what had brought their men down, but they were too slow. I finally caught a glimpse of the pink-colored avatar that was systematically taking down the threats. Three more of them fell to the svelte terror tackling their defenses like a French version of the Black Widow.

Yolo was terrifying in her ruthlessness to get to us. She had switched from incapacitating them to using their own weapons against them in a fatalistic dance as she wove through their numbers. One of the simulated attackers grabbed at his throat as it was run through with his own knife, courtesy of her lethal determination to save her team, her family. Yolo was giving it her all.

...but I could tell that she wouldn't make it in time. Triz and Natasia were still crowding around me, but no one, including Darcy herself, was watching her back.

I made a split-second decision and decided to go with my instinct.

I broke free and knocked Darcy aside with as much force as I could at the same time one of the men yelled out in Bengali, "*Take him!*"

Him?

I had only a small amount of time to be confused about who they were talking about before I felt the magnets in my suit compress and start to pull me stumbling backward.

Chapter 9

I was pushed into a seated position in a small jeep, the door slamming shut cut off the shouts of my teammates. It was very eerie, how realistic the VR program was.

My heart rate was climbing. I was accustomed to being kidnapped by now, and I had the added bonus of knowing that it wasn't even reality—at least not for me.

Someone had faced this though. Someone from Delta had been separated from their team, and I was about to find out what had happened.

I calmed my breathing and stared outside the window, not for the first time wishing I'd had a better sense of direction or even remembered the city of Dhaka better. I might've been able to do or recall something useful. I knew that I'd come here a handful of times, both for Veseli and Ivanov, but that was the case with most major cities around the world. They all blurred together.

The men in the small utility vehicle with me continued to speak in Bengali, more freely now. That was useful.

I tried to focus on what they were saying. It was one of the nine languages that I considered myself more fluent in. However, any language will get rusty if you don't use it often, and these men weren't using everyday common phrases. I had at least been able to deduce that they were only paid locals—mercenaries—and not the actual person pulling the strings. Him, I would be meeting in a short time if these guys were to be believed.

They pulled to a stop on an abandoned street. There were two random bystanders there, but they scattered at a quick word from one of the local mercenaries in the group.

The buildings were old, and there weren't any lights on inside them. Most of the windows were boarded up and the state of them was dilapidated enough to show the bricks from beneath the crumbling finish work. A man helped push me towards the building with two rounded columns, much like the columns that a lot of southern houses had, but these pillars were made of tan brick instead of bright white concrete.

It was so detailed, that I could only guess that this had been the real-life location where Delta hostage had been taken to.

They pushed me inside, and I had to remind myself that it wasn't real as I felt the pressure from the hands through the magnetic sensors on the outfit.

"*Get him in there. Tie his hands and feet to the chair. I will go find our patron,*" one of the guys said.

I was confused once more and thought maybe I had misinterpreted something so basic as gender denominations in a language. Then I remembered that this was an audio recording that had been layered on top of visuals. The program didn't respond to the fact that I was a girl.

The man turned to me, speaking English this time. "Are you comfortable? You'll be here for a long time. There is someone who has some questions about the agency you work for."

"What is his name?" I asked, but the guy didn't respond. Either this part of the program was left as is without any interactive features because it wasn't a part of the evaluation… or the guy had ignored me on purpose. Or maybe he didn't know the answer either. I was betting that it was the former but couldn't entirely rule out the latter.

How would the Cardinals be handling this situation? What would they be doing? What should *I* be doing?

I didn't have long to think about it as new men filed into the room.

There was a noticeable difference in their clothes. That made it easy to pick out the small number of locals from the people that had orchestrated this, even if the differing skin tones hadn't given it away.

The locals wore eclectic colors and prints mismatched together, and they attempted to hide their identities as much as possible since it was their home turf. Their weapons ranged machine guns to knives.

The newcomers wore more uniform outfits of grays with lots of pockets and tactical gear. They all had the same assault rifle weapon secured diagonally across their torsos, pointed downwards and to the left.

Among their group, it was also easy to tell who the head honcho was when he came out. The newcomers had surrounded him, and then when he reached the middle of the large room, they spanned out, keeping an eye out through holes of sunlight in the boarded-up windows.

It left one person in the middle with surprisingly accurate graphics...from the blond, curled hair, dimpled chin, chiseled jaw, and ice-cold eyes...all the way to the scar at the bottom of his jaw and down his neck—the only marring feature on an otherwise handsome face. A face that hid the devil. The face that haunted every one of my nightmares.

Nikolai Ivanov.

My mind disconnected, telling itself that this couldn't be real. I had to be hallucinating. My heart rate increased as I tried to process what was happening, but it was an impossible task. I couldn't calm it down. In fact, my heart only doubled its pace when I realized something.

Where Ivanov was, Dell wouldn't be far behind.

My eyes went back over the men in combat outfits, studying more carefully this time.

I spotted him.

He was by one of the windows, staring out. I had no doubt that he was taking everything in, including the inside of the room. He turned to glance at me, his grey eyes meeting mine. My mind flashed back to those eyes, having the same cold, dead expression as he shot me in that hotel in Paris. The fated mission that had started all of this. His eyes had been that way right before Ivanov had ordered my death.

My mind was going a mile a minute, keeping pace with my racing heart. As disturbing and frightening as the entire situation was, there was one thing that stood out to me—the most terrifying thing of all.

Dell's details weren't nearly as fleshed out within this program.

I had spent ample time with Dell. He'd been my keeper so to speak. He'd trained me on a lot of things. I was the only person that Ivanov didn't have a hold over with no family—no family that mattered—to threaten me to work for him. I hadn't volunteered, and I hadn't signed up. Who better to keep an eye over a hostage worker than Ivanov's right-hand man?

Because of that, I knew how Dell looked, even more so than Ivanov. The scar on the left side of Dell's face that started above his eyebrow and went down past his eye wasn't there, for example. Likewise, the mustache and goatee were there, but the light stubble that he always had growing along his jawline was nowhere to be seen.

This let me know immediately some very important information that made my heart pound.

One, the simulation was based on video feeds as well as audio feeds. There was no way to have that much detail from written or spoken witness accounts. Two, Dell, usually the one getting up close and personal doing Ivanov's dirty work, hadn't gotten close enough to the Delta agent for the programmers or software to add in *his* most defining features. However, Nikolai Ivanov was detailed out down to the exact shadows and highlights of every ridge, bump, and plane on his face.

That meant that Ivanov had been close to this man.

Very close.

Close enough and for long enough to catch and preserve his likeness so well that it was giving me chills.

Which brought me to my third and most terrifying realization: Ivanov had been the one to torture this man. And Ivanov *never* got his own hands dirty. He hadn't even killed his own son, Kaz. He'd instead ordered one of his men to do it. He'd had his only child, a seven-year-old, sweet angel of a child *killed* to teach me a lesson.

I'd long theorized that Ivanov hadn't gotten physical in his 'dealings' since he'd gotten that mysterious scar along his jaw and neck. It would be the type of life-altering thing to make him realize his own mortality and take the measures to prevent it.

So, for him to have changed his ways...to be doing his own dirty work...

I didn't want to think about the implications because the most logical conclusion led back to me. He knew I was loose. He had to be infuriated at that.

Chills ran up and down my spine as Ivanov looked me over. I started struggling earnestly against the simulated rope that was all too real now. I leaned back, only being able to go as far as the chair would allow, my mind not even understanding that it was the work of magnets anymore.

I just knew one thing.

I wanted out. I wanted out now.

I wanted out before Ivanov got closer to the Delta man, to *me. I* was this man in the simulation, and I didn't want to be anywhere near this monster again. I most definitely didn't want to experience this poor, Delta guy's death...because I knew without a doubt that he was no longer alive. If he'd gotten this good of a look at Ivanov, then he had been a dead man before the torture had even started.

I didn't want to still be in his role when that happened.

I went to pull the headset off, but my hands wouldn't move. I was stuck. The magnetics were working well to make the experience as real as possible, and since I was tied up in the program, my arms and legs couldn't move in real-life.

I started breathing faster, unspeakably terrified.

Ivanov started to walk closer to me.

"I want out!" I said, shouting. I knew the Cardinals wouldn't be able to hear me since the little map in the corner showed they were getting closer but still too far away. I was hoping that CJ or Karl would hear me. They were monitoring everything.

Ivanov was getting closer, not responding to my shouts, but his ice eyes were intent on my face. The recognition wasn't there, but it was still terrifying to experience. I was a stranger to him in this world… a disposable means to an end.

"I want out!" I shouted again, my voice breaking at the loud volume. "Now! Please, please, please. Don't make me live through this."

I started mumbling incoherently, tears streaming down my face.

Ivanov crouched in front of me and looked up at my face. Even though it wasn't there, my traitorous mind filled in his unique scent of vodka and bleach making the experience all the more real.

I was crying now.

I could hear and feel the vibrations pounding around me that didn't match the reality I was seeing. No one was reacting to them but me. I hoped it was Karl or CJ.

But nothing happened.

I was still stuck in here.

Nikolai leaned even closer, getting right into my face, staring at me from six inches away. He put his hands on the chair's armrests. I could feel the pressure of it. He leaned up to my ear and whispered, "You're going to tell me everything you know about Delta."

Chapter 10

Ivanov's hand brushed against my leg.

I let out a sob.

The headgear was ripped off of me. The magnetic room came back into view, and I could hear the sounds of reality. However, my mind was stuck in the simulation. I couldn't stop crying.

Karl was yelling at CJ to power the room down so that he could free me from my position. CJ was yelling back equally loudly as he worked frantically to turn the magnets off.

I felt more phantom touches on my suit as the program continued to play out even if the audio and visual were gone. Somehow, the lack of visual was worse now. I could see Karl's worried face, but I knew that it was Ivanov touching me, the Delta guy, in the program.

With the sound of something industrially large powering down, the magnetics gave way. I was set free and Karl caught me from falling to the floor as the "virtual chair" dropped out from under me.

He took me out into the main room. The doors to the other Cardinals' rooms opened.

"What ze hell happened?" Yolo's voice shouted. "We were closing in on ze building where she was taken to. Why did you stop ze sim?"

Sabra was right next to Karl in an instant. "What happened? Why is she crying?"

"She wasn't responding well to the hostage situation," Karl said. "I thought we agreed that Darcy would be the one to be taken. What the hell!"

"We did. But, for some reason, Callie jumped in front of her. It was an accident. But you know this, you were watching the whole time. If you were worried about her, why did you not pull her sooner?" Sabra shot back, now studying Karl's angry visage.

Karl set me down in one of the chairs next to CJ. CJ turned and started looking me over, spewing a geyser of apologies too fast to comprehend but kind enough to feel their warmth in the sentiments. I grasped for one of his hands, and he obliged, cupping my cold, clammy one between his heated ones.

Instead of answering Sabra right away, Karl ran his hands through his hair and crouched down in front of me. He looked up at my face, cupping my cheek with his hand. I had to shake the image of Ivanov in the same position.

Karl studied me as he answered Sabra. "You're right. I'm sorry. I'm angry but not at you guys. When she jumped in, we were surprised and about to pull the plug, but she didn't seem afraid at all. In fact, she calmed down. We thought we'd let it play out and see what happened."

By now the rest of the team was gathered around. Yolo was back out of the magnetic gear and in her dressy outfit. The others hadn't bothered to take them off yet.

"Callie, *a chara*," Darcy said, her Irish brogue thick. "Why did you jump in to save me? Our orders were to keep you protected."

"They were going to take you," I said through my sniffles.

There was a brief silence for a moment as they processed my somewhat irrational explanation. The seemingly random line of didn't seem to stop them though. They connected the dots pretty quickly.

"Well, shit, " Karl said. "You know Bengali? Someone needs to sit you down and write out all the languages you speak."

"We should have known this as well," Sabra said with a contrite look. "We are her team, and we did not know this. I was making too many assumptions, and it cost us all dearly. Forgive me, Callie."

I shook my head and grabbed her hand with my free one; CJ didn't seem inclined to release my other one any time soon. "It's not your fault. Please don't blame yourself. Karl was right. I was fine with the situation. It's not the first or even the second time I've been kidnapped. Besides, I should've told you guys that I could speak Bengali. I was unsure about whether I was supposed to know the language or not, and if we were supposed to act on that knowledge because of the test. But...when they were going to take Darcy...I don't know. I just couldn't *not* react."

"Callie," CJ said with a gentle tone. "Why did you react so strongly if you weren't scared of the kidnapping?"

I let out a breath, looking down. "That man...the Delta one that was taken hostage...he's dead...isn't he?"

"We're not sure. We haven't found him yet, dead *or* alive," Karl emphasized, holding my gaze. "His video feed quit transmitting shortly after you left the program. His team found that building, but the kidnappers had already relocated him by then. We're still following the trail."

I swallowed. "Well, you should be looking for a body."

"Why?"

I pointed at the monitor I'd avoided looking at since Karl pulled me from the room. It was the one that had frozen on the last image from my point of view. "Because that was, without a doubt, Nikolai Ivanov."

There was a moment of silence, and then the tension crashed down in a tidal wave of sound.

Triz moved forward to wrap me in a hug or grab my hand. I wasn't sure. Either way, I flinched, and it stopped her forward progress, freezing her in place with an unbearably sad look in her eyes. CJ had been about to grab my other hand, but he also stopped when he saw me tense up. It didn't stop Darcy though. She brashly stepped forward and put a firm hand on my shoulder, giving me a slight squeeze when I relaxed a bit more. Yolo was studying her nails, and Natasia and Sabra were in a yelling match with each other while Karl was trying to break them up.

Finally, Karl let out a sharp whistle that reined silence over the two leaders. They turned their ire on him, but he didn't back down. "Before you start blaming each other, Natasia, it was a decision of ours to exclude you from the plan. We wanted your reactions to be as authentic as possible--"

"I am in command. I should have been informed," she said frostily.

"Well, you weren't," he snapped back. "Look, I'm sorry. Mistakes—huge mistakes were made today. Only Sabra knew about the plan, but we didn't think it would be a problem because she gave the orders to protect Callie."

"You sent her in with her own Vasily Petrova—her nightmare," she yelled back, not consoled in the slightest.

Yolo, showing more compassion than I'd seen from her before, stepped up and grabbed Natasia's hand in silent support. Natasia turned to face her. Yolo said, "You're okay. It wasn't him. *Monsieur* Petrova does not know about Delta. We have made sure of zat. Ease your mind, *mon Cherie*."

Natasia took a deep breath. "I cannot relax, *sestra*. I heard the stories about this Nikolai Ivanov. He makes my *father*," she spat, "look like an angel. This man took one of our agents. I don't find myself believing in very many coincidences these days."

"You're right," I said, finally able to stop crying though my voice was still thick from the tightness in my throat. "Before the feed cut out, he mentioned Delta. Somehow, Ivanov found out about it, and I'll give you three guesses as to why he's after it."

Karl ran his hands through his hair again. "Double fuck!!" He paced a bit, before drawing himself up with a big breath. "Okay, this is what we're going to do. Callie, if it's not too much trouble, I'd like you to listen in on the feed and translate for us. We obviously don't have anyone here that speaks Bengali, otherwise, we wouldn't have wired the Rosen team up with all of the video feeds and audio to make the training video. Also, we need the people that are working on this informed about Ivanov. We can't keep a closed lid on this any longer. If we had informed everyone earlier, we could've possibly caught this sooner."

I nodded my head.

He continued on, turning to CJ. "Okay, CJ, I need you to look through any electronic trace that you can to see if you can find evidence about Ivanov's movements there or his next actions. It may be a long shot, but it can't hurt. Especially since he's already a lot closer on the trail than we'd thought."

"There was a building," I said, straining my brain for the memory. "Ivanov had sent us to Bangladesh to investigate a building. At the time they told me it was a routine check for potential safehouses, but it was strange because I wasn't allowed to go in. It wasn't the only thing we were there for in Bangladesh, so I didn't think too much of it…but I did note it later. It should be on the thumb drive."

I tilted my head to the side in thought. "Looking back on it, it might've been already been an established safe house for Ivanov. Maybe he's been there this entire time, laying low after we got away with all that information. What if he heard about the Delta people while they were in town and took the opportunity to find out more? They were practically served up on a silver platter the minute they set foot in the capital."

"CJ," Karl said, his eyes never leaving my face.

"I'll get right on it. I already copied the info on the thumb drive to my computer, so I can look it up now."

"Good," Karl said. His blue eyes bounced back and forth between mine. "So…you think this building might be where we can find Ivanov?"

I bit my lip. "I doubt it. He would've washed his hands of Bangladesh knowing that Delta would be on the way soon to find their missing guy."

"So, why do you think this place is important? He wouldn't leave behind any way to trace him, right?"

"No. But…I think that you might find your missing Delta guy there."

Karl was quiet. "You really think he's dead?"

I blew out a breath, looking away gesturing in the general area that had Ivanov's face paused on it. "I think that you're one of the first people in the entire world to catch Ivanov's face on camera. I think that the fact that your guy's feed cut off after Ivanov got close…"

"You think Ivanov spotted the camera," Karl guessed, crossing his arms while he looked deep in thought.

"Yes, and I think that he would've gone into a rage after he found it. I'd be surprised if the local mercenaries survived the ordeal. If your guy was lucky, Ivanov killed him quickly. And if *we* were lucky, Ivanov killed him quickly before he leaked any information about Delta…but I doubt it."

"Why?"

"Because his team is still alive. If he'd needed more information, he would've taken another Delta guy."

Karl wiped a tired hand down his face and adjusted with his tie. "Anything else you think we should know?"

"His behavior is erratic," I said, playing with the twine bracelet. It was hard to see the man that had killed his own son. All the memories I'd thought I'd healed from were playing in my mind. Kaz had been completely innocent, a small seven-year-old boy, born with the unfortunate curse of being related to the devil incarnate.

I could feel all eyes turn to the frozen image on the computer screen. I still didn't look at it. If I looked, I'd lose it and cry about Kaz all over again. It'd been nearly a week since I'd thought about his death while awake.

"That's…erratic?" Triz asked. "His face is stone. Maybe 'erratic' doesn't mean what I'm thinking…"

I licked my lips, unsure.

"No," CJ said, his eyes on me. "You're about to doubt yourself. Don't. You noticed something. What is it? What do you mean?"

I kept my eyes on my hands. "Well, you see the man by the window? Grey eyes, goatee, shorter but built like an ox. That's Ivanov's righthand man, Dell. I don't know his last name. He sounds British, but he could fake his accent. It'd be something he'd do. He's cunning, highly intelligent, and extremely good at his job—which is to take care of all of Ivanov's 'business'."

"He looks somewhat familiar," Karl said, his head tilted as he studied the picture on the monitor.

I bit my lip. "If you have the footage of me in that hotel in Paris, then you most likely saw Dell as well."

"He's the one that shot you," CJ guessed as he breathed out, his eyes intent on the figure in the screen. He looked back at me. "What's so significant about him, other than the fact that he shot an injured, defenseless girl?"

I ignored the ire in CJ's tone for now. "Not much, except for the fact that he never got close enough to the victim's video feed to--"

"Brad." Karl interrupted. "His name is Brad. The uh, the victim. Fuck! I've got to tell his team...". He ran his hands through his hair, making it all stand up in a disarrayed mess.

"Sorry," I said. Another person dead because of me.

Deal with it later, Callie. Focus on now.

I took a deep breath. "Brad was never close enough to Dell to pick up on the single defining feature he has: a scar across his eye. And yet, Ivanov was so accurate that it could've been his passport photo for all the detail."

"Which means that Ivanov..." Natasia said, catching on. She trailed off giving the monitor a more assessing look.

I nodded. "Yes, Ivanov did the interrogating." I shivered, my heart going out for this Brad person's soul. I hoped that he was at peace now. "That's very, *very* unusual. I can't stress how unusual—wait, I can. Ivanov wasn't the one to kill his son. He had someone else pull the trigger, even though he was right there. He doesn't get his own hands dirty. Ever."

With the new information, everyone looked back at the calm facade of a crazy man.

"Okay...new plan. We get Callie trained as fast as possible and ship you guys off to South America for your mission. Even with Callie's luck that's far away from the line of fire," Karl said.

Chapter 11

I was slammed back on the mat once more, knocking all the air from my lungs. I was seriously reconsidering some life choices I'd been making lately.

I'd spent the last week doing physical training with Brock and Jace. The rest of my time had been used going through every audio piece from the Bangladesh mission with the hopes of finding some clue about where the missing Delta person was. I'd also been with CJ a lot in his office working on tracking Ivanov's movements to the best of our abilities.

Using the internet had been nice, but both leads had been a bust. The audio hadn't turned anything else up, Ivanov's safe house had been burned though he left a massacre of dead locals behind, and Ivanov had disappeared into the wind without a trace. In the carnage that had been left behind at the safehouse, there had been one body conspicuously absent: Delta Agent Brad's.

I still didn't doubt my assumptions that he was dead, but I could tell others were starting to.

There were no trails for the missing, presumed-dead Delta member. With the knowledge that Ivanov was encroaching nearer and nearer every minute that passed, Karl decided—and both Sabra and Natasia agreed—to focus on training me up enough to handle a simple surveillance mission with the Cardinals in South America. He was hoping that I would be far away and safe from Ivanov there, but I was worried about Delta.

Ivanov had to have been able to trace us somehow to know about the existence of Delta before actually seeking them out. What all did he know about? Who all did he know about it? He had to at least know about the Tate team and Brock since they went in to rescue me in Russia. Possibly the rest of the Emerson team Ivanov didn't know about, but I wouldn't hold my breath hoping.

I didn't argue my leaving, surprising a lot of them—especially when I agreed.

I had agreed with their plan to get out of the country, not because of my safety, but with the hope that I would create a bigger prize to follow if Ivanov was going to make a move. I could try to give the Cardinals the slip and find a device to log onto the dark web.

After CJ's angry though understandable reaction, I hadn't exactly been comfortable with pulling up certain contacts in front of him. He saw a lot of things as black or white whereas I was gray at best. If slumming it up could save lives, I'd do it in a heartbeat—and who better to find out information on a criminal than other criminals from the dark web? It was sound reasoning in my eyes. I just wasn't sure if CJ would agree with that sentimentality.

Either way, if I found out that Ivanov was closing in, I would leave and give him a chase...make it seem like the people from Delta meant nothing to me if I could abandon them. He might still go after them, but at least it wasn't a guarantee.

"You're not focused, *dušo*," Brock said, bringing me back to the moment.

"I am, honest. I'm just tired. Trying to catch my breath," I said.

"Well, either way. We're going to call our session finished," Jace added. He tilted his head as he recalled something. "Before we forget, starting tomorrow our training session will be in the smaller gym on the 7th floor. We don't need this big of a space, so we booked the second one as soon as it became available."

"I'll meet you by the entrance and lead you there," Brock said, pulling me to my feet and nearly right back off of them as he miscalculated how much force to use. He frowned as he steadied me. "You're small."

I nodded my head and focused on trying to find my water bottle.

"Are you finished with her?" Karl asked from near the entrance to the boys' locker room, startling me.

"Not finished by half," Jace said, staring at me intently. Then he broke our eye contact, freeing me. He looked over to Karl. "But, I guess that you can have her."

Brock growled at that but didn't smack him on the back of his head either. He handed me the water bottle I hadn't been able to find and sent me on my way.

"Alright," Karl said, "I'll meet you out in the hall. Be done in five."

'Be done in five,' I mimicked to myself, but Karl had already disappeared so my sarcasm was greatly wasted. I was feeling somewhat spunky after so many failed training sessions, so I took my time.

Ten minutes later, I met up with Karl and his foot-tapping, watch-checking self.

"What took you so long?" he demanded, sounding exasperated. He didn't give me a chance to answer. He pushed the button on the elevator. "We're going to be late, and I do *not* want to be late. It's going to be hard enough as it is."

"What's going to be hard?" I asked, my hand reaching to my wrist to feel for the reassurance of the twine bracelet. I was feeling bad now for my little rebellion at being told how fast to shower.

"Well, we're adding new training. Your defense classes, though your stamina and strength are building up, are going...horrifically to put it kindly."

"Please, don't sugar coat it."

He chuffed me under my chin. "Hush. It's the truth. You do well with the yoga, but when it comes to defense...well, we're trying to open up more options and praying that one of them will stick."

Not the least bit disgruntled at 'failing' fighting class, I didn't even argue. I asked, "Well, what's the training?"

"Guns," he said. The door opened up to the busy admin floor, and he wasted no time heading straight to CJ's office. He turned to me, something mischievous simmering in his cobalt eyes. "Wait out here."

And then he went inside, closing the door behind him.

The door did nothing to muffle the shout that followed shortly after.

"What? No, I will not train anyone one-to-one," came the deep, growly voice of a very familiar long-haired, massive Russian.

Karl's response was muffled, much softer and calmer. His volume was easily protected by the shut door.

"I do not care if this person is president. I make no special treats! That was my rule to teach classes. I run my program, not others. And I do not want rich dicks think they can tell me what to do."

This time, Karl replied a little louder, but I still couldn't quite make out his voice. I moved a little closer to the door.

"Eavesdropping?"

I jumped and spun around, feeling guilty and terrified all at once. Jace was standing there, freshly dressed in ripped jeans and an intriguingly tight ¾-sleeve Henley that drew my attention. It emphasized his crossed arms and bulging veins. His blond hair was a light brown, still wet from the shower. Already the shaggy curls were defying gravity and coiling back into place. I had the strangest urge to pull on one to see how springy they were.

Jace cleared his throat, shaking me from my daze. I looked up. He had a small smirk on his face.

He opened his arms. "That training was tough today. Give me a hug."

"Why do you need the hug? You weren't the one being slammed into the mat."

"Second-hand pain is a real and serious condition. It was really hard to temper my heroic tendencies, Damsel. Now be a good girl and hug me."

I shook my head, pretending to be upset. I hugged him anyway, practically jumped into his arms. Triz was wreaking havoc on my need for affection. I hadn't even held out for 30 seconds.

Jace gave me a strong squeeze and then set me back down. He smoothed my hair down with his large hand. "How are you?"

"I'm fine? Jace, you saw me not even that long ago." I said, unsure of what he was getting at.

"Your muscles okay?"

I shrugged then nodded.

He studied me a moment before moving on. "What are you doing?" he said, giving a pointed look behind me towards CJ's closed door.

I blushed. "Uh, I'm...well," I started and then noticed the room inside had fallen silent. Aleks had stopped shouting.

There was an inquisitive sound that was muffled from the lower volume—before loud footsteps headed towards the door.

Jace frowned, his eyes shooting to the door. "If that's CJ then it sounds like he swallowed an entire hippo since the last time I saw him."

"More like a bear," I mumbled.

Jace turned in my direction. "What was that?"

I didn't respond, tugging at Kaz's bracelet. I was worried that the bear-like Russian inside the room would direct his earlier anger at me instead of Karl. From the shouted conversation, I'd gathered that Karl was trying to get me to take private lessons, and Aleks was having none of it. "It's not CJ. It's--"

The door swung open.

"*Medvezhonok,* little bear!"

I didn't even get a chance to look him over. I was engulfed in arms so big and thick that it felt like being wrapped in a blanket of solid muscle—a suffocating blanket at that.

"Aleks, oxygen. Remember that stuff? Pretty sure she needs some," Jace said, dryly.

The chest that was squished up against my ear grunted, and the arms tightened even more.

"She can hold her breath for long time. Rock said so," Aleks grumbled, his breath moving my hair and his large chest vibrating me like a massage chair. He buried his nose in my neck, practically submerging himself in my hair, and took a deep breath. He murmured out in Russian, "*I have missed you, Little Bear. You were gone for so long. Don't do that again. Promise me.*"

Aleks was the tallest man I knew, coming in at over six and a half feet. He was also the biggest man I knew. His muscles had muscles. He was one of those solid, stout figures. He was loud and boisterous, with long, wavy hair that was dark near the roots and faded into blonde at the ends. He also had a long beard that brushed his chest. His features matched his body: broad, bold, and masculine. His eyebrows were sharply angled, his nose long and straight, and his ice-blue eyes stood out against his tan skin.

I felt a tightness in my throat. I responded in Russian. "*I can't make promises like that, but I promise to try.*"

"Cute," Karl said, his voice sounding very amused. "Hey, I may not speak Russian, but does that mean you've changed your mind about the private training? Because I can always ask one of the guys from the Henley team to do it. I'm sure they wouldn't mind."

I was put down. Aleks tucked me under his heavy arm and into his muscular side so that when he turned to face Karl, I did as well.

"*Medvezhonok* is the one needing private training? Why didn't you say so?" Aleks looked down at me, a broad, dark grin pulling at his lips. "I will give you private training every day."

My cheeks flamed up, pulling a deep belly laugh from Aleks that shook me as well.

Karl's face was smug as he crossed his arms and feet, so he could lean against the wall. "Why would I tell you her name? I thought you were the all impartial force. You don't play favorites, remember?"

Aleks waved him off. "This is practical. She is spook. Her name needs to stay secret."

Karl frowned. "I said that to you literally two seconds ago."

"Well, it's different now," Aleks said simply. "We can start today, *da*?"

He turned us and started walking down the hall.

Karl straightened up from the wall. "What? You're not going to start now, are you?"

"No time like the now," Aleks said. "Do today what you could do later but not as fun. All those sayings and such."

"Aleks," Karl said. When Aleks didn't stop or turn around, Karl tried again. "Aleks!"

Aleks kept marching us down the hall towards the elevators.

Jace coughed to clear his throat. "I better keep an eye on him as his leader, of course. I would be a bad leader if I didn't take responsibility for his actions." He took long strides to catch us.

Karl sounded unimpressed as he called down the hallway. "Yeah, sure that's why you're going."

"Are you guys hungry? I'm starved. Callie wore me out," Jace said as we went past the little cafe towards the elevators. At my nod, he said, "I'll go order you something. What's your poison?"

I tried my best not to react as I remembered ordering Bryce, Doc Scott, and Brock's favorite sandwiches. No way was I going to reorder one of those. If word got back to them, I would never live it down. And thanks to a certain distracting veterinarian, those were the only things I knew about from the menu. "I don't really have a favorite."

"Okay, I'll pick something out," he said. "I'll meet you guys down at the range."

"Hey," Aleks called. "Order me my bacon and pastrami!"

Jace turned back around. "Is your leg hollow? Aleks, we came here together. You ate one of your gross sandwiches right before we left. How could you possibly be hungry?"

Aleks patted his large but flat stomach. There wasn't any definition to his abs, but it was easy to tell that it was all solid muscle. "I am big boy. I need food."

Jace shook his head and walked away.

"Little boy," I mumbled in Russian in a strange moment of bravery.

Aleks let out a deep, deep laugh. *"You are not supposed to say that to men, Little Bear, but I have nothing to worry about if you know what I mean."*

I was pretty oblivious and sheltered sometimes, but Darcy had been making nonstop sex jokes the past month. It was hard to misunderstand some of them now. Especially Aleks' jokes, it seemed. He was pretty blunt.

"Good," he said, satisfied and full of pride. "I see you know what I mean. When you ready to understand even more better, find me."

I was going to melt inside this small elevator with him if he kept it up. I burrowed further into his side, smelling his spicy cologne.

With my brain not firing on all cylinders and my tongue-tied, the best insult I could come up with was to reiterate my new name for him. *"Little boy."*

"I will be *little boy*, and you will be *Medvezhonok*," Aleks patted me on my head with his big paw, dislodging and messing up my quick ponytail. I glared at him as he smiled back unrepentantly.

The elevator dinged and showed the basement level. It was darker without the walls of windows the other floors had. Some chairs were set up in a corner. Doors lined the far wall in front of us, most of them labeled. The "Bomb Technicians" sign made me a bit nervous. To our left was a large security center, possibly the hub for the entire Delta facility. On the right was the firing range, visible through the shatterproof glass windows that lined the walls. There were about six lanes and almost all of them were being used. I could hear the muted pops of their guns being fired and smell the scent of burnt gunpowder in the air.

I looked up to Aleks. "Do we have to write our name down on a schedule?"

"What?" he asked, "Write down name? Why do that?" He took long strides up to the door and threw it open. I was still tucked under his arm, so he used his free hand to flip a switch. Red lights turned on in each shooters' lanes. The shooters stopped and looked over at us.

"Shooters, listen down," he said.

"Listen up," I corrected since the Tate twins weren't around to do it.

Aleks turned to me. "Up? But I am talking down to them, no?"

I opened my mouth but didn't really have a good explanation for why you had to listen "up" per se. I shrugged.

He turned back to the group. "Listen up and listen down. You all leave now. I will use range for next hour. You come back later," Aleks yelled, no sugarcoating or pleasantries.

The shooters didn't revolt like I had expected them too.

Instead, they packed up, not even bothering to clean their guns. In three minutes, the entire range was emptied out, right in time for Jace to step through and close the door behind him.

He had a bag of sandwiches in his hand. He glanced around the ghost-town the range had morphed into in such a short span of time.

"Aleks, you still have that winning personality, I see." Jace quipped as he handed me one of the sandwiches with a heavy look. I went to grab it, but he wouldn't release it to me until I made eye contact.

"Garbanzo beans, tofu, risotto, and spinach." He stated as if it was very important. Then he turned to Aleks, tossing him a wrapped sandwich. "And your nasty concoction. Don't choke."

Aleks caught the sandwich one-handed, looking happy. "I have big mouth. Is impossible to choke."

Jace's eyes rounded in shock at his statement. "Uh…did you really just say--"

Aleks, enamored with unwrapping his sandwich, said, "Did you get the honey mustard, mayo, and ketchup?"

Jace looked mildly ill. "Yes."

Aleks nodded and dug in.

I went to take a bite of my own, my mouth already watering, but then I paused. Doc Scott had read way too much into a sandwich choice, and now I was paranoid. I looked at Jace, noting on closer inspection that his sandwich looked suspiciously like the one in my hands.

I pulled the sandwich back and cleared my throat. "What's your sandwich?"

"Same as yours," Jace said.

My mouth dried up a little bit as I looked back at the one in my hand with more trepidation.

"What? Why are you looking at that sandwich likc it's going to bite you back?" Jace asked.

"Probably," Aleks said around a full mouth. "Because it is disgusting." He held out his sandwich to me. "Here, try my sandwich, *Medvezhonok*. You'll like it."

Despite Aleks' crazy concoction, both sandwiches smelled good. My mouth was watering, and I was surprised my stomach hadn't started growling yet after my physical training with Jace and Brock. When I didn't immediately take a bite out of either one, Jace cocked his head to the side.

"What's wrong? Are these sandwiches not to your…liking?" Jace asked. "Do you prefer another?"

I narrowed my eyes at him. "Did you talk to Doc Scott? Or Brock...or..." I figured that word had spread by now. "Well, anyone on the Emerson team?"

Jace took a big bite of his sandwich. "Might have. We've done a few missions together now, and they've decided to set Corbin on us. We're bound to run into each other."

"Oh, right. I think Karl said something about you guys working together to get my picture back from the CIA." I paused, replaying what he'd said in my head. "Wait—what do you mean, 'set' Corbin on you?"

"Nothing, eat your sandwich, Damsel."

My stomach growled and made the decision for me in the end. I devoured it. I even took a bite of Aleks's sandwich, pointedly ignoring the triumphant look in both of their eyes. I wouldn't admit it, but I actually enjoyed the unique combination of flavors that made up Aleks's monster of a meal.

Jace wasn't very forthcoming about having talked to the Emerson team or not, so I did test out my theory when Aleks asked how I liked his sandwich.

I shrugged my shoulders. "Eh, it's not my favorite, but it's okay."

Aleks scoffed and looked disproportionately offended at what should've been an innocent comment. He'd even opened his mouth to say something, but a cutting look from Jace and some more of the silent communication stopped that.

They *so* knew.

Chapter 12

Despite his gruff, burly appearance, Aleks was a patient, jovial instructor, and he took the gun safety course very seriously. He wouldn't even let me shoot until I could thumb the safety without looking on several different models of guns. He was also adamant that every gun was a loaded gun and needed to be pointed at the ground at all times until I was ready to shoot.

The shooting part, when he was ready to let me, had gone about as well as my physical training with Brock and Jace...so, not very well at all. I'd shot for 30 minutes—though my jello arms made it feel like much longer—and not one of the bullets had pierced the human figure outline at thirty feet.

I'd like to have blamed it on the fact that Jace and Aleks had stood back, legs spread in wide stances with their arms crossed over their chests, watching. I thought that was at least half of the reason, but I wasn't going to voice that thought aloud.

Aleks hit the button that moved the target up to our shooter's box. He clipped up a new one and looked over mine with jaw-dropping incredulity.

"What?" I didn't see anything wrong with it as I looked over his forearm. Aleks either couldn't or wouldn't answer me.

Jace moved to the other side to look over Aleks's shoulder. A second later, he cleared his throat with a small cough, having figured out what'd made Aleks speechless. His face lit in a small, secret grin.

"Nothing, it's just that...statistically speaking, you should've hit the target at least once. Even by accident. You shot 150 rounds of ammo."

"Not one," Aleks said, shaking his head. He turned back to me, his arms folded. "Maybe gun is defaulty."

"Faulty," Jace said. "Or defective. I'm not sure what you were going for there."

After inspecting the gun, Aleks moved his ice-blue eyes up to my face. I felt like I was in trouble at the principal's office.

"*Medvezhonok,* this was the most bad--"

"Worst," Jace corrected in a chipper voice.

"*Da.* Most *worst* shooting I have seen ever," Aleks seemed a little grumpy, or maybe even slightly disappointed about it.

"Well," Jace said, straightening up. "I'm not going to argue with that, but look at the bright side—"

"There is no bright side. There is only bad shooting side."

"No, really. It just means she will need more classes."

Aleks turned to his teammate. "One on one?" he asked. At Jace's nod, Aleks froze before nodding decisively. "This is okay."

I cocked my head to the side, not sure how I should feel at the moment. There were lots of conflicting things to process from their conversation.

"*Medvezhonok,* what other classes are you taking?"

"Uh, classes? I'm only taking the physical training course," I said, not sure if I was supposed to tell them about the rush to get me away from the country or if the mission in South America was a secret.

"That's it? Perfect!" Aleks said. "We will meet every day right before that. Maybe arms only tired from Jace's yoga, *da*? You shoot better if I get you first."

I wondered if I needed to approve the change of schedule with the Cardinals, but Aleks was still staring at me, so I nodded my head. "O-okay?"

Aleks grinned. "Good. Jace will be assistant."

Did he really need an assistant for one student?

If so, Aleks was doomed to be disappointed. With both of them staring over my shoulders, my aim would never improve.

Jace must have seen my line of thinking because he said, "There needs to be another person present for liability issues." He continued at my incomprehension. "To be a witness."

I tilted my head to the side.

Aleks spelled it out for me bluntly, "He will be here to make sure I don't man-hands or harass you."

"Manhandle," Jace said. "Again. It's manhandle. We went over this in Estonia."

My face went supernova.

Aleks pulled me into his side and started to lead us away. "You have much to learn, *Medvezhonok*. Maybe I teach you other things besides guns. ...or maybe I teach you about different type of gun."

His tone of voice that I was becoming increasingly familiar with was the only warning that I needed. He was making some sort of sexual reference.

But...I was also confused because Jace wasn't saying anything to stop it if Aleks was. Hadn't Jace just finished explaining that he'd be here to make sure nothing untoward happened?

Was I misreading things?

I licked my lips, thinking. "Um, okay," I said, sure now that I had misinterpreted the meaning. "Anything you want to teach me, I'm willing to learn."

Aleks tripped, nearly taking us both down as I was still tucked into his side. He let out a creative string of curse words in Russian—I'd know, considering the type of people I'd been surrounded by many years of my life. Curse words were usually the first thing I picked up. He turned his head down to look at me, studying my face. After a moment he said, "I was talking about dicks. My dick, specifically, but it doesn't have to be just mine."

It was my turn to stumble, but with Aleks holding me, I didn't fall. I choked on my own spit somehow as my body tried to swallow and draw breath at the same time. After coughing the saliva back out of my lungs, I tried to defend myself. "I thought Jace...he *just* said...I thought he was here to make sure things were professional."

Jace shrugged his shoulders, a small smirk on his face. "I said I'd make sure he wasn't harassing you. Do you feel harassed? He'll stop if you do."

I tilted my head as I thought about it.

Did I want Aleks to stop? God help my poor, embarrassed cheeks, but no, no I didn't. Just like I hadn't wanted to explain manhandling because I was afraid he would stop. I liked Aleks the way he was, rough, brusque manner and all. "I don't feel harassed," I stressed, wanting to be clear. "Sometimes embarrassed, yes, but not harassed."

"*Nyet*. All times embarrassed," Aleks said offhandedly but then paused. He was looking at me as if discovering something profound. "That is okay though. I like it. I know you will not always be embarrassed, not if you stay at Delta. I enjoy as much as I can."

He chuckled in satisfaction as my cheeks lit up, almost on cue.

I was reduced to the role of a performing monkey.

Chapter 13

Two more weeks passed.

I hadn't made any progress with defensive training, but my endurance was up higher than it'd ever been in my entire life. My yoga skills were so advanced that Jace was talking about trying to combine my skills into some sort of training that used the entire world as your jungle gym. He said it would be great for getting out of tight spots since I wouldn't be able to fight *or* shoot my way out of a situation—ha-ha. He fancied himself a comedian.

That comment was spurred on by how equally abysmal the shooting lessons were. Jace and Aleks both tried about every gun known to man, even the bigger ones that I hadn't been allowed to shoot before. The idea had been that I'd be able to have a steadier aim with the weight of the gun itself to help combat the recoil.

I still hadn't hit the target. Jace loved to comment how it was some sort of statistical miracle.

CJ and I still hadn't found any leads on Ivanov, but we were still trying. The missing Delta agent from that disastrous mission had been found. His naked body had been dumped outside of town in the wild where it looked like hungry tigers had eaten his remains over several days. Another Delta team had raided Ivanov's headquarters there and found the remains of the Bengali mercenaries he'd hired for local help. He'd got what he needed and cleaned house.

115

The discovery had only solidified my decision to get ahold of my less than legal network to see if I could find out information before Ivanov could hurt anyone else.

Other than that, my life was routine. I continued to spend my evenings with the Cardinals at their home. I sometimes thought Yolo was warming up to me, but then she'd roll her eyes and go back to ignoring me. Triz was a complete 180 of that, and apparently, we were at the point in our relationship where nudity should not be a big deal. That had flown over like a lead balloon.

Somehow, I *still* managed to have the odd run-in with different guys from both the Emerson and Tate teams. It was at least a daily occurrence, usually more.

Although, sometimes I got the feeling that Aleks was intending to ask me something big. I knew a little bit about Russian men. I knew they were sometimes pushy and moved fast. It wasn't a big deal to marry someone the day after you met them.

I liked Aleks and all, but I wasn't ready for a commitment. I'd just finished a lifetime of restrictions. No. Thank. You.

Anytime Aleks even *possibly* looked like he might get serious, I would hightail it away. And I was running out of plausible excuses if his increasingly squinty-eyed, silent accusations were a clue.

I was in the middle of doing just that after another gun training with Jace and Aleks when I ran smack-dab into Karl.

"Whoa, there Callie! Where's the fire?" Karl joked as he steadied me.

I wanted to fling my arm back in the direction of the suspicious Russian that I could still feel boring holes in the back of my head. *There, Karl, the fire's right there*!

I didn't though. I wasn't going to tattle.

"No fire," Jace said with all seriousness. "But maybe a jammed gun."

Even without any inflection, I was able to tell there was at least *some* degree of innuendo at play with Jace's statement. I could blame that new skill on Darcy and now most of the guys that had been throwing sly remarks and hidden messages nonstop around me. I was hearing them everywhere.

It was like learning a new language and being submerged in it for the first time. For a while, it sounded like background noise. Then one day, it was like something clicked in the brain and I realized I could understand the conversations happening all around.

I was hearing innuendos everywhere: the gym, Delta, the hospital, and home. I wanted to turn it off because now I was becoming suspicious and paranoid. How could I have missed something so fundamentally present everywhere that it suffused most adult conversations?

And I thought I was hearing things that weren't there. Especially when Karl ignored Jace's dry statement about the jammed gun, making me second-guess myself.

He looked at me. "Your team is having a meeting. I came to get you."

"What's her meeting about?" Jace asked.

Karl looked over the top of my head to answer. "It's private. Let's go, kiddo."

I gave Aleks and Jace the customary hugs that all the guys now 'demanded' any time I left, and then we headed up to the main floor.

"Will I be late for physical training?" I asked.

"Well, you won't be going to it. We've decided that you're ready enough to leave for South America with your team."

"Ready *enough*?" I frowned. "So...either you found out that Ivanov is in the US or you've given up all hope that I'll make any progress with my training."

Karl flashed me a smile, his bright blue eyes full of mirth. "Well, I can definitively say Ivanov is not in the US."

I groaned, embarrassed. I leaned back against the wall of the elevator and massaged my sore arms that suddenly hurt even more, knowing that it was a pointless pain. All those hours getting slammed to the mat. I rubbed at my eyes, pretending not to hear Karl's chuckle.

We got off of the elevator and headed out, though I was confused when he headed away from the offices and conference rooms. "Where are we going?"

"To the hospital. I'm going to brief you guys there. Your team's waiting."

I jogged to catch up to him as he passed the cafe to the other elevators. He was a man on a mission. "Why the hospital? Why not one of the conference rooms?"

The doors opened. He put his hand on one of the doors to keep them open for me. "Because, kiddo, it's protocol to get clearance from your doctor before leaving the country for a mission."

I processed that and then processed it again. I hedged a guess, my tone hopeful. "Will the clearance be coming from Dr. Harper?"

"He's not a doctor. He's a psychologist."

I cleared my throat. "Technically, neither is Dr. Scott."

Karl grinned at me as if he understood my cautious tone. "Not technically, but he's got more experience doctoring than you might think."

I let out a resigned sigh as my heart stuttered. Doc Scott, the smoldering veterinarian. My *self-appointed* doctor. Self-appointed because he appointed *himself*, if that wasn't clear enough in the title.

Two weeks didn't seem all that long ago when I thought about the mortifying incident at the cafe. He'd made me develop a complex towards sandwiches, of all things. I'd been treating Doc Scott like Aleks anytime he started steering the conversation towards anything resembling relationships or—heaven forbid—marriage. If I had seen even a hint of that mocha, shaved head or blinding-white smile, I would about-face so fast that I nearly knocked people over several times.

Now, it was time to face the music, read: thinly-veiled flirting. My poor cheeks. I could already feel the beginnings of a nice pink forming on them.

We made it to the hospital side on the Delta floor. This was Ms. Hannah's, the not-so-elderly nurse's, floor, so when we stepped out, I shouldn't have been too surprised to see Emerson, her grandson. I was though. He was one of the Delta guys that I hadn't seen in close to three months, so it was like noticing changes in classmates after a long summer break.

His toffee brown hair was slightly longer spiking higher in the stylish-do. He was wearing a dark grey waistcoat vest over a dress shirt and had matching chinos.

The last interaction I'd had with Emerson was holding his hand—on this very floor—so my eyes had no choice but to be drawn down to his long, sinewy fingers. The tendons and veins belied their strength while the fullness of them showed his youth. The nails were well-trimmed and groomed. In my impartial opinion, they were a masterpiece.

Emerson let out a strangled cough that drew my eyes back up to his. Amused jade green met my guilty hazel. "Hello, Callie. You look good."

I looked *good?*

"Uh," I stuttered, and then I realized when his ears tinted pink that Emerson most likely meant I was looking *healthy*. If the rest of the boys and Darcy were here now… I shook my head. They'd be so proud of the progress I'd made—my mind jumping first thing to a perverted message. "Thank you. I feel a lot better. You look um…good, too."

Emerson raised an eyebrow.

I replayed what I'd said. My cheeks blushed once more. "Uh—er! I mean..." I tried to save myself, realizing that I had called him good-looking, only I couldn't explain it away as saying he looked healthier. "W-well, what I meant was..."

Emerson chuckled and put a hand on my shoulder, cutting off my rant as if he'd hit an off-button. His British accent was messing with my brain. "I see Corbin and Aleks have been true to their word about 'schooling' you."

"Bryce too," I said in a quiet voice. "Even Brock has been throwing comments around during our training together. Aleks was already being...um, blunt? But, once Jace saw what Brock was doing, it was like declaring free-range. And Darcy's the worst out of all of them. She's got such a dark, dirty mind." I shuddered. "So, both of the classes I take are basically training with underlying sex education. Well, sexual-references education. Then I go home and get some more sex education."

And… why couldn't I stop saying sex?!

"Well, Babygirl, let me know if you need regular sex education. I'm pretty good at teaching that class. I have access to so many materials. You'd have models and *lots* of hands-on experience."

The raspy voice I'd been dreading to hear had solidified my reasons for apprehension. That was a stellar opening-statement that was quick to make me react.

My face was on fire. Maybe two weeks ago, I would've thought Doc Scott was making an innocent offer. With the guys—and Darcy—all systematically opening my Pandora's box, I could understand the innuendo behind that comment.

I turned to see Doc Scott in a white doctor's coat, standing with his hands in his pockets.

"Duane Scott," Emerson scolded, though it seemed like a half-hearted rebuff.

My eyes narrowed a bit at him. I would've believed Emerson's sincerity before...well, *before* my sex education. But now?

...surely he would've been able to cut Doc Scott off sooner. It wasn't as if the doctor's comment had started innocent and then continued until it was too late to stop. It'd started off with innuendo and downright digressed into a thinly-veiled proposition.

"Thank you so much, Emerson, for saving my virtue and delicate ears from Doc Scott's remark in such a timely fashion," I said evenly.

His jade-green eyes met mine, studying my face. It was hard to keep an innocent look but completely worth the trouble when I managed to. He didn't seem to be able to detect any sarcasm to my statement, so he was forced to say kindly and with a tiny amount of guilt, "My pleasure, Callie."

I looked down then, my cheeks warming at getting away with using sarcasm.

My actions apparently gave away the guiltiness that Emerson had been seeking earlier because he said, "It will *always* be my pleasure, Doll."

His tone was much more sensual that time around.

"Mr. Payton Emerson," Doc Scott scolded in a mocking manner. His eyes were dancing with mirth, so it was unlikely that he really cared about how the conversation had turned out. In fact, if the smug satisfaction was anything to go by, he was quite pleased and even a smidgen proud of his teammate.

"*Both* of you," Karl scolded with a firm tone. "This is an official matter, and despite your demands that you're her primary physician, Doc Scott, we could go track down Dr. Harper. Or even a *real* doctor." He wrapped his hand around my arm, beginning to steer me away. "I have half a mind to do that anyway. This was supposed to be confidential, and yet there's, conveniently, a third of your team here."

"Are you accusing me of having loose lips?" Doc Scott asked, trying to sound put out but looking delightedly devilish.

"Yes," Karl said with blunt admission.

"I'll have you know that Emerson is visiting his grandmoth--"

"I thought she was working the late shift tonight," Karl added but was ignored.

"And he's here acting as the nurse for me when dealing with Callie--"

"You haven't had him around during any of Callie's check-ups the last two months."

"So, yes, I did tell Emerson to be here for the integrity of the patient, since he was already here to see his grandmother--"

"Seriously, I'm pretty sure she's working third shift tonight," Karl said but was once again unacknowledged.

"But I did not tell a single soul that didn't need to know," Doc Scott finished. "I'm a professional."

I was smiling to myself a little bit by the end of the big speech, amused. Not one person in the hallway was buying what Doc Scott was selling, but that didn't stop him from pretending to be righteous.

"Now, I have a patient to assess. Payton, you'll be my nurse, since you're already here."

Karl scoffed but didn't protest. I glanced back at him, and his cobalt eyes were the only thing on his placid face that belied how he actually felt about the situation. They were full of suppressed laughter. He sent a wink at my curious gaze.

We filed in the room, the door shut, and it was like Doc Scott flipped a switch. "Okay then. What sort of clearances will she need for the mission she's going on," he asked, directing his question to Karl, even as he pulled a stethoscope from a drawer to listen to my heartbeat.

"It's a straightforward mission. They're going down to help gather intel on a local gang. It is near and dear to the Cardinals because Triz's family is the one spearheading the project."

"Oh," Emerson said casually, his voice light and British. "So they will be going to South America."

Karl was silent a moment before answering. "Yes." He drew the word out until it was multi-syllabic, laying on his suspicions.

"In that case," Emerson straightened his vest. "I would like to formally inquire if Brock would be able to accompany them on their journey."

Karl let out a few curse words as Doc Scott carried on with the physical, checking my ears, temperature, and reflexes.

"I knew it," Karl said, sounding vindicated and all but waving a finger and saying 'I told you so'. "I *knew* it. I knew you guys were up to something."

"I don't know what you mean, Mr. Westphal. However, it would be a great training exercise for Brock. He's been trying to pick up another language. As luck would have it, Portuguese is not one in his arsenal."

"*That's* your official excuse?" Karl asked, his tone dry. "You want him to learn Portuguese? In a few weeks?"

"You never know. The assignment might go on longer than that. Besides, Brock picks up on languages with relative ease now that he's learned more than three," Emerson said.

"I don't buy it," Karl said. "You guys are up to something. I don't know if it's because you're worried about Callie leaving or what, but you better watch it. Sabra would chew you up and spit you out if she thought you were being sexist about the Cardinals' ability to protect her."

My eyes felt like they were at a tennis match, watching them go back and forth: The ball was in the air. Karl had served. Would Emerson be able to return?

"We would never," Emerson said. "If we were so chauvinistic as to believe that, *all* of the Cardinals would line up to teach us about female equality. And I particularly don't want to ruffle any feathers—no pun intended--"

"Pun fully intended," Doc Scott chimed in as he timed my pulse, giving me a crooked smile.

Emerson continued as if he hadn't heard Doc Scott's comment. "Most if not all of those women are lethal in their own right, and I fear my team would lose. Doubly so because they wouldn't throw any punches, and their misplaced chivalry would likely only further enrage the Cardinals."

"So, say I did believe your excuse—which I don't—and I would be willing entertain this idea—which I might—*you* would be in charge of asking permission from Sabra and Natasia," Karl said, folding his arms and resting against the wall. He was relaxed and enjoying himself as he watched Emerson's reaction.

Emerson straightened his vest as he drew himself up tall. "I would be agreeable to those terms. Duane and I will be the ones to ask the Cardinals for this favor."

"What?" Doc Scott asked, the smile leaving his face. He'd been enjoying the verbal tennis match like me, but he had been much more amused by the whole situation. Emerson's inclusion of him evaporated that mirth in a flash.

Karl was already continuing though. "However, I'll have to ask one of the Tate team to go along as well. To be fair."

"What would make you say that?" Emerson asked his words carefully as if he was tense.

Karl leaned up from against the wall, his blue eyes intense and his thick, black eyebrows furrowed. "You're really going to stand there and pretend that there isn't some weird rivalry going on between the two teams right now? Okay, then, fine. I'll pretend that we're sending people along for reasons other than this competition."

For some reason, Karl shot a look my way before continuing. "Jace has been asking for practical experience for years to learn a new language. He likes being able to speak more than one language and has all but been begging to branch out from German and English. Portuguese would be a nice addition, wouldn't you agree?"

Emerson's jaw clenched like he wanted to say something but was holding himself back. Finally, he let out a sigh and pinched the bridge of his nose. He opened his eyes. "Fine, but I also want to send along Corbin."

"*What*?" cried Karl. "What in the world for? You do realize this is not your mission, right? You can't just invite yourself into it and expect orders to be followed."

Emerson continued. "If they are helping to gather intel on a gang, Corbin would be great at it. He's very adept at getting places where he shouldn't be able to. Plus, he could do with getting some practice reading body language for when we get sent to sneak around in countries that don't speak English."

Karl threw his hands up. "Sure, let's make this a learning experience. Hell, we'll add a dozen more plane tickets to the purchase order. Send the whole fam damily! Why not?"

Emerson ran his long fingers down the buttons on his vest, his jade-green eyes giving away nothing. "We have the funds to do so."

"We have the funds—" Karl gave a couple of stuttering false starts before he let out a big sigh, the dumbstruck expression giving way to suspicion. He gave Emerson an assessing look. "You're not usually this obtuse. You're having me on, aren't you?"

"Indeed, Mr. Westphal," Emerson said. "Why would we pay for a plane ticket when we could borrow the Rost family jet?"

Karl gave him a droll look. "I suppose Bryce would want to go if we're confiscating his family's jet."

"Perhaps."

Doc Scott examined the healing bullet wounds on my stomach and thigh. They were a dark, shiny pink that only continued to fade lighter as the weeks passed.

Karl glared at Emerson. "You're not getting me riled up again. You can send Corbin and Brock, but that's it!" He turned and went out the door. "I'm going to find the rest of the Cardinals. Give them a heads up. Not sure where they went off to. Find us when you're done, Callie!"

Doc Scott patted my knee. "And *that* was the foot-in-the-door technique."

"Very astute, Duane, but I was hardly using anything as nefarious as persuasive techniques. I was merely utilizing the opportunity for our teammates. Karl just happened to agree with the value of the opportunity."

Doc Scott shot him a sideways glance. "Sure."

"What's the foot-in-the-door technique?" I asked Emerson.

Emerson looked back at me. "It's one of two popular persuasion-techniques used mostly by salesmen. Foot-in-the-door is where you try to sell something small, and once you have them on the line to buy that, you add another thing, once you have a foot in the door, so to speak."

One of two?

I tilted my head. "What's the other?"

"Door-in-the-face," he said. "You want to sell something, but you pretend to sell something much larger. When they refuse and slam the door in your face, you knock again and sell the smaller, more reasonable thing that you actually wanted to sell."

"It's like this, Babygirl," Doc Scott said, looking at me from his crouched position. "Pretend I came to you wanting to sell you...oh, let's say a sandwich. It could be any kind of sandwich. For the sake of this scenario, let's say it's a mozzarella panini--"

"Subtle," was Emerson's taciturn interruption. Doc Scott, as seemed to be the habit today, ignored it.

"Say I needed you to buy one. If I was using the door-in-the-face technique, I'd try to sell you a whole case of them. You think that 25 mozzarella paninis are ridiculous for just one person, so you slam the door in my face. Then I knock again, offering to sell you one. You think this is much more reasonable. I make a sale, and you," he pulled a lock of my hair, "get your favorite sandwich."

"Understand?" Emerson asked, ignoring my imminent embarrassment—especially since Doc Scott hadn't stopped grinning at me.

"I think so. Let me see if I've got it right. You *did* use the foot-in-the-door technique to get both Brock and Corbin the okay to go. I have to be careful about anything I say around you because you have an extensive background in psychology that you seem to use on unsuspecting people. And, Doc Scott should maybe try selling a sampler pack of sandwiches. Several of *one* type of sandwich would be a lot for anyone. Maybe they'd like a *variety*."

Doc Scott's mouth dropped open, and I knew that he'd gotten the message.

As a first attempt at throwing around innuendo myself, I was rather proud. He could decipher that statement anyway he wanted to.

Emerson flat-out laughed. He gave me a very enigmatic smile.

"Very astute, love."

Chapter 14

It was intimidating at first, being back in Brazil, but no one had jumped me yet.

The weather was amazing, the people were friendly, and the views were breathtaking. I hadn't been able to appreciate any of it my first go around since I'd been in the country illegally. We'd spent the time shuffling around seedier alleys, abandoned buildings, and shady people.

Now, it was like a never-ending stream of bright, tropical hues, authentic spices, and local music. The art was as colorful as the music. The coconut smoothies were endless, and both Brock and Jace took to the local cuisine with fervor.

Corbin stuck with things he was familiar with, like fried cassava—which was fries made with cassava flour—and *misto quente* which was grilled ham and cheese. He was an adventurous one, that Corbin.

Triz's dad was a warm host and an amazing cook. He'd opened his house to us and was eager to share his culture. He cooked authentic meals and was happy to teach us Portuguese.

The guys had only learned a few phrases so far, but it was progress. They were picking up more and more with each conversation we listened in on. And every night we went to Triz's familial home after a long day of boring stakeouts. There, we'd be regaled with tales in partial Portuguese and partial English. Being so fully submersed like this, it wouldn't be long before the guys would be able to speak conversationally—especially Jace. He was really studious about it.

After a nightmare, I'd get up and go on a walk. The living room lamp would be on late into the night after the rest of the house had gone to bed. I'd peek in and see Jace asleep with a Portuguese dictionary spread open and forgotten across his chest.

It'd become a habit of mine to put the book on the coffee table and pull the blankets up to his chest. One time, I thought he was awake because I felt his fingers brush my arm, but when I checked, his eyes were shut and his breathing was even.

With only three bedrooms, Triz's home was small but cozy. Love and laughter suffused the air. There were pictures on the wall, and Triz's *papi*, spoke of them with fondness, love, and longing all rolled into one—especially when he talked about his true love. I teared up the one time he mentioned how she was with the angels now.

He seemed to like telling me stories. He said I was a good listener, and it was nice that I was fluent in Portuguese. I'd thank him politely. He'd insist on me calling him "Papi" once more, get tired of speaking in broken English, and switch to telling me a story in his native tongue. Rinse. Repeat. And there were a lot of repeats. He had a lot of stories.

Many times, Triz or her older brother would join in and laugh along with him. They weren't the least bit embarrassed by their childhood antics nor the ornery way that their doting father narrated them.

I learned when Triz was younger, she'd been going to school to be an engineer and working at the family-owned mechanic shop. When she was sixteen, she had been caught in the crossfire of a drug war. Triz had almost lost her life the same way her mother had. Her *papi* refused to lose another family member to the local gang. Together, Papi and her brother, Fabrizio scraped together every bit of money that they could to send her away from the danger and violence. Papi and Fabrizio most likely saved her life, and Triz had been determined to return the favor. She continued on until she found her way into Delta and called in a favor to move her family into the house that they had now.

Now, Papi wanted to put together a school in that very neighborhood that had killed his wife. It was going to be named after her *A Escola de Esperança Laura Moreno*, or the Laura Moreno School of Hope.

Her family all had established themselves, not lavishly, but comfortably, and they wanted to pay it forward.

Whenever we weren't staking out suspected gang members, we were helping out on the school. It felt good. I was part of something that I was proud of, and I'd began to feel like a Delta member over the past few weeks we'd been here. And... I was happy about that.

Helping to take out the bad guys for a change... it was healing some part of my psyche that I hadn't thought broken.

It helped me open up more to the Cardinals and even the guys as well. I didn't need to feel guarded around them. I was learning to trust them more, opening up a little, and enjoying our interactions.

"Hey Callie-Cat," Corbin called. He'd taken to calling me that because I always stopped to pet the stray cats whenever we had spare time to help out at the school. The nickname didn't stop me from talking to the alley cats we crossed paths with. I felt a kinship to the tenacious strays.

I turned to Corbin, plaster sprinkled on my head and pieces of dust clinging to the fine hairs of my arm as I worked on the mudding and sanding. Corbin was standing in a freshly painted doorway, his sky-blue eyes locked on my face and making my breath catch. "Yes?"

"What do you call a Brazilian with a rubber toe?" He'd updated his cheesy joke repertoire to match the setting. Somewhat. "Roberto!"

A small smile cracked my face.

Jace, who had been to my left trying to practice his conversational skills in Portuguese with me, stood up to his full height, all six foot of it. " Don't make jokes about Brazilians when we're in Brazil. They'll beat us up."

Completely ignoring Jace, Triz's brother, Fabrizio, said, "Oh, listen, listen! I have another one! How many South Americans does it take to change a light bulb?" He paused for a bit, and then said, "A Brazilian! Is funny, no?"

I actually laughed out loud on that one. My reaction pulled a wounded look across Corbin's face though, so I got back to work, picking up the conversation with Jace, and trying my best to ignore the impromptu joke-battle that had broken out between Corbin and Fabrizio, lest I hurt anyone's feelings.

While we were plastering, Brock would pop in sometimes to check on us. Then he'd pop back out to go help with something else. He was a jack of all trades and was pulled to help on little odds and ends, despite his obvious reluctance to get too far from us.

A warm breeze trickled in the open window, and I could smell the faintest traces of ocean. I closed my eyes and listened to random strangers carrying on conversations as they walked by down narrow streets.

From behind me, Corbin and Fabrizio cracked up laughing, patting each other on the shoulder. I missed the joke that had ended their competition, but I smiled all the same.

I realized that I was content. I was extremely content right here, right now, and it wasn't because of the place. It was because of the people. I liked them. I cared for them.

My thoughts drifted to my plan to get access to the internet. The closer I grew to Delta, the more I worried about Ivanov swooping in, a ferocious dragon, and burning everything down into a molten, chaotic mass of destruction.

I couldn't have that. I needed to see if I could track down Ivanov. If I had to lure him away to save the people that I was growing so fond of, then sooner would be better. The longer I waited, the harder it would be to leave.

I was deep in my thoughts and plans when I heard the telltale sounds of gunshots popping in a loud staccato from outside.

Corbin jerked to attention. Jace spoke loudly in German— probably swearing—and Brock appeared in the doorway within seconds, his eyes scanning the room. Jace pulled me away from the window and the three somewhat encircled me.

Fabrizio seemed to drop out of his shock, because he yelled, "Beatriz! Papi!" and took off running.

My eyes widened. "The Cardinals! Those shots came from upfront!"

"No way! They sounded like they came from back here," Corbin said.

I shook my head and tried to head out into the hallway to follow Fabrizio. "No, the sounds echo in the city like this. I could tell from the way they bounced off the building in front of me."

"It could be Ivanov," Brock said, not letting me pass.

"It could be, but the Cardinals are up there. I have to get to them. *Especially* if it's Ivanov." Tears of frustration and fear sprung up in my eyes. "Please."

Brock seemed like he was going to let the consequences be damned and take me away anyway, but Corbin let out a curse and stepped aside so that I had room to squeeze past. As I was going, Jace grabbed my arm.

I thought he was about to stop me, so I reacted instinctively. My hand knocked his loose grip upwards. I used my other hand to pull his arm over my shoulder as I twisted around to snug my back to his front. Then I leaned forward, pulling and throwing him over my head to the ground.

His back hit the ground with a loud thump, forcing the air from his lungs. He was splayed out flat, coughing a little bit.

"Sorry," I said, meaning it, but also seeing it as a necessary evil.

I went to step past him, but he grabbed my ankle. In a move that was so smooth and fast that I couldn't understand what happened, I was on the ground without even registering my collision with the floor. Jace had somehow managed to roll me to the ground, cushion the fall, and get on top all while he was still trying to catch his breath.

"That wasn't," he coughed again. "Nice."

I started thinking about my options from this position. They were limited in a big way.

"Holy fuck," Brock said, sounding shocked. "All this time training and....what the actual *fuck*?"

"Callie-Cat is a dark angel."

"Why the hell haven't you been using that move in PT with Jace and me? We thought you were a lost cause! We've been trying to teach you that for *two weeks*!"

"I don't want to hurt anyone!" I cried out, frustrated because I couldn't break Jace's hold on me. I hadn't heard any shots in a while, but that could mean anything. One of the Cardinals could already be dying. "Everything I've been taught was chosen to inflict the most damage. Because of my size. Because of what I'd need it for. Because of the types of people that I was surrounded by and would have to use it on. Please, I don't want to you hurt you, Jace."

I was partly bluffing because I wasn't sure I could break loose from the hold, even with the maneuvers that could hurt him.

"You won't," he promised as if he could read my thoughts. "I wasn't expecting it earlier," he said. His dark-chocolate eyes stared into my soul. "I'm expecting it now. And you'll listen to what I have to say."

He stayed right where he was, leaned over me astride my stomach with his hands pinning my wrists to the floor. I wiggled a little bit more, trying to distract the attention from my leg as I crept it up towards his torso.

"Christ! Stop moving," Jace said, lifting up from me the slightest bit so that he wasn't sitting as much of his weight on me. It was perfect because otherwise, I wouldn't have been able to do what I did next. I used my flexibility and new muscles from yoga training to wedge my leg up between us and push him off of me.

I didn't look to see where he landed, knowing that my window of opportunity was small. I rolled over onto my stomach about to push myself up to my feet, but a giant boulder crashed down on me, truly pinning me to the ground and leaving me with zero options from there.

I struggled, but the force was immovable.

"Brock?" I said brokenly, shocked and only barely holding back the feelings of betrayal.

He murmured soothing things in my ear that I couldn't understand because it was Serbian. He kept uttering the sweetest, softest sounds in my ears. It was beautiful. His voice was melodic and calming. It helped me to think straight. I heard him mention Ivanov's name once I had settled down a little more so I thought about the situation.

If it was Ivanov, rushing in there now would only cause him to kill the Cardinals. He would have no use for them, and things only stayed alive around Ivanov if they had a use.

There was movement to my right.

Jace had recovered from his second tumble while I was in the middle of my panic attack. He was there, crouched on the balls of his feet, his soulful brown eyes observing me.

"I'm not trying to stop you, Callie. I just want you to *listen*," he said. At my nod, he continued. "Ivanov is a sort of kryptonite for you. And I don't blame you. None of us do." He gestured to Brock. "We were there when we got you from Russia. We saw the aftermath. It was a fucking bloodbath. I have nightmares about it sometimes. And that was a *fraction* of a moment into your life. The guy wasn't even *there*. He's like every terrifying monster and villain all rolled into one. We know that this has to be tough, but you have to understand that someone needs to keep a level head. That's going to be us. We'll help you, but you have to listen to us. Trust that we're going to do the right thing. Can you do that?"

Back in Russia when Karl had asked me to trust them, I hadn't been able to. I hadn't been able to trust anyone in a long time at that point, not even CJ whom I'd spent a good deal of time communicating important information to.

But now?

After my recovery, the weeks that I'd spent with the guys at Delta and the weeks I'd spent with them here in Brazil? I could trust them at least with this. I could trust them to be my compass when dealing with Ivanov.

"Okay," I said.

Brock got off of me and helped me to my feet, apologizing to me, looking loads more upset about it than I was. I brushed him off, offering my own reassurances that he had done the right thing. Jace wasted no time sticking me with Brock to follow at a distance for backup while Corbin and he scouted ahead.

Using that method, we made it to the front entrance. Corbin and Jace rounded the corner while Brock and I stayed back. When they gave us the signal to come forward, I got my first glimpse of the large glass doors. A lot of them had bullet holes in them, fracturing the glass that Brock and Fabrizio had installed last week. What was really terrifying was the blood spatter on one of the doors. It was still trailing slowly down, searing a red path that would stay burnt in my memory.

"The path leads from outside to the office," Corbin said, letting us know they were going to check that next. They walked up, moving in unison. Brock kept me close as he stood against the wall and kept an eye out the front door. I tried to look out there as well, but I didn't notice anything.

There was laundry fluttering to dry against some of the pastel-colored houses across the dirt and stone alley. The children that had been playing soccer earlier were no longer there. Considering the people we'd been surveilling, it wasn't likely this was a random drive-by. I hoped the kids had taken off before the shooting started.

Only Corbin returned, stopping at the office door. "Hey, guys. It's Sabra. She's been shot."

My legs felt wobbly as my face paled.

"She's fine for now," Corbin said, trying to ease me, but there was something about his tone that kept me from relaxing.

"What aren't you saying?" I asked.

Corbin wouldn't meet my gaze, hiding his sky-blue eyes behind messy, amber hair. He motioned me forward. "You should probably see for yourself. Brock, can you stay and watch the alley? It's unlikely, but they could come back."

"How do you know they won't come back?" I questioned once more, following him.

"Because I think they got what they wanted," Corbin said, pushing one of the office rooms open.

Did that mean it wasn't Ivanov? What was it they'd wanted?

Inside was a scene that was much calmer than I felt. Jace was pressing a bloodied cloth into Sabra's upper arm. Fabrizio and Papi were sitting in the corner and had a grey pallor to their usually vibrant and rich, latte-colored skin. Sabra was talking to Darcy who seemed to be cursing in Gaelic. Yolo was on her phone, studying the screen intently.

Despite the near calmness, I could see the immense pain in Papi's eyes and sheer fury in Fabrizio's.

A cold, dead pit formed deep in my stomach, lodging my heart in my throat. "Where are Triz and Natasia?"

Sabra cleared her throat. "Triz was taken."

I leaned back against the door, trying to concentrate. "A-and Natasia?"

"Got in our van and followed after her."

"This is *so* stupid!" Yolo yelled suddenly. "Why are you not mad that she went off on her own! She should've taken one of us with her. If I had done this, you would be furious."

"I *am* furious," Sabra said very calmly, not even wincing as Jace worked on cleaning her wound. She must have had a pretty high pain tolerance. "However, Natasia has more experience with these things, and I know that she weighs her options before she makes a decision. You are more impulsive."

"Well, maybe that's a good thing! Impulsively, I would've made the same decision!"

"In some instances, yes. In this instance, maybe. Certainly not always. It is what it is, and we have to work with what we've got. Were you able to track Triz's phone?"

Yolo blew out a breath. "Using CJ's program, *oui*, but they tossed it out somewhere because Natasia's phone keeps going, but Triz's has stopped."

"That's good," Sabra said.

"Well, it might have been if she hadn't been circling around not far from where they dropped Triz's phone," Yolo said.

"You think she lost them?" Corbin asked.

"If she ever had them, then yes. It could be that she was too far behind and was trying to use Triz's phone to follow, just like us," Yolo said, more serious than I'd heard her before.

Fabrizio, Triz's older brother, looked up and started speaking in rapid Portuguese with Papi. Papi responded.

"Callie, what are they saying?" Sabra asked, straightening up.

I tilted my head and frowned. "They are talking about how they might know who took her." I stepped closer to them, drawing their attention. I switched to Portuguese. "*Did you think of something? Do you know who took her?*"

Fabrizio turned to me and nodded. He spoke quickly, his eyes huge.

"What's he saying?" Darcy asked, having something to focus on besides her red-hot rage.

"He says that they might know who took her. Triz had an old boyfriend, Rogerio. They grew up in the same neighborhood and were childhood friends. She found out that he joined one of the gangs here." I stopped to clarify something with him and then continued interpreting. "Rogerio convinced her to stay with him, saying that the gang wasn't all bad. It was a way to get protection. Over time, the gang began to demand worse things. He refused, and people assumed that it was because of Triz. So, they targeted her..." I swallowed heavily, my throat thick with emotion. I had a bad feeling that I knew where this story was going. "That was when Triz was attacked in the street. Triz ended it with Rogerio. She left shortly after that for America to get a new start."

I spoke with Fabrizio while the room digested the tale. "*You think there is unfinished business between them?*"

His dad spoke up now. "*Those two invented unfinished business.*" He shook his head, tears gathering in his eyes. He started shouting and swearing about how it was Rogerio's fault that his wife was dead and his only daughter missing.

I wasn't sure how his wife dying was Rogerio's fault since Triz was only a baby when her mother was killed. Maybe it was the same gang? Or maybe Papi was becoming hysterical and not making sense.

"*Do you know where he might be taking her?*" I asked.

"*No. Rogerio stops by the shop every now and then asking about her. He's not welcome though, so the most we've ever said to him is to leave. I don't know where he lives now. Besides, it wasn't Rogerio. He may not even know about what happened today. Unless he's changed a lot, Rogerio wouldn't have done anything that would harm Triz. He wouldn't have shot at her. It had to be the gang.*" Fabrizio said.

"They think it's the gang," I said. "Not Rogerio. They don't think he would've done anything to harm her."

Sabra spoke up. "We could find the gang through Rogerio."

I was already shaking my head no before she finished. "That won't work. They don't know where he is..." I trailed off as an idea struck me. I turned back to Fabrizio and Papi. "Do you know his number? His cell phone?"

"Uh, yes, maybe," Fabrizio said, calming down and regaining his handle on the English language as he sensed the beginnings of a plan in my voice. He pulled out his phone. "I keep it in case. The number is old. It might not work anymore."

"We're about to find out," I said.

He read the number out loud. I memorized it. I turned back to the room and pointed right at Yolo. "I need your phone."

Chapter 15

"What? Why my phone?" Yolo asked.

"Because she said so," Sabra cut in, also sensing the brief hope in my voice. "Give it to her."

"But she's not allowed to-"

"This is an emergency. She's not going to do anything with us right here."

I knew they were worried I would try to track down Ivanov or do something suicidal if I had access to the internet without Big Brother CJ there to keep an eye on me.

Yolo got up and stomped towards me. "This had better not be some scheme to get access to a computer. Triz's life could be on the line here."

She was slightly taller than me, so she was looking down as she was in my face, her expensive perfume wafting over me. She looked fierce, and I had a flash of her taking on people like a deadly pro as a pink-colored avatar in the VR training. I wondered if she could do all of those things and how much scarier it would look in real life if she wore the expression she did right now.

I nodded, and she slammed the phone into my hand. I didn't waste any time.

I'd done loads of phone traces before. It was the most common thing either Ivanov or Veseli had asked of me. However, I thought I'd try something a bit simpler before I got to hacking away. I dialed the number Fabrizio had read to me and held it up to my ear as it rang.

After a few rings, a male answered. "*Hello?*"

"*Hello. Rogerio?*" I asked.

There was a long pause on the other end of the line.

"*Who is this? I don't recognize the number. And that accent... are you American?*" The voice was less nice now.

I could've hung up. I should've hung up, especially if the way Darcy was waving at me to do so was any indication. I didn't though. I glanced at Fabrizio and Papi. They were both pretty level-headed people, present situation aside. Triz was too. She had to have seen something in this Rogelio guy. I was banking on it.

I took a big breath. "*Do you speak English?*"

"Yes," he said. "Explain who are you. Fast."

"You don't know me, but I'm a friend of Triz's."

"I do not know any Triz."

"What? Are you Rogerio?" I asked, more nervous. If this wasn't Rogerio, then we wouldn't have any lead to follow and find Triz.

"*Yes, but you have one minute to explain who you are and how you got this number before I hang up.*" He said in a growl, switching back to Portuguese.

"Please, please. You must remember. Beatriz Moreno. You were together once--"

He cut me off. "Bea? You know Bea? How is she? Her family, they do not talk to me."

"Rogerio, stop. Please, this is an emergency. We were restoring an old building into a school when there were shots--"

It got deadly silent on the line but he spoke up in a low, lethal tone. "Beatriz is alive?"

I swallowed. "Yes. We think so. She was taken. We're trying to find her--"

"You're in Brazil, no? That is why you call me. You think maybe I find her."

I paused, feeling uncertain about confirming our location, but he would find out if I asked for his help. I needed to trust Triz's judgment in men. "Yes. We...we think your gang took her."

He let out a dry laugh. "It is no longer a gang. It is a cartel. And I am not a member. I stopped a long time ago." He let that sentence trail off. "But...I know some people. I will talk to them. I will meet you in thirty minutes."

"Oh, we're at--"

"I know where the school is. It's been in the papers. I read, and I hoped that Bea—uh, Triz, you said, no?—will come. I guess she did."

He hung up the call before I could say anything else. I looked up at the room.

Sabra was all bandaged up. Jace was wiping his hands as best as he could with wet towels. Corbin must've gone out in the hall to check in with Brock. Fabrizio and Papi were watching me with hope. Darcy was back to muttering in Gaelic, and Yolo was glaring at me, her arms crossed.

"Some great hacker you are," she said, snagging her phone back.

"I can trace a number," I said, nonplussed by her comment. "This was faster. It's harder to pull up the programs I need to trace. Too much typing to do on a digital keyboard. I thought you'd prefer faster."

"What if we can't trust this man? He could have changed since our Triz was last with him. Maybe even before."

"He said he's not in the gang anymore."

"That is exactly what he'd say if he was in the gang."

Jace toweled his hands dry. "Surprisingly enough, it's exactly what he'd say if he wasn't in a gang. Go figure. Either way, we'll have to wait and see what happens when he shows up. Unless you want to tie him up and throw him in a lake to see if he floats or drowns? Oh, here's an idea. We could set him on fire and see if he frees himself."

Yolo sent him a glare for the sarcastic comments.

The door burst open, drawing everyone's attention. Yolo had materialized a gun from somewhere on her body and was holding it in a two-handed grip aimed at the door. When she saw that it was Corbin and Natasia, she lowered her arms. "You're lucky I didn't go for my throwing my knives."

Corbin's eyes got big, but he didn't say anything to that. He swallowed, his Adam's apple bobbing up and down. He stepped aside, gesturing for Natasia to go in, though I think it was more out of the weariness that Yolo hadn't yet holstered her weapon than chivalry.

He came up close to me and whispered, "She's crazy."

I licked my lips, debating, and then I nodded.

Yolo was pretty crazy sometimes, and despite her continued aloof demeanor towards me, there were times at the Cardinals' house that I would see a different side to her. A softer side. It was obvious, despite how diverse their team was, how much they all loved each other, and that included Yolo in her own way.

Natasia stepped into the room, looking like she'd gone ten rounds with a tire iron. Her face was cut and swollen in spots. "I lost her," she said, her Russian accent the only hint at how she was feeling. Her face was an ice sculpture of expressionless pain. "They knocked me out. I'm not quite as good as Darcy at taking on a large group of people. When I came to, they were turning the corner. I took the van, but it was too large and bulky to navigate the streets. People kept coming out, getting in the way. If I had a motorcycle, this would've been a different story. I'm sorry."

She held up a cracked phone, handing it over to Sabra.

Sabra looked down at it, clenching it in a tight fist. She tamped down her emotions, her jaw jutting out, and looked up. "It's not your fault. Don't feel responsible for it."

Natasia's face didn't change, but her words belied her thoughts. "I should have been more informed about the local gangs. That's my job! I'm good at it. Some of them I recognized from people we've been trailing. I don't even know why they would target her."

"Well," Darcy said. "It was most likely an old flame of hers. Or at least because of him. He's on his way."

Natasia turned to Sabra sharply. "We have a lead?"

Sabra nodded, and it seemed like Natasia deflated. She closed her eyes for a second, and when she opened them she had seemed to steel herself.

"Would you like something for your," Corbin trailed off, gesturing to his own face. "You know?"

"Nah," Darcy said, going up to Natasia and wrapping an arm around her shoulder. "Let her have 'em. It 'fuels her hate fire'."

Natasia rolled her eyes at that for some reason, but a small smile cracked at the corners of her lips anyway.

There was commotion at the door. Yolo's gun was pointed once more, even faster this time if at all possible since she had never holstered it. When she saw that it was Brock, she swore in French and then in one motion, used her free arm to draw something from her back and throw it. It stuck deep into the wall with a wobbling rattle about six inches from Brock's face.

It was a small knife.

The Cardinals seemed unfazed by this, but Yolo had everyone else's undivided attention, which must have been her goal because she simply said, "Knock next time, *oui?*"

My eyes were huge, and it took the pain of burning in dryness before I remembered that I needed to blink.

"You are a bit of a firecracker, no?" a new voice said, stepping into the doorway next to Brock. He was a short man, especially standing by the nearly six-and-a-half-foot Brock. He had roguishly tousled hair, deep dimples, and cold eyes despite their warm coffee color. He wore a bright white shirt with the sleeves rolled up his arms showing layered muscles underneath. He was small but thick with strength. His goatee was trimmed to perfection, making me think that his messy hair had actually been styled.

By his voice as well as Fabrizio and Papi's angry looks they were shooting towards the man, I knew it had to be Rogerio.

He entered the room, pulling the knife from the wall to study it, despite the fact that Yolo had raised her gun back up and kept it trained on him with the precision of a target lock.

Sabra stepped forward. "You are Rogerio?"

"Yes," he said, twirling Yolo's throwing knife in his hand as he looked around the room. Other than the bloody rags and scattered first aid materials, the room was pretty bare with spots that still needed painting. It seemed to focus him. "I need to know exactly what happened earlier. I called my people still in the gang. It does not make sense for anyone to target her. I have not been in that gang since...since that day, so I hope it is not them."

Fabrizio was up across the room and in his face, spewing non-stop Portuguese like a burst fire hydrant. It was years and years of emotion and anger pouring out, and Rogerio took it. He didn't even react when

142

Fabrizio became more incensed at the lack of a response and pushed him back hard enough to crack the freshly laid plaster on the wall.

I looked around the room. Papi would be of no help. He had a cold look in his eyes that was even scarier than Fabrizio's outburst of hot anger.

I stepped up to them, or I tried to anyway. I was held back by both Jace and Darcy.

"Let them work it out, *a chara*," Darcy said. Jace glanced at our interaction, but Darcy continued on, not even noticing his gaze. "I know a temper when I see one. Let him have it out. We won't be able to get anything done if this doesn't get resolved."

I leaned back causing Darcy to drop her hold. Jace's loosened, but he pulled me closer, speaking in my ear. "*A chara*?" he asked.

I shrugged my shoulders a little bit, watching the scene in front of us.

Fabrizio continued to yell. Rogerio reached the cusp of his limits because he started to stand up for himself. It was at that point that Papi punched the guy, knocking him out cold. I hadn't even seen Papi move, but the older man got all the way across the room in less than a blink. The air was still shifting in the wakes of his path.

He spat on the prone figure of his daughter's ex, shaking the pain out of his hand. "*That was for my almost taking my daughter from me*," he said to the unconscious man.

"Well, great. Now how are we supposed to find out what Rogerio knows?" Natasia said dryly.

This seemed to bring both of the Moreno men out of their red-hazed fury.

Papi gasped and dropped to his knees. "What have I done?"

Sabra put a hand on his shoulder to comfort him.

I pushed between Darcy and Jace, breaking Jace's loose hold. I stepped up to Rogerio's body, glancing up to meet the black eyes of Fabrizio. He didn't seem like he was about to go off the handle again, so I crouched down. My hands patted at Rogerio's pockets until I found his phone. I pushed a button to light up the screen. It was locked.

"Callie-Cat, what are you doing?"

"I'm going to see who he called since he talked to us. It will give us something to do until he comes to. You might try splashing him with water," I said, looking up at Fabrizio. He nodded and left the room, hopefully going in search of a water bottle since the water hadn't yet been turned on in the building. That was why Jace had used wet-wipes earlier to clean his hands of blood.

Rogerio's phone was a newer model, sophisticated. Normally, if I wanted to use it, I'd just do a factory reset, but that might lose the information I wanted. "I need a computer," I said.

"There's a laptop in the van," Darcy said, moving to go get it.

"I'll come with you," Natasia said. "Until further notice, no one is allowed to go alone. Buddy system."

I helped Jace clear the supplies off the table. It was less than two minutes later that Natasia and Darcy returned with the laptop.

"We don't have WiFi," Papi said, speaking up for the first time.

"Not a problem," I said, feeling like my world was centered once more as the technology was placed in my hands. Sabra gave one of her thousand-word looks that told me she trusted me, I could do it, and I had better behave or else, dot, dot, dot…

I opened the lid and booted the system up. It was like child's play to connect to one of the internet cafes. There were so many to choose from being so deep in this part of the city. I pulled up a log of the devices connected to the WiFi and used their IP address as my own to piggyback off of their connection.

I downloaded a program I'd used several times. It was a passcode cracker that would run through all the numerical combinations in a matter of minutes while at the same time bypassing any of the normal security that phones had built-in these days after too many wrong attempts. It only worked through a computer.

I looked at Rogerio's phone once more.

"I need a cable to connect this," I said.

"Is it an iPhone?" Jace asked. "CJ swears up and down by the advanced security of Apple, so that's all we have."

"Same," Corbin added.

"No, it's Android," I said.

"There should be one in the laptop bag," Darcy said, digging it out and handing it to me. "It's in here for emergencies like this."

I plugged the phone in at the same time the program finished downloading. I installed it, only tipping off two alert messages from the laptop's coding. The program wasn't exactly legal, so most computers were designed to quarantine it like a virus. I used a prompt window to access the core processing code to allow the program to run.

"Congratulations," I said as I continued typing, my eyes flying across the screen. "Your computer is now illegal."

No one said anything to that.

I clicked "start" and allowed the computer to do its thing. I stood up straight, waiting and idly wondering what was taking Fabrizio so long to find a water bottle.

My attention was drawn, however, when the computer dinged and files pulled up from Rogerio's phone. I leaned back down to sort through the files, pulling up the *tmp.storage* files. His call logs would be in there.

"Okay," I said, looking through them. It was easy to find Yolo's number. It was the only American number in the file. "Before we called, there hadn't been any communication with anyone since yesterday morning."

"So it's unlikely that he was in on organizing this hit?" Sabra asked.

"Most likely, unless they used burners," Natasia said, coming to lean over my shoulder. "What about after?"

"After he made five calls to local numbers. Three of the calls lasted two minutes or less. The fourth number lasted...just over eight minutes."

Natasia frowned. "Can you pull up the conversation?"

"No, with enough time, we could listen in if it was taking place, but phones don't usually record audio and store them. Even temporarily, it would take up too much space. And unless you feel like hacking into the NSA to get at their database of phone calls…"

"You could do that?" Corbin asked, but I didn't answer.

"What about the last call?" Yolo said, coming up on my other side to study the screen.

"They didn't answer."

"So, he makes a call that lasts a lot longer than his first three. Immediately after he makes a call, and the person doesn't answer. Right. Because that's not suspicious at all," Jace surmised, his arms crossed.

"Jace's right," Sabra said, moving in front of me to look me in the eye. "What was the last number?"

I tried to cross-reference the number to stored contacts in the phone's address book since they weren't immediately labeled on the laptop. "I'll check."

Rogerio groaned as he rolled to his side, stirring on his own. He held his hand up to his jaw, manipulating it back and forth to see if it was broken. "You hit hard, old man," he said, giving Papi a cautious look despite his carefree words. He leaned up against the wall. "The man's name is Tomas Costa. An old friend gave me his number...eventually. He said that he's been gone off and on a lot this week."

"So he's been getting his nails done or something. What makes you think he's the guy that took Triz?" Yolo demanded.

"Tomas and I were enemies, eh rivals, in his head. He was ambitious. I was a hard-worker. I didn't want any trouble, but when you're a hard-worker, the top dogs notice. I guess he holds a grudge."

"But why my daughter?" Papi asked, pain in his voice. It was hard to look at him. The anguish was so strong it seemed private.

Rogerio looked up at him. "Because it's no secret that I still love Bea."

Papi looked like he was about to hit him again, but he held back at the last moment.

"Do you know where he might've taken her?" Sabra asked.

Rogerio shook his head.

"Think! Any warehouses or buildings that you guys might have used back when you were still in the gang?" Natasia interrogated. "I can give you a general area where I lost her signal."

Rogerio ran his hands through his hair in frustration, reminding me of Karl. "He wouldn't use those. The only reason he had to take her was to hurt me. He wouldn't use anything I might find. He knows there are people in the gang still loyal to me."

"What about a house or personal property?" Natasia continued.

"No. Even years ago Tomas wouldn't tell people that. Look, one of the guys I called today says he might be able to help. He said he'd call back."

"How long will that take?" Yolo asked.

Rogerio looked miserable. "He said three hours at most. Look, it's the best chance we've got."

"Well, fuck that," Yolo spat, then she looked at me. "Can you trace his phone?"

"It would be off," Rogerio said. Delta people that knew me waited on my answer anyway.

"It's off," I confirmed, already having tried that route as soon as Rogerio had explained the last call. I wasn't being idle though, and I hadn't given up because of a powered-down cell. Ivanov wouldn't have allowed that as an excuse for failure, so I'd quickly learned to think outside of the box if I wanted to avoid the tank.

While Natasia had been questioning Rogerio, I'd been busy typing away, and Yolo finally noticed. "Callie, what are you doing?" she asked in a careful tone.

I knew that the Cardinals and even the guys would be worried I was trying to do something Ivanov-related, so I was quick to explain. "I am doing a deep search for Costa based on the information we have. Normally, I'd ask for his date of birth, but cell phone numbers are almost as good as a social security number now. Did you know that he has a profile on Match.com?"

"Wait, how'd you get his number?" Rogerio asked, getting to his feet. His eyes landed on the table. "Wait, is that my phone?!" he asked, groping for his empty pockets. "That *is* my phone."

"Yes. And I got Costa's number," I said, trying to modify the password-hacking app to work with the website. If I could hack into Costa's Match-profile, maybe I'd have an address. "Because you called it."

I had once talked to the coder of the password program on a dark-web chatroom, the same chatroom I first met CJ on, actually. I'd admired the creator's work and let him know as much. We'd had quite a few conversations where I was able to pick up a bit on how he had written the program. I was using that knowledge now to re-write the code.

I clicked on the program to run it.

"My phone is locked," Rogerio said, grabbing for it. He lifted it up to unplug it.

"If you unplug that without me disconnecting it from the password program, it will wipe its entire memory," I said in a casual tone, my eyes never leaving the screen as I typed away.

He froze as if I'd threatened to cut off his finger or something. People were so attached to their phones. I hadn't ever had one, so I had a hard time understanding that concept.

"Really?" he asked with rounded eyes.

"No," I said, nearly finished with what I was typing. "I sort of wanted to see your reaction."

"Why?" he asked, trying to hide his embarrassment under anger as he yanked the cord from his phone and unlocked it, probably to make sure everything was okay.

"You wouldn't be that attached to a burner phone, so using one hasn't been a habit of yours. Is it the same, I wonder, for everyone in your gang? Was it not protocol? So, I used a binary code of filtering to search the internet for Tomas Costa paired with the phone number. When it pulled up the Match.com profile, I was fairly positive that it was actually him," I clicked on the tab with the picture. "By the way, *is* this him?"

It was a dark bathroom selfie, taken with the light streaming in from the window behind the figure. The man had his shirt pulled up to show off his admittedly impressive abs. He looked average other than the muscles he was hiding. He could be Clark Kent if he wore a suit to hide his lethal body.

Rogerio nodded. "Yes, that's him."

"I think I found him," I said. "Or at least a place he's been to, if not his actual house."

148

"That's impossible. He's always very careful," he said, elbowing Yolo out of the way to look over my shoulder. There was a GPS location pulled up. "How?"

"By hacking his account. It didn't have his address listed, but he put it in at one point because there were potential matches from the area. When I looked at his settings, I was able to see that he had it set to find people within a 25-mile radius. I used the locations of the matched profiles to triangulate a location for him."

"I understood about half of that," Jace said. "But only because CJ's my brother, and we share a house together."

"Yeah," Corbin said, his arms folded and his gaze on me. "I didn't understand any of it." I shifted a little bit, causing Corbin's playful grin to grow into a goofy smile. "Don't worry, Callie-Cat. I find it cute."

"Can you keep it in your pants for two seconds around her?" Yolo demanded. "It's disturbing."

I blushed since I was able to understand what she was implying thanks to the guys' and Darcy's crash course lessons. Desperate to change the topic, my eyes flew around the room noticing that someone was still missing. "Where's Fabrizio?"

Chapter 16

Papi was quick to call his son's phone when we realized that no one had seen him since he left to get a water bottle. That was over ten minutes ago.

"He's not answering," Papi said after the fifth time trying to call. "It's not ringing, only going to voicemail. Can you do that...that thing? Can you find him, Callie?"

I played with Kaz's bracelet around my wrist, feeling terrible and unsure about how to break the bad news to him. Yolo did instead.

"If his phone is going straight to voicemail," Yolo said. "Then it's probably turned off. She can't trace it if it's off."

"New plan--" Sabra started, but she was cut off when the missing person himself slammed against the doorway, using it as a brake to stop his speed.

He was panting, sweaty, and holding a mostly empty water bottle. He took a second to catch his breath. "Sorry. We were out of water, so I," he took another couple of breaths. "So I went to go to the st-store," breath. "Down the road. The owner, he," another big breath. "He said that he saw the person driving the car was...was Rogerio's old rival--"

Yolo must've gotten impatient listening to Fabrizio's broken speech. "Tomas Costa."

Fabrizio collapsed against the door as if his strings had been cut. "What? How did you...?"

"Callie," Sabra said.

"Well, and Rogerio," Darcy added. "But mostly Callie."

"I'm surprised one of the locals talked. They don't usually tell on the gang because they know they could be risking their lives, their business, and their family," Rogerio said.

"People see what we are doing," Papi said, gesturing around at the building. "They see the good. They see someone trying to stand up for something. Maybe it will have big change in the neighborhood. Maybe being in a gang is not the only thing to respect. Maybe it is not the *only* choice," he said, observing Rogerio.

Rogerio blinked and looked down.

Fabrizio, still looking a bit put out, chimed in, "Yes, but do you know where Costa--"

I cut Fabrizio off, reading the address out loud.

"*Ay, ay, ay, I give up*," he said, swiping his hand down his face to wipe off the small beads of sweat. He was pretty fit, so that store must have been a decent distance away. "*Please, just kill me.* I'm too old for this."

"Nonsense," Darcy said, coming up to him and squeezing his butt, causing him to jump. "You're fit as a fiddle."

"Darcy," Sabra scolded. "Not now."

"Later then," she said, winking at the slightly stunned man.

"Really?" Yolo shouted, getting in Darcy's face. "Triz is missing and you're going to flirt? With a man?" This caused Corbin to intake a quick breath and choke on his own spit. I patted him on the back as he coughed, trying to understand what had shocked him so much about Yolo's statement. "Triz's *brother*, no less?"

"Fuck you," Darcy yelled back, her voice gaining a thick Irish brogue. She gave Yolo a shove. "You know this is how I act when I'm scared!"

"Yeah, you turn into a slut! But this is Triz," Yolo said back.

Darcy threw a punch, but Yolo was quick as a viper. She dodged and popped back up with her own throw swinging in the air.

Then, the fight was on.

"Uh, we should probably break this up, right?" Corbin said, watching the violent fight with a slack expression.

I looked over to Jace. He was in much the same condition. Fabrizio wasn't any better. Actually, on second thought, he still might have been cowed from Darcy's earlier groping.

By this point, the girls were deep in their rage. Yolo had ended up with her legs on top of Darcy's shoulders to try to subdue her. She was latched on tight with her lithe form in true Black Widow fashion. I guess the VR simulation had been pretty accurate about her capabilities after all.

However, Darcy was holding her own. She was pretty scrappy and her temper made her even stronger than normal. It looked like she was all out brawling while Yolo was using her smaller stature and weight with efficiency, calculating her moves before she made them. It was the opposite of her usual impulsive tendencies which made it all the scarier. Blood was actually drawn on both of them.

I knew better than to think that I could do anything to diffuse the situation, especially if Yolo was involved. Not only would I get my butt handed to me—and then some—but it would be like trying to douse a fire with gasoline. I think just the sight of my face made Yolo angry or something.

I turned to Jace. Feeling my stare, he snapped out of his daze, actually needing to shake his head a little bit to clear his thoughts. He met my pleading eyes. He sighed and moved to intervene, but Sabra had made her move a hair's breadth sooner than him.

Sabra was a tall, strong, and fierce lioness as she strode forward and grabbed Yolo up off of Darcy with one arm and pushed Darcy back with the other arm, the one with the bullet wound. She didn't even look like she was in pain as her impressive muscles strained around the bandaging.

"Enough," she said, her voice very deep. She dropped Yolo to her feet and only spoke once complete silence had reigned throughout the room. It was easy to see why she was one of the leaders. "We're going to get Triz back. You can either lose the temper or lose your privilege to go with us. It is your choice."

The two stayed quiet, avoiding eye contact. No one moved in the room.

Well, I didn't have a temper right now. I went to gather up my stuff.

Natasia stopped me when I went to pack the computer. Her ice-blue eyes bore into mine. "We need you here," she said.

I frowned and opened my mouth to say something when Jace interrupted me.

"She's right, Callie. You haven't made any progress in your training classes."

Corbin snorted. "Wait, *she* can't pass her physical training? I find that hard to believe. Have you forgotten how little miss Callie-Cat flipped you not even an hour ago?"

Jace frowned.

Natasia spoke up. "I'm not here to discuss what training she has or does not have. I'm concerned with having you here in case something goes wrong or we need you to hack something else." She spoke directly to me. "It's not a matter of protecting you. For the most part. We need you where you can be the most help. It would be the same for any of us. We're a team, and we have to rely on each other's strengths."

I tilted my head as I thought about it. Since I'd just been thinking about how I wouldn't be able to even help break up a fight between two of my supposed teammates, I conceded rather quickly.

"I'm staying with Callie," Jace, Brock, and Corbin all said in varying tones. Hearing my name come from them all at once sent a shiver down my spine—no matter how poor the timing was.

"No," Sabra said, holding her hand up and cutting off the guys' protests. "Part of the agreement allowing you to come was that Natasia and I were in charge. Jace, you're the trainer for evasive driving at Delta. You will be our chauffeur. Brock, you are the most skilled fighter here. You're coming with us. Corbin--"

"No," Jace said, cutting in. "We can't all leave Callie by herself."

"I was going to say," Sabra said pointedly, calling out his rudeness for interrupting, "That Corbin, you will stay with Callie and Triz's family. Rogerio, you too."

"What?!" both Rogerio and Fabrizio shouted.

"No! I'll have none of it. We are outsiders. We can go in and get her, and this Tomas guy won't try to retaliate once we're gone. That won't be the case if any of *you* go with hearts full of hate and revenge.

You live here. We will be going back to the States. Let us keep it clean and simple. No inciting wars for you to live with."

And that was that. Much like in the VR training, when Sabra spoke, it became law. Those going all loaded into the van after setting me up on comms. I pulled their trackers up on the computer. Then they were gone.

Fabrizio paced, muttering in anger before he stopped to make a call. Papi sat in the corner with his face in one hand propped up on his knee. His shoulders were slumped, and he seemed like he was praying. Rogerio was texting on his phone, stopping every now and then to rub his hands on his jeans, as if he was nervous or sweaty. Corbin pulled up a chair for me to sit on before going to the window and keeping an eye on the street.

Twenty minutes passed before they arrived at Tomas Costa's street. I listened in while they tried to figure out which house was his. With such tight spacing in the middle of the city, it was hard to tell which one was right since the GPS wasn't entirely accurate.

I could hear their anger over the commas. It was frustrating them to not know if they were on the right trail. They could be sitting within yards of Triz or pointlessly staking out the wrong place. There was no guarantee he had taken there.

I held my breath, terrified now that I'd sent them to the wrong place. If Triz was harmed because they'd trusted me, that would be on my shoulders. And if he had taken her there, what if my calculations were wrong? There were only ten or so data points. Granted, three would do in a pinch, but what if it wasn't enough?

The Cardinals continued to argue about what to do while worst-case scenarios flooded my mind.

I looked back at that grainy profile picture Tomas had posted on the dating site. There wasn't a lot of detail, but I didn't need much. I zoomed past his figure to the bright window. Thanks to his novice camera skills, the phone had focused less on him and more on the brighter images, namely the daylight outside his place. I could make out part of a sign with bright red letters on it. It was a supermarket going off of the letters that were visible.

I relayed the information along to the others and sent them a zoomed-in view of the window.

"Got it. It's here," Sabra said.

I melted into my seat in relief. My math hadn't been wrong.

Natasia said. "He's in an apartment building. Second or third floor. We don't see the van, but if Rogerio is right about him not telling people where he lives, he might have had them drop Triz and him off and walked her back. That means there won't be scouts, and we can go in fast." She trailed off for a second as I heard her fiddling with something. "Radio silence, Callie. We're going in, so don't say anything unless it's a life or death emergency."

"She means if someone isn't directly threatening our life," Yolo said, "You better not interrupt, or it'll be your death."

Okaaay, then.

"If you can," Sabra said. "See if there are any cameras in the area you can look off of. Jace will be keeping an eye out from the van, but if you can find any other vantages, that would be most helpful."

You do one technical thing, and they suddenly think that you can access the world.

"I'll try," I said, though I doubted I would be able to do much if they were heading in now. If all went well, they'd be finished before I could pinpoint any cameras in the area, let alone hack into their feeds.

Other than the occasional whispered name or command, they were silent as they approached the building. As I predicted, they had already breached the apartment before I could lock in on any cameras in the area.

We were relying solely on them. In the past, this wasn't a big deal to me, but I was realizing that sitting on the sidelines was not fun when it was people you cared about in danger.

They continued their approach until their microphones picked up voices.

I felt a bittersweet mixture of relief and stress when I heard Triz's voice. It took a minute to place because it was pained and not happy. But... it was her. She was alive and okay, but for how long?

Rogerio must've recognized the other person's voice—even after all these years—because his head shot up to stare at the laptop speakers.

Fabrizio and Papi came closer as did Rogerio. Corbin stayed by the window but glanced over.

"That's my Beatriz, turn it up," Papi said.

I did.

"Okay," Natasia said in a whisper. "We have visual on them, but they're speaking in Portuguese. Callie, if they say anything important, let us know. We're getting ready to go in. We just have to make sure they're the only ones in the apartment."

I listened in on the conversation being carried out. Someone was hit, and someone whimpered.

The three men around me growled or swore.

"*Why do you continue to lie, Beatriz? I know that Rogerio still loves you. He sent you away so that you would be free.*"

I had to guess that it was Tomas Costa's voice coming in on the speakers now. The Cardinals must be moving in.

Someone spat something out, before Triz's voice filtered through the speakers, causing the men to tense. "*I told you. I left on my own. I wanted to get away from this hell.*"

"*Yes, yes. You keep saying that, but I don't think it's true. You see, Rogerio left the gang not long after you disappeared. I can't help but wonder if he sent you away to protect you.*"

Rogerio swallowed at being mentioned.

Triz spoke up, spitting the words out in her anger. "*No. My brother and my papi protected me. They worked their asses off trying to scrape together enough money to send me to college.*"

"*So you say, and yet, he still loves you.*"

There was a moment of silence. "What?" Triz asked, shocked enough to speak in English.

"*He still loves you. I find it hard to believe that a man could pine for one woman for so long if there was nothing to hope for.*" Tomas said, sounding sly.

"No, no, no," Triz started murmuring to herself. "You must be wrong. I don't believe you!"

"Believe it or not, dear Beatriz," Tomas said, seeming to get a smug thrill about speaking the language she had gone to for comfort. "I know it's the truth."

"He nearly killed me. I was caught in the crossfires of a bad deal," she said, sounding desperate.

Tomas seemed confident and relaxed. "No, the gang did that. Rogerio would never do anything to harm his precious Bea. That was the leaders."

"No," Triz said, her voice broken. It sounded like she was crying.

"Wait, you think you were in the wrong place at the wrong time? Did you really not know?" Tomas asked in mocking disbelief. "No, you must know. How could you not know that you were the target? Those other people were just collateral damage, little Bea, to make your death look like an accident. Of course, you ruined that plan by not dying."

I looked over at Rogerio to see what he was feeling about this. Both Fabrizio and his father had tears rolling down their faces. Rogerio was more composed but barely. His eyes were watery, and the pain on his face was unbearable.

Another sob broke free before Triz spoke up again. There were heat and anger in her voice. "I don't care what you say. Rogerio is dead to me. He knew gang wars killed my mother. He might not have ordered the kill, but he joined in the first place. Nothing good ever comes from gangs. It is his fault, and I will never forgive him."

Rogerio startled me as he put his hand on my shoulder to catch himself. The battle with the tears had ended as his face scrunched up, and he clutched his hand to his chest. It was fundamentally heartbreaking to see that much pain and despair on a grown man. Triz's Papi actually reached a hand up and set it on the young man's shoulder.

I didn't know what to think or how to react. Triz was right. Someone almost died just by being associated with him. Did that make it any less his fault?

Rogerio ripped away and went out in the hall to lean against the wall, his face buried in his hands. Fabrizio and Papi shared a look. They both had held so much anger towards a man that had been given tough decisions in life as a young boy.

There was commotion over the speakers as the Cardinals and Brock made their move. They stormed the apartment in a great calamity authority.

It wasn't long before it sounded like they had Tomas Costa subdued and Triz freed.

And then, Tomas started laughing. He laughed loud and long until it sounded unhinged and maniacal, raising goosebumps on my arms.

"What the fuck's so funny?" Brock's voice demanded.

"If it really is true, and you don't love him, letting you live, Bea, with that hatred, still blaming him...that's worse than killing you off. At least now, Rogerio will have to live with the fact that you can never forgive him, and he can never have the love you once gave him so freely."

Brock must have punched Tomas because the laugh cut off into abrupt silence. "Creepy fuck," Brock grumbled.

I tuned out the rest of the conversations on the other end of the comms and looked back at the broken man in the hallway. Rogerio's face was buried in his hands and his shoulders were hunched over.

Triz would be home safe soon, but it felt like Tomas' words were true. It probably was a worse pain than death knowing the love of your life and childhood best friend would never be able to forgive you.

Chapter 17

The aftermath of everything that had happened left us in a state of anxiety.

Tomas Costa had been picked up by an anonymous tip from his house, conveniently gift-wrapped with bloody ropes that had been tested as belonging to a female. It was enough to put him away for a while, though no one believed for a second that he wouldn't get back out soon, what with the lack of a body to go with the blood and Tomas' ironclad conviction to keep silent. It would take months though.

From our surveillance, we figured that Tomas was a big enough head to cripple the gang with his absence.

So... as horrible as it was, Triz had expedited our departure by getting kidnapped. We could go home weeks ahead of schedule because with Tomas out of the picture, the school would get built and established without the influence and pressures from the gang.

My kidnappings usually only complicated my life. These helpful ones were a nice change.

It would be good to go back home, but it also had cut my timetable down by a lot. Tonight was the last chance I had to sneak out and find internet. I had to know what Ivanov was up to.

My decision was solidified. The new departure date lit a fire of urgency, but it was Yolo's blatant distrust earlier that banished my guilt. How could I betray their trust if there wasn't any in the first place? She thought that I would put my issues ahead of Triz's life just because I had a piece of technology in my hand.

I got up from my spot on the floor and started navigating through the sleeping bodies. All the Cardinals were bunked in Triz's room, and it was nerve-wracking trying to find my way through the minefield in the dead of night.

The door opened without a sound, and I closed it behind me with a soft click before I could breathe again. Brock and Corbin's room across the hall was shut. Papi's room was at the back of the house on the first floor. I wouldn't even have to go past it. The last obstacle I had was Jace in the living room downstairs.

Jace was stretched out on his back, the Portuguese-to-English dictionary open on his chest, not a blanket in sight. I was halfway to the couch, blanket in hand, before I stopped myself. He'd have to be cold tonight. I couldn't cover him up, turn out the lamp, and put the book away for him. It was too risky.

In a stroke of great luck, the front door was silent as well. It wasn't long before I was outside with the night breeze winding through the narrow city streets carrying the scent of the ocean.

My luck didn't hold out though. I walked down narrow streets for a long time before I gave up hope that I would find a library with public computers. I had turned to head back to Triz's house when three guys and a woman stepped out of an alley, blocking my way back home.

I changed course a bit to pass. When they stepped to match my side-shuffle, I looked up. And I knew then that I was in trouble. All four of them were on the long list of people we'd been surveilling since arriving in Brazil.

It was the woman that stepped forward to speak. She had a mean look on her face with long, dirty blond hair and tan skin from being raised in the South American sun. She spoke in Portuguese. "*Beatriz, we didn't think you would be so stupid as to go off on your own after putting Tomas in jail.*"

They thought I was Triz?

We both had brown hair and were short, but the similarities stopped there. Surely, they couldn't mistake me for the curvaceous Brazilian beauty with that luscious mane of curly hair. I was a pale, twig version of her.

I didn't have to pretend the stutter when I spoke, but I did pretend that I didn't speak Portuguese. With some fast thinking, I acted like I didn't even speak Spanish. A lot of people assumed the official language was Spanish since it was a South American country. "Uh, y-yo no ha-hablo e-español. P-please, por fav-or, I d-don't have any dinero," I put my hands down and patted my pockets. "No m-money."

My accent was horribly American. They bought it hook, line, and sinker.

"How long has she been here to not know that Spanish is not the local language? Ignorant Americans! This is obviously not Triz, you fools," the blond hissed at the guys.

"How were we supposed to know? She came out of their house!"

The woman turned back to me, a speculative look in her eye. She leaned in close. "What is your name?"

I leaned away a bit and then thought better of it. I channeled my best impression of loveable Triz and bumped into her, giving her a hug. I slipped my hand into her pocket. "Oh, thank goodness you speak English. My name's Callie. I'm so lost. Could you help me?"

I was so nervous about trying to steal her phone that I actually blurted out my real name. I wanted to face-palm almost immediately after.

The woman didn't answer. She pushed me away and turned her back to me, presenting the perfect opportunity to slip her phone into my pocket while the guys were watching her. *"This is a waste of our time. You interrupted my night for nothing."*

She took off down the street with her dainty, elegant heels clacking. The guys gave me one last glance. The shortest guy stepped closer and gripped me by the arm so tightly that I knew right away it would bruise. He pulled me in, close enough that I could smell spices on the heat of his breath.

I prepared myself to maim and run as fast as I could. I was sure they'd have guns. Everyone we'd surveilled had carried, and the group of guys in front of me was no exception. A voice stopped me.

"If she says leave it, let's leave it," one of the remaining guys said. He gave me a disgusted, knowing look as if to say that he knew I was far from innocent. *"It's her funeral if it upsets Costa."*

The short man moved his grip to my shirt, manhandling me until I stumbled into him. He murmured something to me in Portuguese that I wished I really didn't understand—instead of just pretending to not understand. It raised the hairs on my neck and made me shiver. He got a knowing glint in his eye, and I knew that I'd blown my cover. He knew I understood exactly what he said.

Instead of ratting me out, he only grinned, leaned forward, licked my ear, and left with the others.

"I will see you, Callie," the guy said in heavily accented English.

The men hadn't bought my ignorance so easily which wasn't a surprise. I didn't doubt that they had watched me leave Triz's house. They just weren't saying anything because the woman had so much power over them.

I was lucky we were leaving tomorrow—well, today.

I trembled, replaying the man's threats in my head once more.

I was *really* lucky.

It was also a good thing that they hadn't done anything more to Triz's "ignorant American friend" just to send a message.

That was just fine by me.

I pulled the woman's phone out of my pocket, doing a factory reset as I looked around for a safer place to hack. She hadn't noticed me lift it when I bumped into her. It surprised me because I had zero experience picking pockets. It seemed I had all the dumb luck tonight.

I wasn't sure how I felt about staying out in the open after the run-in with Tomas' guys, but I didn't want to risk taking the phone back to Papi's house where it could be traced.

A noise at the end of an alley made me jump. My eyes flew up. It was just a cat, but I couldn't relax either way. Every movement reminded me that the woman could put two and two together to come up with a red-handed thief that had played her. Then I would be in big trouble—like end up a dead Callie-Cat trouble.

I pocketed the phone, letting it finish resetting as I left the area. It was a balance, trying to play the ignorant tourist while at the same time studying every face that I passed in case they were some of the people we'd surveilled as potential gang members. It wouldn't do a whole lot of good to leave the area the woman and her entourage last saw me if I was spotted by some other scout from Tomas' gang.

I ended up sitting on a well-lit bench next to an Americanized hotel I'd passed on my search for a computer. The place probably had the best WiFi in the city. In no time at all, I was connected and delving into the dark, slimy world of the deep web.

Pesky guilt rose back up as I thought about all that the Cardinals had done for me. It almost stopped me. Then I made myself remember the way Yolo had been so distrustful of me having a phone. I couldn't betray their trust. I didn't have it in the first place.

I entered the website. It was a hangout for hackers. Sometimes people would go here as a way for prospective employers to find them. I had met other hackers here before. I'd done some of them favors. Hopefully, they would remember that.

WICKED_1: Byte-Syzed? Thought you died.

This hacker was one that I had talked to a lot before I met CJ as an undercover hacker online. I didn't know this hacker's real name, but I knew a lot about him. For example, he was a hacker-dad that had done a lot to help me write programming when I first started out. He was pretty moral for being on the dark web. He thought of himself as a "hacktivist," one of those people that used their genius computer skills to expose corruption and challenge big powers. He was actually the hacker-dad that I'd used to help adjust parental filters to suit my needs back when I was eleven.

I typed back.

BYTE-SYZED: Nearly did.

WICKED_1: What happened?

BYTE-SYZED: Not enough time. I need a favor. A dangerous one.

WICKED_1: We both know I owe you big. This favor have anything to do with the people that had you?

BYTE-SYZED: Yes. And before I tell you anything else, it's very dangerous. If you mess up or get caught, you will be killed. Your family as well.

WICKED_1: I don't get caught.

I bit my lip. He didn't say whether he had a family or not. If he had, I would've asked someone else. I hoped I wasn't dragging another family with me in my downfall.

BYTE-SYZED: His name is Nikolai Ivanov.

After filling in Wicked_1 on everything I could, I ditched the phone and snuck back to Triz's without running into any more of Tomas Costa's gang.

It felt like I'd only just laid my head down when it was time to head off to the airport. I wore the longest sleeve I had to cover the hand-shaped bruise I'd gotten from my nightly encounter, but other than that, I'd gotten away with it.

Triz was quiet and somber. No one was there for the conversation between Triz and her ex-boyfriend, but the way Rogerio came out looking even more broken was a clear indication of how it had gone. And Triz...she wasn't the bubbly, free-loving person that I had grown used to.

Normally, she was the one that would bring me out of my shell since she was so outgoing. The rest of the team was more reserved, except for Darcy.

But, I didn't see Triz smile even once on the entire flight home, and instead, I found myself seated between Brock and Corbin. Jace sat in front of us so that he could turn around in his seat and talk to us.

I didn't talk. I had a lot on my mind, like whether I should stay with the Cardinals or not. Sabra might think it was too late to save them by leaving, but I wasn't so sure.

Even with all that happened, I kept replaying the fact that someone as fun-loving and kind as Triz was unable to forgive someone that had been so close to her at one point.

It made me wonder if I deserved a second chance myself. Lots of people had lost loved ones because of me, and they didn't even know me. I was sure they would never be able to forgive me. And that was what mattered, right?

How could I ever be guilt-free knowing that?

I didn't remember much of the conversations the guys tried to engage me in even though I could subconsciously tell they were trying to cheer me up.

I was in a quiet, morose state that lasted all the way through the customary goodbye hugs. I piled into the back of the Cardinals' van, careful not to sit next to Triz, my usual seat partner. Instead, I forced myself into the back corner, next to Darcy.

I stared out my window, watching the more familiar scenery of Virginia as we left the airport and headed back to the Cardinals' house.

I barely noticed as we passed through the main parts of Norfolk and reached the outer limits of the city. It wasn't long before we arrived.

"There is a car following us," Sabra said out of nowhere, startling the van into action.

"What?" Natasia asked, direct and to the point as she checked the side mirror.

"A silver car with tinted windows. It's been with us since the airport."

My heart slowed and then picked up double-time.

Who could be following us?

Darcy put a hand on mine as she leaned forward. "What are the odds of that? We live out in the middle of nowhere."

"I can tell you that they're not good," Sabra said. "That's why I mentioned it."

She turned her turn signal on and pulled onto a county road. Darcy and I turned around to watch out the back. Three seconds later, the person drove on by, not even slowing down.

"Huh," Darcy said. "False alarm? Right girls?"

No one said anything.

Sabra got us back out on the road, heading for the house. She turned onto our long, isolated driveway, obscured by trees. I let out a deep breath, feeling safer now that we were off the road.

Sabra pulled in, parking in the garage, and the worry I'd felt at thinking we were being tailed morphed into a pit in my stomach as I returned to my previous line of thought. I knew that Natasia hadn't been happy with Triz's decision to not forgive Rogerio. Natasia had said as much, even as she said that she would respect her decision as a friend.

Natasia was the only one that had verbalized her opinion. The others hadn't said anything, making me wonder if they agreed with Triz.

I felt ostracized. I was a guilty person—a murderer. Was I was among people that would despise me if they knew the real me?

A knock on the van startled me. I looked up. The van was empty now. They'd left without me noticing.

Natasia was standing there, her face blank, but her icy eyes held a hint of warmth. "Are you coming in?"

I nodded.

"Triz isn't mad at you, you know."

I nodded again. I knew she wasn't mad at me. She didn't even hate me. Intellectually, I knew that her cold shoulder wasn't a cold shoulder at all. She was trying to process her own ordeal as well as deal with painful memories of her past. But still. If she knew, she *would* hate me. How could she not? I would be just like Rogerio. No, I was worse than Rogerio. Rogerio had been a young child making decisions that he couldn't have understood would lead to so much pain. Even if I'd been a child, my actions had caused real suffering.

"Come on, Callie," Natasia said with a firm tone. "There's no use dwelling on the would-be. Let's head inside and deal with what's happening right now."

I moved to get out, feeling the cool, damp air of the garage engulf me. My body started to shake as my nerves grew, and the lead became even heavier in my stomach. My adrenaline was spiking, and we hadn't even made it into the house yet.

I took a deep fortifying breath and frowned.

I stopped in my steps and took another deep breath.

I turned my head towards the house. There was the slightest smell of… something. It was so subtle, even for me, but it was definitely unfamiliar to the house I'd grown accustomed to.

That is, it was unfamiliar for here but familiar to me *somehow,* and it had goosebumps rising on my arms.

I passed Natasia to make it into the room. I looked around. Everyone was there except Triz.

"Where's Triz?" I asked, not worried about being so direct.

"Upstairs," Darcy answered as she looked through the cabinets for something to cook.

Sabra was frowning though as she looked from me to Natasia. "Yolo, go get Triz. Now."

Oddly enough, Yolo didn't argue once. She was up, like a lithe panther sprinting up the stairs.

Sabra turned back to Natasia and me. "Natasia? What's wrong?"

"I don't know. Callie?"

I took another deep inhale. "I...I smell something. It's familiar, but it shouldn't be here...It's hard to tell what it is. I can hardly smell it under everything else."

Darcy looked up by now and was making her way over to us from the stove. I blinked as the scent seemed to shift around.

"Focus, Callie. It could be important," Natasia said, grabbing me by the shoulders to face her.

Yolo came down the stairs, dragging Triz behind her.

"I..." I pushed my lip in and tried to concentrate. "I don't know. Earthy, like charcoal maybe and... some kind of chemical?"

"Get in the car," Natasia said in an urgent voice before I had finished speaking. She pulled me along behind her.

Everyone else followed without question. We were buckled into our seats as per Natasia's orders in less than ten seconds.

Natasia was in the driver's seat this time. She had her arm up on Sabra's seat to help her turn and look out the back window. She paused, frowning. Natasia clenched her teeth and squared her jaw.

"Hold on," she said and, without opening the garage, slammed the gas down. The tires smoked and squealed before we were rapidly moving.

We slung forward, caught only by our seatbelts as the van backed up. With a crash that shattered the back window, we burst straight through the old garage door. The van's shocks absorbed a good portion of the impact, but there was a lot of tossing and vaulting as the vehicle traveled over the broken debris.

Yolo started cursing under her breath, and Triz looked more alive and terrified than she had since she was taken.

Darcy gave a whoop of joy from beside me, punching one hand in the air like we were on a roller coaster. The world tilted, and my head nearly slammed into the window as Natasia expertly maneuvered the van in a 180 turn that I didn't know was possible with a vehicle so large. The force slid Darcy across the bench seat into my side, knocking the air out of me as she let out a breathless chuckle.

Yolo turned in her seat to frown at me. "What did you say to her?" she accused as if I knew what had triggered Natasia's deadly focus and urgency.

The car slammed back into drive, the gears grinding and tires throwing rocks as we started to propel forward away from the house. When traction caught, we shot off like a rocket.

And it couldn't have been too soon either, because we had only driven twenty feet when the house behind us exploded.

The sound was deafening, and a shrill ringing blocked out all noise.

A blast of heat chased after us and shot through the busted-out glass of the hatch with so much force that it would have shattered had it not already been broken by the garage door. Hot wood and metal pelted the back of Darcy's head. I was short and had already been somewhat lower in the seat, so most of it missed me. The others had taller headrests, so they were protected.

Natasia dodged falling, flaming debris that had scattered all over the place as she kept up a white-knuckled, fast pace. I gripped Darcy's arm and the window-side cup holder as I tried to brace myself from smacking into either the window or my seat buddy.

The ringing disappeared, and sound returned with an alarming clap.

"Head to Delta if we don't have a tail," Sabra said, her voice projecting in a loud volume without sounding like she was shouting. She was easily heard over the din of the whining van as it bounced on the driveway and lawn while Natasia steered the juggernaut with precision. "We need to get somewhere safe and contact CJ. He was the one that installed our security. He should be able to pull up our feeds and see if we can find out who was behind the attack."

The van made it onto the road, swerving into the lane with a spray of gravel.

There seemed to be a collective exhale as we made it off the long, stretched-out property. We were still secluded away from civilization, but it was still better being on a public road.

I let go of my lifelines, giving Darcy an apologetic smile at the red handprint left behind from my terror-induced grip. She just winked.

I turned to look out the back of the van. There was dark, black smoke billowing up and out of the treeline where the house was, or rather, where the house used to be. No one was behind us though, so that was a good thing.

"You knew," Yolo said, and I felt dread settle in my stomach. I thought she was talking to me. She wasn't. She was facing the front, staring at Natasia in the rearview mirror. "You knew that someone might be watching to detonate if we tried to make a run for it. That's why you kamikaze-ed your way through the garage door."

Natasia met Yolo's angry, grey eyes briefly in the mirror before she looked back out to the road.

It was Sabra that answered. "Yes, she did. We wanted to give us as much leeway as possible. If they'd seen us opening the garage, they might have detonated."

"We were lucky we had enough time to get away from the house," Natasia added. "They must not have built their explosive correctly. There was too much lag time."

"Well, their fuck-up is our gain," Darcy crowed, bouncing in her seat.

Yolo turned around. "We lost our house," she snarled. "How could that possibly be our gain? Everything. It's all gone."

Triz spoke up for the first time since Brazil, her voice soft, "We're not. We're still alive."

"Too true, Triz," Sabra said sagely, her dark brown eyes meeting mine as she turned around to address us. "And no matter what we find out when we get to Delta, we will stick together on this."

Yolo rolled her eyes.

Apparently, she had also understood whom Sabra's words were meant for.

Me.

They suspected that this was the work of Ivanov.

I had my suspicions as well. I would have to get my hands on a device to see if my friend had dug up anything yet. If it was Ivanov, I wasn't sure what I would do.

We made it to Delta without a problem, though Natasia did risk stopping at a car wash to remove the large, smoldering debris that had landed on the car. She also swept up all the loose glass from the trunk area. While she was doing so, Darcy went into the gas station to buy junk food, and Sabra made some calls. One was to Karl, another to Dr. Harper, and the last one was to CJ.

CJ and Karl were both going to meet us at Delta to try to pull footage of what had happened.

By the time we parked the van, both Karl and the Tate team were there at the elevator doors to meet us.

CJ and Jace stepped forward in an uncharacteristically coordinated move that made me able to see how some people might not be able to tell them apart. I hadn't seen them look so much like twins since the first time when CJ had given me a minor concussion by accident. They wrapped me up in their arms, my feet not even daring to pretend to brush the ground as I was held aloft in their six-foot embrace.

I'd always had a close connection to CJ, and I was glad that the trip to Brazil had at least managed to forge a stronger bond between Jace and me, even as I was still distraught about Triz.

"Are you okay?" CJ asked.

At the same time, Jace said, "How in the world did you manage to find trouble between the airport and now? It was an hour drive. All you had to do was go from Point A to Point B."

I took in a deep breath of CJ's lemony scent. I hadn't smelled it in weeks, and it was comforting.

Karl jumped in with, "Alright, alright, break it up. I've seen your new 'routine' with her. We don't have time for all of you to hug her right now," he said, pulling me along by my arm and sending a warning look towards Aleks.

Aleks...big, dark, deadly Aleks looked angry. "We have not seen *Medvezhonok* for more than month. You think you stop *me*?"

Karl tilted his head in thought as he regarded the big guy. "Okay, you make a valid point, but may I remind you that possibly Ivanov has somehow found out where they live, and we're not entirely sure how much information is compromised. We need to find out. Stat."

Aleks kept his stare leveled at Karl's face. "*Da.*"

I pushed my lip in, uncertain as I looked between their faces. Finally, Karl sighed. "You've got one minute--"

"Five," Aleks said.

"Fine, two minutes--"

"Four."

Karl threw his hands up and ran them through his hair. "Are you seriously negotiating right now? At a time like this?"

"Is important matter," Aleks said with a one-shouldered shrug.

"Fine," Karl said. "Three minutes to--"

"Five," Aleks said.

Karl's jaw dropped. "You do know how a negotiation works, don't you?"

Aleks's lip twitched the slightest bit in amusement. "Russian negotiations."

Natasia, the Cardinal's very own resident Russian, stepped up and said in a no-nonsense manner, "Three minutes. And it starts now. If you argue that is less time you have."

Aleks frowned and opened his mouth, most likely to protest, but I cut in. "Deal," I said and ran into Aleks' chest. He opened at the last minute, off-guard from the rapid direction of the negotiation. He caught me with a booming laugh. I could smell the masculine cologne. He moved his trunk-like arms under me and lifted me off my feet, holding me so tightly that I could hardly breathe. But I didn't care.

This was becoming a comforting place for me. If he noticed my tremble as the adrenaline wore off, he didn't mention it. I took as much in as I could and tried to commit it to memory in case this was the last time I would be seeing them.

Chapter 18

It didn't take us very long to log onto the cloud where the security videos for the Cardinals' house were stored.

CJ pulled up a feed.

"Okay," he said. "We're in." He projected it to a flat-screen TV in the corner of his office so that everyone could see it. There were several different angles and shots of various rooms in the Cardinals' house. I was uncomfortable to see that there were even shots inside the bedrooms, even knowing they were there beforehand. Was everyone here going to see all of that projected on the screen?

"Okay, so you guys left on the 29th last month...I will go to that point. It's most likely the time that someone came in." He pulled up the logs, and it showed them all labeled with a date and hour. He let out a breath of frustration. "This might take a while. There are separate files for every hour. If it was one big file, we could fast-forward until we spot something. Because of the upload function, we'll have to click on each individual file. Sorry, I didn't know that was the setting when I installed it, and I never went back in to double-check."

"How many files are there?" Sabra asked.

"Well, 24 hours, for each of the days you were gone the last month or so...so something like..." he looked up and to the side as if he was trying to calculate it in his head.

"768," I said absently. "768 files for the 32 days we were gone." I pointed to the screen. "But it looks like they were backed up twice every hour, so it would actually be double that." I met Karl's stunned face. "I like math?"

Jace coughed a bit though it did sound suspiciously like a chuckle.

"Well," Yolo said, "What the calculator lacked in her computations was the logic that the person who planted the bomb was there today, so most likely you would only need to search through the last few hours or so."

I bit my lip, resisting the urge to defend myself. Everyone was having a bad day, especially the Cardinals. They'd lost everything.

Karl unfolded his arms, straightening up a little. "Wait, what? How do you know he was there today?"

"Because," Natasia said, "The house didn't blow up when we went in. It blew up after we left."

Aleks tilted his head. "Double trigger on garage door opener maybe? Only go off after door opened twice. Make sure he wasn't caught in blast if you got there early?"

Natasia shook her head and looked at him. "I didn't open the garage door when we left. Even so, the house blew as we were leaving."

Jace raised an eyebrow over his dark chocolate eyes. "Okay, just for giggles, let's clarify something really quick. Exactly how far away were you when it went off? Are we talking you saw a small, mushroom cloud of smoke and fire in the rearview mirror, or are we talking like you could cook an egg off your car you were so close to the heat?"

Darcy pulled her poofy, curly hair up and turned her back to the room. She had shucked her jacket from the plane and kept the tank top. It left the freckled, alabaster skin bare for all to see the small burns and cuts from her shoulders up.

Glass dislodged as Darcy let her hair fall back down. "Close enough. If the window hadn't been damaged when Natasia plowed through the garage door like some Russian Duke of Hazzard, it might've blown out from the explosion."

Karl ran his hands through his hair, seeming stressed. I worried that being around me would cause him premature gray hairs.

"Do you need a car?" Jace asked, looking concerned. "Where'd you park?"

"In the hospital's garage," Sabra said.

"I'll go check it out, see what the damage is," Jace said, catching the keys tossed his way. He waved his hand back and forth at the computer screens. "I'm no good with...all of this stuff anyway."

I felt like he had a derisive, almost self-deprecating tone to his voice just then, but he was out the door before I could analyze it. No one else seemed to have noticed it either. They were watching CJ scroll through the hours of video files until he got to the near end of the list.

"Now, we may still have missed it if the guy came in right before you guys got there. The feed might not have been able to upload after the explosion, so if he came in within that half-hour time frame, we're out of luck." He clicked on the last file in the list, deciding to work his way back. He hit play and set the speed all the way up. "So much better than CCTV," he said.

It showed a smoking house, three of the cameras were completely black.

It took a minute for us to realize what we were seeing, but when it clicked, there were noises of excitement. Apparently, the cameras had still been rolling, despite the explosion.

"Well!" CJ said, sounding both pleased and surprised, "Maybe you do have a bit of luck." Yolo had glared at him during his speech, so he trailed off and cleared his throat. "Never mind."

"How is this possible?" Karl demanded.

CJ shrugged. "I installed a central hub for uploading the files on the upper levels. The bomb must've been downstairs and didn't damage the room. That's the only explanation to why we're still getting new recordings."

Sabra nodded, "It was a fire-resistant room with its own generator and WiFi connection."

I stared slack-jawed at her statement.

"What?" Natasia said. "If you knew my father, you would know that so much surveillance is not an overkill. And our paranoia paid off it seems."

"Good to see it actually worked. Okay, we'll start with the time of the explosion then," CJ said, hovering his mouse between some of the uploads and waiting on us with an expectant look on his face.

"The bomb exploded at 14:19, give or take 30 seconds depending on how accurate your watch is," Natasia said.

"Well, that's disturbingly specific," Karl said.

CJ clicked on the correct file with the appropriate timestamp.

The video started from the beginning. It scrolled through, with the only movement being from afternoon light as it filtered in. Clouds rolled across the sky, causing shadows to dance along the ground. There were cameras in each of the main rooms and hallways of the house—one was in my room. They'd warned me about it so I would get dressed in the closet or bathroom. It was a temporary protocol when someone was at high risk for kidnapping, Karl had told me.

With a lack of movement in the other cameras, our eyes were drawn to the garage when it lit up from the opening door. Sabra pulled the SUV into the garage to park.

CJ slowed down the video to a playback speed only slightly faster than normal time.

On the screen, the car emptied out of everyone but me. I felt my cheeks heat in embarrassment as more than one set of eyes came my way. I'd wanted a private moment to myself. I hadn't realized there would be a need for the world to view it. I avoided catching anyone's eye.

Motion and activity burst through the other camera angles as the Cardinals spread throughout the house, unloading their suitcases into their rooms. My eyes went to Triz's room. She'd left the door open, so the hallway camera was able to catch her on video. She was curled into a ball on her bed, her eyes blank as they looked into space while she held her knees to her chest.

It wasn't long after that Yolo mentioned something that made everyone in the kitchen look around. Natasia stood up and headed back out to the garage in search of me.

I already knew what happened there, so instead my mind focused on the fact that Yolo had been the one to notice my absence. I wondered why that was. Was she so annoyed by my presence that she was only able to relax if I wasn't around, making it extremely obvious to her when I was gone?

Natasia walked me inside, and then less than a split second later on the semi-fast speed, Yolo was running upstairs to get Triz. Triz seemed to protest at first, but Yolo grabbed her hand and yanked her along down the stairs.

I was focused on those cameras since I'd been there for the other POV, so it surprised me a bit when Karl said, "What was it that tipped you off? We thought you saw the bomb, but you're all looking at Callie."

My eyes went back to me on camera. I looked thin and ghostly, my head tilted to the side as I frowned, deep in concentration even as I could see movement on the corner of the screen that let me know Triz and Yolo had returned.

"She could smell it," Sabra said.

CJ's jaw dropped a little bit as he leaned around the computer screen to look at me. "You could *smell* it?"

"You know what bombs smell like?" Aleks asked at the same time.

"Err," I bit my lip. "No. I mean, I had smelled something like that before a couple of times on someone. I'm not sure who, maybe more than one someone. I just described what I smelled, and Natasia figured it out."

Sure enough, on-screen, Natasia was dragging my confused self behind her as the others followed.

We loaded up into the SUV, and then Natasia backed out of sight, busting through the door as bright daylight filtered in and illuminated the garage. It wasn't even a second later that something happened on the kitchen camera.

The stove door blew open from a small fire, displaying what could only be the bomb.

It had been in the *oven*.

I felt chilled and nauseous at the same time; it had been so very close.

The oven door stayed down, giving us a good look at the explosive. It was a large box with a few short pieces of pipe on the outside. It burned for a few seconds before the small fire seemed to ignite into a large inferno that blasted the camera as well as a few other cameras on the screen.

I jumped a bit.

"Defaulty bomb," Aleks said, presumably because the bomb hadn't gone off right away. "Amateurs."

"Faulty," Jace corrected. "That or defective. Again, defaulty is *not* a word. No matter how many times you use it."

"It is word. I combine like craptacular or cankles or Brangelina," he looked at me with a wicked grin, playing with his curly beard a bit. "Or Caleks or Aleksie."

Yolo let out a sigh. I tried to avoid blushing by looking back at the screen.

"Brangelina hasn't been a thing for years," CJ said absentmindedly, distracted by something he was doing on one of his other computers.

No one answered him as most of them hadn't stopped studying the screen. I turned back to it.

The kitchen camera was dark, as were the cameras in the rooms closest to the kitchen. The hallway cameras on the second floor, as well as my bedroom camera, were jostled and titled, showing the disarray in the aftermath. Little keepsakes and knickknacks were knocked from their places, shattered along the ground. Some of the windows had exploded outwards in the blast.

"You smelled a bomb... from over fifteen feet away... in a closed oven," CJ said slowly.

"Callie," Triz said, her shaky tone drawing my immediate attention. I looked at her, but she was pointing to the screen. It was my bedroom that had caught her eye.

I hadn't paid attention to my room because I didn't have any possessions there. I had Kaz's bracelet and that was all that mattered to me. Because of that, I hadn't looked at my room, but it was hard to miss the message. After the explosion, the camera had tilted in its position, so it was pointed directly at the black lettering scrawled across the cracked vanity mirror.

It read: Where are you, Callie?

Goosebumps spread along my arms as the hair raised on the back of my neck.

"That person is definitely an amateur," Darcy said, going for humor when no one knew what to say. "Don't they know they're supposed to write that in blood red?"

"Darcy," Sabra warned.

"So we *did* lose the house because of her," Yolo said. "Just wanted to verify."

My legs went numb, and I leaned against the wall.

Everyone in the room turned to face Yolo, but it was Sabra that yelled. "Yolonda! What is wrong with you? You know that we all agreed to this. We knew it was a risk! And, it's not Callie's fault."

"*Oui*, some agreement! What was I supposed to do?" Yolo asked, unfolding her arms and taking a defensive stance. "I didn't want this! I knew it was a bad idea, but you all wanted it. I couldn't say no, not with the rest of you already on board!"

Sabra's face lost her fierce anger. Instead, she took on a stony expression, worthy of Natasia. "You did that because you care about us. You trust us and love us. You respect our decisions. Am I wrong?"

Yolo seemed to pause a little bit, pushing out her chin as she squared her jaw. "*Non*. You are not wrong."

Sabra studied her teammate. "Then you should focus less on the fact that you were the only one that didn't want this, and instead try to understand why the rest of us did."

Yolo glanced over at me for a second, causing Aleks to shift. I hadn't realized he'd moved to stand beside me. Yolo didn't look long enough to trigger his protective instincts into offensive action—of which I knew from experience he had in bounds and leaps. Yolo gave a curt nod to Sabra before she headed outside.

"She is going to cool down," Triz said. "I'll keep an eye on her."

"Okay," CJ said, "Let's keep working our way back to see if we can't find this amateur bomb tech that threatened you guys." He stopped typing a bit, his cheeks lighting up in a slight blush. "Uh, that is to say—I didn't mean you guys like you were all guys or something. Or that you're manly! Or that you don't like guys!! I—er, well," he rubbed the back of his neck, the tips of his ears red by now. "I'm--"

"But what if we *don't* like guys?" Darcy husked in a deep brogue, her Irish accent coming through loud and clear. "Are you implying that's a bad thing?"

CJ looked absolutely flummoxed. His jaw dropped as he stopped to stare at Darcy who had moved up to Natasia and put her arm around her waist. Natasia, with her stoic face, even leaned into Darcy's embrace a little.

The room was dead silent.

I almost laughed at the expression on the Tate team's faces, but by some stroke of luck, I managed to keep it in.

Natasia ran her slender, pale hand down Darcy's untamable, red curls while she stared down CJ. "Well, are you going to continue to stare like a little boy, or are you going to work your computer?"

CJ coughed and choked a couple of times, his eyes flicking over to me for some reason, before he started to right himself back on task. "Okay," he said in a low voice.

I felt something serious suffuse the room. I had missed something.

I fingered the twine bracelet, uncertain, but I couldn't figure out what had happened. Two minutes passed before I gave up. My mind was still focused on: A. The Bomb. B. The Mirror Message., and C. Yolo's words. There was already too much to process.

CJ only had to go through four video files before we saw a large man, clad head to toe in black, enter the house right through the front door that had been locked. He moved around, looking through random things before heading upstairs. From the hallway, we watched as he entered both Triz's and Natasia's bedrooms to give them a perfunctory search before reaching mine.

When he opened the door and looked inside, he paused. He seemed to have found what he'd been after because he entered and started going through drawers and closets. It felt wrong and unnerving seeing this dangerous man touching and looking at my stuff, and I wasn't even attached to anything there. I couldn't imagine how much worse it was for the Cardinals.

After he'd searched through everything, he went to the vanity. There was makeup spread out there that Triz had bought me, though she insisted I didn't need it; it was just in case.

We couldn't see him actually do it. It was out of view from the camera, at least until the bomb jostled the view. But the man picked up a black eyeliner and scrawled out the message we'd already seen: Callie, where are you?

The message seemed even eerier now that we'd seen the giant man that had drawn it.

Then he went down and assembled the bomb inside the kitchen oven from his pack. It was unnerving to watch.

"Darcy had been right there," I said to myself, feeling the significance of the situation starting to settle in. Not only that, we'd all been in the kitchen. Triz might've been okay on the second floor, but the rest of the team had been in danger.

CJ rewound the feed and played it again. I watched the stranger move through the house, feeling something nagging at me. He was so tall and broad he brushed the door frames on all sides. In fact, it looked like he angled his body and ducked his head at the same time to enter a room, but it was so smooth and fluent it was hard to notice. I certainly hadn't noticed it before.

"He's tall," CJ said. "Maybe 6'7", 6'8". Aleks has to duck down like that sometimes to get through doors."

The guy bent down to assemble the bomb in the oven. He seemed to gather himself, his back and shoulders shaking a bit from something he did out of view with his hands before he got to work. He was quick and efficient, hardly stopping as he pulled tools out of his belt without even looking. The moves were well-practiced.

This guy was supposedly an amateur? I frowned.

"Callie, what is it?" Karl asked, startling me.

I met his electric blue eyes. "Nothing." I looked back to the screen, watching the man efficiently work to assemble the bomb, a niggling feeling in the back of my mind like I was missing something but didn't know what. I tilted my head to the side, watching the imposing figure work, assembling a bomb that should've decimated the team. "It's probably nothing."

Chapter 19

"You need a house," Aleks said out of nowhere. Well, considering the blown-up bits of the Cardinals' house on the screen, it wasn't entirely out of the left-field, but it was certainly a bit of a jump in the conversation.

"Yes, you need a safe house. Isolation didn't work out too well," Karl said, one arm folded across his chest and the other propped up to scratch his chin in thought.

"No safe house will be truly safe," Natasia said, a heavy tone in her voice. "I at least got a new start by leaving the country, but if this is Ivanov's work, then he is willing and able to follow her to a new continent."

I gulped at the thought, wondering if I could adapt to the life of an Eskimo in the Arctic. Or maybe I could go to Antarctica. Over half of the world's population of killer whales lived in Antarctica. Killer whales were nice.

At least everyone would be safe with no chance of collateral damage. And if Ivanov was willing to follow me *there*, then… heck, he'd earned it. Maybe he'd put me out of my misery before I froze to death.

"Well, there is unit open at Trainer's Facilities," Aleks said.

"You mean at Hartstrait? There is?" CJ asked, turning to face his teammate. CJ's expression changed quickly. "I mean, we do—err, there is. I remember them saying something about that last week. It had slipped my mind until now."

There was an awkward silence that followed. I looked around. The Cardinals were giving the guys unamused looks while Karl, on the other hand, looked highly entertained with his arms folded across his chest and leaned back against the wall.

Natasia raised a perfectly sculpted eyebrow. "There is an opening at the most sought-after Delta housing?"

"And on such short notice, too!" Darcy said with a small grin on her face as she elbowed me.

"How convenient," Sabra said in a dead-serious tone that was hard to decipher.

"Freshly opened up," Aleks said, either oblivious or uncaring of the pointed remarks the Cardinals had thrown his way.

For the most part, Karl was watching the discussion go on like me, as if it were a tennis match, only instead of wide-eyed horror, his face had grown more and more entertained. He was tickled pink with the whole conversation, whereas I was worried that the two teams were going to start yelling at each other or actually *physically* fighting.

And I wasn't sure which team would win—most likely the Tate team, but it was a close call.

If Yolo and Triz came back, they'd doubtlessly tip the odds in favor of the Cardinals. I'd seen Yolo in that simulation. She was a real-life Black Widow. And Darcy… Darcy had a red-hot temper that dulled her pain in a brawl and made her an unstoppable force. I hadn't seen the other three fight, but I bet they could hold their own, especially Sabra with her large muscles and powerful frame. Together, the Tate team would definitely have a run for their money.

"Uh," I said, hoping to break the tension. "How many bedrooms are there?"

CJ and Aleks exchanged looks before CJ said, "Two. Two bathrooms as well."

The Cardinals exchanged their own look, before Sabra said, "We'll move in after we're done here."

"Are you sure?" CJ blurted out. "That fast? We could get you a hotel for a couple of days or so. Then you could move in."

"Move in where?" Jace asked at the same time, returning from the parking garage.

"The Trainer Facilities at Hartstrait," Darcy said with a twinkle in her grass-green eyes.

Jace frowned and went to open his mouth, but CJ beat him to it. "They had a new opening last week. Remember? Some of the trainers talked about having too much space so they wanted to move in with some of their friends."

A single, blonde eyebrow went up on Jace's tan forehead. "Oookay." He seemed confused, but he shrugged it off and tossed Sabra the keys. "I took your car key. I'll see if I can borrow a trailer from someone and bring the van to the Emerson team's house. Corbin should be able to work on it there to fix it up. It'll be good as new. In the meantime, I put a copy of my SUV on your key ring. You should be able to use that while we do the work on your car. We've still got CJ's Mini Cooper."

"And my car," Aleks added.

"Ya, no," Jace said without explaining further.

"Thank you," Sabra said. "Let us know what we can do in return. We owe you."

CJ shrugged and scratched the back of his neck a little bit. "Don't worry about it."

"No, we'll repay you back somehow. Just let us know," Sabra said, insisting. She always held her head high and kept a tall standard of pride about her. I wasn't sure if it was subconscious or based on her upbringing, but she didn't like to get help from others.

"Easy," Aleks said. "We take Callie."

"*Nyet*," Natasia said, giving the large Russian a frosty glare. "Callie is not a negotiation chip."

"Also," Sabra said, ignoring everyone's antics. "I think that it's time for Callie to get a phone."

My shoulders sagged as guilt tried to rise up. My entire reasoning for sneaking out in Brazil had been that the Cardinals didn't trust me, so how could I betray them? If they got me a phone, that ploy would go right out the window.

Should I tell them about sneaking out? Should I not tell them?

Karl lost the amused look in a second flat. "She needs a phone? What? Why?"

"You need *more* reason than the fact that a scary man is after her?" Natasia asked in a dry tone.

"Well, no, but it was your decision to do this in the first place to protect her."

It was? I hadn't been sure who had ordered me not to have any access to the internet. In all honesty, I thought it'd been CJ since he had the best idea of what I could do with internet at my fingertips.

"Yes," Sabra said. "But she's been living with us and a part of our team for several months now. She's saved our lives, and we've saved hers. She understands the sacrifices that we made tying ourselves to her. She wouldn't leave us because Ivanov might target us to draw her out. She knows how he works. Together, we have the best chance of surviving and bringing him down. She's our best protection against Ivanov now, and I trust—*we trust* that she wouldn't do anything to jeopardize that."

My eyes were big and round in the silence that followed. I was battling my morals and trying to figure out how to feel less guilty about this situation.

Sabra nailed me on the spot with demolition-sized sledgehammers and industrial-strength nails. Clever woman.

Karl cleared his throat. "This is a team decision?"

"Yes," Darcy and Natasia piped in. Natasia added, "And we know that Triz and Yolo would agree."

I raised an eyebrow at that last bit about Yolo agreeing, but then I mentally shrugged. If she thought I'd use it to disappear or sacrifice myself as Sabra had so bluntly put it, Yolo would be over the moon with the decision.

Karl bobbed his head back and forth as he thought about it before nodding. "Well, okay. I'm sold. CJ?"

CJ hopped to action, pulling a small phone out of his desk. "It's not a smartphone, per se, but it'll be good if you need it for an emergency," he said, handing it over. "You handled that other phone pretty well with the CIA agent--"

"Agent Petya," I said at the same time that Karl did.

"Right, Agent Petya," CJ corrected. "So I'm assuming you know how to use a phone."

I hadn't had one of my own before, but I did nod my head in assent to let him know I could handle one. He placed it in my hands.

"And we're not making the same mistake again," Karl said, almost immediately taking it back out of my hands. He started typing on it. "Last time you didn't have our numbers or addresses. We're checking that off our to-do-list right now."

He put his number in and texted himself before he went to hand it back. "I also put in the Cardinals' numbers as well."

I reached out to grab it, but Aleks snatched it up before I could. He started typing on it. "We will be neighbors. You need our numbers as well."

"Why?" Darcy asked. "You worried she's going to need to borrow a cup of flour?"

"*Da*," he said, hitting a button that made the twins' phones chime in their pockets. He put the phone back in my hand. "You girls go out. Eat. Shop a little. All your stuff fried. We go to admin office for you. You can move into Trainers' Facilities when you are ready."

"Go out to eat? Our house was just blown up! And you think, what, that we should have a girls' day? Like this is any other leisurely day?" Yolo asked as she made her reappearance, a small hand on her hip. "And what does he mean they're getting everything squared away with admin? There aren't any spots open at the Trainers' Facilities. There never are."

"It's a recent development," CJ said. "And you can still have a girls' day if you want. You can eat at the Cafe, and then borrow some clothes and stuff from Delta reserves. Let us focus on securing your room. It's the least we can do. You can head over in say..." he trailed off and glanced back at the others for some reason. "Two hours?"

"Two hours," Aleks agreed since Jace just looked confused and put on the spot.

CJ nodded. "Two hours. We'll meet you at the front entrance to escort you up. There'll be furniture and stuff, all you need to bring are blankets, pillows, and clothes. Oh and some bathroom stuff," he said, waffling his hand back and forth as he scrunched his nose up.

"Simple enough," Sabra said, "We can find most of that stuff here at Delta to avoid going out in public until we know we are safe again."

Aleks got a dangerous look in his ice-blue eyes. "And, to make it official girls' day, I will supply pillows and panties."

Darcy, not missing a beat, stepped in close to crowd Aleks' space as she spoke in a low tone. "But we usually pillow fight..." her eyes trailed up and down his form, "Naked."

I choked on my spit and was happy I wasn't the only one.

Aleks grinned. He clapped his hands. "Perfect. See you then. And *Medvezhonok*?" I looked up at him from my phone. "You need anything, you text me."

"Us," CJ said. "He means us."

Aleks grin morphed into something wicked. "I say what I mean."

Before I had to come up with a response, Natasia wrapped an arm around me, leading me out of the room. "Let us know, dear Karl, what the bomb techs find out at our house. And keep us updated on when we can go in to get our stuff."

"What? Why me? Why am I in charge of that?"

"You're just so good at it," Darcy added, passing him by and giving him a hearty, solid pat on his back.

"Oh, and if you could be a dear, *mon cherie*," Yolo said. "I wouldn't mind it if you could find someone with a connection to a good laundering service, *s'il vous plaît*. I'll need it to get the smoke smell out of my wardrobe. *Merci*." She patted his slack-jawed cheek.

Karl blinked at her. Triz giggled as she passed him by with a little wave—actually looking like her normal, happy self, and Sabra nodded at him, not saying a word about her team's antics, definitely *not* berating them. Her silence clearly endorsed their behavior, and yet she somehow managed to keep an admirably serious expression, as if they hadn't just treated the CIA agent like a bellhop boy.

"Okay," I heard CJ say to his team, but then they trailed off in a private discussion.

I heard Jace shout out, "*What*?! In two hours?!", but that was all I could make out over Darcy's uproarious laughter. Sabra cracked a smile, and Natasia looked like the cat that got the canary.

"What's up with the twins today?" Yolo asked. "One was twitchy, and the other was oblivious."

I was surprised and confused when I found out that she'd directed the question to me. She didn't usually talk to me, only bothered making indirect digs. Not this time though. She'd asked a serious question, and she'd asked it to *me*.

I toyed with my hair nervously as I tried to think of a response. I didn't know what was up with the twins either, and I wasn't sure why she expected me to know. "Uh..."

Yolo rolled her eyes. "Never mind."

Sabra led us all down one floor to the third floor.

It had a huge cafeteria and numerous tables that reminded me of a school. It was set up buffet-style with different entrees and sides already plated and set out. People were in line to get their food, aged young adult to well into retirement. I was surprised that Delta catered and collected such an eclectic bunch of people.

There was an enticing mix of foods in the air, from pizza to Salisbury steak to an impressively stocked salad bar. People were chatting, and trays and silverware were clanking as they were being washed in the back part of the kitchen, creating a pleasant hum of noise that was a balm to my frayed nerves.

All of us met back at the register, Sabra swiped some sort of ID card, and we were good to go. A group of young boys had just left a table, so we all sat down there, not speaking much as we ate our food in silence. I was sure the Cardinals were processing the fact that they'd lost their home. I knew that they'd worked a lot to be able to get such a remote location that would be safe for Natasia.

I'd taken that safety from them, destroyed all their hard work and ruined their home. They'd have to start all over.

The pizza seemed to congeal in my mouth, so I forced myself to swallow quickly through my tight throat. I looked away to blink back the tears that were trying to gather in the corners of my eyes.

When I felt like I could look back at the forlorn faces without crying, I noticed that only Darcy and Sabra had much of an appetite. Yolo was picking at her salad, Triz was staring into her rice, and Natasia was sipping a water, no plate in front of her, as her eyes kept scanning the surroundings.

Sabra cleared her throat, breaking the silence. "We will go to the storage area in the back and pick out some stuff that we will need for the next few days or so. We will not be going to our cover jobs, so Triz, Darcy, make sure you call in." She held up her hand to stop their objections. "At least until we get the all-clear from Karl. Until then, we will be going from the Trainers' Facilities to Delta and back again. We will not be making any other outings, so just make sure you are prepared for that."

Triz turned to Darcy. "Do you think they'll have any mousse in the back?"

I scooted a small plastic bowl towards her from my plate. "It's not mousse, but you can have my pudding," I said, trying to help her feel better any way that I could. She'd changed countries, been kidnapped, found out her once true love *still* loved her, and broken his—and her—heart. If she wanted chocolate, I'd darn well give her chocolate.

Triz stared at me for a long moment, a slight frown on her face. I shifted in my seat, feeling my eyes start to water again. She didn't want anything from me.

She hated me.

My downward spiral of self-loathing was cut short as Darcy was startled enough to let out a surprised laugh. I looked her way. Her head was thrown back, and she had an arm across her stomach. "Callie, she was talking about mousse for our hair—not chocolate mousse, though I wouldn't turn that down either."

Triz looked at Darcy in confusion. "Chocolate mousse?" she asked at the same time I asked, "They make *hair* mousse?"

Darcy gave me a wink. "We use it to keep our luscious, untamable curls in check."

I blushed for some reason and looked down. "Oh," I said, somewhat lamely.

Triz gave me a bright smile, the first genuine one I'd seen on her send my way since we'd gotten back. "Don't feel so bad Callie. I didn't know about chocolate mousse."

I nodded but kept my eyes downcast.

We finished lunch in silence.

After gathering supplies from a place nearly as well-stocked as any Walmart, we headed to the parking garage. Two hours had already passed because Yolo tried on every single piece of clothing from Delta storage before putting it in her bag.

We transferred our ashy suitcases from Brazil into Jace's SUV along with our new...borrowed...items.

I wasn't sure how far away the Trainers' Facilities were, but we'd be at least on time if not a little bit late.

A small spring of excitement welled up inside. My heart beat a little bit faster than it should as energy suffused my body. I felt as if I'd slammed back six espressos in a row.

We would be neighbors with the Tate team.

Chapter 20

We parked outside the Trainers' Facilities.

It seemed to be in a nice part of Norfolk. The area was in town, but close to the bay. I could smell the salty breeze and hear the roar of jet skis and speed boats as they played. It was a gated community on East Beach that led right to the ocean. People were swimming and enjoying themselves in the sun. The sign at the gate didn't say "Trainers' Facilities", but it did say Hartstrait Senior Community.

Senior community?

It must've been the right place though because we didn't pull away.

Natasia drove up next to a panel by the gate. There were several buttons and house numbers that you could push, as well as a button to ring reception. Natasia didn't even get a chance to push a button because Jace was there, walking through a pedestrian gate to meet us.

"Ladies," he said, pushing a house number button. CJ or Aleks must've been waiting to buzz us in because the light above the gate turned green. "Welcome to the Trainers' Facilities," he said in a somewhat hushed voice. I noticed that his eyes kept darting over to the empty gatehouse where a guard should be sitting.

I fiddled with my hair, "Are we supposed to sign in and fill out a form?"

"No!" Jace said. He cleared his throat and spoke in a softer volume. "I mean, we took care of the paperwork and everything already. All you have to do is move in. So, let's get your happy little butts on up to your new house." He hopped in the van, squeezing into the back row beside me.

The gate seemed to be on its last leg. It probably needed oiled or something. It screeched and struggled to opened. It was a far cry from the high-tech design of the Delta headquarters.

"Come on, come on," Jace said under his breath, impatient with the slow-moving gate.

"It's on its way, Tate," Natasia said, glancing at him in the rearview mirror with a Cheshire grin. "Calm down. What's the big rush?"

"No rush," he said, shooting a mild glare her way. "I just don't want you guys to have to meet the gate guy. He's a really mean old man, that Larry. We did you a big favor, getting all the paperwork taken care of. He's got this huge, hairy mole on his upper lip that wobbles up and down like the bouncing ball on a sing-along movie to every word he says." He shuddered.

Sabra had the slightest smile on her face. "I have some friends that live here. I thought the gatekeeper was a woman."

Jace coughed, letting out a sigh of relief when the gate finally opened enough to drive through. He seemed to relax as the gate closed us in and we started up.

"You never answered Sabra's question," Darcy reminded with a wicked smile.

"Huh?" he asked before he shook his head. "Oh, right. No, the gatekeeper is a scary old man. He's new actually. It's probably best if you avoid him, or better yet, pretend that you are just visiting and don't live here. So, we've got you in a two-bedroom apartment. It was the only one available on such short notice-"

The Cardinals all started to ask questions at once, losing their amused grins.

"Calm down," he said. "It's fine. The rooms are large, and they both have their own bathroom. You can sleep two or three in each room. You can even stay in the living room if you wanted to. It'll be fine. You won't have to rough it for very long."

"Yes, we'll make sure of that," Yolo said.

The houses were built one right on the other, squeezed together so that they felt more like apartments. It looked like a garage made up the ground floor, and the house part made up the upper floors.

Natasia found a spot for the big SUV to park. We went to the back to get out the luggage that we'd grabbed from the Delta storeroom as well as the stuff from our trip to South America that Jace had thoughtfully transferred over to the SUV for us before taking off.

All in all, I now had two backpacks, so I put the heavier one on both shoulders and slung the other over one like a purse.

I looked around, wondering which of the houses we'd be staying in.

Yolo didn't seem to share my confusion.

"The two-bedroom one, right?" she asked without waiting for an answer. She headed up a walkway with determination. I frowned when she stopped in front of a door and turned the handle. It didn't open, but she stayed her ground, instead turning on the stoop to lean against the wall and wait for us to catch up.

Confused, I turned back to Jace, catching the glare he was sending Yolo's way as he mimicked her words in a high falsetto. His face smoothed out as he met my gaze.

I cleared my throat, trying not to get distracted from his eyes. The brown was so deep and chocolaty. I had to look back to Yolo before I could speak. "How does she know which house we're in?"

I felt more than heard Jace shrug his shoulders. "Who knows?"

"She probably was familiar with the people who so recently moved out," Sabra said sagely.

I looked back at her only to spot Jace now casting a glare her way.

Natasia smirked. "You going to let us in, Tate, or should we find the other Tate brother to do the honors?"

I tilted my head at her. "Why do you think CJ would have the key?"

Natasia moved up to me, wrapping an arm around my shoulders as she steered us towards Yolo. "Just a hunch, *mladshaya sestra*."

Yolo was frowning, a pouty moue on her face that made her lips look bigger than usual. "I can't believe there are only two bedrooms."

"It'll be okay," Sabra said. "Besides, there are two full bathrooms. We only had one full bathroom at our house."

Jace wedged himself in between us and the door, brandishing the keys like a great prize. "We've got two copies for you, but we'll get some more made."

"What do the 'A' and 'C' stand for?" I asked, catching the etchings on the brass surface when they glinted in the light.

Jace moved his hand slightly, covering them up.

"Yes, do tell," Darcy said with a grin, propping her chin on my shoulder so that even though I couldn't see her face, I could clearly hear the mischievous smile in her tone.

Jace cleared his throat. "The 'A' stands for "apartment," obviously. And, and the 'C'... stands for, uh, COPY!"

I jumped back a bit at the volume in his last word, right into Darcy's gentle grasp.

"So what would the 'J' one stand for?" Darcy prodded, tilting her head to the side, her red, vibrant curls brushing against my straight brown locks.

"What? I thought there were only two copies?" I said, trying to look at Darcy but she was too close for me to turn my head without bumping noses.

"There is! I mean, there are only two copies. Let's get you guys settled in," Jace said, quickly opening the door before the Cardinals could ask anything other questions.

I glanced behind me at the girls, unsure about their strange behavior. They all had this...this spark in their eyes like they were amused. Even Yolo had lost the pout to give a very satisfied grin. I was trying to put together a puzzle but was missing half the pieces.

Jace gestured us in, and I was practically shoved in first as the Cardinals lurched forward as a collective group.

I passed a door to the garage, climbed the stairs, and looked around.

The place had to be freshly empty because I could detect the smallest traces of pizza and cleaning chemicals still in the air. Other than that, the area was spotless.

The living room was carpeted in a neutral beige color, the piles of the carpet vacuumed and standing up in neat order. From looking at the tracks left from the vacuum, it was easy to tell that the carpet was the plush kind that would show footprints like a yellow, brick road.

The kitchen was open to the living room, and there was a small table pushed against one of the walls in there as a sort of frat-boy dining room. Beyond that was a hall that led to three different doors. Considering they said it was a two-bedroom house, I could only assume that two doors were bedrooms and one was a bathroom. The other room must have an attached bathroom.

I stepped out of the entrance hall and headed with determination toward the couch. It was my fault that they no longer had a home. The video feed had confirmed it. I would not let any of them sleep on the couch—especially if Ivanov had been the one to plant the bomb. He could trace us here with ease. And if that happened, I'd be the first one they'd run across if they busted down the doors.

I put my bags down with a resolute thud. I didn't take a stand often, but I was firm on this decision.

"What do you think you are doing?" Natasia asked, a sharp, platinum-blond eyebrow raised.

"It's my fault you don't have a house. Triz and Darcy were already sharing a room back at the house anyway, and so were you and Sabra when I moved in. I'll take the living room, and Yolo can be in one of the rooms with you guys. It'll at least be more private than out here."

Natasia stared at me a moment longer as if something was bothering her. "Fine, *sestra*, but don't think I don't know the real reason you are offering to stay out here."

I swallowed under her frosted look, her icy eyes cutting me down to my guilty core until I was fidgeting and looking away. She held her gaze long enough to make her point but kept her word and didn't call me out on it. For now.

The Cardinals split up, heading down the hallway. Yolo, Darcy, and Triz ended up in the bedroom with the attached bathroom. It had been painted recently—I could still smell the chemicals and latex in the air—making me wonder what had happened to require painting. I only hoped it hadn't been the scene of a gruesome murder. The apartment *had* opened rather suddenly after all.

Sabra and Natasia took the other room, and after a pointed look from several of the girls, Jace got the hint and left to let us settle in. Sabra caught his arm and told him a strong and sincere thank you before letting him leave. On his way out, Jace made sure to emphasize that they were in the house right next door. He said if I needed anything from any of them that I had their number.

The reminder that I did actually have a phone made me pull it out. I laid back on the couch—my new bed, listening to Darcy bustle around in an oddly well-stocked kitchen. Natasia and Sabra pulled up some chairs and started talking over their laptop at the small dining table. Triz stayed in their bedroom, and Yolo had emerged some time ago, dressed up and ready to head out. She'd left with the copied key and a strict warning from Sabra about going straight to Delta and back.

I leaned back against the pillows on the couch, pulling my socked feet up and tucking them into the cushions. I turned the phone over in my hands, feeling the sleek, smooth surface of the device. CJ was right. It wasn't fancy by any means. It may not even be built to access the wifi as a smartphone would be, but I had a feeling it could be tweaked a bit to fix that problem if I wanted to.

But I was at a conundrum. Sabra had all but stated that if I contacted Nikolai and offered myself up, I would not be saving them. I would be leaving them on their own to fend for themselves against an enemy they didn't know. And she was right. That's exactly what would happen.

I couldn't leave Delta either. They were shocked by the Cardinals' house being blown up. And, even at the virtual training, they were surprised to find out that Ivanov was *still* after me and had somehow found out about Delta.

Delta would need me. I was sure of it. They were all such intrinsically good people. They wouldn't understand the depths and depravity that Ivanov could and would sink to. I didn't want them to have to think about it either.

Sabra was exactly right. I had to stay to protect them. No matter what my hacker friend found out now. It was too late to leave.

Ivanov had to be taken down, or he would destroy Delta, the entire institution. It would be unaccountably heartbreaking because, from what I'd seen of Delta, they were authentically good people.

I would go online later to find out what Wicked_1 uncovered, but I wouldn't be doing it to try to run away. The phone slid into my pocket with ease.

I got up and joined the Cardinals in the small kitchen, despite wanting to go find Triz and make sure she was okay after everything. I wanted to confess all my sins to her just to get it out of the way. At least it'd be easier to deal with the hate now, instead of waiting for her to find out about it later.

I didn't though. I was too cowardly.

Instead, I headed to the kitchen and sat down at one of the four mismatched chairs at the table. "What are you doing?"

Sabra glanced up at me in slight surprise. Her expressions were always more stoic and subtle, but I'd been getting better at reading the small nuances to her thoughts as they occasionally crossed her face.

"What?" I asked at her look.

Sabra's eyebrows went up, letting me know I had somehow surprised her again. "Nothing, sit. Please."

I pulled a chair closer, and Natasia made room for me. Sabra moved the computer so that it was between the three of us. They were looking at the video feed from earlier. "We're trying to see if we can identify this man."

I glanced at the man on the screen. Because I knew the proportions of the house, I could tell that the man was very, very large, as CJ had guessed, at least 6'7" or 6'8". He was filled out, tall, and just all around massive. It wasn't a man that I had seen working for Nikolai before, so he could be hired muscle.

I frowned, watching him move on-screen through the house at normal speed.

"He was in there for a total of ten minutes," Natasia supplied.

The man moved around with calculated movements. It was how black-belt Brock moved, letting me know that the man was well-trained.

"He moves like he is or was military," I said, in the spirit of not wanting to withhold anything. After all, if Natasia hadn't dragged out my thoughts, we would've blown up earlier today.

"I was thinking the same thing," Natasia said. "In fact, he's not regular military. He's had some sort of advanced training, perhaps black ops or special forces. Whoever hired him, they aren't pulling out any of the stops. They want you bad."

I swallowed through the lump in my throat.

"Stop it, Natasia," Sabra scolded. "Think about what you are saying from an emotional point of view instead of being so pragmatic all the time. You are not helping by scaring Callie."

Natasia turned from the screen to look at my face. Her face softened. "I am sorry, *mladshaya sestra*. I should have been more sensitive to how this is affecting you. People do not call me after an ice princess for nothing."

My eyebrows rose on my forehead. She knew that people called her an ice princess?

Natasia smirked. "Yes, we are aware of that rumor. Along with certain *other* rumors..."

I frowned. "What others?"

"Don't you worry yourself about that, Callie," Sabra said. She pointed back at the screen. "To be clear, you don't recognize him from Ivanov's men, correct?"

I shook my head. "No, I don't recognize him..."

I trailed off as something he did on the screen caught my attention.

He was standing in front of the oven, ready to assemble the bomb, but he was facing away from the camera, making it hard to see his exact actions.

"It bothers me that the bomb took so long to go off, and yet, he assembles it not like an amateur but a professional," Natasia said.

"Could you rewind it a bit?" I asked, transfixed on the figure's back. He was head to combat-booted toe in black, so there wasn't any information to gain from that other than his size.

"How far back?" Sabra asked, not questioning me.

I played with my hair. "Back to where he opened the oven. Right before he starts to make the...the uh, bomb."

Sabra rewound the video, going back a little bit farther than that.

"What's bothering you, *sestra*?"

"I..." I frowned. "I'm not sure."

Darcy stopped cooking, coming over to lean on the back of Sabra's and my chairs. "It must be instinctive or subconscious. Your brain remembers something that you can't."

I felt nervous now. If it wasn't anything, then I would be letting them down.

A hand slapped the table. My head snapped up.

"No, *sestra*," Natasia said, reading my face with annoying accuracy. "If you hadn't mentioned anything while we were there at the house, we would be dead. Your instincts are good. Do not doubt yourself."

"Ya. What she said," Darcy said, watching closely.

I looked back myself. Sabra had rewound it to when the figure entered the kitchen. He looked around for a couple of moments before heading to the oven with decisive steps. He pulled the oven door open slowly, though we still couldn't see his hands. He hunched down a bit, then stood back up to height. And then...

"There," I said, quickly and loudly, startling everyone, including myself.

"What?" Darcy asked, confused. "What was it? I must've missed it."

I was frustrated because I couldn't explain it. Sabra rewound it again a few seconds as she saw the mounting anger on my face at my inability to articulate or even understand what my brain was nagging at me. Natasia sat up straighter in her seat, leaning forward.

The man hunched down a bit then stood back up to height. And then... "There," I said, watching the quick movements of his shoulders.

"He's doing something with his hands," Natasia said, pushing Sabra's hands away and rewinding the video to watch it once more.

It played out again, niggling at me. His shoulders moved in a quick, halting movement before he got to work pulling pieces from his belt to assemble the bomb.

"Wait, *that*? That is what caught your eye? So what, he was snapping his fingers or something," Darcy said, heading back over to the kitchen. My eyes followed her as she stood in front of the oven and stove combo.

"Darcy," I said. She started to turn to face me. "No! Don't turn around. I mean, can you face the oven, please?"

"Do as she says," Sabra said, curious about where I was going with this but knowing me well enough to know I didn't normally boss people around, ever.

Darcy faced the oven.

I bit my lip, glancing from the computer screen back to the Irish spitfire. "Can you, uh, move your hair to the side so I can see your shoulders?"

Darcy pulled her large mane of untamed, red curls to the side, giving a clear view of her burnt shoulders.

"Okay, now clap," I said.

Darcy shook her head a couple of times, but then she clapped her hands.

The movements were close, nearly identical. It was still missing something else, but the man in the figure had definitely clapped his hands.

"How did you know?" Natasia asked, turning to me.

"I...I don't know," I said, frowning.

"Okay," Darcy said. "So he clapped. Why is that important, Callie?"

I looked back at the frozen image of the man that had nearly killed us all. "I'm not sure..."

Chapter 21

We laid low for a total of two days before Triz lamented enough to Sabra to get her to cave. We were all allowed to go back and forth between Delta now—not just Yolo. It hadn't been Triz's exact goal per se, but it was enough to appease her. She was going through withdrawals not being able to go to work at the mechanic shop.

Darcy told me that Triz usually worked her frustrations and issues out through oil changes and car modifications. I imagined that with everything that happened in Brazil and when we returned home, she would be needing to log a lot of time.

Without access to the shop, she signed up to teach some auto-shop classes to members at Delta.

Darcy seemed to be okay not going to the bar where she tended. She said she enjoyed listening to funny drunks and putting mean drunks in their place, but she was also liking all of the time to binge-watch Netflix. She took any opportunity to kick her feet up on the coffee table and chill on my "bed."

So... I was somewhat glad to be going back to Delta as well.

And, that was where we were headed now. I sent a couple of last-minute texts to the Tate team.

They'd been messaging me quite a bit the past two days. Twice, Aleks had come over to borrow a cup of sugar and invited himself into my "bedroom" to just talk. They had a key to the outer door, so they always climbed the stairs to knock on the door at the top of the landing.

One late night Aleks had shown up with CJ in tow after everyone was asleep. Darcy had been up, so she'd answered the door. She had stared at them standing in the doorway. Her wild, untamable hair was mussed and twice it's normal volume, and she'd been in the kitchen to get a glass of milk.

Aleks and CJ had frozen, confused that she'd been the one to open the door—at least that's what I assumed. Darcy stood there in silence for a moment staring back at the guys as they looked at her, transfixed by her bright red curls that seemed like an untamable entity, defying gravity and creating a massive volume.

"Your hair…" Aleks said. "It is wild beast."

Then Darcy said, "No, just no," and, without letting them utter a word, she'd slammed the door in their faces. Apparently, it was too late at night for her to deal with their antics.

The whole thing was quite amusing, but it couldn't top what I was feeling now.

I was pretty excited about today. The girls were in a better mood, their spirits lifted just because they were no longer cooped up.

Karl, along with whomever he'd assigned to work on our case, hadn't found anything yet about the explosion or bomber, but he wanted my training to continue. And he said that I could take one of the electives that I'd chosen myself to start today: motorcycle class.

Well, Karl had said I could pick from the electives I was *allowed* to take. Apparently, I was still banned from a technology class—and no, I wasn't sullen over that *at all*. Technically I still had my kiddie phone, and after finding out I was still banned I most definitely would be modifying the little guy to suit my needs.

Yep. I was not upset one bit.

Either way. I was excited that I could take a class that I would be somewhat prepared for. I'd had to drive a scooter in a pinch when I was on the run from someone in a crowded city. While trying to stay alive, two wheels lent much more freedom than four. If bad guys were already using armor-piercing rounds anyway, a car wasn't going to offer much more in protection, so the maneuverability of two wheels was more advantageous.

I was excited to learn the real tricks of driving one in the safety of a controlled setting versus the life-or-death crash course.

Darcy told me that I'd be back on the 8th floor for the class, so that was where I was headed, using the elevator that didn't require a key code. Normally they used the top level of the hospital's parking garage to hold any driving course, but Karl wanted me securely within Delta due to recent events...so I guess he'd pulled some strings.

The doors parted, and the open floor that I remembered from the VR training came into view. The rooms for the simulation training were empty, their doors open. In fact, the entire level was empty except for two motorcycles and a group of guys.

I paused in the doorway, nearly getting shut in the elevator doors.

Unable to close with me standing in the way, the elevator doors stiltedly clanged back open. As if I hadn't heard the first chime to announce the arrival, it dinged impatiently trying to take off.

The commotion drew everyone's attention to me. So much for sneaking in or giving myself a moment to collect my nerves before going to greet such a group of what I knew to be very attractive guys.

I was mortified now, trying to get out and feeling like they might think I didn't know how elevators worked. It was way more than halfway tempting to get back on the elevator, go down to Karl's office, and beg him to let me change classes.

It was way too late for that though.

"*Dušo,* what are you doing? You'll get squished," Brock growled, pulling me out of the way.

Thanks, I had *no* idea.

It was probably my imagination that the doors dinged shut with a rather huffy tone as the elevator was finally able to close and leave my inept self behind.

Brock pulled me forward to the rest of the guys.

Corbin stepped up and engulfed me in a hug. He smelled like his usual sandalwood and pine, but there was also an undertone of engine grease that I was used to smelling on Triz. I wonder if he worked on cars too.

"Callie-Cat," he said, as he pulled on a lock of hair with a playful, little tug.

"Babygirl," a raspy voice called out. I looked over, spotting Doc Scott. I didn't even have time to turn around as his arms wrapped around my waist from behind. He pulled me into a hug, lifting me off my feet. I hadn't been hugged by him before. I'd done my best to maintain a nice, healthy distance since he was my *self-appointed* doctor. The strong arms and deep voice of his raised goosebumps all up and down my arms. I swallowed. Twice.

After a beat, I patted one of those corded, thick forearms to let him know he could put me down.

Doc Scott wasn't done with me yet because, in an incredible show of strength, he turned me in his hold without letting my feet touch the ground once.

My legs dangled there since I didn't know what to do with them. I felt like a ragdoll, unmoving, but Doc Scott didn't seem inclined to let me go anytime soon. I gave a mental shrug. *C'est la vie*—one of the few French sayings that I knew—I thought, resigned... kind of.

I squeezed my arms around his neck and buried my embarrassed face in his chest, taking in a big inhale and trying to enjoy the moment. He smelled like spearmint.

He leaned down and murmured something too low to hear. The vibrations of his chest sent tingles that danced up and down my spine, doing nothing to lessen the goosebumps on my body. He definitely noticed them too because he took one hand from my back and rubbed up and down my arm with a chuckle. That, of course, only exasperated the goosebumps further.

"Alright, alright," Brock complained. "Let her go before you break her. Fuck, you see her every week you stingy doc."

"And you spent over a month with her," Doc Scott shot back fiercely. "Besides, I would never break her."

Doc Scott put me down on my feet anyway, giving me a wink and a knowing, roguish smile when it brought a blush up to my cheeks like clockwork. "And, there's never enough time when it comes to Babygirl."

I turned around to face Brock, my heart pounding.

He was scolding Doc Scott in another language, looking over the top of my head to do so. I didn't understand what he was saying, and it didn't seem like Doc Scott did either. He sent me a sly wink when he caught my questioning gaze.

I looked away.

I spotted long brown hair and cobalt blue eyes like sparkling sapphires.

Bryce.

I grinned at him and gave a small wave. He nodded back at me and did the same. I wanted to go forward and hug him since he was the only other guy here—besides Brock—and I didn't want him to feel left out. However, he along with Emerson and Doc Scott were the ones that I wasn't as familiar with.

Besides, I was horrible at reading body language. How did I tell if he was open to a hug or not? I hadn't seen him in over a month. And the time before hadn't been that long either.

I looked down and used my toe to draw invisible patterns on the ground, avoiding his gaze.

Brock stopped speaking a foreign language. I knew because his deep voice said, "*Dušo?*"

I looked up into his winter grey eyes, so light they were nearly white. He hadn't changed much since I saw him at the airport a few days ago. He had a darker 5 o'clock shadow on his face than normal though.

He studied me for a moment, and I felt like he was cataloging every inch of me, looking for injuries. When he finished and trailed his eyes very slowly back up to my face, he didn't say anything. Instead, he held his arms out.

I could read *that* body language loud and clear. I took quick, short steps forward and hugged him, not giving myself time to think about it and make it awkward as I had with Bryce.

Brock wrapped me in close so tightly that I had trouble breathing in his aftershave and rain scent even though my face was smushed against it. I gripped the thick dark green material of his long-sleeved shirt and relaxed. It brought up the feelings of safety he'd fostered in me while in Europe and South America. It was exactly what I needed.

He gave me one last squeeze, kissed the top of my head, and stepped back, holding me by my shoulders. "It's so damn good to see you, *dušo*."

Corbin rolled his eyes. "It's only been three days."

We ignored it.

"I've missed you too," I said with a small smile.

Brock smirked at me.

Doc Scott cleared his throat and stepped forward. "If the greetings are over now, I'm going to be coaching you on motorcycle lessons. Are you ready?"

My eyes had a mind of their own as they went back to Bryce. I still wanted to give him a hug. Bryce cleared his throat and looked away before my eyes could meet his. I turned back to Doc Scott, nodding my head rapidly.

Doc Scott glanced over Bryce's way, making me want to die of mortification as I realized he'd seen and known the nature of my glance. He stared at Bryce a moment longer before he said, "Well, okay. Let's get started. Follow me."

I turned to follow, ready to leave the awkward situation behind. Loud footsteps sounded out as if someone had stumbled, so I turned around to see Bryce a lot closer to me than before. My heart would've been going crazy at his proximity if he hadn't been turned away from me, glaring at an angelic-looking Corbin.

Corbin gave an unrepentant shrug and a goofy grin. Bryce went to turn back forward and froze when he also noticed how close we were. He coughed into his fist, glanced down, and went to open his mouth.

My eyes widened, and I was terrified I would be reprimanded for hugging so many members of his team. Doing so had seemed so natural since that was how everyone on the Tate and most of the Emerson team had been greeting me lately. Now, I wondered if it wasn't.

I didn't wait to hear what he was going to say. I fled the scene with my tail between my legs, unwilling to stick around if he was to chastise me.

Doc Scott was in front of me, holding up a helmet. "Okay," he said when everyone had gathered close. "First things first. Safety."

He went on to explain about riding gear and helmets.

When he'd finished up, he paused. "Okay?" I nodded. "Good. Any questions?"

I nodded again. He motioned for me to ask it when I didn't on my own. "Um, not that I'm complaining because I'm not. But, if you're teaching the class, why are there so many people here."

Corbin bumped me with his shoulder. "We're here for moral support."

"It's non-negotiable, *dušo*."

"Uh..."

"Ignore the peanut gallery," Doc Scott said. He shook his head but continued on. "We'll get the helmet on you and then we can talk basic controls." He stepped up instead of handing over the helmet until he was very close to me.

I could feel the warmth surround me as his large form displaced the cooler air around me. He leaned down to catch my gaze and lowered his voice. "Callie, if the others are making you nervous, then let me know. I don't want you to be too stiff while you're riding...uh, I mean...I don't want you to be too...tense? Ya, tense when you're handling...the..." Doc Scott scratched the top of his shaved head in resignation.

I bit my lip wondering how he'd gone from calm to baffled.

"Well, shit," Doc Scott said abruptly, making me jump.

"Problems, Doc?" Corbin asked, appearing from nowhere, which was quite the feat in an open room the size of an entire building. Doc Scott shot him a fierce look, not as surprised by his presence as I was.

They spoke to each other.

I tuned them out and took the time to look over Doc Scott. I hadn't known he rode motorcycles. It showed me how little I knew the flirtatious vet.

Doc Scott was wearing a long-sleeved navy shirt tucked into black jeans, and black combat boots. The shirt was stretched tight across his chest, shoulders, and arms, showing well-built muscles. And his pants...his pants weren't Bryce-tight, but they were close-cut enough to hug the two powerhouses of his thighs, hint at sculpted calves, and... I could only guess about what they did for his...ahem, derriere.

Someone cleared their throat breaking me from my thoughts.

I blinked a couple of times and looked back up. Both Doc Scott and Corbin were grinning at me, and much like their looks, their smiles differed greatly. Doc Scott's crooked smile was more a smirk of satisfaction; Corbin's was a sinfully sweet, playful smile. He even winked at me for good measure in case my face hadn't already been fire truck red—which was highly unlikely.

"You promised you wouldn't be a distraction," Doc Scott warned, turning back to their conversation before I'd got caught staring.

Corbin held his hands up. "I'm going. I'm gone."

I watched Corbin trail off to join up with the others.

"Well," Doc Scott said. "Do you want me to make them leave? I'll do it. Just say the word."

I studied the guys where they were grouped together, smiling to myself as Corbin snuck up on Bryce while he was distracted on his phone. Bryce jumped a little bit and glared at him over his shoulder. Brock smirked at the two of them, his arms crossed as he leaned against a pillar to enjoy their antics.

It was fun to see them all at once again. It melted my heart. They were more like best friends than a secret government team. The only person missing was Emerson.

"No, you don't have to. They can stay," I said, a soft smile on my lips. I turned back to Doc Scott.

His gaze was heated and focused on my lips. I went to lick them, self-conscious, but before I could, he stepped up to me, distracting me from the action. "Okay then," he said and shoved the helmet down on my head without warning. He grinned a one-sided, blindingly white smile at my frown.

And that was when lessons began.

Doc Scott didn't help me secure the helmet. He wanted to make sure that I could fasten the belts on my own since this was a stunt driving course. It was assumed that I wouldn't be riding for leisure.

After that, he had me get on the bike and point out all of the controls to him and explain what they were. Since I'd rode several different models in a pinch, it was easy to point out the main ones like the clutch, rear and front brakes, and throttle. He filled in the gaps.

He told me the process of taking off, slowing down, braking hard, swerving to avoid an obstacle, and turning both slow and fast. When I nodded with no questions, he raised an eyebrow.

"You've had experience before, haven't you?"

Wanting to speak to him, I tried to pull the facemask of the helmet up with the bulky gloves on my hand. I couldn't feel out the plastic tab through the thick material on my fingers, and Doc Scott grinned, flashing his movie-star teeth as he reached to pull it up for me.

"Yes," I said. "Kind of. My experience was with smaller scooters, and that was as an emergency."

He frowned. "What do you mean, 'emergency'? Driving a motorcycle is not something you can learn in an emergency."

I wanted to reach for Kaz's bracelet, my go-to comfort device, but I couldn't with the gloves.

When I didn't answer Doc Scott's hands clenched and unclenched a couple of times at his sides before he opened his eyes back up.

"Okay, I don't want to know...*today*. One day when you're ready, but I *will* want to know Babygirl. I'll want to know everything," he said, holding my gaze for a couple of seconds. It was long enough for me to break contact and nod my head. He wasn't just talking about my scooter experience. "For now, drive around the perimeter of this floor a couple of times. Don't go any faster than second gear."

I nodded, pushed the facemask back down, and prepared to take off. I went to put it in gear when I froze. "Wait," I said, but I knew it would be muffled. I moved to take my gloves off, and that was what drew Doc Scott back up to the bike. He lifted the helmet mask up off of me so he could hear.

"What is it?"

I had gotten the gloves off, and I was digging around in my pocket. "It's my phone. I don't want to break it. Can you hold onto it for me?"

"You have a phone now? I thought you weren't allowed to have one," Doc Scott said, grabbing the phone up from me.

I paused in my search. I hadn't told him that.

I shouldn't have been surprised that the guys talked about me with each other, but I still felt a little flutter in my stomach at his simple statement. "Uh, ya. They changed their mind after...uh..."

I trailed off, not sure if I was supposed to tell the Emerson team about the house blowing up. Only the Tate team, Karl, and Karl's CIA people had been aware of the situation as far as I knew. And if Doc Scott was surprised about me having a phone, then his team hadn't been told about the reasoning behind it either.

"Well, they changed their mind," I finished lamely.

Doc Scott nodded, turning the phone in his hands. He went to ask me a question but was distracted when Corbin came up behind him and quickly slipped the phone from his grasp.

"I'll hang onto it for you, Callie-Cat. That way Doc Scott won't get distracted if it rings. Don't want him taking his eyes off you," Corbin said with a wiggle of his eyebrows, and then he headed back to the group.

Doc Scoot looked like he was ready to go after him, but I stopped him. "It's okay, Doc Scott. He can keep it safe for me, right?"

He sent me a side glance before staring back at Corbin leaning over my phone, the screen lighting up his goofy grin. Doc Scott shook his head, and then seemed to drop it when his own phone chimed in his pocket along with everyone else's here. Doc Scott pulled his phone out, checked the notification, and then took a moment to type on his phone.

"Never mind," he said, once he'd pocketed it. "Are you ready?"

I nodded, feeling nervous energy fill my body as I pulled the gloves back on. I grabbed the clutch and brakes. I started it.

Doc Scott walked around the front so I could see him. He held his hands up in front of him to let me know to stay still. He checked one more time, asking with a thumb's up if I was ready. At my nod, he moved out of the way.

I took off. The bike was wobbly as first, but the faster I went, the smoother it was. So, I kept up a brisk speed, keeping it right at the max speed he'd told me. It wasn't long before I'd completed two laps.

I made it back to where Doc Scott and the others were standing when he flagged me down. I stopped short of where he was, feeling let down a bit at my lack of precision, but he didn't appear to think anything of it as he jogged over.

He lifted the mask. "That was good. Do two more laps around and see if you can make shifting any smoother. Make sure to use that friction zone. You can feel the motor revving up and the gears starting to engage as you let off the clutch."

He was so poetic when he talked about motorcycles. I had no doubt that he was passionate about them.

I nodded since I knew I wouldn't be able to raise my voice loud enough to be heard over the motor. He put the mask back in place and patted the top of the helmet a couple of times, making my head wobble a bit. He stepped back and gave me the go-ahead.

I took off once more. I tried to use his advice, though I still wasn't sure what a "friction zone" was. I played around when I was in the farthest corner from them. It would be less embarrassing if I wiped out at a distance. I experimented using different levels of clutch versus throttle as I shifted the gears. I still couldn't say that I felt the friction zone, but my timing did seem to get better as my shifting became more seamless.

I went to enter the last turn and saw cones out, spaced in a straight line. I glanced to where I'd last seen Doc Scott, and he motioned for me to take the cones.

I entered the cones, weaving in and out, slowing down quite a bit, and dodging back and forth to miss them. I sweated as I nearly took out the last cone but leaned so far to the side to avoid it that my foot peg actually brushed the ground. I missed it though. I straightened the bike up and accelerated as I completed a lap around the floor, stopping by Doc Scott once more. He made a slicing motion across his neck, so I powered down the bike.

He had a small, surprised smile on his face as he shook his head in amusement. He lifted the helmet. "I've never seen anyone dig so hard into those cones, Babygirl. You were great at maneuvering, but you were overcorrecting by far. Stand up."

I made sure the bike was out of gear and stood up. He pointed at the tires. "You were dodging those cones like you were in a sedan, but you're on two wheels. You don't need to go so far to miss them. You have a small tire. Okay?"

I nodded, and he patted me on the helmet again.

He had me sit back down. "Alright, when you do it again, keep your eyes up. If you hit a cone, you won't wreck or anything, so I don't want you staring at the ground. Going that fast, you won't need to lean or turn the handlebars. All you'll have to do..." he straddled the front tire of the bike and put his hands over the top of mine on the bars. He pressed lightly down on one of my hands and then the other. "Is press."

I shivered a little, feeling the weight of his obsidian eyes resting intently on my face, checking for understanding. I tried to focus. We were talking about... what again?

"Got it?" he asked, leaning down until we were level so that he could meet my downcast gaze.

Did I?

We were about to find out. I nodded.

He pushed my helmet back down. I shook my hands, feeling almost nauseous now with the adrenaline from driving combined with the butterflies from Doc Scott.

I tilted my head trying to take some of the tension from my neck before I took off. I did an extra lap around because it helped to center my thoughts.

Press, he said.

I entered the cones, pressing lightly on the handlebars instead of turning them. It was in fact much easier, but my timing got off. I took out the last three cones as if they were suicide-jumping right under my tires.

I did a lap, and Doc Scott motioned me to not stop and take the cones again. Someone had already reset them. I took the line, only hitting the very first cone before I got my timing.

He had me run it again, and this time I was ready for it. I made it through, dodging and weaving like a king. It was actually very fun and quickly became my favorite part.

He had me run the gauntlet a few more times before pulling over. He was suited up on his own motorcycle. I nearly wrecked at the sight of him in a leather jacket.

I could see outlines taped on the floor in a rectangle. He was going to demonstrate the figure eight.

The box seemed quite small. I looked back at where Doc Scott was sitting on top of a large, dark behemoth of a machine. He jumped up and kicked down, impressing me as he kickstarted the beast with a loud growl.

I looked back at the taped box. How was he planning to maneuver that beastly thing inside that teeny, little box?

Doc Scott shifted into first and took off with ease like the bike was an extension of his own body. He entered the rectangle, lining his tire up with the very edge of the box and preparing to turn as he reached the end. Because he was going slow and turning sharply, he had to both turn the handlebars and lean the bike while shifting on the seat to counter his weight. He turned and then immediately had to counterweight the other way to make the other loop of the eight and ended up exiting the rectangle the same direction he'd started. He went ahead and did a fast loop around the room.

Doc Scott finished by pulling to a perfect stop next to me that made me drool with envy. He took his helmet off, his shaved head coming into view. His strong, jutting jawline and defined throat were very distracting. He turned to me and gestured that it was my turn.

He made it look so easy. I wasn't fooled though. I'd driven enough to know that this was going to be a real challenge. I took a deep breath and took off.

Chapter 22

"I can't believe he made you do that!" Darcy yelled, pacing back and forth in the small room.

Triz was leaned against the far wall, watching the irate Irish girl with a small grin on her face. "Callie's already said it wasn't his fault. I teach those motorcycle classes sometimes. Doc Scott didn't *do* anything that I wouldn't've done. Calm down, Darce."

"Don't you 'Darce' me, Beatriz Josefina Catalina Moreno." Darcy snapped.

Natasia let out a long, low whistle at the use of a very long full name.

Triz wasn't offended at the use of her full name. She only looked even more amused, but Darcy carried on waving an arm at me. "Look at her! She's so small!"

"I'm half an inch shorter," Triz said, more amused than anything.

"Yeah, but you've got more to you than she does!"

Triz raised an eyebrow. "Are you calling me fat?"

"Oh, don't even play that with me," Darcy yelled, turning directions once more as she paced. "You're built like a sex goddess, and you know it. I'm pretty sure the song, 'All about that Bass,' was made for you. Callie doesn't have as much padding," she said, stopping next to me and pinching my side.

"Hey!" I said, moving away from her. "I've already got scrapes. There's no need to add bruises to the list."

Sabra gave Darcy a stern look, instantly calming her down, but then she riled herself right back up again. "I mean, he made her pick her bike back up when she wiped out. And then, he made her get back on it!"

Triz waved away her concerns. "She wasn't going fast if she was doing the figure eight. We always make them get back on when someone wipes out, and there's always at least one that does for each class. It's no big deal."

"If it's no big deal, then why are we here waiting on the doctor?" Yolo asked, examining her nails.

I looked up from the cold compress I'd been instructed to hold to my elbow. "I actually agree with Yolo on this one." Yolo stopped her examination of her nails to raise a single eyebrow at me, her grey eyes locking on mine. She seemed impressed that I'd had the nerves to call out our mutual neutrality towards one another.

"Well," Natasia said. "At first it was Brock that insisted she get checked out. Then it was Darcy. Now...well, probably still the Emerson team, but I think that most of it is Doc."

I froze. Natasia always, always called Dr. Harper by Dr. Phil. That meant that...my eyes got big. "Wait, you mean that Dr. Harper isn't going to see me? But—"

"What?" Darcy asked. "You mean that we're here waiting for that fecker that caused this in the first place? He's got some right bloody brass ones, he does. I dare that bollock to show his face her. Ah dare him!"

Her accent had grown thicker and more pronounced the longer she talked.

"Curse of the seven snotty orphans on 'im!"

"Whoa, whoa, hey now," Yolo said, picking at her nails. "Don't go pulling out your Gaelic curses now. I think it was a character-building experience. Good to Doc Scott."

The door to the room opened, cutting my protests off. I didn't have to look to know who it was.

"Nice to see you too, Darcy."

"*Trasna ort féin!*" she said back, getting restrained by Natasia and Sabra as she tried to intimidate Doc Scott.

"Ouch, doctor," Natasia said. "She just told you to go f—"

"Thanks, anyway, Natasia. I think I got the message, loud and clear," Doc Scott said. He turned to me. "Babygirl, I heard that you tried to have me replaced." I heard and felt him shut the door behind him. "That's not nice. Don't worry, I won't take it personally. It's probably from the head trauma."

"You know she didn't suffer any head trauma. You had her wearing a helmet," Natasia said with a dry look on her face. She still kept one hand on Darcy even though she seemed to have calmed down a bit. She was still muttering in Gaelic every now and then.

"And she was going about as fast as a snail," Yolo added.

"Hmm...well, you must be suffering from extreme dehydration," Doc Scott continued, coming into my line of sight as he studied his clipboard. "Thirsty people have been known to make poor decisions. I should've checked to see if you were hydrated."

I winced. I think I'd somehow managed to hurt the flirty doctor's—err, vet's feelings by trying to make Dr. Harper take over the check-up. I hadn't thought about it from Doc Scott's perspective.

"Doctor Duane Scott," Sabra said, her African accent coming through. "I have had 11 younger brothers and sisters in my life, seven of which are still alive. That does not include my sisters in the room with us that also need managing time to time, begging your pardon." The Cardinals gave half-hearted shrugs, waving her off to show they weren't offended. "That said, I have a sixth sense about knowing when someone is throwing a temper tantrum...even if you are trying to be professional about it."

There was a short silence before Doc Scott straightened up. "You're right. I'm sorry, Sabra. Brock insisted that she get this exam even though I checked her over as soon as it happened. I agreed because who in their right mind would turn down spending time with her?"

There he went, saying things that lit my cheeks on fire.

"But then you asked for Dr. Harper." He turned to me. "Babygirl," he said, pausing until I managed to drag my eyes up to his. "I'm sorry if I made you uncomfortable with me. I have this tendency to flirt, and it gets especially out of hand when I like the person."

Cue the cheeks.

Doc Scott continued on. "What I'm trying to say is that I don't want you to be uncomfortable with me in any way. It could mean life or death with you if the stories are to be believed." He gave me a light chuff under the chin. As if physical contact would help my blushing situation. Yeah, no. "So, as your appointed doctor--"

"Self-appointed," Natasia added, a comment he studiously ignored with his 'selective hearing.'

"In order to get us more comfortable with one another, and make sure that nothing like this happens in the future, I am prescribing that you go on a date with me."

My mouth dropped open. I was sure it did. The room was completely silent as I stared up at Doc Scott's face. It seemed dead serious for once.

I floundered about what to say or do or act. I mean, he'd just asked me out. I'd never been asked out in my life. Did I accept? Did I deny? Was it legal to date one's own patient? And...what about the others?

I was broken from my frantic, racing thoughts by a groan.

"You've got to be kidding me," Yolo finally said, getting to her feet. "You mean we were all dragged here as moral support for an injured teammate, only to find out that you orchestrated it all to ask her on a date?"

I went inferno red, being so blatantly reminded that the Cardinals were in the room and had witnessed my being asked out.

The door opened, once more, and there was Emerson. He was in a pressed outfit, complete with a waistcoat that matched the light beige chinos. The white dress shirt was rolled to his elbows, showing off sinewy arms and long, graceful fingers. His toffee-brown hair was combed until every strand was in its place. He was a lean, trim form wrapped in a proper package.

He paused as his jade green eyes took in the tense postures in the room.

Doc Scott seemed surprised and a little wary about seeing Emerson. "What are you doing here?" he asked.

Emerson finished entering the room and shut the door behind him. He shot Doc Scott a look that I couldn't decipher before turning to me.

"I came as soon as I heard Doc Scott needed an assistant. Are you okay, Callie?"

His British accent made me melt.

I collected myself and went to open my mouth, but Yolo had only been cut off from her earlier rant. Apparently, she wasn't finished. "Of course, she's fine. She only got a couple of scrapes on her elbow and knee. Darcy probably hurt her more than that waiting on you clowns."

Emerson's gaze came my way as if to have me confirm it. I nodded. When he was satisfied, he turned back to the room at large. "Then what--"

"Because your teammate wanted the chance to ask her on a date!"

Emerson's eyes widened infinitesimally before they narrowed a bit. It was all very subtle, but with him, the smallest of movements had the biggest impacts. He zeroed his gaze in on the unabashed vet.

"It's for her health and safety, Payton," Doc Scott said.

"Is it now, Duane?" Emerson asked, his voice dry.

Doc Scott ignored him and turned to me. "So Babygirl? What do you say? Tonight work for you?"

My eyes rounded out once more. "Uh..."

I didn't want to turn him down. I'd already hurt his feelings once today. At the same time, I knew I wouldn't be able to survive a date with him. He was a professional flirt. And I had to respond in front of everyone here?

Emerson cut off my response. "She can't go on a date with you, Duane. Fancy that, she's already agreed to accompany me to dinner tonight."

My head whipped back around to Emerson. His gaze was on me, steady and reassuring. I wanted to push my lip in, but my hand was too busy holding the cold compress.

"Oh, the plot twist. Oh, the drama," Darcy said, quickly over her temper in the face of my duress. She was over-the-top concerned when there was only a perceived threat. Now that I was in real emotional terror, she was going to kick back, watch, and enjoy herself?

"Can we get some popcorn?" Triz asked. My head whipped in her direction, feeling distinctly betrayed. She was always so smiley and kind. She only winked at my gobsmacked expression and blew me a kiss.

"Is that true, Babygirl?" Doc Scott asked.

I turned back around. "Uh," I looked between Doc Scott and Emerson. My brain worked through different equations and scenarios.

Emerson was relaxed and calm. I knew I would most likely be able to survive a date with him. He was always so proper—well, except for the ploy he was pulling right now. That seemed somewhat out of character.

Why was that?

I thought about it some more. Emerson was probably only doing it to save me from the situation he'd aptly assessed as he walked in the room. Thank goodness for his arrival because the Cardinals certainly weren't doing anything, the amused traitors.

That he was only doing it to help me out solidified my decision. He might not even hold me to the fake date. It was only for show to help Doc Scott save face until he could reprimand the flirtatious doctor in private.

"Yes," I said. "It's true."

Doc Scott studied me a moment before his face cleared up, and he got his usual one-sided smile back on.

"Betrayed by my own friend," he said, putting a hand over his heart. For someone supposedly betrayed, he didn't sound very let down. "Next time, Payton. Next time. And the same goes for you, Babygirl. I'll get that date with you," he warned.

I gulped at the promise in his amused, obsidian eyes.

He cheered back up. "Okay, you're free to go. I'll go find a nurse to get you release-papers, so Brock won't complain," he said.

We all moved to clear out.

"Callie," Emerson called out to me as I was leaving. I turned back around. Without speaking, he nodded at the door, asking me to close it. "A word, if you please?"

I shut the door after a quick nod to Sabra that I would catch up. I turned back around. The silence in the room made me think about how the last time I'd been alone with him, he'd asked me to join his team. I wiped my hands on my jeans.

"Thank you for that."

"For what?" He asked, his head tilted to the side.

"With Doc Scott. I wasn't sure what to say to him."

"No need to thank me," Emerson said.

I nodded, wanting to get out of there before I made it awkward, like usual. I turned, thinking we were done.

"Callie," he called.

I turned back around, my hand on the door.

"Aren't we forgetting something?"

I frowned. "Uh..."

"I'm hurt. Our date? Can I pick you up tonight at 8 o'clock? May I presume that dinner is fine?"

My eyes were wide once more. "Uh...I don't think--"

"Of course, I'll send Bryce over to help you dress for the occasion. He likes to deny it, but he is quite good at knowing what the current fashion is. After all, those high-society dinners at his parents' house have to be good for something. What's the address to the Cardinal's house?"

I couldn't process fast enough to keep up with what was going on, so I focused on the easy question.

"Uh, we had to move. In fact, I don't think I'm supposed to go out--"

He was an unstoppable force though. "Oh, no problem. I know somewhere, very discrete. What's the new address? I'll send Bryce there. Do you know it?"

"Well, I, yes. I know it. Since Grinley, the Cardinals always make sure I have that information memorized before I leave the house," I said.

"Perfect. What is it?" he asked, looking down at his phone.

I recited it to him automatically.

He paused, before looking up at me. "That's the Trainers' Facilities...isn't it?" I nodded. "What's your house number?"

I told him.

He stared at me for a long moment. "I look forward to dinner tonight. You can tell me all about how you ended up there. Bryce will be by about 6. See you then, love."

"But-!"

He left.

After a minute of watching the door, waiting on him to come back in and let me know this was all some elaborate joke, I picked my jaw up off the floor. I tried replaying the conversation—if it could be considered that—in my head.

Apparently, I'd stared too long off into nothing because Natasia appeared in the doorway to check on me. "Callie? Are you okay?"

Numb, I nodded my head before I swallowed so thickly that it was almost, almost a gulp.

I had a date tonight.

My heart fluttered, and energy suffused my body.

I had a date tonight.

With Emerson.

My eyes rounded in shock. I looked up into Natasia's perfectly sculpted face, her features sharp and smooth. Her ice-blue eyes trailed over my expression. I wasn't sure what exactly she saw there because my face felt numb like the rest of me—numb, but it caused her own expression to thaw a bit.

"Come on, *mladshaya sestra*," she said, entering to help guide me out of the room I'd been frozen in. "It seems like you have a date to prepare for?"

She phrased it like a question, but it didn't feel like one.

I nodded. "But how is that going to work with us not being allowed out?"

She shrugged, pulling me into her side as she steered us out. "It's Emerson. He's a planner. When you gave him our new address, he immediately sought out Sabra to get more information. She only told him that we're sticking to Delta and home places, so I think that you will be going for dinner here at Delta later. Sorry, it's not the best place to have a date."

She paused to study me. She seemed curious about something. "Especially," she hedged, drawing the word out, "Not a first date."

I blushed crimson.

She grinned, cracking her frozen exterior even more. "That's what I thought."

We met up with the team and headed to the car before Natasia spoke again, digging into her jacket for something. "Before I forget," she said, pulling out my phone. "Corbin Myers said you gave this to him? For...*safekeeping*? ...*him*?"

I nodded, grabbing the phone up, happy that I'd asked him to watch over it...well, kind of asked him.

"You must have a lot of trust in him."

I nodded again, pushing a button to see that the phone was completely dead. It was odd the battery had drained so fast. I'd only had to charge it once in the few days I'd had it. "Yeah, I guess. He's a part of the Emerson team, and I trust them. Personally though, I don't know Corbin that well. I actually tried to give it to Doc Scott, but Corbin said Doc Scott needed to concentrate. So, Corbin held onto it for me."

"Hmm," Natasia said in a suspicious tone.

I turned to her, but her face was an emotionless mask. "What?"

"Nothing," she said, but her tone implied that it was *anything* but nothing.

I looked back down at the phone in my hand more carefully. For some reason, my mind started recalling the time I'd been at the Emerson team's house. I remembered all of those stories about pranking, noting how Corbin had starred in majority of them.

There wasn't anything wrong on the outside, and I wouldn't be able to tell anything more about the inside until I charged it. Unable to find any noticeable difference, I gave it one more weary look before slipping the phone into my pocket.

I wondered what I had done, handing over my phone to Corbin.

Chapter 23

I knew that I was dreaming. I even knew what the dream was about. I should not have been scared, and yet I couldn't stop the emotions and terror from swelling up inside me as I recognized the surroundings.

To any other person, it was an abandoned warehouse, but to me...it was so much more than that. The details were muted and fuzzy in the way that old memories sometimes were. Who could blame me? I hadn't been to this place in years, and I'd done my best to try to forget it.

I was being restrained. It had taken embarrassingly little to subdue me, despite all of the practice and training both Andrea and Veseli had put me through. A lot of that was because I was trained in trying to escape. I hadn't done well with offensive moves, especially against the massive man that Andrea posed as a teacher. Despite knowing them for going on four years now, he still seemed as big as I remembered him that first day he came to kidnap me from school in Pennsylvania—still as big of an enigma since then too.

Veseli had opened up much more so than Andrea. I'd picked up little snippets of information about both of them between their conversations in Albanian—a language I had been very careful not to let on that I'd learned. Even after four years, I still hoped to one day escape and go back home. Hopefully, my stepfather was still in Pennsylvania. I could come back, we'd finish the adoption, and I could live with him. Maybe my mom had even forgotten about me by now. A person that would cheat on their husband and lie about it for years probably wouldn't have any problem forgetting their own daughter.

I hadn't been treated horribly since being with Andrea and Veseli, but I still wasn't free. I had no choice about being here.

That was important to me. I wanted a choice.

In a world where my decisions were made for me, I had to hold onto something that would keep me fighting. So I'd secretly learned Albanian because if there was one thing I'd learned since being kidnapped, it was that information was power. I hadn't learned anything that could help me yet, but they spoke of things in their native tongue that they didn't share with me. It would only be a matter of time.

But, that's how I also knew that the current situation was not part of any crazy plan of theirs. We'd been ambushed, plain and simple.

My head was shoved forward facing the ground. My arm was wrenched up even higher behind my back—a none too subtle warning to be still or have it dislocated. I had no doubt that the person would follow through.

Andrea and Veseli didn't have the same hang-ups as me about subduing people...permanently. Whereas I hadn't been willing to kill, they had both the physical and mental means to deal with it. And they hadn't been slacking off. Already I'd witnessed them deliver fatal blows to at least ten men apiece.

Now that I was being forced to look down, I could see that there was at least double that estimation of men lying on the ground.

I tried to slow my breathing while more lifeless bodies continued to fall to the ground as Andrea and Veseli only continued to pick up momentum. With my head still forced down by a hand big enough to keep me in place with ease, I could only roll my eyes up to try to see what was going on.

Veseli was using knives fisted in his hands as he swung out. He was drenched in blood, and his eyes were feral. Even as I watched, he swung out once at three guys approaching and was sprayed by the high pressure of their carotid arteries. He sensed two trying to come up behind him. He kicked out to back them up before throwing his knife at them. The knives embedded themselves deep in the men's chests.

Veseli didn't waste even a second as he charged forward, plowing between the two and freeing his knives from the stunned, shocked men as they dropped to their knees. He threw one of the knives at a man that had snuck up on his partner. It skimmed Andrea by mere inches before finding its target in the enemy.

Andrea himself was using his hands and fists. He had guns strapped on him, but he was his own weapon and preferred to use that in close combat. He somehow heard or instinctively knew that Veseli had saved him. He gave Veseli a quick nod as he took a man's head in his large hands.

Even with a helmet on the guy's head, Andrea's hands were so large that they were close to overlapping themselves as he positioned them. The man's eyes widened. He sensed his own mortality and the alarming position he was in as he noticed how big Andrea was.

Andrea didn't give it a second thought. He gave a sharp twist. The fear left the man's eyes as his spinal column snapped. The man dropped like a puppet with its strings cut.

Andrea casually stepped over the fallen body, eyes locking on his next target. Because of his style of fighting, he was still immaculate and clean, a stark contrast to his blood-soaked partner. And, though Veseli was a terrifying sight, Andrea, somehow, was even scarier. He seemed like an untouchable Goliath, spotless in a sea of blood and guts. Veseli fought with rage, and Andrea was cold and meticulous.

The men around us started to shout in what I recognized as Russian.

Without turning to me, Veseli yelled out, "Callie, what are they saying?"

I tried to listen in, but there was too much chaos. I had only started learning Russian a few months ago, and I was good, but I wasn't on par with the speed of a native, let alone several natives that were shouting in terror and fury. Not only that, I was most likely in shock at seeing the men I had somewhat grown to trust killing in such an efficient, easy manner. Other than the fact that they had kidnapped me, I had forgotten that they were bad men. Veseli had been sheltering me a lot the past two years.

I felt a strange sense of loyalty well up in me towards him. I tried to block out the sounds of the pain and suffering as I tried to focus on deciphering the Russian words. They could be regrouping or calling in reinforcements. I needed to let Veseli know if they were. I finally understood a snippet of conversation, but I had to be misinterpreting.

Why would the enemies be falling back?

I went to voice it anyway, after hearing it doubly confirmed by others repeating the same thing.

"Don't even think about it, pet," the man behind me said, an English accent to his voice. I felt the cold press of a gun on my temple.

I stilled.

"Callie!" Andrea yelled in confusion, trying to prompt me to speak as the Russians actually did start to fall back.

When I didn't respond, Veseli did another swipe with his knife to clear the immediate area around him so that he could chance a look my way.

He froze when he saw me. His eyes traveled my form, checking for injuries of which there were none, I was sure. Again, I hadn't been fighting long before I was subdued. Finally, Veseli's eyes settled on the gun pressed to my temple.

"I see I have your attention now," the English voice said from behind me.

Even from a poor vantage, I could see that Veseli was furious. He let out a slew of curse words in Albanian and, quick as a whip, threw his knife towards one of the men to my left. The man dropped with the lethal blow.

The guy with the gun to my head hadn't even flinched.

"Are you done with your little temper tantrum now?" The voice was unaffected, almost mocking at the life that had been lost, supposedly his comrade. If it was, there wasn't any love lost between the two. Even though the man had been murdered, the guy behind me wasn't bothered in the slightest.

Veseli shrugged, kneeling down to wipe his remaining knife clean on one of his victim's shirts since there literally wasn't a spot on himself that was free of blood. He talked calmly as he cleaned his knife. "Had to see if you would cringe away and drop her."

"Thereby freeing her and signing my own death the second I stepped out from behind her," the English man said. "I know. I'm not green. I've been in the business for a while, same as you."

"So it would seem," Veseli said, getting to his feet. He finally looked at the man, studying him. "Who are you, and what do you want with us?"

The man behind me chuckled a bit as if the whole scene was any other day at the office to him.

I wanted to scream and yell in frustration as tears welled up in my eyes. All around me, bodies were strewn around in garish, uncensored detail, and I felt the weight of the foreshadowing looming near like it was a physical entity. I would look like them, with my insides out. I would be a lost life, just like them. It would only take the pull of a trigger. With the barrel of the gun already pressed against my skull, it would be over in seconds.

...and the gunman was laughing about the whole situation.

"You just stay right there, Andrea. Try to sneak up behind me, and I'll shoot her brains out." He gave me a hard shake to emphasize his point. My heart leaped to my throat, terrified he would twitch and make the gun go off.

Andrea held his large hands up in a placating manner, but it only made him look like a grizzly bear rearing back on its hind legs. It wasn't very reassuring.

The Russian men around us shifted in unease.

"Whoa, whoa, hey. Calm down, calm down. Don't hurt her," Andrea said.

I felt tears spill down my cheeks, but I was frozen on the spot. I didn't dare to breathe for fear of upsetting the man holding me. I didn't even know his name or what he looked like. Was I going to be killed by someone I didn't even know? It somehow seemed more unfair that way.

Veseli and Andrea had stopped fighting, but more men kept pouring into the building with us.

This job was supposed to have been so simple. We were to meet with a businessman and talk about what we could do to help bring more money to his empire. I'd researched for weeks after they contacted us. They'd seemed legitimate and not completely unethical, which was what Veseli had been looking for in clients more and more lately: ethics.

It seemed satirical in hindsight. Veseli had been turning more legitimate and on the up-and-up. And yet, fate had brought him right back to the life he'd tried to leave behind, standing bathed in blood amidst a volley of corpses.

It was supposed to be so simple. Talk to Russian businessman Nikolai Ivanov. Offer our services. Get his trust and business. Close the deal.

Andrea hadn't even brought any rocket launchers which was traveling light for him. We'd been so sure it was a clean and easy job.

How could everything have gone so wrong?

The mysterious man spoke up again, tearing me from my thoughts.

"Who I am doesn't matter, but my boss is the one you should be worried about," he said lowly.

I could see Andrea scanning the warehouse as men filed onto the catwalk and trained their guns on them. Veseli was still looking at us, avoiding my gaze.

"So take us to him," Veseli said. He let out a sardonic smile. "It so happens that our schedule has opened up, and we're more useful alive than dead."

The man behind me chuckled again. "Unfortunately, my boss has men like you. You're a dime a dozen."

Veseli made an aw-shucks face and shrugged, indicating the dead bodies around them. "Really? Surely you don't think we're so easily replaced, do you?"

"Well," he said. "You're good. I'll admit that. Ivanov was quite impressed when he found out that this big business of yours was only a two-man empire."

Veseli closed his eyes and shook his head, holding up a hand for him to stop. "Wait, wait, wait. Just wait a goddamn second—did you say 'Ivanov'? As in Nikolai Ivanov? Why the hell did he pull this fuck-fest of a stunt?! We were already willing to meet with him! Is this how he does business? Because, if he does, let me just say, full disclosure, I'm not impressed."

"Well, it's not exactly how he does business...at least, not yet. But it's still too early. You'll understand soon."

There was some unspoken signal that I missed from the guy behind me because the Russian men all brought up their guns, taking better aim at Andrea and Veseli.

"You see, Ivanov does business with a body count. He doesn't like to have any pesky witnesses running around. You could say it's, well, pardon my pun, bad for business."

"So, you're going to kill us?" Veseli laughed, more relaxed than I would ever be under such a large firing squad.

"You can go ahead and try fuckheads!" Andrea yelled, vibrating with pent up strength and energy.

"Why work so hard to set a meet if you were just going to kill us?" Veseli asked, his eyes roving over the masked gunmen, calculating.

"Because," the man said. "He did need something from you... and now we've got it."

I frowned in confusion, but for the first time, Veseli's gaze flew to my face. He looked horrified as realization dawned in his dark brown eyes. I'd never seen that much emotion on his face, especially aimed my way. It was almost like he...like he cared.

I was too busy trying to decipher his emotions, so I jumped when Andrea bellowed out, "Callie, run!"

Gunshots started up, and I was deafened. Instinctively, I hunched in on myself, thinking that they had turned to aim at me after Andrea's warning. But that wasn't the case. I'd never been shot before—hoped to God it never happened—but I was sure I would've been able to feel it by now if it'd happened.

The man behind me forced me to turn and marched me towards the door. I could still see the flashes and feel the vibrations of the shots ricocheting around the warehouse even though I couldn't hear them going off.

It was like everything was in slow motion, and my brain was wading through a frozen sludge trying to think about what to do.

At the same time, it was like time warped another way because I blinked and was suddenly inside a dark limo, staring at a man that was terrifying. He had blonde hair, icy gray eyes, and a stony expression that gave way to an easy smile.

"Hello, Callie," he said.

I gulped, scooting back in my seat, shaking and terrified.

I looked around, trying to find an escape, but the English man that had led me here climbed in the back with us, giving me my first glimpse of him. He was a black hole, void of emotion. Veseli and Andrea seemed like open books compared to these two.

The man, I assumed was Nikolai Ivanov, turned to the guy. "Good work, Dell. I assume that the other two will be taken care of shortly."

Dell nodded. "I shot Andrea myself. It won't be long before Veseli falls as well. Your men should be calling to confirm."

My eyes watered at the news. My heart tightened into a clenched fist within my chest. With Andrea dead, even if the odds hadn't been so grossly stacked against him, Veseli wouldn't last long.

I hadn't realized how much those two had come to mean to me. I'd been their hostage, yes. But since I'd deleted myself from existence, they were also the only two people that knew about me other than my mom and stepdad, and now they were gone.

Ivanov smiled and leaned forward, studying me.

"I'm hoping that you can show us your worth. People around me don't last long if they don't," he said, brushing a finger against my cheek that made me flinch back as if he'd sliced me. He smiled a cold smile.

" Papa," a sweet voice said from beside me. I jumped in shock turning to see the boy seated next to me. He couldn't have been more than three or four. He had blonde hair so light that it was almost white, a cherubic face that only the young have, and curious blue eyes. He was speaking in Russian.

"Yes, my son?" Ivanov asked, staring at me but addressing the boy.

My mind caught up with the meaning of the words, finally able to translate them. I looked back at the boy, wondering how someone so angelic-looking could be related to the person across from me.

"Who is this girl?" he asked, looking up at me.

Not letting Andrea and Veseli know I could speak Albanian had been an advantage, so I thought that I could pretend that I didn't know what they were saying.

"Callie," Ivanov answered, switching to English. "Practice your English, son."

The boy frowned in concentration, biting his lip. He looked up at me. "My name Kazimir," he said slowly.

I swallowed, feeling terrified and like this was all surreal. I was in a limo while the two people I'd grown to see as protectors were killed amongst a horde of dead bodies. And they were trying to carry on a civilized conversation?

Ivanov grabbed me by my throat in a flash. "Say hello to my son, Callie. It is polite."

I couldn't even cough. My throat was gripped too tightly. I stared up into the cold, blue eyes in front of me, trying to speak. I could hear the little boy next to me crying and shouting at his father, but I couldn't concentrate to tell what he was saying since he must've switched back to Russian.

I moved my mouth to let Ivanov know that I would talk, but he still didn't let up. I managed to nod the best I could with my neck in his vice-like grip. Only then did he let up and sit back.

I took a few gasping breaths, unsure of what had just happened. My mind was going into shock if not already there.

"You are trying my patience, Callie."

Not wanting to be choked again, I quickly turned to the boy beside me, but I flinched back when my face nearly brushed his. I only just held back a scream. He was in my face, his head inches from my own. He looked older now, about seven or eight. His skin was deathly pale, and there was a huge bullet hole in his head.

I tried to shrink away, but his small hands grabbed my shirt and pulled me close. "Why Callie? Why did you get me killed?"

My mouth opened and closed a few times. I didn't know what to say. It was like I couldn't even speak. Had I spoken at all?

A loud shot echoed around the limo, lighting it up.

I turned my head, only to see that Ivanov was pointing a gun at me. It was still smoking. I felt around, my hands going to my forehead. I gasped when they brushed across something wet—a small divot, the size of a nickel. Warm rivulets of liquid began to trail down along my face from it. My fingertip disappeared inside it, making me nauseous. It wasn't a divot; it was a hole.

I pulled my hands away as if I'd touched a hot stove... as if I could forget about it and be fine. But I could feel the warm liquid, the blood, trickling down my shoulders and back, cooling as it traveled down my body. With tears in my eyes, I reached my hands up, running them through my hair, trying to feel the back of my head to confirm what I suspected.

Just as my fingers started to brush against the rough, wet edges of a crater, I felt the air move.

I gasped and woke up.

Chapter 24

I shot up off of the couch, shaking and sweating. My throat burned as I tried to choke back tears and gasp in breaths at the same time. My muscles protested the strength it took to hold me up.

I glanced around, trying to figure out where I was.

There was a moment where the open floorplan living room and kitchen combo confused me, but then it clicked.

Trainers' Facilities. Hartstrait.

I was at the new apartment with the Cardinals.

A loud voice spoke from nearby, causing me to jump and turn. It was Darcy.

"Jesus, Mary, and bloody Joseph! Callie, you scared the ever livin' daylight right outta me, ya did. I lost ten years just now," she said, taking a seat across from me in one of the two mismatched armchairs. She had a large bowl of cereal and took a bite before continuing around her mouthful of Cheerios. "How'd you know I was comin'?"

I sat up all the way, putting my feet down on the floor and my head in my hands. "I didn't. At least I don't think I did."

Why had my dream been so different? Sure, dreaming about my guilt for Kaz had been par for the course. It'd been going on three months since his dad killed him in front of me, and the nightmares still hadn't stopped.

But to dream about Andrea and Veseli? That was unusual. I hadn't dreamed about them in nearly three years—not since Ivanov introduced me to the tank. I'd had new fodder for my nightmares then.

"I agree with Darcy," Sabra said, her voice coming from the kitchen. She was sitting at the small dining table, watching captioned news on her tablet and sipping some sort of hot herbal water. "You've been tossing and turning for a while now, but you only woke when she approached."

Despite her calm demeanor, her voice was tense.

Dr. Harper had *strongly advised* me to tell the Cardinals early on about my nightmares. He wanted to make sure that none of them woke me up, harming me or themselves by doing so. Because of that, they knew not to wake me. But I knew it was hard on them, especially now that they could see the product of the nightmares happening out in the living room.

I didn't get to answer. A knock on the door made Darcy flinch in her chair, spilling cheerios on her black shirt that she had to wear for a shift at the bar.

Her cursing was fast and in Gaelic as she shot up to attempt to pat herself dry. It was rather ineffective, so she gave up, heading to her room.

Sabra went to answer the door, giving her irate teammate a pat on the back as they passed each other. I sat up, pushing my sweaty hair back and turning to see who was at the door. I couldn't see around Sabra's tall form, but I could recognize the voice.

Jace.

Ooh, Darcy was *not* going to be happy if Jace had startled her and soiled her work shirt just to borrow another cup of sugar.

Sabra let Jace in and shut the door behind him.

Jace made a beeline for the couch, plopping down on it close enough that I fell into him when his weight settled.

I turned to look at him, trying to smile.

He had a lopsided smile on that dropped when he saw my face. "Callie, what's wrong?"

I blew out a breath, leaning back into the couch and not feeling the need to scoot away from him. I stayed where I had settled with my arm brushing against the side of his torso and his arm behind me on the back of the couch. "You're going to be dead if Darcy finds out that it was you at the door. That's what's wrong."

He scoffed, relaxing back some more, wiggling down in the cushions until his arm had fallen from the backrest to around my shoulders. It did a lot to help my nerves from the dream settle and another type of nerves flare up.

"Please, she can do her worst. I'm a trained Delta member. Hell, I'm a *trainer* at Delta. All three of us are. That's how we got our place here at Hartstrait apartments. We're the creme de la crop. Amazing. Aca-awesome. Besides, you weren't answering your phone. I was worried and being neighborly."

I groaned. "How could I forget?"

"Forget what?"

I fished my phone out of my pocket. "I forgot to charge it when I got home."

Jace snagged the phone from me, testing the power button out himself. "You guys got home before noon. How could it already be dead? Did you forget to charge it last night?"

He handed the phone back to me.

"No, well, yes. I mean, it's not a smartphone, so I haven't needed to charge it as often as the Cardinals seem to need to charge their phones. I didn't charge it last night, but I should've had enough battery to last me another day at least. But who knows, maybe it was updating or something." I stood up to plug it in. After a couple of seconds, the screen lit up showing the empty battery.

I went to head back to the couch, but then the phone started going crazy. It was vibrating nonstop and making a notification sound that kept cutting itself off halfway through as more notifications came in.

My eyes widened as I turned back to the phone resting on the entertainment center. It was counting up the missed phone calls and messages.

I shook my head, wiping the shock from my face. "Jace, how worried were you?"

His eyes widened as he held his hands up in innocence. "Whoa, whoa, I didn't text you *that* many times. Stalker isn't exactly one of my favorite colors," he said, gesturing to the spastic phone. "In fact, I didn't text you at all. I called you. Like *twice*."

The phone was still going off though, so I approached it.

I picked it up and look at it: 24 messages and 7 missed calls.

I unlocked the phone and looked at the first messages. There were three all from Corbin.

"Hey, Callie-Cat."

"You were awesome riding that bike today."

"Until Doc messed it up."

Brock had sent me a message, calling me "*dušo*" which I quickly translated now that I had the spelling.

It was Serbian for "sweetie."

He'd been calling me sweetie.

It made me blush, but I figured that he had to know that I would translate it when he sent it. The nice thing to do was to send him back his name so that he could translate it. The only problem was, I'd called him "broccoli" on accident. It'd been the first thing that'd popped into my head. I was still regretting it.

Would he notice a difference if I changed it?

I figured it wouldn't hurt to try. I bit my lip, thinking hard and then typed out, "*Byapok*."

I tilted my head. That sounded like *Brōkali*…right? …especially after hearing it *one* time so long ago. I hit send.

Almost immediately, I got back a reply. "You speak Bengali?"

I sent out an affirmative.

Before I could open one of the other messages, he sent back. "Extensive? Your nickname for me is… extensive?"

I laughed, forgetting what a translator app would show. I responded, "Literally, yes. But colloquially it means 'thoroughly awesome.' I thought that fit you to a tee."

Brock: "Colloquially. That's a fancy word."

Me: "I try."

Brock: "Thoroughly awesome. I like it. But it's different from what you called me before…?"

I blushed.

Me: "Yes."

I didn't say anything else as an explanation. I opened one of the other conversation threads.

Other than one message from each of the remaining Emerson team letting me know who they were, save their numbers, and text anytime—I coughed—the rest of the messages were from Corbin.

I skimmed through them, but the gist of it was asking me questions about what I liked and what hobbies I did. He also asked me about my upcoming date with Emerson. He wanted to know if I needed help getting ready.

I sent him a quick text to let him know that the date wasn't for hours. I had plenty of time.

After that, I looked to see who the calls were from.

One from Brock—that made my heart pound—four were from Corbin, and two from someone called Thing 2.

I bit my lip. "What's a Thing 2?"

Jace frowned. "It's a part of *The Cat in the Hat*."

"Oh, right. I remember. They were twins, right?"

He studied my face. "You could say that. Why do you ask?"

"Well, you said you called twice...so…process of elimination," I said, responding to a new text from Corbin. He was giving me a hard time because of my "blasé comment" about the date not starting for a while.

Jace frowned. "What do you mean? I thought I programmed our numbers in there already."

"Yeah," I said, offhandedly. "I think that Corbin probably changed all of your guys' names around in my contacts. I'm starting to understand why Doc Scott and Natasia gave me such weird looks when I told them I let Corbin hang onto my phone for a while."

Jace was across the room, standing next to me in an instant.

"Let me see," he said, pulling the phone from my hand. He scrolled through the contacts, and I looked over his arm as he did so. I had all of the Emerson team in there, along with Karl and the Cardinals whose names remained untouched. It was the Tate team that took the brunt of the damage, their names being altered to Alexa, Thing 1, and Thing 2. Jace snorted when he saw Aleks' name but didn't find his own contact all that funny.

"Okay, Aleks' name is actually pretty clever. I'll give it to him, but I'm changing these back. No buts, Callie."

"Hey, they're funny," I said.

"I said no buts!" He typed on my phone for a while. It seemed to take a lot longer to change back three names than I would've imagined it would take, but how would I know? I technically hadn't programmed any of the numbers myself yet.

As Jace was typing, Corbin must've been fed up with waiting for me to text back because the phone started ringing.

Before I could say anything, Jace pushed a button to answer it. "Heeey, Corbin," he said in a cheery voice. "What's up?"

I tried to get the phone back from him, but he put his free hand on my face to hold me back, and the sad truth was his arms were much longer than mine. Mine were windmilling in the air like a tire looking for traction.

"What? No. Yes, this is Callie's phone...I have it because I'm over here.... a date? No, why would you think that...Where? Her house. That's where," he gave me a look and rolled his eyes. Then he stopped, stiffening a little bit. His voice was uncertain when he responded to Corbin's question. "Uh...yeah. Yes, that does mean that she's awake and decent. Why do you--"

He got cut off by the apartment door bursting open behind us. I turned my head the best I could with Jace still using my face to hold me away from my phone.

"Because we're coming in," Corbin said from the doorway. "Hey Callie-Cat, did ya miss me?"

Chapter 25

Corbin entered without waiting for a response.

I was at a loss for words as Bryce came right in afterward, a bag in his arms.

My heart gave a flutter like it had when Jace came in and sat beside me on the couch. There were so many guys in the living room—very good-looking guys—and I didn't truly appreciate how much space a male body takes up until I saw the three of them in the small room.

It crowded up fast.

Jace frowned. "Decided to forgo all boundaries now, eh Myers?"

"What?" Corbin asked.

"The downstairs door was locked. As far as I know, you don't have a key. Not like I do."

Corbin waved him off like a pesky gnat. "Maybe you forgot to lock it."

He put his hands on his hips to survey the room. Noticing a hallway, he beelined in that direction, opening doors and familiarizing himself with the place. He was rather forward. But it seemed to fit his personality since he **had** just let himself in.

I heard him open Natasia and Sabra's room. No one was in there since Sabra was out here with us, still looking through her laptop, and Natasia was at Delta.

I finally found my voice. "But… I thought Sabra locked the door. She always locks the door."

Bryce coughed into his fist and turned his head, hiding his expression.

"I *did* lock the door," Sabra said, sounding not very upset or shocked.

I frowned at her, "Then how did…"

She looked up. "Ask Corbin."

I was distracted when shouts came from the other Cardinals' bedroom.

Speak of the devil… We all turned in that direction in time to see Corbin shoot out into the hallway, a terrified expression on his face. I could hear Darcy shouting up a storm behind him, speaking in Gaelic as she chased him, batting at him with a brush.

"Callie! Save me!" he said, trying to shield himself as Darcy whacked him repeatedly. "Ouch! Stop it, you she-devil. Crazy-tempered red-head."

Even I knew that was the wrong thing to say to her as Darcy stopped cold, her face smoothing over.

My eyes rounded, and I darted over and wedged myself between Corbin and the volcano that was about to erupt.

And I got there none too soon either because Darcy lunged forward, her blazing eyes set on Corbin's horrified ones. "You think I'm mad because I'm redheaded! What next! Are you going to say because I'm Irish that I have a bad temper!!"

"Whoa, holy fudge, shitake mushrooms," Corbin said, backing up until he couldn't anymore. "Callie, help! She's morphing into her true form!"

I was too small to stop the angry surge of Darcy. I wasn't willing to step out of the way either, so I was backed into Corbin until we were all squished against the wall.

A quick glance around the room for help showed that Sabra was amused, her arms crossed as she leaned back in the kitchen chair and watched on. Bryce seemed to share Corbin's horror at the situation, as he looked on in wide-eyed fear as well, not wanting to step in. I fought the urge to panic, seeing there wouldn't be any help from them. I mentally squared my shoulders and turned back to Darcy.

"Darcy, calm down. What did he do?"

She didn't even bother to look at me as she answered. "This *boy* is the reason I got cheerios all over myself. And to top it off, his lack of boundaries led him right into our bedroom and bathroom!" She punctuated her statement with another jab of the brush to Corbin's shoulder, the only thing peeking out from behind me. I heard him cry out again.

My eyes involuntarily flicked to Jace's direction at the mention of the Cheerios, but he had somehow mysteriously vanished.

I turned back to Darcy, trying to figure out what to do to diffuse the situation. I pushed my lip in. "Uh, that doesn't sound so bad. He was just trying to look for a place to get me ready for my d-d-...ahem, d-date with Emerson."

"He walked in while I was in the shower!"

Bryce shouted Corbin's name, reprimanding him.

Corbin straightened up a little, "I didn't see anything!"

"Not the point, Cor," Bryce said with an arched eyebrow.

"I'm sorry, okay!" he cried out when Darcy deftly whacked him again with the brush. "But I didn't make you, 'Spill me Lucky Charms'."

He had adopted an Irish accent and a girly voice as he mimicked Darcy's voice.

My eyes widened. He had a death wish, that was all there was to it.

Darcy paused before going ballistic.

How was she missing me completely every time and landing such powerful hits on him? We were pressed so tightly together it was hard to tell where one person ended and the other began.

I didn't want to do it, but I couldn't let Corbin take the blame for everything, especially since he was at least halfway innocent. I prayed for forgiveness for what I was about to do, but Corbin had dug himself into such a deep hole that it was the lesser of two evils.

"Wait, Darcy, wait!"

She stopped and looked down at me. It was then that I quickened my breath, realizing how incredibly close we were.

"Uh, um, well...." I stuttered. I felt Corbin's hands reflexively tighten on my hips and pulled me further into his strong chest behind me. His breath on my neck was not helping the situation either. "W-w-well, you see, Corbin's telling the truth about the Luck—uh, *Cheerios*. It was Jace at the door earlier, and--"

Darcy didn't even let me finish my sentence before she was off of us and scanning the room. "Tate! Where are you? I saw you here!"

A door slammed. Darcy ran towards the front hall.

"Wait!" I said, feeling guilty about throwing Jace under the bus, even though he'd been the one to scare her. I went to go after them, but Corbin tightened his grip on my hips and pulled me back into his chest.

"Just...holy ginger balls, Callie-Cat, let them go. Maybe she'll calm down. Just stay here a minute. I nearly died. She almost killed me. Just… let me calm down."

I heard muffled thumping from the hallway as Darcy took the stairs to the ground floor. She yelled out, "You can't hide from me, Tate! Corbin's not the only one that can pick a lock!"

Alarmed male voices could be heard through the walls from the house next door. It sounded like the other two-thirds of the Tate team were home. And they didn't sound all that happy either.

Sabra must've seen the terrified look on my face because she said, "Calm down, Callie. Darcy won't seriously harm him. Your boy toy is safe."

"Boy toy?" Corbin perked up. He tightened his hands on my hips. "Can I be your boy toy, Callie-Cat? Please? Pretty please?"

I coughed and choked before I could get out a response. "Um...sure?"

Corbin jumped and pulled me into a hug that made my feet leave the ground when he straightened up.

"Cor, do you even know what a boy toy is?" Bryce asked, his voice dubious.

"Yes," Corbin said, turning so that he could address his friend without letting me down. "And she already said that I could be it, so don't even think about asking, Bryce."

That seemed to have been the furthest thing from Bryce's mind... until Corbin forbid him from doing so. He got a deviant look on his face. A smirk spread.

"Yeah, well, Jace's her boy toy. She can have more than one. Tell him, Cal."

Corbin put me down on my feet so he could look at me. His blue eyes were as clear as the summer sky, and they were so...so beseeching.

My brain stumbled. "Uh..."

"Hey, no fucking fair! You can't pull puppy dog eyes on her. Knock it off, Cor." Bryce met my gaze. His sapphire blue eyes were so...so pleading.

"Um..." I brain-stalled again.

"Hey! If I can't pull puppy eyes, neither can you!"

"You're being ridiculous. Leave her alone," Bryce deftly caught my hand, pulling me free from Corbin. I wanted to drop down on my knees and thank him. It was suffocating so close to Corbin "Why do you even *want* to be a boy toy?"

"Wait," I said, frowning now. "What's a boy toy? Is it something bad?"

It had to be if Bryce was acting this incredulous for Corbin wanting to be one.

Bryce gave me a heavy look, his eyes searching mine for answers that weren't there. "Never you mind that. Just don't let anyone say that they're your boy toys, and you won't have to worry about it. Trust me."

He said to trust him, but he had such a devilish smirk.

"I could Google it for you," Sabra said.

"NO!" Bryce said, alarmed. At the same time, Corbin said, "Sounds like a good idea to me! I'll help."

I frowned at the normally serious leader of the Cardinals.

I could tell she had no intentions of actually doing it, but...Sabra had a very serious look on her face when she'd said it, and it'd caused Bryce to lose the smug smirk.

"No, that won't be necessary," he said, slow and calm. "Just remember. No boy toys. You'll be fine."

Corbin led me back to the couch. "We can have my sisters get you ready in here. It has the best lighting."

"Wait," I said, backing away. "We've still got at least three hours before Emerson's going to be here. Why do I need to get ready now? And… you have sisters?"

"Yes, three of them, and they said that three hours is not even close to what they wanted to get you ready for your first date," he said. "It is your first date, right?"

I pushed my lip in. Should I tell them that I wasn't entirely sure if this was a real date? Emerson hadn't even asked me out, and I was pretty sure that he'd been only doing so to get me out of the awkward situation with Doc Scott.

But then Emerson had insisted on going through with it...

Instead of explaining, I nodded. I noticed that Bryce's smirk had turned into something softer.

Corbin cleared his throat a couple of times. "Right. I thought so. My sisters want it to be special. 'And you can't rush art'," he mocked in an overly girly voice. As if he hadn't almost died doing the same thing to Darcy. "Now, go shower."

I just nodded, doing as he instructed. My mind was empty and racing at the same time. As I passed by Sabra, she winked at me, offering no help whatsoever with the unexpected Emerson team ambush.

I shook my head. Some teammate.

Even so, I found myself smiling.

Sometimes it was hard to get used to the reality of my life. I kept waiting for something bad to happen to mess it up. It usually did.

Chapter 26

arcy had calm and what **D** returned sometime during my shower. She was smirking, leaving me both fearful and curious of exactly she'd done to the Tate team. I'd tentatively asked, not sure I wanted the answer, but she hadn't been in a sharing kind of mood. She just gave me a smacking kiss on the cheek and went to her room.

Her action had drawn the dual, undivided attention of both Bryce and Corbin, making me fidget where I stood.

They'd studied me for a long, uncomfortable moment but then changed the subject.

Corbin's sisters were supposed to come here, but when I asked him about them, he held his hands up and pointed at Darcy. She'd decided to take over when she found out, claiming it was her right as my teammate, and Corbin hadn't stood in her way, probably because he valued his life and had angered her enough for one day.

Sabra had disappeared the minute Darcy volunteered herself to help me get ready. It wasn't even thirty seconds later that Darcy then commandeered Corbin to help her since the rest of the Cardinals were gone and Sabra had vanished.

Bryce claimed that he had to text the saleslady about the outfit he'd brought, so he got out of helping.

Corbin mostly leaned against the walls and watched while Darcy worked. The bathroom was small on a good day and downright microscopic with a crazed-teammate and a good-looking guy crammed in there.

Sometimes, Darcy would ask Corbin to hand her something, and I think Corbin would grab the wrong thing on purpose just to ruffle Darcy's feathers. But it never failed to make me laugh, and once I started laughing, Darcy stop cursing Corbin and his unborn children to a life of abundant harvest and no harvesters—I was paraphrasing, of course. She would glance at my smile, shake her head, and get back to work, grumbling under her breath. When she was distracted, Corbin would send me a secret wink.

All in all, Corbin's absent sisters had been right. It'd taken Darcy every bit of the three hours to get me in the "perfect" outfit, wash and style my hair, and add some light makeup.

I'd never worn makeup before, so when she'd brought it out, it all of a sudden hit me that I was going on a date.

With a boy.

No, with *Emerson.*

It was a good thing that Darcy hadn't finished until the last minute. If I'd had to wait around and twiddle my thumbs, I would've made myself sick with nerves and self-doubts.

Corbin, when he wasn't messing with Darcy, was taking pictures and texting a lot on his phone. Bryce brought in the garment bag from living room, and the boys were promptly shooed out so that Darcy could help me change. Corbin might've even taken a video when Darcy did the big reveal, moving aside to let me see myself in the mirror.

I wasn't sure how good of a reaction video it ended up being because as soon as I caught my reflection, I was gone in my mind, lost to the world around me.

Darcy had pulled half my hair up into an artful updo, somehow got my pale skin to glow, and managed to make my eyes pop out with depth and allure. And the dress was...beyond gorgeous—beyond anything I had ever worn before. It was a knee-length, A-line, spaghetti-strapped rose-gold piece that shimmered. It cinched in at the waist with a matching metallic sash tied in a large bow around my waist.

I studied the reflection staring back at me, trying to process the thoughts running through my mind. Since my mind couldn't react fast or lucidly enough, my body decided to step up to the plate.

And apparently, my body thought tearing up would be an appropriate response.

Corbin's phone lowered. "Uh, Callie-Cat?" He put his phone down and led me away from the mirror and to the living room couch. At his insistence, I sat. He knelt in front of me. "Callie, what's wrong?"

I sniffled a bit. "I don't know," I said thickly, trying desperately not to ruin the makeup Darcy had added, but the stress of failing and ruining all of Darcy's work only added to my surging emotions. I wanted—no—*needed* a hug.

"Callie, *a chara*. Don't worry about the makeup. I can fix it. I can take it off. I can start over."

"N-no," I sniffed. "It's almost eight o'clock."

"Emerson can wait," Corbin said. "If it happens, it happens."

Bryce smirked. "You're supposed to make them wait anyway," he drawled.

I stilled, processing his words. "I am?" I asked, my own voice becoming very high pitched at the end as the tears seemed to be crescendoing into what might turn out to be some pretty spectacular waterworks.

Where was this book that contained all of these rules for dating?!

I was teetering on the edge of hysteria. It was hopeless. What was I thinking? How could I dream that I was ready to go on a date? I didn't know the first thing about it.

Bryce's eyes got round. "Oh, shit. No, Callie, I was just making a joke--"

I started crying in earnest now. I couldn't even tell that he wasn't being serious.

That was it.

The makeup was ruined. If I kept it up, it would get on the gorgeous, expensive dress that Bryce had brought.

"Fuck me sideways, you guys were supposed to fix her," Darcy said, angrily.

Bryce came up so that they were sitting on either side of me now, rubbing up and down my back.

"I-it's not his fault," I said, "I just...I-I just d-don't know any-anything about d-dating. I h-ha-haven't even worn make-up be-before. H-how can, can I g-go out with s-someone like Em-m-merson?"

"Uh, well, if you're going on a date with him you probably shouldn't call him Emer— oomph!" Corbin was cut off by Bryce reaching around me to hit him on the back of the head. "What? I'm just saying that she should call him Payton since that's his—" Bryce gestured at me. Corbin turned, his glare softening and disappearing altogether as he caught my face. "And I'm still not helping, am I?"

"I-I shouldn't call him Em-merson?"

There were too many rules, and I was too ignorant. I was staying home. Sorry, Darcy, for wasting your time. Sorry Emer..., uh...Payton, for standing you up on our not-really-a-date date. And, thank you, Corbin, for making me see reason before I could embarrass myself— more than I already was.

"Okay, I'll bite. What's going on?" came a British voice at the entryway. "Why is she crying?"

All three of our heads whipped around to stare at the front door. Sabra was there—out from her hiding spot and holding the door open for an immaculate vision of poise.

Emerson was standing there in a full suit—not just his normal slacks, dress shirt, and vest. The material of his vest matched the exact shimmery gold of my dress. He had a bouquet of purple daisies in his hands.

I hadn't even heard him knock.

I sniffled and then burst into tears once more, hiding my face in my hands. The makeup was a hopeless cause now, and I didn't want Emerson to see what a mess I was.

Through my sniffles and hiccups, I could feel the air shift as Bryce and Corbin retreated. They were replaced by the scent of coffee. Em— Payton was kneeling down in front of me.

"Love."

I didn't look up, even when he raised his fingers to one of my wrists.

"Callie," he said softly. He put a finger under my chin, lifting my face. "Come on, pet. Let me see those lovely eyes of yours."

I looked up. "I'm not a pet."

He sent me a soft, enigmatic smile. "My apologies. It's just a term of endearment." He took a handkerchief, a real cloth fancy one, out of his pocket. He unfolded it carefully and used it to gently dab at my face.

"Tell me what's wrong, darling," he said soothingly.

"No-nothin--"

"Do not lie, Callie," he said, his jade-green eyes pinning me in place with a look.

I glanced away as he continued to dab at my face. "I d-don't kn-know. I-I was looking at m-myself in the mirror and...and...Darcy made me l-look so p-pretty!" I burst out, starting up the tears again.

I was making such a stellar impression on my first date.

Chapter 27

The scent of coffee and hazelnut was much stronger as I found myself suddenly held to Emer—Payton—aww, screw it, Emerson's shoulder.

His grip was strong and reassuring as he embraced me like a gentle doe. "Shh, shh. It's okay. You look very beautiful, love—with or without makeup." He continued to soothe me until my sniffles calmed back down.

The thoughts that I wasn't worthy or ready for even a fake date hadn't changed, but, the embrace helped calm me down more than anything. I started to breathe more slowly against his chest.

"That's better," Emerson said, leaning back. He gently swiped any of the remaining tears from my cheeks before taking the sides of my face in his hands to study me. I wanted to fidget as I felt his intense gaze travel across my cheeks.

Before I could get self-conscious, he said, "Perfect. Now, I have dinner reservations," he looked at his watch on his wrist, "In approximately 40 minutes, but they can be changed if you prefer. Would you like me to change the reservation to give Darcy time to reapply makeup, or would you like to go as is? You are breathtaking either way."

I played with my hair, somehow not embarrassed by his statement since I knew without a doubt it was nothing more than poetic flowery. "Well, I don't want to cause any trouble with delaying the reservation. What if they can't get you back in?"

Emerson quirked a smile at me. "I have a feeling that it won't be a problem."

I thought about it some more. "No, no, I'll be fine. I've never worn makeup before anyway. What's another night going to kill me? I would like to go ahead if it's alright?"

He sent me a smile that took my breath away.

"Of course, love." He got to his feet and offered me a hand.

I took it as he helped me stand.

"Oh, hey," Corbin said. "Em, mind giving Bryce and me a lift?"

Emerson stiffened a minute amount. I nearly missed it. If he hadn't tucked my arm away into the crook of his elbow, I wouldn't have even noticed.

"Of course, Corbin. I'll drop you off on the way," he said.

Corbin waved him off as he started heading for the door. "No need. We're feeling rather peckish ourselves. Mind if we crash?"

Emerson let out a slow breath as if he was searching for strength. "Actually, yes, I do mind." At his teammate's unrepentant grin, he let out a small sigh. "But, that won't change your mind. Will it?"

"Glad you are so understanding, Em. Oh," Corbin said, noticing the flowers in Emerson's hand. He came forward trying to grab them. "Let me get those."

Emerson yanked his hand back and away from Corbin's reaching grasp. "These are for Callie."

Both of them froze, Emerson with his hand pulled back and into the air and Corbin with his arm outstretched to get at the bouquet. There was a small stare down where they communicated something that had Corbin backing away a bit with his hands up and deferring to Emerson.

Emerson straightened out his slightly ruffled suit, patting down his tie. He turned me to face him and held out the flowers. They were dark purple daisies. I felt my heart melt at the gesture. Likewise, his voice was impossibly soft as he spoke to me. "For you, Callie."

I reached out to take them, hardly believing how I'd ended up here in life. Thinking about this time last year...they were two completely different worlds.

Some days I woke up, expecting to be back in the tank or working for Ivanov once more. Some days I believed I really had passed away and gone on to heaven. This was one of those moments because it was so hard to believe that my present life could be real.

I grasped the flowers like they were made out of the most precious, delicate glass in the world. The petals were velvety, smooth, and incredibly vibrant. "Thank you, Emerson," I whispered.

"You're welcome, and please, call me Payton," he said.

I beamed up at him, feeling happy, trying to show my thanks at the weight of his gesture even if he had no clue why it was so important to me. With his permission, maybe it wouldn't be so bad to call him...Payton.

Payton's mouth parted a little bit in surprise. He averted his gaze from my face and fiddled with his cuffs.

"Hey, can we call you Payton too?" Corbin asked, squeezing between the two of us and slinging his arms around our shoulders.

Em—err, still was going to take some getting used to—Payton cleared his throat before turning a stern look towards Corbin. "I'm so glad you asked. No, you may not."

Corbin shrugged before slipping forward and heading to the kitchen. "I'll just get these in some water, ya?"

I frowned, staring after him. He had the daisies—*my daisies* in his hand.

My mouth dropped open in shock. I turned back to look at Em—Payton, but he was shaking his head in resignation. "It's going to be a long night."

"Not long enough," Sabra said, coming up to us with her arms folded and a stare fixed on her face. "You just pretend she is Cinderella. She needs to be back by midnight. If not, you will have quite a few high-ranking Delta teams on the lookout for her. Got it, *Payton*?"

She was talking to him like he was some juvenile delinquent and not the formal, suit-wearing young man that he was. I wanted to sink into the couch in embarrassment.

Payton didn't let it ruffle him too much though. He was back to his calm, collected self.

"Of course, Sabra," he said. "Shall we, Callie?"

I nodded, eager to escape into the darkness of a vehicle. It was starting to feel like this was equal parts the best and most embarrassing night of my life.

Outside, we passed by the Tate team's door on the way to the car. It looked as if they were heading out.

I bit my lip.

The Tate team all seemed to be dressed somewhat fancier than normal, but not so much so that I could say for sure. It was little things you might've missed if you didn't know them. Instead of a t-shirt, Jace had on a long-sleeved shirt with the sleeves rolled up. CJ's hair was actually combed. And Aleks...well, his was even more indiscernible, because it wasn't a visual change. He was wearing some sort of new cologne.

Payton narrowed his eyes at the group, but they just said that they were heading out anyway and would walk with us. Bryce and Corbin brought up the back to finish our assembly line.

Our dinner for two was starting out with quite the crowd.

The seven of us—no, wait, ten—Darcy, Triz, and Natasia were walking up from their parking spot when they saw us. With a quick word, the Cardinals joined up with the long procession.

I was half-worried the tag-alongs would try to go with us, but the Tate and Cardinal teams split off, going to wherever they were parked. The only add-ons with us now were Bryce and Corbin. My shoulders relaxed a bit.

We walked up to a navy blue, impeccably clean car.

Payton held the door open for me, letting me sit in the front, and Bryce and Corbin got into the back seat. Corbin fought an uninterested Bryce for the spot in the middle so that he could lean forward and talk to us. He kept up a steady banter not giving Payton and me the time to talk. It was actually a blessing because I was too much of a nervous wreck to carry on a conversation.

On the drive, Payton kept glancing in his rearview mirror and letting out a sigh. I could tell it was from whatever he saw back there because his jade-green eyes were lit up from the vehicle or vehicles behind us.

"Problem, Em—err, Payton?" I asked.

He looked over to me for a moment, picked my hand up in his and brought it to his lips slowly to kiss it.

It felt like he'd brushed me with a livewire that shot straight up my arm and to my core that set my heart pounding and stomach tingling. He put our hands back down on the center console but kept my hand clasped in his. "No problem at all."

I couldn't possibly say anything after that with my nerves so frayed, so I just looked out my window.

And it was only because I was looking out my window that I noticed the silver car. The headlights were maybe ten feet away from my door, blinding me as their bright beams filled the cab of the car.

"Payton!" I screamed.

With reflexes a Nascar racer would be envious of, Payton swerved away from the impending collision. The car tilted, shifting on its suspension. We veered left. Payton couldn't go too far though without going into oncoming traffic. He came back into our lane, picking the lesser of two evils.

I braced myself as we impacted.

Metal crunched.

I was thrown to the side, my head banging into something hard. It could've been the window or the dash. It was so disorienting; I couldn't tell up from down.

The car skidded. Horns sounded.

I was thrown in the opposite direction as a second deafening bang went off. It was like firing a cannon in an enclosed area.

My hearing went a little fuzzy as I tried to process what'd happened.

Were we safe? Were we in the oncoming traffic? Were the horns blaring at us to get out of the way?

It was hard to tell. I wanted to turn off some of my senses to concentrate. The pain was making me dazed. I didn't move, sitting there for what felt like minutes but was probably seconds.

I blinked feeling someone shaking my shoulder. I looked up.

Corbin was leaned over the seat, trying to say something to me.

I blinked again. I looked over to the driver's seat. Emerson was laying over the steering wheel. Just beyond that, his window was shattered, and I could make out the large, crushed grill of some massive truck. Its hood was out of view, higher than the roof of our car and not visible through the busted out window. The truck must've tee-boned us as we skidded after the impact.

"—ou okay? Callie, are you okay?"

That was Corbin, his voice worried. He was pale, making his freckles stand out starkly across his cheeks and nose. I'd not seen him so serious before.

Moving hurt, so I turned back to face the front.

I licked my lips. "I'm fine," I rasped.

That small reassurance was enough. Corbin's eyes lost a little worry as he went to check on his teammates. He shook Emerson but got no response.

"Bryce?" I asked.

"I'm here. I'm okay, Cal."

"Emerson?" Corbin asked, sounding a little hysterical. "Emerson, wake up!"

I heard a loud, booming sound cursing in a very familiar Russian voice.

"Aleks," I murmured to myself, feeling great relief.

I didn't even care how he'd gotten here. When last I saw them, they'd been heading to their cars to go somewhere. It was enough to know that the Tate team must've been nearby, heading in the same direction as us.

"Did she just say 'Aleks'?" Corbin asked, his head snapping towards my face. "Callie, are you sure you're okay? The glass is cracked on your window. Did you hit your head?"

Bryce leaned forward, his face coming into view. He had blood running down one side, matting into his dark brown hair. When the truck hit us, he must've hit his head too.

Recalling that I'd been asked a question, I shook my head, regretted it when the pain flared up a little bit, and then spoke. "No! It's Aleks. I hear Aleks."

But I knew they now heard him too because their faces cleared, losing the worry.

Bryce opened his mouth to say something but was cut off by a horrible wrenching sound.

My door rattled and vibrated. Glass shook loose, raining down on my hair and arms.

"Callie!" Corbin yelled.

I turned. It was the silver car that had hit us in the first place. It had started up and was backing away.

It barely looked scratched. Both the frame and the body had to be reinforced because it was barely damaged after the crash. As the driver reversed, my door fell to the ground with a loud clang, letting more of the chilly night air in.

I jerked away, looking out my open side of the car.

One of the silver car's headlights had survived the impact. With the light glaring and bright, it was hard to tell, but it seemed like the windshield was tinted black. I couldn't make out the details of the driver. All I could see was my own reflection staring back at me as if reflecting my mortality in a mirror of doom.

The car stopped, three car-lengths away. I held my breath. My air rushed out in an exhalation of fear when the car went back into gear. It turned sinister as it revved its engine to a loud growl instead of continuing to back away.

The hairs on the back of my neck stood up on end.

Something was wrong.

"It wasn't an accident," I realized.

"What?" Bryce asked, looking over at me from where he was hunched over the front seat trying to wake Emerson.

"It wasn't an accident," I said louder.

"Oh God," Corbin pounded against his door behind me, but it must've been wedged shut. "Callie!"

The silver car's engine screamed as it topped out its RPMs.

I realized how very vulnerable I was right now.

There was nothing standing between me and two tons of lethal metal machine not even thirty feet away from me. I scrambled for my seatbelt, not taking my eyes off of the car, glinting like a deadly silver bull ready to charge.

I prayed that I would get unbuckled and away from the gaping hole where my door had been.

But there wasn't enough time.

The car lurched, racing forward.

I couldn't get the seatbelt unhooked. I was trapped like a gnat in a web.

I closed my eyes, resigned, seeing the one remaining headlight shine through my eyelids as it got closer. The snarl of the engine was deafening.

I pictured Kaz, feeling his bracelet on my wrist.

Hands were reaching down next to me, trying to unfasten the seatbelt I'd given up on.

It would be too late.

I held my breath, bracing for impact.

Another loud crash sounded. More glass pelted me, like razor-sharp sand.

The glass hurt, sure, but I wasn't flattened.

I opened my eyes.

A very familiar van, newly repaired after the bombing, had rammed itself into the car, pushing it off track and parking between me and the danger. Natasia was in the driver's seat, abreast of my seat.

I let out a half-cry of elation and hysteria.

Beyond, I could see Aleks running in front of the Cardinals' van, his gun out and pointed as he yelled at the still undamaged silver car. Without a doubt, it was reinforced. Natasia had plowed into its side with enough force to knock it clear sideways, and it still didn't show much in the way of body damage.

The driver's windows were tinted as black as the windshield. Aleks belting out orders at his own reflection while I held my breath. The driver could have a gun pointed at him, and we wouldn't know it until it was too late.

There was a long moment, where everything seemed to still as if the driver was debating his options.

I held my breath.

Then, motion seemed to pour back into the scene. The driver stomped the gas, peeling out with screeching tires as he fled the area.

Aleks' face flashed orange as he fired his gun off two, three, four times into the retreating shape of the car. All four made their mark with unerring precision, but all four bounced off.

It was bulletproof as well.

This had been no accident.

We were lucky that apparently the Tate team and Cardinals had been tailing us… because…

Whoever that was, they'd come prepared.

Prepared to kill.

Chapter 28

I let out a big breath and looked over to my left.

Emerson still hadn't moved. Like Bryce, he had a trail of blood crawling down the side of his face. The truck that impacted us must've hit much harder than the silver car as they'd both taken quite a bit of damage.

"He's breathing. Don't worry," Corbin said.

I nodded, shifting around to test my functionality. I was sore everywhere. It wasn't too bad. I knew it would be much worse tomorrow, but for tonight, I could move around without much pain. I put my hand up to my forehead.

My fingers trailed across a tender spot, sending a jolt of pain along my nerves that made me hiss.

I turned back to the missing door, remembering the feeling of staring towards that one headlight and wondering if I'd met the end. I shivered, cold and jittery. It felt like I had the energy to jump a car, but I was also unstable enough to fall over at any minute.

"—llie might be in shock," Bryce said, causing me to tune into the conversation. "She hasn't responded to us in a while."

I moved a little bit, already feeling my muscles seizing up from sitting still too long.

How long had I been out of it?

Natasia had pulled the van away, parking it only a handful of feet away to act as a shield in case that battering ram of a car came back to try to finish the job.

Jace—no, CJ was kneeling on the ground beside my open door.

Open door. That made me snort.

Open door.

The "open door" was an unrecognizable mess of twisted metal laying on the ground where it'd fallen.

"Callie," CJ said, using his hand to help me stay still. "Are you laughing?"

I coughed a little and then pointed to the metal on the ground beside him. "Open door," I said.

CJ looked beside him, an eyebrow rising on his forehead. "Yes," he said, drawing the word out. "Your door is open. Is that the door?"

"Yup," I said, leaning my head back against the headrest. "I'm dizzy," I said.

Footsteps sounded, scratching and grinding shattered glass into the pavement. I turned, my vision wobbling at the fast movement.

"Whoa," I said. Then I frowned. "Not again," I groaned, closing my eyes.

"What?" Corbin asked from somewhere in the backseat. "Callie, what's wrong?"

I pointed out the open door, nearly hitting CJ in the face because my depth perception was off. "Double-vision. Again." I stopped, catching a whiff of oranges. "Oh, no, wait. Never mind. There's actually two of them."

"Callie," one of the twins said, crouching down next to his brother.

"Jace," I said back.

He took my hand. "Damsel, we have to get you out of here before the cops show up."

"We do?" I asked, my head tilting to the side.

"Yes, we do. You don't exist, remember? Now... can you stand?" CJ asked as he went to work with his brother to help me from the car.

"Yeah, sure. Okay," I said, and then I passed out.

I woke up, hearing beeping next to my head. Ironically, it was almost in time with the pounding *inside* my head. My pulse felt like it was being squeezed through a spiked straw, constricting painfully with every second.

I went to sit up and groaned. Every single part of me hurt. My fingers hurt. My stomach hurt. The lights hurt my eyes...

I frowned.

My stinking ear hurt, and my ear wasn't even a muscle.

"You have a concussion," someone said from beside me. The voice was deep, soothing, and British.

I jerked to the side, nearly toppling over the side of the bed. That would've been exactly no fun at all considering the quick movement let me know that I was hooked up to many sensors and lines. The most painful of all had to be the needle from the IV, jammed into and taped on the delicate skin of my wrist. It earned a baleful look from me.

It wasn't honestly necessary for a little bump on the head, was it?

I looked around.

We were at Delta. Sunlight was filtering in the window, making me do a double-take. It had been night last time I recalled.

I glanced beside me, taking in the image of Payton Emerson, awake and healthy, other than the nasty bruising on the side of his forehead. It took me a second to realize he was in a hospital gown, in a wheelchair.

Noticing my gaze, he gave me a rueful look. "Don't fret, love. I'm not hurt. Duane gets this way whenever one of his team is in trouble. He refused to allow me anywhere without the wheelchair."

A smile tried to pull at the corners of my lips.

He narrowed his eyes. "Don't you go thinking I'm some poor sod that can't stand up to my mates. Duane started to wheel my IV line with me," he gave me a mysterious smile. "But I won that argument."

Kaz's bracelet was still on my wrist, even though the other stuff I'd been wearing was gone—including the beautiful, rose gold dress.

"Do you think you could get me unhooked too?"

Emerson raised an eyebrow at my question, looking downright haughty. "Is the sky purple?"

I choked a bit on my breath. "Uh... no?"

Emerson paused what he was doing. That upset me because he had been rolling forward in his wheelchair to unhook me from that tortuous IV. I gestured for him to continue on, but he looked crestfallen. "I'm partially colorblind. Is the sky truly not purple? Well then," he said, sounding as if he'd come to some great, life-changing revelation.

He went about trying to unhook me, but I kept my narrowed eyes on his face. He was good. He was *really* good. He looked innocent.

"I feel like you would know that the sky was blue, even if you were colorblind."

"You think so?" he asked, pressing down on the IV needle with a cloth as he slid it out of my wrist.

I paused. Surely, he would know. Even if he didn't see blue, knowing the color of the sky was elementary. He would've heard it in conversations, on movies, in songs, as descriptions in books if he read a lot.

"Yes," I said with resolution. "There's no way you've missed hearing people reference it as blue, not once in your entire life."

Emerson peaked under the wrapping, seemed satisfied, and pulled the gauze away. He met my eyes with his jade-green ones. "Well, love, beautiful and clever. I'm in trouble, aren't I?"

I looked away, fiddling with my hair. My head snapped back around to him. "Wait, how did you pick out the purple flowers for our date?"

"Callie, love," he said with some superiority. "I've been colorblind all my life. I think I know a few tricks to deal with it by now— especially since I'm only partially colorblind."

I leaned back against the scratchy, white pillows that felt like they were crafted from cardboard. I pointed at them. "What color are these?"

He gave me a look that spoke volumes. "I'm not playing this game with you."

"What game?"

"The game where you ask me what color something is. When I get it right, you don't believe I really can't see colors. When I get it wrong you try to explain what the color is. Corbin had a grand old time when he first found out. Drove me mad."

I sat back up. "The flowers! Our date!" Then I remembered why I was in the hospital in the first place. "The crash!"

"I must say… your order of importance intrigues me, love."

"Please don't therapize me. What happened? Did the police show up? Did they find that driver? Where's Bryce? Is he okay? Is he alive? Was his head injury worse than it looked?"

Emerson cleared his throat, holding up a finger to stop my endless questions. "Therapize?"

"It's a word. You're changing the subject."

"Oh, I know it's a word, love. It *is* my area of expertise after all. However, I'm impressed that you know it. With all the languages you've learned, I thought that you would have more holes in your vocabulary. Contrarily, you handle your words quite well."

"You're—"

"I know, I know. Changing the subject. Let me see... We were in a car crash involving two other vehicles. The police did show up, but you were safely ensconced within the Cardinals' van by that point, so you're not in any police reports. The van is right back at the repair shop. You're hard on vehicles. No sign of the driver. Bryce is fine. His parents could afford to buy out the entire floor here, but Duane stuffed him in the same room as me. He is okay, physically. Also, yes, he is alive—see previous answer, but not for much longer if he keeps whining about that bloody guitar of his. Did you know he has a name for it? Billie Joe. He calls the guitar—"

Emerson stopped, cleared his throat, and composed himself. "What was your last question? Oh, right. Was Bryce's head injury worse than it looked? I fear for his sanity, so it's very possible he is suffering some sort of internal brain trauma."

"You just called your teammate damaged."

"Did I?" Emerson asked with a careful tone in his voice. "What's a bloke got to do to get a decent cup of coffee around here?"

He looked around the empty room.

There wasn't much in the way of furniture other than a couple of dark green armchairs.

"I can see the question in your eyes, love. Just ask."

"What color are those ch—"

"Not," he stressed, "That question."

I opened my mouth and then closed it. Then I said, "I thought you would like tea."

He gave me a droll look. "Why, because I'm British?" His accent became more pronounced, overly posh. "Top o' the mornin' to you, ol' chap. Nice day for a full-English breakfast and a full-bodied Earl Grey tea, wouldn't you agree, darling?"

My lips twitched.

He frowned, not getting the reaction out of me that he'd expected or wanted. "Love, I don't sound like that. I don't even have an accent anymore. I lost it from living here so long."

I stared. I mean, ya, his accent wasn't so strong, but it was certainly there. Could he not tell? Was he deaf as well as blind?

"Don't give me that look, love. Now, do you want to know about the driver or not?"

I didn't want to drop it, but I really needed to know about the driver. "You said there wasn't any sign of him."

"True, but... Well, this is what we have so far," he pulled a grainy photo out from a folder. "Somehow CJ was able to backtrack the car's movements until he found this, and that was only after hours of digging."

"Hours? What time is it?" I asked, studying the picture.

There wasn't a lot to go on. It was a gas station. The picture showed a man in nondescript clothing. He was not the same person that had blown up the Cardinals' house.

"It's about 4 in the afternoon. You scared quite a few people by not waking up."

"I haven't been sleeping very much lately," I said. "So, does CJ have any leads on who the guy in the photo is?"

"Impossible to tell, I'm afraid. He was able to parse out that the man was about six-foot-tall, maybe 180 pounds. We were actually hoping that you'd have some insights since it appears they were after you."

"Welcome to my life," I said.

Six foot, slim but muscled...the list wasn't too long, but the options were disturbing. I doubted it was any of Tomas Costa's gang come to get me even though, after already eliminating the B&E guys, they were the most recent threat. They would have to be psychotic to follow me to the US after one measly encounter.

I blew out a breath. "It could be Grinley."

"We've been keeping tabs on him. It's possible but unlikely. That was the first thing Karl checked after watching the footage."

I looked up from the photo. "There was footage?"

"Traffic cam, the same thing that CJ used to track the guy in the first place."

I almost hated to look, but I had to. I had to know.

I leaned closer to the photo in my hands, inspecting. The person's jaw was visible, as well as part of his neck. Ivanov had a scar down the right side of his neck, and I just had this feeling…

The silver car flashed in my mind as it revved towards me, coldly trying again for that fatal blow.

"You see something. What?"

It was too blurry. Unless the image was mirrored, it was the right side of the figure, but I couldn't make out the shiny scar that ran down the length of Ivanov's face. Still though…that didn't mean it wasn't there.

"It's more of a… gut feeling. That person came at us from a side-street. They couldn't have been tailing us. That implies long-term surveillance or a team of people in your ear with access to some good technology. And the car… it was barely damaged. That's not cheap."

"Yes," he said, letting the word hang in the air.

"It was abandoned, wasn't it? The armored car?"

"Yes, it was dropped at that same gas station. He went inside to pay and never came back out. CJ thinks that they had already scoped the place out and discovered the holes in the camera coverage."

I took a long, slow blink. "I think…" My heart raced. "I think it might be Ivanov. Honestly, who else could it be? No one would go to such lengths to come after me. Any enemies from my past probably think I still work for Ivanov. You don't get on the wrong side of a guy like him. Not and live."

"So…the man trying to kill you is also keeping you alive?"

"It's possible. I've been in the crime world a long time. Even before Ivanov… Those people hold grudges like a hoarder with their collections. I'm sure there are other people out there that aren't too happy with me, but Ivanov would be the only one to make a move—other than Grinley—if they think I'm still 'his'."

"You know, one day, you're going to have to sit down and talk about your past."

I didn't contradict him out loud. Instead, I stared at that picture, wondering if it *had* been Ivanov in that silver car.

I paled. "Oh god, what if it *is* Ivanov? He could've been watching us for weeks."

Emerson rubbed the back of his neck. "More like months."

I dropped the paper. "What?"

He had my full attention, that was for sure.

"Well, it could be a coincidence, but Yolo seems to think that this particular car was at the Delta parking lot on your first day of training. There was a car that honked at you. She thought it was over a parking spot dispute at the time, but she said that it was a silver Mazda of a similar style with blacked-out windows."

I fell back into the pillows. "The whole time? He's been here the whole time?"

"It makes sense. You said that he would've gotten that information from that Delta agent that you believed to be deceased."

I had been nodding my head when I remembered something else. "That car that followed us from the airport..." I trailed off, looking in askance at him.

He must've been told about it as well because he nodded his head. "We haven't found footage from either incident, but it won't be long. Not with CJ on the case."

"So, it really was Ivanov behind the bombing. He almost followed us right to their house that day." I wiped a hand over my face, trying to figure out what to do. What *could* I do? I wanted to scream and cry and shout and demand to know why I was still alive.

I had a feeling I knew the answer though.

Nikolai Ivanov was *studying* me. He was taking notes, calculating and planning. He'd found where we lived, where we worked, where we traveled. He had to know about every person that I cared about by now.

Sabra was right. I couldn't leave them on their own. There wasn't a doubt that Ivanov would follow, but he wouldn't be leaving the Cardinals or the Delta teams alone like I'd originally hoped.

No, if Ivanov had known where I was this whole time, and I was still alive, it was because he wanted to make sure I hurt. He wanted to make me watch as he destroyed the small taste of freedom I hadn't even dared to hope for but had become so dependent on.

Ivanov would take out everyone that I cared about first. He would torture them, kill them, make them suffer for having ever shown kindness to me.

Maybe that's how Natasia was able to intercept him before the car could hit me. It wasn't just dumb luck that the Cardinals and Tate team were there. There was no such thing as dumb luck with him. He knew they were there. He was sending me a warning. He wanted me to worry and stress about what was coming.

He was going to kill them.

He was going to kill them all, and save me for last.

I shut down for a few hours, lost in my head and trying to come up with a good solution. Nothing was forthcoming.

If I left now, they'd all die. Maybe I could slip Ivanov's grasp, and I wouldn't be forced to watch. The outcome was still the same. However, if I stayed, maybe...*maybe* we had a fighting chance. Maybe Sabra was right before. We could work together. With their skills and resources combined with my experience with Ivanov... maybe.

A nurse had come and gone, going over my vitals. The sun had moved steadily across the sky, chasing shadows around the room. It was dark out now.

Emerson was back, sipping a coffee and pestering me to eat.

The good news was, surviving a car crash with him had made me much more comfortable around him. I was slowly coming out of the haze I'd been in, drawn to the sounds of the English man complaining about his wayward teammate and his never-ending pleas for his guitar.

Emerson paused what he was saying, giving me a look. "You're listening now. I can tell. Do you want me to continue?"

I bobbed my head a little bit and folded my hands across my lap. "Yes, please," I said, imitating what I thought it would sound like if he'd said it.

Emerson watched me for a moment, hesitating. "You're taking the piss outta me, aren't you?"

"I don't know what you're talking about."

"That! That right there. You're speaking with an accent."

"I don't have an accent."

"Yes, you do. Stop it."

"Hey!" a deep, raspy voice said from the doorway, cutting us off. "Good to see you awake, Babygirl. And Emerson, you're here. You ask her yet?"

"I was just getting to it," he said.

"He was just getting to it," I repeated.

"Callie," Emerson growled.

Doc Scott grinned a lopsided grin. "I see. You making fun of Emerson's accent?"

"I don't bloody well have an accent!"

I gave a slight smile. "He doesn't bloody—"

Emerson leaned forward, putting a hand over my mouth. His lips brushed against my ear. "You know, love, in England we believe in corporal punishment. Are you wanting spanked?"

My face went pale and then bloomed with red. I gulped and shook my head.

Emerson smirked, took his hand away, and leaned back in his wheelchair, more than satisfied with himself.

"What in the world did you say to her to get *that* kind of reaction?"

"Nothing for you to worry about, mate."

"Riiight," Doc Scott said. "Hey, whatever you say, man. I don't need your help getting reactions out of her anyway."

How very true. My face helpfully proved him right by changing to a new and uncharted level of red.

"See?" Doc Scott said with a roguish smile.

"What were you wanting to ask me?" I asked, desperate for a change of subject.

Emerson sat up, jutting his jaw out a bit. He adjusted his elbows on the armrests of the chair. It was when he went to smooth out his hospital gown that I realized he was fidgeting.

"Emerson," Doc Scott said, folding his arms across his chest. "You gonna chicken out now? After you had no problems swooping in earlier when I was trying to ask her out?"

"I had already—"

"Don't lie to me. I know it's not true. Besides, I'm the one hooking you up with outside food. One phone call. That's all I need to make, and your raincheck date will have to suffer through hospital food."

"Raincheck date?" I asked.

"Yes love, you see, we missed our date, so I wanted—" Emerson was cut off as the door to the room opened.

In came Corbin, dressed head to toe in black, wheeling a cart with some empty glasses on it. I was speechless. He winked at me, rolling the tray right up beside the hospital bed.

"Madame," he said with a phony French accent. He brandished his cell toward me. There was a picture of a vending machine pulled up. "My name is Corbin Myers. I'll be serving you today. May I take your beverage? As you can see, we have a wide variety of options that we chill specially for your enjoyment."

I blinked a couple of times. It was hard to take the 180 that my day had taken. I'd woken in a hospital after a car crash. Emerson and I had just been discussing the likelihood of it being Ivanov behind the incident, and then, bam. Now I was on a date? A raincheck date for the first date—which was fake. And neither of those times had I actually been asked out by the man himself.

Corbin cleared his throat and leaned over the side of the bed to gesture to his screen. "I prefer option D8 myself. A nice cran-apple juice that should pair nicely with your meal."

I shrugged and nodded, handing him back his phone.

"And for you, sir?" he asked Emerson.

"I'm good," Emerson said, holding up the paper cup of coffee he'd managed to get his hands on.

"Of course," Corbin said, spinning back to me. "I'll have your drink right out to you. By the way, you look simply ravishing today."

His outlandishness made me crack a smile. I was in a hospital gown, my hair was knotty, and, from the feel of it, I had an ugly bruise on my forehead.

"If you're done flirting with my date, mate," Emerson said dryly, but a quick glance his way confirmed that he was more exasperated than upset.

Corbin turned to him. "Aww, Emerson, don't be jealous, you look ravishing yourself." He leaned in close and pinched the fabric of Emerson's hospital gown. "Is that Armani?"

Emerson smoothed down the seafoam green gown, dislodging Corbin's hand. He sent him a narrowed look. Corbin withstood it a grand total of about two seconds before he hastened a quick retreat.

"Whelp," Corbin said, "That's my cue to go. If you need me for anything, don't hesitate to ask." He turned to me, grabbed up my hand in his, gave me a smoldering stare that was only intensified by his sky-blue eyes, and kissed my hand. "I'll be ready to serve you. Anything you want. Just ask. *An-y-thing*."

"Corbin!" Emerson's voice had risen in pitch as if he was losing his cool at the persistence.

I had a feeling his teammates, especially Corbin and Doc Scott, were some of the only people that could pull off the feat of ruffling his feathers.

Corbin darted away out into the hallway.

I turned back to face Emerson and felt something in my hand. It felt like paper. I cocked my head to the side and started to unroll it as Emerson spoke up.

"Callie," he said, seeming somewhat out of sorts and not noticing what I was doing. I continued unfolding the paper, curious about where it had come from and when it'd gotten there without my noticing. "I must apologize on behalf of my immature mates. They gave me their word that--"

"A phone number?" I blurted out, staring down at the scrap of paper in bafflement.

"And I—beg your pardon?"

I showed him the paper.

Doc Scott burst out laughing, having some idea about what was in my hand and why.

Emerson's jaw clenched before he let out a resigned sigh. When he saw that I was still confused, he said, "Corbin's doing, I presume."

"B-but...I already have his number," I said, perplexed beyond belief.

Why would he go to the trouble of slipping me his phone number when he'd programmed it into my phone right before we left? He couldn't have forgotten so soon that he'd given it to me.

"I--" Emerson cleared his throat into his hand, but I thought that I caught a hint of that enigmatic smile. Even when he'd gotten himself under control, his jade eyes betrayed his amusement. "Forgive me, love. I'm not laughing at you. It's just that your face is an open-book. I can see your thoughts, and I find them very endearing. You see, Corbin's actions were more directed in jest at me."

When I only felt more bewildered, he carried on, his smile growing larger.

"When a person is out on a date, sometimes a waiter or waitress might try to slip their phone number to one of the people on the date. This is an invitation to leave their initial date and be with them. It's also a sign of disrespect towards the person that they are with since they are propositioning their date right in front of them. No, don't feel upset, love," he said at my distraught look. "Corbin was only playing a prank, and he did it without ill intentions. I believe he intended to get a laugh out of you, though he got a laugh out of me instead."

I felt relief at that, holding out the piece of paper, "Well then, maybe he should've given it to you," I said.

He gripped the paper and pocketed it, a small smile playing at his full lips. "Indeed, Callie, indeed."

Chapter 29

I was a lot more relaxed after Corbin's prank. Emerson had been amused but not at my expense. He had been kind and explained things to me instead of laughing at my ignorance. I knew that if anything else happened on our impromptu, raincheck date that I didn't understand, he would take care of me.

My shoulders loosened a little bit.

"Duane, you may leave at any time," Emerson said, reminding me that Doc Scott hadn't left.

Doc Scott gave a crooked smile, his onyx eyes landing on my face. "Why would I leave? Remember? I'm hooking you up with outside food. You've got to play nice."

"If that's your idea of an ultimatum, then we'll take our chances with the hospital food," Emerson replied, not missing a beat.

"Ouch," Doc Scott said, clutching his chest. "You hurt me deep, man."

"That's what she said," a voice drawled from the doorway.

I looked over. Bryce was there, dressed in tight black with some maroon accents. He had a bandage on his forehead, but that was all that showed from the crash.

"Why isn't he stuck in a hospital bed? He hit his head," I pointed out.

"Because Babygirl," Doc Scott said. "He didn't lose consciousness, and both you and Emerson did."

"Trying to hospitalize me?" Bryce asked, walking into the room. "You ought to be ashamed, especially since I come bearing gifts."

He tossed me a bottle of cran-apple juice, fresh from the vending machine. I took one of the empty glasses from the rolling cart Corbin had left behind and poured my juice into it.

Emerson rolled closer. "Is Corbin not brave enough to bring that himself?"

Bryce whipped his head to the side to get the hair out of his eyes. "More like he's not stupid enough to bring it himself after giving your date his phone number."

"Well," Doc Scott said, leaning up from the counter he'd propped himself against. He straightened his shirt. "I've got to get to the clinic. Someone's bringing in a mom and her litter of pups because they aren't feeding from her. I'll talk to you guys later. Babygirl, enjoy your date. Because I'm next."

My eyes got big, wondering what exactly that meant.

I avoided his eyes immediately, unable to hold his gaze as he stared so intently at me with those obsidian eyes.

It was only after he'd moved that I was able to look up. Doc Scott had turned his back my way as he bent over the counter to write something on my chart, and my eyes were drawn down without a choice. The dip along the spine of his back, his massive, muscled shoulders, and his—I coughed and looked away.

When I heard a deep belly laugh, I turned back around to see Doc Scott giving me a knowing smile.

My eyes widened in realization.

He'd done it on purpose, and I'd fallen right for it.

"Next time, Babygirl," Doc Scott said, his raspy voice thick and deep, making me shudder. He was a man built for activities done in the dark and every action was geared towards making it as hot as possible.

Doc Scott turned away and left, a strolling saunter to his steps, but I adamantly kept my eyes on the glass in my lap. No way was I going to give him the satisfaction of knowing I'd watched him leave.

"Are you alright, Callie?"

My eyes flew up to Emerson. I replayed my actions in my head and winced, guilt showing on my face. I was supposed to be on a date with Emerson, even if he still seemed nothing but amused and still a little exasperated at the antics of his friends.

Was it normal for a person to not feel upset when their date was so blatantly checking out another person? Then, the answer came to me.

This wasn't a real date. I knew that. It was just Emerson following through on his plan to save me from the wicked Doc Scott. And it was a raincheck date at that.

I was able to relax once more with that reasoning and carry on a conversation with him. I started off with an explanation about what had happened to the Cardinals' house, skimming over certain details and describing how we'd ended up at Hartstrait.

Emerson was alarmed to find out that Ivanov had discovered the location of Cardinals' house so fast.

He also asked about how we were liking the complex. Unfortunately, to answer him truthfully, I had to explain how Yolo wasn't a fan of the small, cramped space. He just nodded his head, his eyes calculating something I couldn't begin to guess at. He moved the topic of conversation to how my training and classes were going. I explained the best that I could because, frankly, they weren't going that well.

He was a perfect gentleman about my shortcomings because— sensing my unease—he changed the topic. He started talking about himself and what he liked to do in his free time when he wasn't haranguing his team to keep them in line.

I found it endlessly fascinating to learn more about the mystery that was Payton Emerson. It was also much more comfortable to have the pressure off of me to carry on the conversation.

It was after fifteen minutes of talking that I realized Bryce had stepped out at some point.

Emerson had just finished telling me about how he grew up in England with his mom when my phone started blowing up.

"Oh, I'm so sorry!" I said, scrambling to reach it on the bedside table and silence it.

I hadn't known it was on sound in the first place, and my cheeks inflamed when I recognized the words, "Kiss de Girl," being sung by a Jamaican voice followed by a high-pitched caterwauling male that was terribly off-key.

I opened the phone, pushing as many buttons as possible, trying to get the thing to stop. It wasn't working, and eventually, it cut off only to start back up again. "Sha-la-lalalala don't be scared—"

"May I?" Emerson asked, holding his hands out.

My cheeks were bright red. I offered no resistance, eager to get the device away. I practically tossed it at him. "Please!"

He took it in his hands, hit a single button, and the devil-device stopped.

"Emers—Payton, I'm so sorry. I don't even know what--"

"Who is: The Irate Irish?" he asked, bringing my thoughts to a screeching halt.

"What?" I asked.

He turned the phone to show me that I had two missed calls from someone called 'The Irate Irish.' My mouth opened and closed as I fished for an explanation. "I-I don't kn--"

I was interrupted again as another incoming call lit up the screen. This time, the caller ID said, "Hottest Guy in the World."

In slow motion, I watched as Emerson started to turn the phone back around to face him and see who was calling. To be honest, I wasn't entirely sure who it was either, but I knew that I didn't want Emerson to read *that* caller ID.

What would he think of me? I was on a not-really date with him and being called by someone I'd supposedly dubbed as the hottest guy in the world.

"No—don't!" I blurted out, my brain deciding that the last minute would be an ideal time to start functioning again.

It was too late though.

Emerson raised an eyebrow, shooting me a quick glance, before answering the phone. He put it up to his ear, listening. His eyebrows both raised as recognition dawned in his eyes. "Ah, Jace Tate. I should've suspected it was you." He was quiet for a moment before he frowned. "No...What do you mean that Aleks--"

The rest of his sentence was cut off as the door to the room banged open, revealing none other than Aleks. Beyond Aleks, CJ was just barely visible as he peeked around his massive teammate's body. He had an apologetic look on his face.

"I'm sorry," CJ said. "We tried to stop him."

There was a sincerity in CJ's warm caramel eyes that made me believe him, even as it also made me realize that same sincerity was missing from the other eyes in the doorway that I could see.

My thoughts were confirmed when the Irish Cardinal moved up to enter.

"Speak for yer-self there, boyo, I didn't," Darcy said, going to one of the few chairs in the room and plopping down. Triz gave a bright and happy wave at me, and Natasia gave me a solemn nod before joining her sisters at the far side of the room.

"Don't mind us," Darcy called, looking at her phone.

I wanted the floor to swallow me up. It was too much. I was so embarrassed. There was no way that I could look at Emerson's face to even try to gauge his reaction to the crashers.

"You can mind me," Aleks said either boldly or mistakenly. I wasn't sure which it was. He came up to stand right next to Emerson and me. Ya, I was leaning towards boldly.

Aleks picked up Emerson's coffee and took a long sip. I had no doubts that if there were any other chairs left unoccupied Aleks would've drug one up to the bedside to join us.

CJ came up and grabbed Aleks, dragging him over to the wall next to the door.

"Where's Jace?" I sputtered out to CJ, thinking that if their leader knew of this, he wouldn't have allowed it to happen.

"Glad you're thinking about me, damsel," Jace said from the door. "We were in the area, saw the lights on, and thought we'd stop by."

He went to join CJ and Aleks at their corner of the room. I went to follow their progress with my eyes and spotted balloons and flowers that blocked them. They were out of my line of sight and that made me nervous.

I looked at the Cardinals over Emerson's shoulder. The girls were settled in, opening a laptop and discussing what was playing on the screen.

I didn't have to stress about trying to figure out what to say for long, because at that moment, the door to the room opened once more and Brock entered, carrying some bags of food. They smelled heavenly, like spices and coconut—maybe Pad Thai.

Brock paused in the doorway. His winter-gray eyes took one look around the room, and he summed up how I was feeling in one simple sentence. "What the fuck?!"

Chapter 30

Brock forcibly put the carryout bags down on the rolling cart beside us, causing the silverware and glasses to tinkle and jingle at the strength of it, but his eyes were already on his first victims, the Tate team.

"One second," he gruffly said to Emerson and me. He headed the Tate team's way.

I shrunk down into the hospital bed, not able to look back and watch the scene unfold, my mind repeating over and over endlessly, 'Ohgodohgodohgod...'

"What are you fuckers doing here?" Brock boomed out.

"Checking on *Medvezhonok*," Aleks said.

"Fine, you checked on her. Now get out."

"Why do we have to leave? You leave."

"I brought the food. I don't have to leave!"

"Wait, excuse me?" Emerson said, jumping into the conversation. "You're *not* leaving?"

Brock looked back at us, his thick, black eyebrows furrowing down. His look clearly said that his teammate should drop it for now.

"Well, are you going to kick the ladies out as well?" CJ asked.

"Fuck yes, I am," Brock said.

Movement across from me caught my attention, and I looked up to see the Cardinals were about to join the argument. My eyes rounded, and I tried to get them to stop, but they either didn't see me or weren't all that worried about my sanity.

"The fuck you are, Brock Johnson," Darcy said, her cheeks turning pink. I was able to recognize her classic "I'll brawl you and maybe I'll lose, but it won't be easy" look as it started to spread across her face.

Brock shouted back towards them. "The fuck I am! Callie and Emerson are on a date!"

"So nice of someone to remember that," Emerson said in a calm voice, but it was largely ignored.

Darcy went to jump up, but Triz was on her lap and hadn't moved to let her up.

Triz turned her exuberant smile on. "We want to be here with Callie. It was getting boring out in the waiting room reading magazines." Triz continued on, looking innocent. "Besides, your team has been crashing their 'date' the entire evening."

"Yeah, but--"

"No," Natasia said, smoothly getting to her feet. "No, it is okay. We will go," she said, pulling out keys. "Come on ladies," she said.

Darcy and Triz gave her a strange look, looking like they wanted to protest, but they listened.

There was silence around the room as everyone watched them get ready to leave, waiting for the other shoe to drop. It was like we all knew that it was too easy.

They were almost to the door when Natasia stopped, pinning me with her ice-blue eyes. "Callie, I'll get your clothes. I talked to one of the nurses, and they said that you're cleared to leave if we can be there to take care of you."

"What? Me?" I asked.

"Fuck NO!" Brock boomed. His sentiments were chorused by several voices behind me. I turned back to see the commotion had drawn the rest of the Emerson team to the open doorway—including Doc Scott who had supposedly left for his vet clinic to help out some newborn puppies.

"Yes, you," Natasia said to me, a secret smile on her face as she ignored the reactions of the others. "It was Karl's orders that we keep an eye on you while the threat of Ivanov is so high. If we are to be kicked out, I'm afraid you'll have to go with us, *mladshaya sestra*."

There was silence in the room as Natasia efficiently dropped that atomic wrench in everyone's plans.

Of course, who else would break up the silence, but...

"Well," Aleks said loudly, slapping his palms against the wall and pushing up. "If *Medvezhonok* is not staying, then neither am I."

Voices started up again, and I realized with a surprising amount of clarity that even if I looked to Emerson to settle the whole thing, it wouldn't go over all that well. He would be accused of favoritism one way or another. I was the closest thing to an impartial party in the entire place. The Cardinals didn't back down easily, current case in point. I'd have to start standing up for myself eventually.

I took a big swallow of cran-apple, and sat up, avoiding looking at Emerson for fear that I'd clam up. I turned over towards the Tate team, watching as Brock and Aleks argued back and forth, nearly at each other's throat. I pulled my legs over the edge of the bed, made sure my gown was in order, and walked up to them. I placed a hand on either of their biceps.

They were two of the biggest guys I knew, and it was amazing to me how a simple touch got them to stop. They turned.

I looked at Brock.

"Brock," I said, noticing that I didn't have to speak at a loud volume because everyone had quieted. "I would really like to eat with Emerson. Would it be okay if they stayed?"

Aleks's muscles bunched and shifted under my hand as he crossed his arms and smirked at Brock in triumph.

Brock on the other hand, only tensed up further and was practically grinding his teeth as he gritted out, "Sure, *dušo*."

I turned back to look at the victorious look on Aleks's face when I had a thought. I knew I'd have to stop doing this. It wasn't fair to the guys, but right now, it was the only thing I could think of to take one of the guys down a peg or two, other than—well, throwing them over my shoulder as I'd done in Brazil.

I leaned up to Brock and kissed him on his cheek. "Thank you, *Byapok*."

I went back to the bed and sat back down, knowing that Aleks's self-satisfied smirk had vanished even without looking back to check.

Corbin groaned from the doorway. "What the Hello Kitty! Why does he always get the cute cheek-kisses?"

Brock rubbed his cheek before he headed back to the hall, hopefully to finish cooling down his temper. The Cardinals returned back to their seats.

Only when conversation resumed and the rest of the Emerson team disappeared back into the hallway, was I able to let out the tension in my shoulders and take a deep breath.

"A commendable job, Callie," Emerson said, smiling at me once more.

It did a little to soothe my worries, but it didn't erase them completely.

"Eme—Payton, I'm sorry. This hasn't exactly been a good date." His expression became guarded, and I realized that my lack of social skills had landed me in hot water. I rushed to explain. "What I mean is you seemed to plan out the perfect evening yesterday, the flowers, the restaurant, the dress...even if it wasn't a real date, I can tell you had everything planned down to the last detail. And--"

"Callie, I can assure you that—even if this started out as a way to save you from the likes of the devilish Doc Scott—I had considered this date to be real. Very much so."

I froze, thinking about the implications behind that. He wanted to date me for real? Or was going on a date different from dating? It was, wasn't it? Did he want to be dating? Trying to determine which one it was, I remembered something that caused me to frown. "But you didn't get angry when Corbin flirted and stuff. I mean, you seemed angry but not really."

"How very observant of you." His jade eyes studied me for a moment as he picked at his food. He seemed to be thinking something over, weighing it in his mind before coming to a decision.

He leaned forward and lowered his voice to give us some privacy. "Callie, I have always been completely honest with you and have tried to be transparent when it comes to my team's intentions for you as long as that transparency wouldn't stunt your growth as a person. I find myself debating whether this would be one of those times where it would, in fact, be detrimental to your progress. I won't deny, you've grown tremendously as an individual and a team player. I don't want to jeopardize that."

I nodded but only felt all the more confused. Slightly disappointed at what had to be the politest dismissal ever experienced, I went to lean back in my seat, but he gripped my hand. I was trapped, prey to his intense gaze.

"And it's only because of that truly impressive growth that I am willing to leave you with this: Any interactions between yourself and members of my team should not be over-analyzed. We are a unique group of men that find it more pleasing to...share and not let things come between us as a team."

My mouth dropped open as my mind went to the absurd conclusion that he meant they all wanted to share...well...me.

Then my logic and sanity came back as I reasoned that couldn't have possibly been what he'd meant. There was five of them! It was insane.

Payton leaned back, going to open the carry-out containers and cutting off any more discussion. I envied his ease in the aftermath of the bomb he'd just dropped.

I couldn't taste the food they'd ordered as I mulled his words over and over.

He'd opened a Pandora's box of his own inside my mind. It was an idea that was festering and growing. Being with them, with all of them...it set a yearning down deep in my soul. I remembered the family pictures at their unfinished—at least, as far as I knew—house. I mentally implanted myself into those family pictures right along with them. I thought about how each of the guys was so unique and dear to me. Could Payton *really* have meant for me to be with all of them?

The bite I'd taken turned to ash in my mouth as a thought came to me. He'd said everyone on *his team*. I only just managed to stop from turning—only just. The Tate team was very near and dear to me as well. Would they not want to be friends anymore if I was with the Emerson team? Would I even see them anymore? I forced down the bite I'd taken.

No, if I had to choose, I'd have to be with the Cardinals. There was no way I'd be forced into any more ultimatums. I cared too much, too equally for both groups of men. And, honestly, I was Free-Callie. I could choose what I wanted. I wasn't being controlled by Veseli, Ivanov, or even Delta. I didn't want that. And if I wanted to be with them, even if it was just as friends, then that's the way it would have to be. I refused to feel guilty for any of my interactions with them. I had too much lost time and experiences to make up for in my life.

Firm in my resolve, I finished my dinner with a little more gusto, feeling like a weight had been lifted.

The evening was perfect, even with—or perhaps because of—the hectic additions.

After dinner, they'd cleared the rolling cart and moved it to the side as Bryce pulled up music on his phone. With our gowns fastened, Doc Scott cleared the two of us to dance, with the caveat that he got a turn as well. The dance with Payton went off well, and Doc Scott stepped up to take over but then Corbin cut in. Not one to be left out, Aleks had bodily picked me up at the end of Corbin's song and started doing a high-energy dance to a waltz song no less. He didn't let that stop him though. He was throwing, dipping, and spinning me in a breathless, dizzying experience. He lifted me so high one time that I nearly hit my head off the ceiling, drawing the ire of Doc Scott. My muscles loosened up more and more the longer I moved them, and I ignored the headache from the bruise—giddy on nerves and excitement.

I'd kissed Aleks on the cheek, thanking him and also silently sticking to my determination not to favor Emerson's team. Then I laughed out loud as he pointed to his other cheek in demand. I indulged him and kissed it as well but had to draw the line when he pointed to his lips.

It was like an unspoken rule was broken, and after dancing with a person each from both teams—other than my original date, the rest were lining up for their chance—err, dance.

I'd cycled through dancing with everyone except Doc Scott who'd—ironically, since this had all started because of him trying to ask me on a date—had to leave halfway through to go deal with that litter of puppies. Apparently, they were a real thing.

The Cardinals had finished the night, by trying to teach me some...ah...girl moves in a group dance.

Natasia had smirked as she cut in on a shocked Corbin, his jaw dropping as she led me over to Darcy and Triz. I tried to keep up. I did, but at the first pop and drop, I'd frozen, very aware of every male in the room. I made the excuse that I was too sore which no one believed after the jitterbug moves Aleks had pulled. They didn't call me out on it though. The girls had laughed and pulled me close until we were a jumping, dancing mass of giggles.

It might not have been a typical date or even an atypical date, but it was perfect.

...especially when the night ended with my very first kiss on the lips.

Epilogue

Well, I think that went rather well," CJ said, flopping down on a chair.

They'd all made sure that Callie was home from the hospital and settled into the apartment, Emerson-Team-free, before they decided to call it a night.

Jace had to agree. "Ya, but I'm worried. I've never known the Emerson team to pursue something so fiercely. They're really set on this." He pulled out some cards for a game of solitaire.

CJ pulled out his laptop, doing something on it. Jace eyed his twin's screen out of the corner of his eyes. He'd noticed that lately, CJ had been working on something with determination, but whenever he'd asked his brother about it, CJ clammed up and shouted some random excuse. It was starting to worry him.

"Well, that's okay because we're determined too," Aleks said, "They may have got the droplets on us with first date, but we stop it." He bellowed out a laugh. "Ha! Did you see Rock's face when we came in room?" Aleks chuckled a full-bellied laugh. "Money-less!"

"Priceless," Jace grumbled, too preoccupied with recalling the night and playing his game of solitaire to put any effort into correcting his teammate. He bit his lip, and then realized what he was doing and who exactly it reminded him of. He wondered how he could possibly be picking up one of Callie's habits. Sure, they were neighbors, but had they really been spending that much time together? "So..." he hedged carefully. "Is this something we all agree on then?"

The room quieted, turning serious.

Jace carried on, "I mean, after Bridget, I wasn't sure how you all felt about...you know."

"Sharing?" CJ offered.

"Ya, that," he said, somewhat awkward and scared to put his feelings out on the line. He'd thought Bridget had been the one, but in the end, their relationship had been too much for her and, months and months later, Jace was finally able to admit that maybe she had been too much for them as well. It'd taken him that long to come to the conclusion, but there it was. Healing.

"I don't want to scare her," CJ said, speaking up for the first time in a soft voice. "What if she doesn't realize that all of our touches mean we want something more?"

Aleks clapped CJ on the shoulder. "We have been working on that, remember? Pretty soon her mind will be muddy like mine. Maybe muddier."

"Dirty," Jace said offhandedly but sitting up quickly in thought, "But...I think that CJ has a point. I mean think about it. Callie hasn't had any friends...at least not that we know of and certainly not as an adult. She was taken when she was young, right?"

CJ nodded.

"Well," Jace continued, "What if she doesn't know that our touches are anything but how friends interact with each other?"

The room was quiet again in thought.

"It's possible. Of course, she could know what they mean but not be interested in us that way at all. You said it yourself. She's on the Cardinals' team. Aren't they all...together? Or, she's been through so much. Maybe she's not interested in any relationships right now, period," CJ said at length. "I guess that if we do plan to continue, we'll have to make it more obvious. That way there's no question."

"You give me permission," Aleks said, grinning, poking at CJ's ear and making him jump and swat at the air. "I will be almost illegally obvious about intentions for *Medvezhonok.*"

"Which brings us back to the previous problem," Jace said, "Not to get ahead of ourselves, but I don't want things to end up as they did with..."

'Bridget,' their eyes all said but no one mentioned it out loud.

"It won't. We jumped onto Bridget too fast. We have known *Medvezhonok* for months. We do this slow. The right way. No sleeping together after first day."

"Okay, okay, stop, stop," Jace said, holding up his hands. It was hard to predict what would come out of the shameless teammate, so it was better to head it off before it got too far.

"What? You don't want me to talk about sex? Is no big deal."

"I don't care. My brother is here you idiot."

"I'm your *bratva*."

"My *real* brother."

"That hurts."

"Get over it," Jace said, rolling his eyes.

Aleks got over it in a flash, showing he hadn't been offended in the first place. "Wait, so you two have never...you know..." he waved his hand between the two of them.

Jace and CJ's eyes both shot wide open followed by adamant disgust. "What? No way!" they said at the exact same time, probably one of the first times they'd had such uniform and twin-like reactions.

"That's incest!" Jace said.

"And besides, I don't think of Jace that way," CJ said.

"Same, brother."

Aleks chuckled, "You agree on something? World must be ending. But that is not what I mean. I mean...there's that twin thing. Guys like twins, *da*? It is on all American shows. Why would not girls feel same way? Are you saying you wouldn't do that if Callie asked? It might be good. For her."

Jace spoke up, "You have met Damsel, right? You don't think she can recognize our flirting but you're worried that she might one day ask CJ and me to be the middle of a twin sandwich?"

"No, that's...well, *da*, I guess that's what I'm saying."

Jace rubbed a hand down his face. "Not answering that. Moving on. We're getting off-topic, or at the very least way ahead of ourselves here. Do we agree on our thoughts concerning Callie?"

"Wait, wait, wait," CJ said. "Does anyone else feel weird about this?"

"About what?" Aleks asked.

"I don't know...discussing this and planning it out. It's like we're trying to trap Callie or something. It feels...presumptuous? Preemptive? Slightly predatory?"

"I disagree. This is not anything you would not think about to yourself before seducing someone. It is an old game of men and women. Men pursue and strategize, and sometimes the pursuing is done by the woman. And then the other party can choose to be wooed or not. You learn what a woman likes, you plan out dates, you think about your intentions for her. This is all before anything might become official." Jace shrugged. "It's normal. We're just externalizing a normally internal process."

"That's what she said," Aleks said.

Jace gave him a long look. "Have you been hanging out with Bryce a lot?"

"*Da*, we were stuck in that closet for hours during CIA mission to get Callie's picture. He taught me phrase."

"Moving on, then. It's not anything that you don't plan or think about mentally. It just feels odd saying it all out loud," Jace said. "...as off-topic as Aleks may have got, it brings up something important. We already know the Emerson team has discussed this among themselves. We winged it a bit with Bridget, but we need to discuss things both among ourselves, and, when she's ready for it, with Callie. This is not a normal relationship. But none of us are normal. That doesn't mean that it'll poof and magically work. We have to be prepared." He paused here to let the significance sink in. "And that means be prepared for anything. Even if that thing might be threesomes or, help us— foursomes."

Aleks let out a loud whistle, "Whoa there, *bratva*," he waggled his eyebrows. "Pretty ambitious there. Who knew you had these muddy fantasies wiggling around in your mind?"

"I'm not ashamed to say it," Jace said. "I may not have been thinking them particularly, but since your raunchy mind brought it up in the first place—we need to consider the possibility and the likelihood of it. What kind of guys would agree to share a girl among them? You both are at least okay with knowing others will be having sex with your girl. It's not exactly that big of a leap to jump to sharing together if all parties are consenting."

They thought about it, contemplating his words.

CJ spoke up after a moment. "So, with that being said, on the topic of consent--"

"You're not going to pass out rape whistles, are you?" Jace joked, earning him a pillow in the face from his twin.

"Anyway, I know we don't usually do this, but...I think that we should take a page out of the Emerson team's book."

"Since when did we start having to learn from the rookies?" Jace asked with an eyebrow cocked.

"Since they've most likely been talking with Corbin's family that successfully raised four kids with three dads and a mom," CJ said.

"Corbin has three dads?" Aleks asked, surprised.

"Yep, and they've all been together with his mom since before his oldest sister, Rebecca was born."

Jace made a disgruntled noise. "And like the good boys they are, they've probably been doing their homework. But I guess we can learn a thing or two from them. I know we're sort of black sheep amongst Delta, but even the rebellious ones have to know the rules to know exactly how far they can be pushed. Don't want them to have any advantage."

CJ said, "We need to get it out in the open to avoid any doubts or insecurities. We don't normally talk about feelings and stuff, but I'd like to on this. So...do you all wish to try to...uh, court? Sure, do you all wish to court Callie? We've been on a date with her, kind of, so I feel like you should have an idea about what you feel."

Aleks instantly responded. "*Da.*"

Jace was a little slower to go. He was like that: slow with his heart, but also slow to let go. He'd taken Bridget's departure the hardest. Finally, he said, "Yes."

"That's fully agreed then," CJ said. "To also be clear, do you agree that our end goal is to bring Callie onto our team as well?"

The yeses were even faster this time.

"Should we call Emerson team? Make them sweat?" Aleks asked. "Let them know our intentions for *Medvezhonok*?"

Jace grinned. "No, let them have their night. Let them think they won something by sneaking in a date with Callie. Corbin may not have made any major pranks against us yet, but there's no need to poke the bear or even alert them to our plans. We'll go for the sneak attack. They won't know what hit them."

About the Author

A little about me. I love to read, write, travel, and drink tea. I especially love it when I can do more than one of those at a time. I have too many different series started, but all of them are definitely reverse-harem. It took me years to finish my first book, but I'm so glad I did!

My style is very dark and leans towards paranormal and thriller themes when I write and read. If I'm trying to write, and I don't have time to read until I get inspired, I like to listen to music. That'll usually get me out of a block and back to writing!

Keep an eye out for the third book in the 6-book series about Callie Jensen, *Cardinal of Hope.*

For more information, go to https://www.miasmantz.com/

Other places to follow:

OTHER BOOKS BY THIS AUTHOR:

Reverse-Harem Series

The Cardinal Series:

The Cardinal Bird (Book 1)
Cardinal Caged (Book 2)
Cardinal of Hope (Book 3) – Spring of 2020
The Cardinal Sin (Book 4) – Coming Soon!
Cardinal Rose (Book 5) – Coming Soon!
The Red Cardinal (Book 6) – Coming Soon!

Paranormal Reverse-Harem Series

The User-Friendly Guide to Ghosts Series:

Before the Guide (Book 1) – Spring of 2020
Prewriting the Guide (Book 2) – Coming Soon!

Sneak Peek at Book 3 of the Cardinal Series: <u>Cardinal of Hope</u>

Available: Spring of 2020

Cardinal of Hope
By: Mia Smantz

Book 3 of The Cardinal Series

Prologue

Goosebumps pricked my skin, raising up and down my arms in the over-cooled room. The office was already near frigid temperatures, and I could *still* hear the sound of the AC running. I was at Delta, the secret facility established by the CIA for their agents to work outside the laws and red-tape.

Of course, that could be bad, but it wasn't. It was less black-ops and illegal and more about bending the rules and expediting things that would otherwise be barred by mounds of paperwork. It worked surprisingly well.

Take me, for instance. I'd been one of those cases that had benefitted said expedited process when they'd gone in and saved me from near-death in Russia. After finding out all of my acts of terrorism and hacking had been committed while under duress, they'd even made sure to help clear my existence from the CIA while I was still hiding from my kidnappers.

My gaze was automatically drawn to the movement in an otherwise motionless room.

Dr. Harper leaned back in his chair, his fingers steepled together in front of his chest as he eyed me.

He was an older man as proven by the salt-colored strands that were starting to season his copper-toned hair. He was my appointed psychologist at Delta even though he'd only minored in it. His doctor title came from his degree in fine arts which was appropriate since he'd made reading me an art form over the past few months since I'd come here.

I eyed him back.

The clock ticked on the wall. It created a staccato rhythm that punctuated the hush of the room, joining the gentle swish of the air conditioner. The clock seemed to say that time was wasting away in the extended silence.

However, whereas I was content to allow the minutes to slip away, Dr. Harper was probably feeling every wasted second. At least, that was what I was hoping for. Then maybe he'd ease off a bit.

His light blue eyes, almost as bright as Corbin's, studied my face.

I tried not to fidget in my seat.

Birds chirped away outside, though none of them ran into the glass, thank goodness. Dr. Harper's office was on the outermost perimeter of the building, affording him a wall of glass that left a tremendous view. Because of the one-way mirror that made up all of the windows, we could see outside, but people on the streets would only see an abandoned building—a false facade for the secret organization that served them well.

Norfolk was a beautiful place to have such a view of, so it was great that the CIA had footed the bill for the special windows. Delta was in a tall building. Depending on the room we were in, we could peek out and see through the megalithic giants of some of the other buildings in the city and catch a glimpse of the ocean as the sun glittered and sparkled off its surface.

Dr. Harper's office was set up so that his desk was beside the glass instead of in front of it. I didn't blame him. If I had an office with the view he had, I'd do the same. I had never understood why people would put their desks facing inwards when they had a wall of glass to view out. The layout meant that I was also beside the glass. I could look down at the people on the street far below as they moved about with their daily lives, unaware of being so close to the hi-tech facility.

I watched as a group of teenagers walked by, out of school for the summer. The heatwave had hit with a ferociousness that reminded me of my time in Pennsylvania as a child. I'd suffered many hot summers there before I was kidnapped.

Based on the beginnings of the Norfolk summer so far, I could tell that summer here wasn't going to be as hot or muggy as Pennsylvania, not with the cool, constant breeze coming in off the Atlantic Ocean. However, I'd been locked away in Russia for a good part of my life where the temperatures ranged from cold to colder. Any type of prolonged summer heat was going to take some getting used to.

My legs weren't sweaty, thanks to the frigid temperatures in the building. That was good, otherwise I would've been sticking to the seat of the chair what with the short shorts Triz had included in my ensemble for the day.

Triz liked trying to bond with me through clothes even though neither of us had a modicum of fashion. She was a 5'0" Brazilian goddess with hair as voluptuous and lush as her perfectly-portioned body. She drove a motorcycle when there wasn't a threat hanging over our lives, so—according to some of her teammates—she was the ultimate male fantasy.

However, Triz's motorcycle had been destroyed when Nikolai Ivanov, the Russian mob I'd been saved from, had bombed the house. Triz had turned her free-time to trying to be girlier and dragging me along for the ride. Even though I'd much rather be creating a new code online or trying to replicate C.J. Tate's beast of a computer, I felt guilty enough to pander to her wishes without protesting.

Well, I pandered without protesting *much.*

Thoughts of Triz led to Darcy, the fiery, redheaded member of the Cardinals—a team of five trained women on the international payroll of Delta for their ability to speak multiple languages. They were named after the Italian cardinal Guiseppe Mezzofanti. He was a hyperpolyglot said to have known as many as 70 languages and able to switch between them as easily as toggling between apps on a computer.

Because Ivanov was still at large, I was staying with the Cardinals on a trial basis. Then they'd found out that I knew several languages myself. Now, I wasn't sure if they'd let me leave, or if even I wanted to.

Darcy had been the one to help me get ready for my very first date. She had a knack for coaxing out people's natural beauty with a subtle hand and a lot of finesse.

The thought of Darcy was a dangerous one that I knew would lead to other dangerous thoughts, so I focused once more on the clock. I was a horrible liar, and, if I focused on my first date, I wasn't sure I'd be able to stay strong against Dr. Harper's inquisitive study of me.

I was cognizant enough to realize that I was trying to focus on mundane things and avoid the topic...to stand my ground so to speak. However, my eyes kept being drawn back to Dr. Harper.

He looked so relaxed, reclined back in his chair as he was, his gaze steady.

What exactly was he trying to pull here?

My eyes went back to the clock. Neither of us had so much as uttered a word in over five minutes—five minutes!

Didn't he care that our time together was being wasted in silence?

I opened my mouth and ask him that very question but then stopped as I realized what I'd almost done.

I steeled myself, shoring up my resolve. I refused to speak on the topic—flat-out, not happening.

Dr. Harper could sit there all day, not saying a word and studying me with his all-too-knowing eyes. I wouldn't cave.

One thing that I didn't have to do was watch him do it. I looked down, picking at the material on the arm of the chair.

The silence reigned supreme. It became a sentient being that was looming over me, breathing down my neck. I brushed against the hair back there, refusing to turn.

He's just using another tactic on you, I told myself. Stay strong.

It was important that I not give in. I had to stand my ground on some things. It was a lesson I'd learned living with the Cardinals. And, I was determined to follow through with it...this time.

But, minor in psychology notwithstanding, Dr. Harper was *good*.

My desperate eyes flew back to the clock. I'm sure my face flashed a quick glimpse of disbelief at registering the time. Only another *two* minutes had passed.

Still though...that was seven minutes of nothing but silence. I didn't even think Dr. Harper had moved an inch other than to keep up his steady breathing. He was still studying my expression when I snuck a glance up.

My eyes jerked away, unable to meet his expression.

We only had ten minutes left in our session. If I had to wait it out for ten more minutes, then fine. I would. It wouldn't kill me.

Probably.

Maybe.

My thoughts ran to another doctor-slash-veterinarian that I knew—one that was as prodding and inquisitive as this one. I wondered if Dr. Harper had been a mentor of sorts to the roguish Dr. Scott, or Doc Scott as he continued to persist I call him. It would actually make a lot of sense. They were both bound and determined to bulldoze their way into my life and snag a piece of my thoughts.

A throat cleared, drawing me out of said thoughts.

It had come from Dr. Harper, but he hadn't stopped his stare-fest or made any move to speak.

I frowned. How in the world had he known that I'd actually been able to forget about his presence for a second—literally, only a second? It was unfair.

My eyes went back to the clock. There were still eight minutes left. I could feel myself start to sweat despite the artic efforts of the industrial-grade AC unit.

I started reciting arithmetic in my mind. It'd been a while since I'd resorted to working complex math to preoccupy myself, but...well, here we were.

It took a couple of false starts to center my focus long enough to start working an equation, but perseverance was a great quality that I possessed in great quantities. I was deep into my mind calculating out the area of an imaginary triangle when Dr. Harper cleared his throat again.

It didn't shock me as much this time, and I mentally stalled, somehow arriving at the answer. I'd had a lot of answers scared out of me, but I'd never had an answer appear because I was scared. I cocked my head a tiny bit as I marvelled what'd happened. Then I wiped the imaginary slate clean, starting on a hexagon. It was more complex. It might keep me busy for a few good minutes. There were only six more of them left, after all.

The process was working well.

I knew it would. I'd used it before to keep quiet on certain things before, but I'd not tried it on Dr. Harper. Dr. Harper had been so built up in my mind after all of our sessions together, I'd begun to think that he was, in fact, a mind-reader.

But that wasn't going to be the case this time. I was going to beat him. The taste of victory was sweet on the tip of my tongue. The session was almost over. My heart raced. I'd found out that Dr. Harper wasn't infallible.

A small smile lifted one corner of my mouth.

Dr. Harper must've noticed he wasn't going to prevail because he changed tactics, letting out a large sigh. "Callie—"

Even though there was no actual time, the minute the second hand of the clock hit the twelve, I heard a mental "ding."

Our time was up.

I jumped out of my chair and was halfway across his office before I said, "See you next week, Dr. Harper."

"Callie! Don't you—"

I shut the door gently behind me.

I took a moment to lean against it and get my bearings.

When I opened my eyes, I thought I saw a flash of mocha, muscled skin wrapped in a white doctor's jacket.

Doc Scott!

He was the reason I was in this mess in the first place! If he hadn't tried to ask me out, I wouldn't have been asked on that date with his teammate, Payton Emerson.

Which, okay, for that I could thank him for that because he'd help facilitate my first date—no matter how much I'd believed in the beginning that it was only a ruse to help protect me from the wiley, dark veterinarian. It had been an amazing, awkward, embarrassing, and lovely first date. As uncomfortable as some parts had been, I wouldn't have changed it for the world. The problem was that somehow Dr. Harper had heard about my date.

And like the prying, elderly grandfather type he portrayed himself as—despited his mid-forties age, he had asked me for...for *details*.

My mind flashed to my first kiss, a deep flush suffusing my cheeks even as a smile lit my lips. I recalled the absolutely perfect moment. Everything had gone right, and it was like the planets aligned. A person couldn't have hoped for a better first kiss.

I snapped out of my thoughts and realized that I'd taken a couple of steps toward where I'd seen a flash of the veterinarian. I'd been about to give him a piece of my mind. Only, my mind wasn't worth much at this moment, having both barely survived a session with Dr. Harper and also locked in the memories of my first date...and the kiss...

My cheeks heated up again.

Simultaneously thanking and confronting Doc Scott didn't seem like such a good idea when my mind was being too mushy to think straight. My stomach was giddy, and my heart was bubbling with excitement.

Instead, I made the wise decision to turn away and see if I could track down a ride home.

I'd had enough of trickster doctors for one day. I'd take out my frustration—and gratitude—on him another day.

The only real concern now was how long Dr. Harper was going to hold out for me to spill about the date. I only met with him once a week, but if he kept it up, I'd be a frayed mess before the month was out.

I'd hold out as long as I could.

I added to my list of things to do. I'd need to look up some more complex math equations to mentally complete during next week's session with the well-meaning but nosy doctor. I'd need them if I planned to stand strong.

And I did.

Honest.

Chapter 1

I was feeling...perturbed.

The phone was ringing in my hand, but I hadn't answered it. I couldn't.

After, or well, *during* the date with Emerson—and company—I discovered the contact names had been changed on my phone.

...again.

I blamed Jace since he'd started the whole mess.

Jace Tate was the darker, more sarcastic version of his computer-geek twin, C.J. Tate. Along with their third team-member, Aleks, they seemed to have started up some sort of rivalry with the Emerson team. This led to my phone becoming a repeated victim of the two teams' most tricky members—Jace of the Tate team and Corbin Myers of the Emerson Team.

Between Jace and Corbin, it was getting out of hand—especially since Jace had taken the *additional* liberty to change my default ringtone to "Kiss de Girl." There was nothing like a Jamaican singing crab and a caterwauling seagull to draw attention to oneself. I'd thought I'd die of embarrassment when the thing had gone off during my date with Emerson.

But it wasn't only the ringtone that was giving me problems. They kept giving each other's teams insulting names on my contacts list. It was amusing at first, but I wasn't entirely sure who was calling me right now.

I'd figured out all of the new names but two. For instance, on the date, I'd figured out that the "Hottest Guy in the World" was Jace. Even if I hadn't guessed that he'd changed everything when he'd been on my phone that day of the date, his contact name was a dead giveaway to the culprit.

The other names were pretty easy as well.

"BIG Russian" was undoubtedly Aleks. He was the biggest person I knew.

Then there were the names for the Emerson team. "Boulder" was Brock Johnson. Aleks used to tease him and call him Rock until he discovered the existence of Dwayne "The Rock" Johnson. That had been a rude awakening for him, knowing that he'd been giving Brock a backhanded compliment the whole time. So now he was called Boulder.

Then there was "Dr. Dolittle" which could be no other than Doc Scott after the wacky movie vet that could speak to animals.

"Bloody Brit" was Emerson, named for his origins and the slight English accent he still had no matter how much he denied its existence.

"Rockin' Rost" was Bryce Rost, a trust-fund baby that enjoyed annoying his doting parents as much as he enjoyed playing in a rock band with his guitar, Billie Joe. Yes, he *had* named his guitar.

"The REAL Hottest Guy in the World"—due to the process of elimination—could be no other than Corbin, in direct retaliation to Jace.

Easy.

But, Corbin, the devil, had swiped my phone at some point—I was still trying to figure out when—and saved CJ's and Jace's numbers as the exact same name. It was hard enough to figure them out when they were Thing 1 and Thing 2, courtesy Corbin via round one, but now, they were both Doublemint Twin. There was no number, no designation, no different upper or lower case letters. They were. Exactly. The. Same.

And one of them was calling me right now as I stared down at the phone like it might jump up and bite me.

I was nervous that I wouldn't be able to figure out which one it was by voice alone. Usually, I could tell from their personality or their scent. Lemony cheer? CJ. Sarcastic oranges? Jace.

But, I didn't have those through the phone.

I was going in blind here.

"Are you going to answer that?" Yolo asked, startling me a bit since I hadn't heard her come back to the kitchen.

Yolo was another female on the Cardinal team. She was petite, a few inches taller than me, with medium brown hair and sultry, brown eyes.

All of the Cardinals were nicknamed after Disney Princesses. For example, Darcy was Merida, and Triz was Moana. I myself had picked up the name Wendy Darling because of the "lost boys" that were always following me around.

Oddly enough, all of the Cardinals actually matched their personalities somewhat except for Yolo. Her moniker was Belle, and she wasn't bookish in the least. Her full name was Yolonda but she had it shortened because it matched her life's philosophy that "you only live once, y.o.l.o."

There was a bit of friction between us at the best of times. Our personalities didn't mesh well at all. She wanted me to stop endangering her team just by existing, and I wanted to do the same. Only, I wasn't nearly brave enough to leave or stupid enough to think that my leaving would save them from being a target in Ivanov's eyes. He'd kill them anyway on the off chance that I had liked them. Because of that and my timid personality, we weren't all that close.

"Yeah," I said, watching the screen. "I'm just not sure who it is. I mean...I have an *idea* about who it is, but..."

A spoon clattered to the table, drawing my attention.

Yolo was staring at me, and after a beat or two of silence, she finally said. "Well, Callie, I didn't know you had it in you." She seemed...proud? "Just do what I always do, give the shortest answers possible. If they're calling you, he—or she—obviously enjoyed themselves. So when you're not that forthcoming, they'll become more talkative. You should be able to figure out who they are if they talk long enough."

I stared at Yolo for a moment, trying to decipher her meaning. Despite the rough start and still rough ongoing relationship, we'd become somewhat more tolerable to each other. But that only meant that the young baroness-to-be tolerated me slightly more than something stuck to the bottom of her shoe. That was real progress for us.

However, at the moment...everything I'd thought I'd learned about her was becoming shaky.

Not only was she being pleasant and affable, it felt like we were talking about two completely different things. I didn't want to upset her or be lame in front of her since it was one of the first times she'd opened up to me, so I instead hit the answer button on the phone. Yolo, in her own way, had made answering the phone the lesser of two evils.

"Hello?" I said, trying to ignore the knowing wink Yolo sent my way as she went about her business...still in the kitchen.

My bedroom was the small living room in our apartment at Delta's undercover gated community, Hartstrait.

That meant there was zero privacy. I didn't doubt that Yolo was paying attention even if she tried to look like she wasn't. I was a teenager without a bedroom door.

"Callie," one of the twin's voices came through the speaker. "I'm glad I caught you. I have something I need to talk to you about."

Oh no, I didn't get enough info from that!

Panicked, my eyes strayed of their own volition to Yolo. She was leaned forward on the counter, propped up on her elbows, her short, light brown hair styled in loose waves. She was doing nothing now to pretend that she wasn't listening in. At my look, she waffled her hand back and forth and then mouthed, "Keep it short."

I pulled at the ends of my hair. "Oh?"

That was short, right?

Yolo gave me an approving nod, sipping two-handed from her oversized coffee mug filled to the brim with chamomille.

"Yes, something came up..." he trailed off. "Callie, are you okay? You sound...different...cautious. Is it Ivanov?"

I wish you *sounded different. From your brother.*

"No, no, nothing like that. There's still no word from him, not from Delta or the CIA. No...I'm f-fine. It was a long night," I said, but then my eyes widened when I saw Yolo was shaking her head and waving her arms frantically.

What was wrong with that answer? I strained my brain to try to say something else. If what I'd said was bad, maybe I could distract him. "Uh, what did you want to talk about!" I shouted.

Yolo smacked herself in her forehead and closed her eyes.

"Well, I don't want to talk about it over the phone. Are you next door?"

My eyes glanced around the room as if I didn't know where I was. Yolo was quick and must've understood his question based on my very blatant look around the place. She started shaking her head and pointing her finger at me to stop.

I paused. But...why should I lie? I couldn't think of a reason, so despite Yolo's silent warning, I stuttered out, "Y-yes?"

Yolo clunked her tea down with a solid thunk so she could throw her hands up and roll her eyes.

"Can I come over?"

My eyes rounded once more, and I looked to Yolo. She had her hands up as she raised her eyebrows. I was on my own, her look said. I'd dug my own grave.

I gulped, but then I thought about it. They, whoever it was, would come over. I'd see them face-to-face. It would be perfect. Then I'd be able to figure out who it was. "Sure! That would be great!"

"Okay, see you in two," the mystery twin said and hung up.

I looked down at the screen to memorize the number. I was going to memorize *all* of their numbers. It wouldn't be difficult for me. Memorizing was my thing, whether it was code or languages.

And then...*then*, I was going to booby trap my phone. I wasn't sure how I would do it, but it was happening, the first chance I got. Corbin and Jace were going to be in for a nasty surprise if they thought they could keep messing with *this* girl's technology. I was a wanted hacker in several countries. I'd remind them why.

I caught movement out of the far corner of my eye.

Natasia, dubbed Queen Elsa to some and Ice Queen to others, was dressed in a light blue that brought out the icy brightness of her eyes and made her snow pale skin seem to glow as she entered the kitchen. It only took her sharp attention a second to realize something was up as she stopped to assess the situation from Yolo's exasperation to my pent-up nerves.

"Alright, what did you do to *malyshka sestra?*" She asked, calling me "little sister" in Russian.

I shrugged.

Her gaze settled on the fed-up French.

"*Mon amour,* why do you so quickly assume that I did anything? I'm offended. I was only trying to help her out."

Natasia raised her perfectly sculpted eyebrow and gave a pointed look.

Yolo shook her head. "I was! Oh, *mon Dieu,* you should've seen the trainwreck that jus-"

She was cut off by a knock on the door.

It was the upper-level door, which made sense to me because all of the Tate team could get passed the bottom door with their copy of the key.

The houses at Delta's gated community, cleverly disguised as housing for old retirees, had garages on the first floor and housing above. After Ivanov had the Cardinals' house blown up, the Tate team had been helpful about getting us into the coveted houses. I wasn't sure how or why they had a key to both the downstairs door and the upstairs door at the landing, but they did.

Yolo was not so blasé about the situation.

Their heads turned around to stare at the door. Natasia was merely curious, but Yolo glanced back at me while her face changed to concern.

"Callie," she said, her French accent becoming more pronounced. It did that when she was experiencing strong emotions or trying to flirt her way into someone's bed. "This is ze man from ze phone?" At my nod, she lowered her voice. "Send heem away. Zis iz not good. He obviously was lurking and broke into our house. I have dealt wis crazy people before. He must be one of zem, and if not, he is one of Ivanov's."

"Uh..." I was so confused. She knew the twins. They weren't crazy. I pointed at the door. "I'm just going to go...yeah," I trailed off awkwardly, still trying to figure out why Yolo was acting so crazy herself. Instead of finishing my sentence, I stood up and headed towards the door.

"Callie," Yolo whispered. When I looked over, she was shaking her head adamantly. Natasia was also giving her a puzzled look, but Yolo wasn't paying any attention to it.

"Callie," she whisper-shouted at me when I didn't stop. "I am being serious." Her eyes got bigger the closer I got to the door.

"It's okay," I said turning away. I reached out to put my hand on the door to open it. She muttered in French, but I didn't know what she'd said, so I went to explain. "It's one of the tw—oof!"

I was pushed to the side by an unforgiving bundle of lithe muscles, squishing my face to the foyer wall. I caught a whiff of jasmine and the expensive, heady musk of Chanel No. 5, letting me know that it was Yolo that had tackled me. She had come out of nowhere, not giving me time to release my grip on the handle. So when I was pushed, the door was actually pulled open.

The jasmine mixed with lemon.

I didn't even have time to turn around and visually confirm that it was CJ at the landing before a male voice was making a similar "oof" sound out in the hallway.

Realizing that I wasn't pinned anymore, I scrambled to get out from where I had ended up lodged between the door and the wall to look at what'd happened.

CJ was flat on his back in the hallway. His blonde, curly hair was long enough to be in a disarray after being tackled to the floor.

The petite French girl had pulled a Black Widow-worthy move and "Romanoffed" poor CJ before he even knew what hit him. Yolo had to be half his weight, so I knew she'd done some full-bodied acrobatics to get him to the floor so quickly.

Natasia joined us to see what was going on.

Yolo had CJ's long-sleeved shirt in a two-handed grip and was crouched over his torso, using an outstretched leg and her bent knee to keep his arms supine and incapacitated.

"Listen hear, *monsieur*. Callie may not know it, but I know your type. You leave her…" she seemed to pause as she finally took in the person's face.

"CJ," I said, worried, moving to step forward, but Natasia held out an arm to stop me. Her face was confused, but amusement was starting to crack through the fissures in her icy armor.

"CJ?" Yolo repeated in a slow, incredulous voice, her light brown eyes turning to look at me in question.

"*Yes*, CJ," the man in question said. "Mind telling me what's going on?"

Yolo ignored him, her eyes on me but keeping him hostage in her grip. Her mouth opened and closed a couple of times before she shook her head and repeated, "*CJ?*"

I fiddled with my bracelet, wondering why she was so shocked. I didn't know that many people, after all. Only a limited amount of people had access to my number, and she knew every single one of them. "Uh, yes?"

"But...CJ's almost as innocent as you." She looked down back at the indignant twin, unwilling or unable to move and let him go.

I was confused.

CJ was also. He seemed to have had enough because he sat up, doing a sit-up...with her still on his chest.

My mouth dropped at the display of athleticism.

He stood up and put her on her feet before taking two good, large steps away from her. To be honest, his wariness was not unwarranted.

Yolo was standing there, staring, assessing—or rather *reassessing*. Her eyes ran up his body at the muscles that without a doubt had to be there. Her gaze became more appreciative.

"CJ," she said, her voice huskier, a smirk on her face. "You've been working out, *non?*"

He stood there unsure while she stepped forward to grope his arms. He went to push her away, but she had already moved onto lifting his shirt up to show abs.

"Hey," he protested, but Yolo was already looking back at me.

"I'm impressed, Callie. Good job," she said as she began to saunter my way.

My eyes rounded. A drop of fear shivered down my spine at her odd behavior.

Wait, no, go back to CJ. Don't turn your attention on me!

I took a step back in alarm but was stopped by the wall.

Yolo leaned in close. "I'm very impressed, you, how do you say...you dirty dog," she purred intimately. "I didn't know you had it in you, *ma petite*. Perhaps you are not so bad after all?"

"Wait," a voice from the stairwell said.

Oh no. Witnesses.

I turned my head to see the last two Tate team members, Aleks and Jace, had gathered in the hallway.

The person who had spoken was Jace because he carried on when he saw he had our attention. He cocked his head to the side so that his own blond curls, identical to his twin's, fell into his dark chocolate eyes. "Didn't know she had *what* in her?"

Yolo turned back to me and patted my cheek with some affection. "Why, your brother, *mon cherie*. They had the one-night walk."

Everyone was confused except for Natasia and apparently Aleks.

Aleks's head snapped to the still somewhat traumatized CJ. "You had one-night walk with Callie and did not tell us?"

CJ looked lost and terrified. "Wh-what? I don't even know--"

"Oh," Jace shouted as he seemed to understand something. "One night stand!"

"What?!" CJ cried, his head whipping back to Yolo. He avoided my gaze as his cheeks heated up.

Then the hallway erupted into chaos.

Chapter 2

Natasia was full-on laughing—which I was pretty sure I hadn't seen before. Jace was interrogating a confused and increasingly embarrassed CJ. Aleks had folded his massive, massive arms across his broad chest to stare at me. His eyes were intent, not only because of the unique color—a blue lighter even than Natasia's, so light that they were nearly white—but also because he was a big, burly, intimidating guy. He stood at over six and half feet tall and was filled out with hulking muscles that weren't chiseled and defined but were impossible to miss. He made the twins look like wiry kids even though both of them were six feet tall and had their own significant muscles.

Yolo leaned back away from me. "Callie, how many others have you had sex with to have forgotten your own neighbor's name?"

"What?!" I cried out, my cheeks flaming hot. That's what this was all about? She thought the phone call earlier had been from a random one-night stand?

Silence ensued as heads whipped in my direction.

I started shaking my head, as I realized what Yolo had been talking about earlier in the kitchen. I raced to explain. "No, no, no, you don't understand! See Jace--"

"Jace too?" Natasia asked innocently, only egging Yolo on. "You pulled twins? Was it at the same time, *malyshka sestra?*"

Beyond mortified and caring at this point, I turned my head to glare at her. "You stop. You're always my ride to and from Delta. You haven't left my side since Ivanov tried to run us off the road with his armored car. You'd know if I'd s-slept with anyone because I'd practically have to do it in front of you!"

Several coughs sounded out in the hallway at that while Natasia winked at me. "I'm not denying it."

Augh! She was so—so impossible! She knew exactly what she was doing. "You were even on my date with Emerson! How could I have--"

"Wait. That date was real? You actually nailed Emerson?" Yolo asked. "In front of Natasia?" She turned to her teammate. "Did you join?"

I wanted the floor to swallow me up. I really did. I'd thought my date had been embarrassing, but I had reached a new level of mortification. Dr. Harper and his pestering, bothersome questions had nothing on Yolo and Natasia teamed up.

CJ looked like he was having an asthma attack. Jace's eyes were so full of shock that he actually had no sarcastic comebacks for once. Aleks...well...Aleks looked like he couldn't settle on grinning or killing someone. I could see through his blond beard that his lips were twitching to split into their signature, broad grin.

Yolo needed to stop talking. I rushed forward, acting on instinct.

I hadn't managed to land any moves in defensive training at Delta, but I was half-decent when motivated enough. Just ask Jace whom I'd tomahawk-thrown over my shoulder once before when I'd felt like the Cardinals lives were in danger, and he wouldn't let me get to them.

I was beyond that level of conscious thinking now. I'd gotten motivated enough, apparently. Even as pushed to the limit I was, my mind still analyzed the situation.

The landing at the top of the stairwell was limited in space, but I could use that to my advantage. I had no chance of subduing the Black-Widow level fighter, but I hoped to at least let her know that she couldn't get away with everything scott-free.

I grabbed Yolo's arm and turned my back into her chest to throw her over my body.

She flipped over me. She landed on her back with a loud thud but didn't stay down long. She pulled her legs up into the air, reversing her momentum, to swing into a handstand, kicking out at me as she did so.

I dodged to the left, keeping my movements tight and efficient to stay fast. I'd seen Yolo's pink avatar in the simulation, trying to fight her way to me. She was too fast to be overly flamboyant with. Instead, I matched her steps, taking the time to study her instead of rushing in while she was still upside down.

CJ had been corralled to the stairs with his teammates when we'd started fighting which gave us more room. Natasia stayed in the open foyer, not moving to intervene, but a potential threat for me to keep an eye on nonetheless. I had known the girls a matter of months whereas they went back years together. Her loyalty would lie with her teammate, her *real* one.

Yolo finished flipping over, putting her feet down to stand up, but I did a spinning crouch, sweeping my leg out to trip her. She jumped, barely managing to avoid it.

I had put a lot of power behind that sweep, and my momentum kept me from stopping the spin. I had no choice but to turn away from her, but I could feel the next hit as it came through the air. I was able to take my crouched turn and morph it into a sideways donut roll. I finished the roll and sprang to my feet.

As I came up, I was already bobbing left and right as she sent punches my way.

I timed her rhythm and caught one of her arms. I went to pull her forward and off-balance, but she had a bit more muscle and weight than me. And she'd had a *lot* more offensive training than I had.

Trying to salvage the failed move, I went to throw her over my shoulder again, but she'd already wizened up to that move.

She reversed the throw on me, landing on her feet and pulling me over her shoulder like the most advanced game of leapfrog in history.

Even though I was surprised as I was yanked forward over her head, I didn't think she'd let me pull her own trick on her. Instead of sailing all the way over and trying to land on my feet like she had, I hooked my legs around her neck, catching my weight and stopping the chain of shoulder-throwing. I gripped with my thighs as hard as I could and threw my torso forward to the side, swinging like a pendulum from her neck.

When she couldn't brace for the force of my body weight, she had no choice but to topple over. She managed to do a swan dive to roll out of it though so that by the time I somersaulted and was back on my feet, she was right there with me.

I kept dodging and weaving, and she kept coming at me. She swiped her feet. I jumped. I swung at her head. She ducked. She punched at my stomach. I caught her wrist and pulled her to me. She used my grip to slam me into the wall. She pinned me.

Literally, between a rock and a hard place, our fight lulled.

We were both breathing hard. My wrists were captured and pushed above my head. Our chests were brushing with every inhale she was so close to me. Her brown eyes bored into mine, and then, the look in them changed from focus to mischief.

It was enough to shock me out of my anger. The whole fight had been fun to her.

Admitting to my own limits, I went to call a ceasefire and surrender, but she stopped me before I could utter even the first word.

Yolo moved in, bringing her soft, rose-colored lips to mine in a gentle kiss. My eyes rounded in surprise, and my body tensed up. Her hair was sweet-smelling as it brushed my cheeks. Her expensive perfume washed over me. Everything from before dropped away as I was suffused in the moment.

And all I could do was remember the kiss from my date.

Instead of Chanel No. 5, I was smelling hazelnut and tasting the coffee on his lips. Instead of rounded, supple curves, I was feeling hard planes and muscles. Instead of smooth cheeks, I was feeling a strong sculpted jaw and the start of stubble. Instead of the soft feminine hands, I was once again feeling the strong, sturdy grip on the back of my head and long fingers threaded through my hair.

I wasn't kissing Yolo. I was kissing Payton Emerson—my first real kiss.

My eyes closed as I went limp, returning the affection as I remembered the way he'd walked me out of my hospital room to a staff room that night for some privacy. He'd been so accommodating the entire evening throughout all of the shenanigans. He reached his limit because he'd whisked me away, studied my face for a moment once we were secluded, and had gone in for the kill.

He'd fisted my hair and angled my head where he wanted it, leading me and teaching me by a passionate fire that consumed my soul and made my lower belly tingle.

All of a sudden, it was as if the passion reached a limit. The shift was subtle, but little clues showed that he was beginning to ebb away. He'd taken me to a whimpering, quivering high, and then he'd gently guided me back down until he was giving sweet pecks and nibbles on my bruised lips. He stopped and tilted my forehead to rest on his as we breathed together.

Enough time passed for our breathing to even back out. He kissed me with a gentle brush of his lips on my hairline and said, "Goodnight, love," in a husky voice that nearly brought me right back up to the level of starving frenzy I'd been at.

I hadn't minded him calling me "love" one bit. Neither did he seem to mind it when I returned the favor and called him by his first name, Payton. It was a rare privilege he'd afforded me and didn't regret one bit if the lustful flash in his jade-green eyes was any indication.

It was the small nibble to my lip, mixed with the jasmine and musk that brought me back out of my memories.

I broke the kiss, staring at Yolo to gauge her face.

She studied me for a long time before breaking out into a smile that morphed her from lethally beautiful to breathtakingly gorgeous.

"I think I may like you, after all, Callie Jensen," she purred. She softly brushed the back of her hand along my jawline before stepping back and heading into our apartment without another word.

I was left alone and bereft against the wall at the top of the landing. I was still breathing hard, both from the fight and the memory of my first kiss.

I looked up to the only other Cardinal still out here. Natasia was studying me, calculating as she tried to solve some puzzle I'd presented. I didn't dare look towards the Tate team even though I knew they were still at the top of the stairs. I couldn't.

No one was saying anything.

Focus. Focus, Callie, so you can change the focus of everyone else.

I had to clear my throat a couple of times. "Uh...um, CJ, you wanted to see-"

"What the. Actual. Fuck," Jace said, drawing my gaze without my permission. I had fully planned on avoiding everyone's gaze until the end of time.

My stomach dropped at the look of anger and indignity and...betrayal on his face. I nervously licked my lips as if doing so could erase the evidence and the event from their minds.

Jace had an eyebrow raised with an incredulous look on his face. "Brock and I have been working with you for months. Months! And it's like Brock's got some magical forcefield up around him so that you can't lay a *single* hit on him. And then you go and take on Yolo? I mean, come on, it's Yolonda Bernard, the French baroness-to-be in a small, lethal package. And don't get me started on those moves. I know that neither Brock or I have taught you those moves, and don't you dare tell me they're yoga!"

It took me several beats and owlish blinks to realize that he was upset about my performance with him in defense training and not the kiss I'd just shared with Yolo.

The hallway quieted until CJ cleared his throat.

"That's what you want to focus on? Her *fighting* abilities?" CJ asked.

"I'm compartmentalizing here! Give me a break," Jace turned back to me. "You've got some 'splainin' to do, Lucy."

I didn't understand the Lucy reference, but him wanting some answers was easy enough to comprehend.

"I can't explain it," I said in a thick voice. At Jace's look of disbelief, I continued. "I can't. I was trained in a lot of defensive moves and stuff. Because of my size...it was all about how to incapacitate and get away. I'm not very good, and fighting brings up a lot of bad memories. I was always being punished for losing."

"Wait, so how did they train you? You obviously don't feel threatened enough to pull out those Matrix moves around us."

"The answer is in your question," I said. "I don't feel threatened around you guys."

CJ's face was somber as he probably understood then that I had been trained against my will.

Jace seemed nonplussed though. He seemed to shake off my response. His raised eyebrow became more sinister. "We'll have to change that."

To be continued...

Release: Spring 2020

Printed in Great Britain
by Amazon